PRAISE FOR LUCRETIA GRINDLE

"Grindle is a craftswoman of delicate, evocative psychological thrillers."

— *THE DAILY TELEGRAPH*

"One of Grindle's distinguishing skills is characterization and dialogue... exhilarating."

— *HERALD*

"A beautiful evocation... Delicate, and with a narrative style that deserves the greatest respect."

— *DAILY MAIL*

THE DEVIL'S GLOVE

SALEM BOOK ONE

LUCRETIA GRINDLE

ISBN (eBook): 978-1-960610-00-3
ISBN (Paperback): 978-1-960610-01-0
ISBN (Hardcover): 978-1-960610-02-7
ISBN (Large Print): 978-1-960610-03-4
ISBN (Jacketed Edition): 978-1-960610-04-1

Cover Design Jane Dixon Smith
Cover Image © Rekha Garton / Trevillion Images
Marketing by The Book Whisperer

For Maisie and Emma

PROLOGUE

August 2, 1718

Sun cracks the purple dark and for an instant, something less than a breath, the bay is a field of fire. Then it is misted white. Swaddled like an infant, or a wound. Another breath turns it silver as the underbelly of a fish. So each day of the world begins.

This morning, the tide creeps across the wide ledge below the meadow then slithers back, coy and silly as a girl. If I climbed down I would feel it, slick and silvered with newness, as if the ocean had not been here all night but had only just arrived. I know that isn't true, of course. I know the sea is always here, eternal as the stars. As a child I tried to outwit its arrival. Running the track through the golden-rod, I was sure I could beat the sun, snatch the moment before the ocean birthed in flames and keep it for myself. It was wicked, I knew even then, to wish to look upon Creation in its nakedness. To wish to look at all. And yet, a secret seed of me still longs for just one glimpse, one eye-blink, of what is hidden. I dream of a world laid bare.

It's why I come, I suppose. Why, even in the dead of winter, I pull my cloak around me and lift the latch. Pick my way through the darkness across the track to the meadow that fronts the bay. In truth, I no longer believe that I will glimpse or snatch anything. Now, I come for comfort. Standing here above the rocks as the sun rises, I close my eyes and listen to the panting of the tide and let it lick the wounds of time.

Today is the same, yet different. Because today is my last birthday. My climb up the stairs has ended. I will not set foot upon another step. I could play a dodging game, with the wasting that will come, and the dreams. And perhaps I will. Or perhaps I will do the other thing. It would be easy enough. It would take no great effort to untie the wherry, and set the oars, to climb in and settle myself and row out. I have always been at home on the water, and I am still strong enough to brace my feet and bend my back. To pull with both arms at once, not looking over my shoulder but instead keeping my eye fixed on where I have come from, so I may reach where I wish to go. I could do that.

I could row, and row, with my eye fixed upon this place until it is nothing. Until there is no scent of earth nor animal and not even a bird circled above me. I could row until I stopped, alone on the empty silver plate of the sea, and rocked like a blown flower with the petals of my life strewn all about me.

But I will not. At least, not yet. Because I have a secret. And a confession. I am a thief. All my life, I have snatched and hoarded stolen words. Now I wish to set them down. But I cannot just loose them to the four winds, let them blow and snare where they will. Instead, I must gather them, and spill them out. Examine each one, then pin and re-pin them like butterflies to parchment until they make the correct pattern. This is the final task I set myself, to tell the truth of what happened in Massachusetts.

Even the name sounds like a snake moving through grass. It sounds like the hiss of my skirts as I turn and start back across the meadow. Thinking on it, on both the labor of the telling and on the place itself, I become careless and trip and dart my foot on a scrub-rose. The thorn comes out on the first pull. Cradled in my palm, it is no bigger than a mouse's tooth, the prick so small that I can barely see where it went in, which is no surprise. Even in the winter I come here barefoot, and though the rest of me is clean and soft, my feet are my exception. They are the filthy witness to my journey.

Nor are my calloused pads the only thing I hide, for we are, all of us, wheels within wheels. Shells within shells. Take me. On first glance, you would not guess that I have been called Whore, along with Mad, and Damned. You would not suspect that I have been told I can fly. Or that I suckle imps, and talk to serpents. Nothing in my fine face suggests that I have stepped through the gibbet's shadow, or reached for the feet that dance on air.

Run your finger across my cheek and along the tilt of my nose. You will find no scent of the men in their white collars who spoke of God and governed Hell. Trace the curve of my ear and the crest of my lips. You will hear no whisper of the secrets I traded with death, nor taste its dark ridges. Nothing will lead you to guess what sweet familiars we were, thirty years ago in Massachusetts, where they called me Witch.

PART I

BAD CAT

Northern New England
Summer, 1688

CHAPTER ONE

Small, white, and perfectly formed, the child's hand reaches out of the dark. The fingers, their nails pearly and shining, stretch toward me. And I know that, no matter what, I cannot let them touch me. So, I back away. And away again. Then I'm caught.

I can't see what it is that snares me. I can't see anything in the thick darkness, except the perfect white shape. Tangled like a bird in a net, I twist and writhe as the tiny hand comes closer. And closer. Until finally it reaches out and strokes my cheek with a touch so cold that it burns. That it presses its frozen mark into my skin, branding me.

Trying to shake it off, I open my mouth, and scream. But nothing comes out. Just a gasp as I jerk awake, panting. The room is so close that it is too hot to breathe, never mind scream. Yet my throat is raw with trying because I have had this dream four, five, six, I don't know how many times tonight. Every time I close my eyes. All I want now is for it to be dawn.

❧

It is the year sixteen hundred and eighty-eight, and we are in the settlement of Falmouth, barely one hundred souls of us, if dogs have souls, clustered in the shadow of our fort. The blue blanket of Casco Bay swaddles our neck of land, cradling us in the sea. While on either shore, at our backs and to our sides we are sheltered, and bound, by the endless forests of The Eastward. Maine.

Winters are long here. Locked in snow and ice, we dream of summer. But this year it came too early, and has been too hot. By July, the fields were shrunken and dazed. Now, in August, the milk sours in the churns and the spiders grow fat. At night they stir themselves to knit the mallow stalks and the speckled faces of the barn-lilies. But come morning, no dew spangles their webs. Last week, fire buckets were ordered, six for every house. We whitened our arms with the salt and blistered our palms on the stiffened leather straps as we passed them, hand over hand, up the beach. Every night at dusk, the sun sinks like a cannonball. This is how it was at the dying of Avis Hobbs.

My mother and I live outside the village, so we did not even hear that she was ill until yesterday afternoon. I was drying fruit. I'd split a basket of apricots and was laying them on the table, getting ready to string and hang them and swatting away a persistent wasp when I heard the garden gate and boots on the gravel. We leave the kitchen door open these days because of the heat. Glancing up, I saw the small dark shape of our minister, George Burroughs, weaving through the beds of lavender and overblown chamomile. He was in his shirt sleeves, and had obviously run the whole way because he was panting like a bull. When he stopped and leaned against the door jamb, he had to catch his breath before he could even form words.

I like Mister Burroughs. He insists we call him that because, although he preaches and marries and buries us, he has never been ordained. So he is Mister, not Minister, although I wonder if God cares. The point is, George Burroughs is a kind man. He has befriended my mother and me since my father left for

London. So, when he told us Goodwife Hobbs was ill, and asked if we would come to her, we could hardly deny him, although we do not know the family well and they have never been particularly kind or gracious to us. Or to anyone else.

The Hobbs are not particularly well liked, especially since the twins, a son and daughter, drowned some years ago. They are not shunned, but people tend to avoid the unfortunate, perhaps because they think bad luck is contagious, and life is fragile here. The Hobbs are tenants, and have a farm in Massachusetts, which is where Avis's husband is. Avis Hobbs had recently discovered that she is to be blessed with yet another child, and so chose not to make the long, hot, journey to Topsfield. She stayed here instead with their youngest daughter, Abigail. And it was Abigail who woke the Burroughs yesterday morning at dawn, hammering on their door.

The child, George Burroughs told us, was terrified. White with fear and barely able to speak. Sarah Burroughs went at once, then summoned the neighbors. No doubt a gaggle of goodwives descended on the Hobbs house, bearing teas and ointments and poultices. But nothing they tried made any difference. Like a creature struggling in deep water, Avis Hobbs thrashed, then sunk and thrashed again, until finally the minister set prayer aside, took matters into his own hands, and ran for my mother.

We heard all of this as I fetched the baskets from the stillroom and the three of us set off, hurrying out through the garden and up across my father's meadow along the path that leads to the village. My mother keeps the baskets prepared and packed for just such emergencies as this. Filled with jars of her ointments and oils and distilled teas, with clean linen, and bandages and sharpened knives and sipping bowls and anything else she might need, they are heavy, and in the past, she always took pride in carrying them herself.

Then, last spring, my mother became unwell. Now she is a pendulum that swings and dips. Sometimes she is almost her old self, and I think surely I am mistaken. There is nothing wrong with her but this infernal heat. Then, without warning, she is half a stranger, herself yet not herself at all, as if a great shadow has bloomed inside her and seeps out, coloring her like cheap dye. On those days, I carry the baskets. And she smiles, and says I am her 'strong hands', and that I live up to the name she gave me when we came here, which I suppose is true. I am her daughter, her only child. Resolve, born of Deliverance.

❧

WE HAD REACHED the lower edge of the common by the time George Burroughs finished his story. My mother stopped then, and looked at him. She did not say a word, but she did not need to. The question, and the accusation, was written on her face. *Why so slow to call me?*

Stopping to examine the toes of his boots as if he found them suddenly fascinating, Mister Burroughs muttered, "Goodwife Skilling." Which was all the answer we needed.

My mother can set bones. She can draw the poison from a wound, and stitch broken flaps of skin back together. She can break fevers, and save babies who would otherwise be born dead. She has had this gift all her life, and has never stopped perfecting and enhancing it. But, like all gifts, it is coveted. And sometimes feared. And often the cause of jealousy. Some—mostly the goodwives who are as bothered by my mother's looks as by her skill, and by the fact that my father is gone—whisper that her knowledge is not natural. That her gift does not come from God at all. None do so more loudly, or more often, than Mary Skilling.

A small woman with crow eyes who fancies herself a healer, Goody Skilling would resist my mother being called if a dog was ill. Plainly, she had hoarded Avis Hobbs to herself, until she thought the woman was dying. Then, like a crow dropping carrion, Goody Skilling was more than happy to let the minister fetch my mother so this death could be dropped at our door.

I had nearly collided with George Burroughs when he and my mother stopped. I came so close that I could see the red patch of sun rash at the back of his neck and smell the sharp odor of sweat that soaked his linen shirt, making it cling like a second skin. My arms and shoulders ached, and my collar itched in the heat, and at the mention of Goodwife Skilling, I wished I was anywhere else.

There are days that change your life. Most of the time, you do not realize it. But sometimes you do. Yesterday was one of those. As George Burroughs took my mother's arm and they turned toward the Hobbs house which came into view beyond the dry overgrown grass of the common, I felt my stomach twist. For just a moment as I stood there, the world seemed to pause as if it was giving me a choice. I could step forward and follow my mother into whatever waited for us, or I could drop the baskets, and turn, and run. Gather up my skirts and race back down the meadow, toward our grove of birches, and the cove beyond, and the sanctuary that has always been our house.

But as quickly as it came, it passed. Because, in truth, it was no choice at all. I could no more abandon my mother than fly. Even if I had, it would have done no good. She would have gone to Avis Hobbs whether I followed her or not, whether she was welcome or not, whether the minister asked her or not. Because her 'gift' is also her duty.

So, we walked on, the three of us, my mother, George Burroughs, and me under the furnace of the sun, none of us knowing we were on a fool's errand. Although that would become clear soon enough.

❧

THE HOBBS HOUSE, though solid, is mean and unkempt. The gate sags. Hens squabble in the door-yard where the paving are stones are webbed with chick weed. Scrubbing them should be Abigail's job. She is ten, so past old enough. But Abigail, and her mother, apparently think her too precious for labor. My mother calls Abigail Hobbs 'Avis's poppet'.

Even recalling that, I felt a splash of guilt as I lugged the baskets up the path, and reminded myself that the poppet—though she is spoiled and has a tongue twice her age—is surely, like her family, not among The Blessed. Her older brother and sister drowned. There is another older brother, but he is gone away, signed to the militia. And everyone knows William Hobbs is a useless drunk. So for all intents and purposes, Avis and Abigail, like my mother and I, were alone in the world.

We crowded in through the door, which Goodwife Burroughs promptly slammed behind us. The house was shuttered. Dark and hot as a forge, it smelled like a stinking oven. Goody Burroughs was barely a shape as she skittered ahead of us up the narrow stairs to the room where Avis Hobbs lay, sweat-slicked and glassy-eyed, her hands twitching in her marriage bed. Almost as if she was afraid, Sarah Burroughs stopped abruptly on the landing. My mother stepped past her into the open doorway. Then, she too stopped.

Once my eyes adjusted to the gloom, I had begun counting the tops of the jars in the baskets, concentrating on them, trying to distance myself from the stink of sickness that had thickened as we climbed the stairs, so again, I almost ran into her. Over my mother's shoulder, I saw Mary Skilling standing by the bed, staring intently at the floor, trying to pretend we were not there, while behind us on the landing Goody Burroughs hissed at her husband, who hissed back, trying mightily not to snap. So, no one except me heard what my mother said.

"Why?" She whispered as she stared at Avis Hobbs. "Why did they not use charcoal?"

Her words were barely more than a breath, but my head snapped up. Because charcoal is the antidote to poison.

CHAPTER TWO

Sensing me behind her, my mother glanced over her shoulder. For the blink of an eye, the meaning of her question hung between us. Then it disappeared like smoke.

The room we stepped into stank of sweat, and of the pig smell of cheap tallow, and of sickness. Edging along the wall, I placed the baskets on the unswept hearth. Again, I counted the waxed tops of the jars as if the very fact of them would take me away, back to the stillroom with its sweet smells and cool stone floor. Still refusing to acknowledge us, Goody Skilling was pressing herself into the wall as if she had been nailed there. Shoving past her husband, Goody Burroughs pushed into the room and began to babble about ointments, making the already cramped space smaller and hotter and louder. Any trace of weakness suddenly gone, my mother wasted no time in shooing them out.

"Fix the latch. Lock it," she ordered as George Burroughs herded the women down the stairs.

I did as she said, then leaned against the closed door, wishing I could have gone too. Because I did not want to see what was beneath the faded quilt that had been darned and re-darned, then ripped again with thrashing. My mother lifted it gently. Standing very still, she looked down on Avis Hobbs, then bent and pulled back the woman's lips. Her gums were pale, her tongue dark. If Avis Hobbs' knew who we were, or that we were there at all, she gave no sign of it.

My mother waited a moment before lifting the stained linen shift and pressing the barely swollen belly, which was gray and slick as the belly of a fish. She did not speak or look at me when, a moment later, she re-covered the worm nakedness of Avis Hobbs. Instead, she crossed to the hearth. At the sight of the sight of her rigid back as she bent over the baskets and the stiff movement of her arms, my stomach tightened. Once, I was knocked into a field fence by one of the cattle. Caught across my waist by the rail, I could not breathe, and felt a sort of living death. All the world was bright in front of me but utterly still, as if suspended inside a glass. Watching my mother as her hand hovered over the jars, I felt the same thing, and blinked, and opened my mouth, trying to suck in the air in that was as thick as soured cream.

Again, without looking at me, my mother waved toward the window. "Open it," she said. "For heaven's sake. Open it, so we can all breathe."

The hinges on the narrow, leaded frames whined as I push them wide and leaned out. The heat of the afternoon hit me in the face. Grateful even for that, I opened my mouth and gasped like a fish, which was when I felt it. It started as a flutter across my shoulders, before skittering down the outstretched length of my arm and hesitating in my upturned palm as if asking me to cup it in my hand. Without knowing how, I recognized the baby's soul. For a second, I was sure I could see it, shimmering in the furnace of the afternoon. *Go,* I told it, and moved my fingers to hurry it away. *Go! Go well and fast from this place*. Because I had glanced over my shoulder, and seen which jar my mother lifted from the basket.

❧

TWO MONTHS ago at the waning of the Milk Moon, I stripped and stewed the bark of an alder. A month to the day after that, I collected the first choke-cherries. They had stared up at me, black and shiny as babies' eyes as I stood in the stillroom, staining my fingers with their hard fruit as I plucked the stones out and sucked each one until all the flesh was gone. Only then did I bite down, cracking each choke cherry pit before I spat it into the jar. Some say it is safer to use a grinding rock, or the flat of a knife. But the crack will not be clean. You risk shell fragments tainting the liquor. My jaw was sore when I finally covered the opened stones with the alder tea that lures the poison from their tiny hearts.

We have known this recipe for a long time. When I was very small, we lived south, in Duxbury where my father traded with the local sachems and their people. When King Philip's War broke out and the fighting worsened, he commended us to their safekeeping. I still remember how, after he rowed us up-river to the village led by the she-sachem, Ashawonks, my father lifted me from the wherry, swinging me the way a ship swings from its anchor.

"I am hiding you here," he said as he put me down, "because you hide your most precious jewel in the last place anyone will think to look for it."

For the three years that the war raged, during the raiding and the burning and the battles, we were safe with Ashawonk's people and my mother learned all manner of new things. Among them, how alder was stripped and stewed, how the choke cherry stones were cleaned and cracked, how long they needed to steep, and how the recipe was used. When it was used at all, which was not often, only as a last resort when everything else had failed, and even then, only on the young and strong. Because this is a cure that walks the blade between healing and death. The convulsions it induces, the bringing-up which is also the cure, is fearsome, and can stop a heart.

"Are you sure?"

The words felt thick and sticky on my tongue, because I almost never question my mother. But I did yesterday, and when her eyes met mine in that dreadful room with the slick fish body of Avis Hobbs laying between us, I saw that she was not sure, and the realization made new sweat blossom on my chest.

"What else can we do?" Her voice was so low that the question was as much in her eyes as in words.

We both looked to the door, then back to Avis Hobbs—to her waxed skin and blue tinged lips. I thought of charcoal, and my mother saw it, and shook her head, and she was right. It was far too late. Like salt water, charcoal must be given at once to seize the poison and carry it from the body. Avis Hobbs had been clutching her belly all day. With the recipe my mother held in her hand, she might die. Without it, she surely would.

As if sensing what passed between us, Avis Hobbs shuddered. Then suddenly, she twisted and bucked violently. Straightening her arms and legs, arching her back, she jerked. And just as suddenly, stilled. Her head dropped as she bared her teeth and her eyes rolled back.

"Quick!" My mother knelt, measuring from the jar into a sipping bowl and I tried not to notice that her hands were trembling as I climbed onto the bed.

Rucking my skirts up, I grabbed the dying woman. Avis Hobb's shoulders, bony as wings, poked at my chest. The smell of her was sharp and sweet at once. Her skin was as slick as a side of hung beef. Pinning her with one arm, I felt with my free hand for the dry rim of her lip, pressing her tongue down with a finger, holding her mouth open the way you hold open the mouth of a calf that refuses to suckle. Sweat sheened my mother's face as she stepped to the bedside and poured the liquor.

I felt its oily coolness on my fingers, and on the dry husk of Avis Hobbs' tongue. It got into her mouth, and down her throat.

I felt her swallow, and hoped it was enough. Then Avis Hobbs choked and writhed, and spat in my mother's face.

My grip loosened as she lashed out, catching the bowl, knocking it from my mother's hands. She screamed as I snatched at her skinny bare arms, finally grabbing one, trying to stop her from falling off the bed. Which was when I looked up, and saw Abigail standing in the open doorway.

She was so small, and so perfectly still. Her little hands were folded in front of her, and her cap and apron glowed bright white against the gloom of the landing.

"Get her out!" A reddened stain was running down my mother's cheek and into the hollow of her neck. "Get her out now!" She hissed. Because already, Avis Hobbs was on her hands and knees, beginning to gasp and scrabble.

My mother grabbed for the woman, trying to support her as I slipped off the bed, my skirts tangling in the ripped quilt. Finally, I half fell, half scrambled across the floor, kicking the drooling bowl aside as I thought, *This is my fault. If I had fixed the latch properly, if I had been certain the door was locked, Abigail could not have pushed it open. She could not see this.*

When I did finally reach her, Abigail refused to budge. Fastened on the sight of her mother, who by then looked more like a creature than a woman, the child was stuck tight as a fence post. Finally, I half lifted and half shoved her out of the doorway. But not fast enough. Not before Avis Hobbs screamed, and the scream was cut off with retching.

Staggering onto the landing, I knelt and pulled Abigail Hobbs to me. I said her name over and over again, as if calling her name might erase what I had done. Might turn back time, lock the door, and wipe away the terrible picture of her mother she would now surely see forever in her nightmares.

"Forgive me," I said. "I am so sorry!" And then added, inanely, "Don't cry," although I was on the verge of tears myself by then. Because I already knew that, unless we were very lucky, or my mother was truly strong enough to bend the warp and weft of time, we had been too late. Abigail Hobbs would be motherless by the night bell or, more likely, before.

The knowledge churned my stomach, whipping up my own fear. So, in truth, I did not know which of us I was speaking for, or if I was speaking for both of us when I held Abigail Hobbs on that grubby dark landing and murmured, *Don't cry, Don't cry,* as if they were the only words I would ever say. Nor do I know how long it was before they finally dried in my throat and I realized that the only sound coming from behind the closed door of what was surely by then a death room was silence.

My cap was askew and my hands were grasping Abigail's shoulders as I leaned back and looked into her face.

"Don't cry," I started to murmur again, before I noticed that she was not crying.

Instead, standing as still as Lot's daughter turned to a pillar of salt, Abigail Hobbs was smiling.

I rocked back. As I put a hand out to steady myself, I realized that I had never really looked at her before. Now, even in the half light of the stinking shuttered house, her skin, tinged with summer, seemed to glow. A golden curl strayed from under her bright white cap. Her nose and cheeks and brow were so smooth that they might have been porcelain. As her small, white hand reached up to stroke my cheek, I remembered the word my mother used—*A Poppet.* A made thing. A perfect form.

She was right. Abigail was perfect. More than that, she was undeniably beautiful. And the most beautiful thing about her was her eyes. I couldn't look away from them, from their depths, which were an exquisite blue. But it wasn't the blue of the sea, or the summer sky. It was the motionless blue of deeply frozen ice.

❧

NOW, I raise my hand to that same cheek and tell myself that I am being ridiculous, that what feels like cold is merely numbness left over from a bad dream. A nightmare, brought on by the horrible day, and the heat, and the ghastly death of poor Avis Hobbs.

Beside me, the wide bed is empty. This is not unusual. My mother has always liked the night, and it is no great secret that the hour just before first light is when all manner of things must be cut and picked and plucked. In that magic space, as night has dripped and distilled and is about to be poured away, the earth is at its most potent. My mother often goes out then, if there is not snow on the ground, and sometimes even when there is, to seek and reap her harvest before it is drained by light. Other times, she simply stays up to watch the stars. I've often found her standing, motionless in the garden, or on the bank above the cove, her head bent back, studying the pattern of the heavens as if she can read what is written there.

I swing my legs over the edge of the high bed, and pad to the window. The sanded boards, warm under my bare feet, still hold the heat of the day. As I push the shutters open, I realize it is almost dawn. There is no wind. Beyond the paddock and the milking shed the outlines of the birches are dark scribbles against the lightening sky. Watching them, I think that their leaves and branches are as still and limp as the wings of broken birds, and in that moment, I know exactly where my mother is. I see her, standing in the Hobbs' unkempt garden. The picture wavers, like a footstep in sand when the tide comes in, then vanishes.

When I get downstairs, I find the kitchen door ajar, which means she must have left quickly, driven by some sudden thought. Some time in the night a mist rolled in from the cove. There is not enough of it left to smell of brine or drip from the fence rail, but I can see my mother's footsteps. A trail, so small they look almost like paw prints, weaves through the beds, leaving a dark trail on the gravel before they disappear through the garden gate. Following, I can feel the familiar pull of her like a string in my bones.

❧

By the time I skirt the common, the sky has made its turn from night to the beginning of day. The dog star is running down the horizon and I can see that, although it is barely hours since Avis and her unborn went to God, all life has leaked from the Hobbs house. I have no idea who has taken Abigail until her father returns, but no one is here. Even the chickens are gone. I push and lift the broken gate then, setting it aside, pick my way to the back of the house where I know I will find my mother.

"Clever," she says, as much to herself as to me.

The Hobbs' kitchen garden feels as if it is hovering just beyond darkness. A mouse skitters by, followed fast by another. I can smell a tangle of mint, and make out a mat of thyme that has spilled over the stones. My mother gestures toward the overgrown stalks of tall flowers that edges the fence. Avis had obviously given up any pretense of caring for them. Once, though, they had been a high stand of monkshood.

Few plants bloom as late in the summer, and in the growing light I can see that these are heavy with buds. The blossoms will be lush, and especially inviting as everything else around them has withered. Monkshead is beautiful. Its flowers are the blue deep of a summer midnight. But every child knows, we are all taught from before we can waddle and pluck, that this is a plant you never touch. Not the beguiling blossoms, nor the stems, nor the roots, nor even the leaves. Because every part of it is poison.

As I step closer, peering, I see what I don't expect. None of the stalks have been cut. No buds have been pulled away. Not so much as a leaf has been clipped.

"Clever," my mother says again, and opens her fist.

Curled and dead, no bigger than a large pebble, I am not sure at first what she is holding. Then, as she watches me, I understand. It is a dried hellebore. Lenten Rose. The death flower, which kills as surely as monkshood. The pretty little blooms emerge as the snow melts. Their roots are ground and laid out to poison rats.

I look to my mother's feet, past my own toes grayed and soft with dust, and see where she had been kneeling, and what she has found. Hard against the wind-stripped boards of the house, hidden by a scramble of mint she pushed aside, a patch of dead leaves and earth has been scraped back, either with a tool, or the sharp edge of a stone. The roots of a patch of hellebore had been exposed, dug up, and re-covered. You would never notice. Unless you thought to look.

My mother's gaze meets mine. Her eyes are flecked with amber, and in certain lights look almost gold, as if they have trapped the fragment of a star. She shakes her head, closing her fist around the deadly curled thing. Then, without speaking, we pick our way back around the empty house, down the path, and through the broken gate. The sky lightens and the crickets begin to jump as we make our way around the common and down the meadow, our secret rocking between us like a shell whose shape I cannot begin to imagine.

CHAPTER THREE

"Tell it again."

Judah White's dress is the color of a dove's wing. From the corner of my eye, I see her hair has escaped her cap and sprigs across her cheek. We are laying on our backs in the grove of birches below our house, counting clouds. Small, and floating very high above us, Judah says the clouds are angels' kisses.

Judah White and I are the sisters of each other's hearts. Three summers ago under the full Buck Moon, we sliced our palms with a razor shell, and held our hands together and made our blood mingle. Judah pokes my cheek with a piece of thatch she has plucked from the long grass that is so dry it is turning itself to hay without even being cut. She walks the prickly stalk towards my nose.

"Tell it again," she says, and laughs.

Judah is indentured to Joseph Ingersoll who owns The Ordinary. She arrived five years ago, to replace poor Elizabeth Bourne. Like my parents and also Judah, Elizabeth, whom we called Eliza, came from Jersey, one of the string of little islands that float between England and France.

Eliza Bourne had also been my friend although she was much

older than me and more a nursemaid, a helping hand for my mother when she was not at The Ordinary. Until she was accused of theft. Eliza did not do it. But Goody Burroughs decided she did, so the truth did not matter much. By the time Mistress Ingersoll found the table linen stuffed in the wrong chest where she had forgotten them, Elizabeth Bourne had been gone three months. Banished, with a T for thief stitched on to the back of her dress, she was forbidden to return to Falmouth unless she wanted to be whipped. She only avoided the lash before leaving because my father paid her fine.

I do not know where Eliza went. Perhaps to Boston, although my mother says more likely farther south, New York or Philadelphia or even Virginia, where no one knows her and she might begin again. So, Judah came from Jersey to take her place. Philip English, another Jerseyman who is my father's partner and friend, arranged her passage as he had arranged Eliza's. The island of Jersey is not big. As she had known Elizabeth Bourne's family, my mother also knew Judah's. When Judah arrived here, my mother, determined not to let the same thing happen again, took her in, and vowed to watch over her. In truth, Judah has been so close to us since she arrived that she may as well be my blood sister. Or my twin, as we are of an age, although we do not look alike.

Even if I did not love her, I would say Judah White is beautiful. Every time he sees her, Captain John Alden laughs, and calls her The Jersey Maid, and says he will trade her for barrels of beer. Judah's hair is as black and glossy as the bottom of a well. Her eyes are the sometimes gray and sometimes green of the sea she crossed to come here. When she is angry, you can hear a trace of Jersey, and beyond that France, in her voice.

It is four days since Avis Hobbs died, and gone noon. Morning chores are long done. My mother is in the stillroom, grinding burdock to paste. Mr Ingersoll is with Mr Burroughs, walking the boundaries of the fields to the marsh edge where the fence has come down. I have finished milking, and raked the shed floor, and it is far too hot for anyone to miss either Judah or me for an hour yet. I pull my cap off and squint up, tracing the silver columns of the birches. Above them the clouds have vanished, melted into the pale green scatter of leaves that dapple the sky.

The story Judah wants me to tell again is very good. And it is mine. Even Mercy Lewis, who is not at all beautiful, but sly, and anxious to have all the best stories, would like to have it. I know because since Avis Hobbs died, she has slithered close to me and smiled. Sweat soils the brow of Mercy's cap, and her hands, when they are not at work, twist and writhe like snakes in the sun.

William Hobbs returned from Topsfield yesterday morning. But he was far too late. Already, Avis Hobbs had been laid in the earth. In this heat, and with the state of her, there was no time to wait on grief. George Burroughs and the Cloyce brothers dug her grave through the night she died. She was set free to God with all of us on hand to witness her going before the sun reached noon the next day. The Cloyces and the Lewises, cousins as they are and living side by side and landlord to the Hobbs, saw to the cakes and funeral wine. But the death room was my mother's province.

We went straight there from the burial, and went again the next morning, clearing and sending the linen for burning, sweeping and salting the hearth and the sills. Mercy Lewis followed us to the Hobbs' house, saying she had to call for Avis's cat. A small orange thing named Percy, William gave it to his wife as a kit and the whole town knows she doted on it. So Mercy was set on finding it as everyone was sure William Hobbs would wish to have it with him.

"Percy, Perceeee!" She had yowled.

Pleasing as an ill-tuned fiddle, Mercy Lewis's voice made my teeth hurt. Perhaps feeling the same way, Percy did not appear. Then, because her mind is like an unsettled bird that cannot light on anything for long, Mercy forgot about the cat, and turned her attention to me.

She had asked already, trailing after me as I made my way up the town beach with the salt pan that morning, how it had been with Avis? How had she conducted herself in her going to God? Then, I had pretended not to hear. But I could not play the same trick yesterday at the Hobbs' house as she sidled close and complimented me on my apron and on the pattern I was making with my sweeping.

Mercy Lewis does not like me any more than I like her. Yet, she thought she could have my story for a smile and a compliment because my father is away and my mother is sometimes ill. She could have saved her labor. The third time she asked, pulling on my sleeve, I turned and glared at her. When that did not make her go away, I crossed my eyes and bared my teeth. Then I swung my broom so suddenly it caught her hem, causing her to step back and begin wringing her hands and muttering about idiots.

The only person I give my secrets and my stories to is Judah. So, as she prods me with the stalk of thatch, as she walks it across my forehead and pokes it in my hair and I swipe at it, I tell her again about the dying of Avis Hobbs.

I tell how George Burroughs told us of William's leaving, and of Avis's illness, and how Abigail came pounding on their door. I tell how I smelled his sweat, and when I nearly ran into him was so close I could have licked the red sun patch on the back of his neck. I tell about Goody Burroughs and her arguing, and Goody Skilling who was too jealous to look up because jealousy is a kind of fear and she is terrified of my mother. I tell about the rips in the quilt, and the stink, and how, when I opened the window, the babe's soul glimmered over my shoulder and along my arm and took its leave of my open hand. And I tell her too, about Abigail. How she stood in the doorway, and would not let me move her. How she studied me with her icy jay's eyes, and how her cap and apron were bright white. I even tell about the dead gray fish of Avis Hobbs' belly.

I make Judah a gift of these things, give them to her to hold and run her finger over the way we run our fingers over the edges of the shells we pick from the cove beach. As I do, I know that she will carry each thing I tell her home, and pull each one out later when she is alone so she may examine it and decide if it is worthy of keeping or should be discarded.

Because this is what we do. Judah and I hoard, and pick, and keep only the best, only the most perfectly formed secrets and tid-bits and lies. Then we choose a shell for each one. And when we have enough, when each collection is complete, we bring them here. If it is spring or autumn and the earth is soft under the birches, we clear a patch and arrange the shells. We pattern them into the loam, and let them rest until the leaves fall or the mat of violets or long grass grows through them and all our secrets are swallowed by the earth.

Or, if it is summer and the ground is hard as it is now, or winter and it is frozen, we go down to the beach and walk the packed sand at low tide until we find exactly the right place. Then, we set the shells out. We form them in lines, or spirals, or sharp edged squares, grooming them until they are the shapes of the stories they hold. And when at last we are finished, we step back and wait for the tide to creep up and run her fingers across our offering. Then we watch as the sea reads every story, every lie and hidden shred of our days, before finally she carries them away.

This is our habit. There is nothing we do not dissect and share. But today, for the first time, I do not give Judah every single thing.

I tell myself this does not matter. That her pattern will still be complete. That I have not robbed her, or dropped a story and cracked its meaning. Judah will not miss what I have not told her because she will never know what she does not have. She will never know how my mother stopped in the door of the death room, never feel the flutter of her words as she first looked on Avis Hobbs, or see the curled deadly blossom and the broken root my mother found buried beneath the overgrown mint.

Nor will she know how, in the cloying dark of that night and each night since, I have sat up with a scream drying in my throat as I finger the icy patch on my cheek, feeling the stroke of that small pearly hand and remembering how, as her mother died not feet away, Abigail Hobbs fastened her ice blue eyes on me, and smiled.

CHAPTER FOUR

"A Trisket, a Trasket. Four kittens in a basket."

I stop, my hands wrist deep in the crumbling earth. It is not a good day for digging. With the weather so hot and dry, it is hard to fashion the walls of the holes. Hard to pack them tight and smooth so they will not fall in on themselves before they hold even a single memory. My mother and I learned this too, in The Greening. The earth cradles every act played upon it.

In the years we passed under the care of Ashawonks, as we lived nestled among her people in the jewel box my father chose for us, my mother and I came to know the forest. We learned the thickets and ponds and streams, as well as the shore, and the opened ground that was burned each spring before the last snow melted so planting could begin. And, as we did, as I followed my mother, my short footsteps never out of her long shadow, we saw that along every track and path, at any place of meaning, a memory hole had been dug—a repository fashioned to hold what had happened there.

Sometimes, they were as deep as an elbow and as far across, if the event remembered was large—a battle, or a feast, or an alliance.

Sometimes, they were no deeper than a wrist or wider than a hand and commemorated nothing larger than a meeting, or a hunt, or an extraordinary sight, a great stag or a huge pair of snowy owls. No matter its size, each spring every hole would be carefully tamped and re-tamped. And each time a memory hole was tended, the story that lived there was tended, too—told to anyone who happened to pass by, who would in turn re-tell it. In this way life was remembered. Names and events tethered to the earth that birthed them.

We commit memory to books. Scratch the nib along the paper, blot the ink, and trust written words to cradle all the fragile past. I know that is what civilized God-fearing people do. I can read, and my penmanship is good. My mother has seen to that. We have ink and quills and parchment in the writing box where we keep my father's letters, those that reach us, and the accounts and records of the earnings from the sawmills he has built and ships he has launched with Captain Alden. My father has been gone two years, and all his absence is written down. So, perhaps I should know better than to do this. But I cannot help myself.

After my father left us, Ashawonks took us to the spot where we saw him last. The she-sachem was a small woman, but fearsome. She moved through the forest as if her feet did not touch the ground. Some said she was a shape changer, that under a lesser moon she would vanish for nights at a time. That day, above the river bank where my father took his leave of us, shape changer or no, Ashawonks showed my mother how to find and hollow out the space where his boots stood. She knelt, and dug with a clam shell wider than my hand, then helped my mother firm the sides of the hole so the earth would not fall in and swallow what had been.

Ashawonks taught my mother how to smooth my father's smile. How to tamp the booming sound of his words into the soil. How to fasten his touch to the earth so when my mother missed him most she could return and kneel beside the memory hole, and place her hand on its damp floor, and know that she would find him there.

Now, since spring when my mother's unwanted suitor began tapping at our window, I have done the same. As soon as the earth was soft enough to yield, I began to look for the right place. When I finally found this spot high on the point that stretches above our birch grove, I became a thief. I began to pluck the brush of my mother's lips when, thinking I am asleep, she bends to kiss me in the night. To cup my hands around the sound of her voice as she speaks my name. To steal and hoard the sight and smell and sound of her. Then, when my pockets are full, I come here, and tamp the soil, and smooth the edges of the holes, and imprison her in a ring of memory.

This clearing was made by the tribes. I have found fragments of shell at the bottom of some my holes, and blackened stones that, unless they lie, came from fires that smoked mussels pulled from the rocks below. But since we have come with our forts and our houses and our fences, no one has used it. When I found it, this place was almost lost. It is still my secret. No one, not even Judah, knows about it. No one comes here, save me. Or so I thought. But it seems I was wrong.

"A Trisket, a Trasket. Four kittens in a basket."

The singing voice is unfamiliar, strange and deep. But surely a man would not sing such a ditty? Although it is true that some men sing with the voices of angels. You come across them from time to time in the fields, sowing or driving cattle, when they think they are alone in the world with God. Then, the singing they make is as alien to their large bodies and rough hands as a goldfinch's song to a mule. But this does not sound like that. This song is not spiraling to heaven. This voice is deep and thick. Dreamy as a slow-sinking stone. But with a sour edge. This voice sounds like turned cream running down a basin.

I pull my hands from the half-finished hole and wipe them in the grass. This far up, the point climbs and narrows until it sticks into the sea like the prow of a ship. If you look down through the wind-stunted trees, you will see nothing but rocks, hard and pinked, as if the dawn they face is always on them. In winter or in a storm, the waves out here thrash. Now, in this heat, the sea, like the rest of us, can barely bestir itself. It strokes and rocks, half-hearted, making almost no noise at all, which is why I can hear the singing.

"A Trisket, A Trasket—"

The song begins again, sounding closer. So close that, like a doe with a fawn, I realize I must quit this place in order to protect it. I have a sudden vision of being caught here—discovered on my knees with all my memories revealed. I get to my feet, trying not to scramble, to be both as silent and as fast as I can.

The path that runs up the point is barely a path. In most places, it is little more than the echo of a track. No one from the village bothers to even try planting here. The soil is too thin and too salted and the trees too wind lashed and poor for cutting. But despite their frailness, in the summer they are thick with undergrowth. The voice is louder now.

"A Trisket. A Trasket. Four kittens in a basket—"

I reach the far side of the clearing and duck under the low branches. My skirts snag on brambles. Through the scrim of leaves, I can see the glittering lazy sea far below, deep green and darted with sunlight.

"A Trisket. A Tras—"

The singing stops, and I freeze. Without warning, my skin turns cold. Out on the water, the brightness of the sun is suddenly sharp and dangerous as shattered glass. As if pushed by a giant hand, I sink to my belly. Without knowing why, only that I must, I make myself as flat and small and still as I can.

My heart is throbbing like something being squeezed. I am sure I can hear it. Then I realize something else is throbbing, too. Beating like the beat of a drum. I close my eyes, but it gets louder, until it is a sound and a shape at once and I know that if I stretched my hand out, I would touch it.

"A Trisket. A Trasket—"

There is a tease in the song now, as if it knows I am here. As if it can see me, and is daring me to show myself. To crash through the brambles, bursting from my hiding place like an animal set on by hunters. Cold sweat blossoms on the back of my neck.

"Four kittens in a basket."

I open my eyes, somehow knowing what I will see. Blanketed by the low twisted trees and the brambles, surrounded by a haze of green, I can just make out the track a few feet in front of me. A dark figure stands on it. With the shattered sun and broken glass of the sea behind it, it looks huge. But it cannot be. Because Abigail Hobbs is only ten years old.

CHAPTER FIVE

I should not be able to see her through the thick undergrowth. But I can. She comes into focus like someone stepping out of a fog. Abigail is holding a bouquet in her small perfect hands. Sea roses splash, bright red against her white apron, backed by the deep, verdant, blue of monkshood.

Both of us are absolutely still. More than still. It feels as if we have been smote, struck to stone, a sinew pulled tight as an Indian bow stretched between us. Laying in the brambles like a terrified animal, I understand with absolute clarity that the throbbing is the beating of Abigail Hobbs' heart. And that if I can feel hers, she can feel mine.

The idea makes me ill. Dizzy. My tongue is so thick I can barely breathe. When Abigail bends and looks straight at me, the world vanishes. Flat on my belly with my chin in the scrub, I am pinned by the blue jay screech of her stare.

I do not know how long we stay this way. It seems forever. I am not breathing, not moving. I am willing my heart to stop. Abigail smiles. Then she straightens, and turns away. She begins to sing again as she moves up the track towards the tip of the point, the strange sloping notes of the song winding themselves into the trees as she disappears.

I wait until they fade. Until I cannot hear them any more, and the world returns to itself. When at last the air is filled with the lap stroke of the sea and the chirr of birds, I crawl forward. Almost falling through the bramble, I stagger to my feet, reach the track, and bolt like a frightened horse.

❧

THERE IS a jangling in my head. I am still running, scrambling down the point, bursting into the birches above the cove, when I realize it is the town bell, tolling. No. Not tolling, ringing frantically, as if someone is hauling the rope, jumping up and down pulling it every which way. The fear in the sound is so palpable that my first thought is *Fire!*

As I reach the paddocks, the bulk of my father's house rises before me. I feel a selfish burst of relief. No flames lick its gables or finger the fine panes of its glass. Ahead, at the top of the meadow, in the gap between the houses that sit between us and Broad Street and the common, I can just make out figures running. But there are no flames on those roofs, either. The pale mid-day sky is undisturbed. No black smoke spirals upwards. I run on up the meadow, pulled by the sound. Darting along the side yards, I burst into Broad Street, and turn towards Ingersoll's where I can see a crowd gathering. The whole village is converging on The Ordinary, which can only mean both that there is news, and that it is bad.

We have a meeting house. George Burroughs preaches in it, but he is not ordained so we, and it, are not truly blessed. We are not Boston, or even Salem. John Alden says the Eastward is more interested in fishing and trading than praying. So it is the tavern, Ingersoll's Ordinary, that is the heart of the village. This is where everyone comes when there is news.

The bell subsides as I reach the outskirts of the crowd.

Thomas Cloyce, who like all the Cloyces considers himself important for no reason anyone knows, is standing on the front steps beside Joseph Ingersoll. With them is Anthony Brackett whose farm is across the neck, fartherest out on the road before it turns south. I bend to catch my breath, then look for my mother and find her standing with Judah and George Burroughs and his wife.

The crowd smells of sweat and fish. I work my way through the gate and across the door yard, edging around clumps of people. Thomas Cloyce is shouting at everyone to be quiet. When nothing happens, Joseph Ingersoll raises a pot and bangs it with a poker. As I reach Judah's shoulder, Anthony Brackett shoves him aside and begins to speak.

"A rider came, going north," he shouts. "Bare an hour ago. He needed to get inland, so he left the news with me." A heavy man, red faced, in scuffed boots, Brackett is puffed up like a turkey cock. He stops for breath.

"News! What news?" Someone shouts, urging him to get on with it.

"Yesterday, at sunset, in Saco," Brackett croaks, his voice suddenly hoarse, as if the heat and the words are too much for him. "Savages!"

The crowd quiets as if sea water has been thrown over them.

"A band of them," Brackett's voice gathers again. "Armed. Well armed! They fired on three men and their sons bringing in cattle. Captain Blackman, the militia commander sends warning from Saco, that we should arm and be ready!"

There is a silence, then an intake of breath. Saco is not a day's ride south.

"How many? How many were there?" Someone shouts.

"No telling!" Brackett's eyes swell until they are so large they look as if they might meet across his nose. "No telling! Half a hundred. Perhaps more! It was sunset, and they came out of the forest where they hide. Out of the trees where they'd been lurking like demons, waiting for the God-fearing to fall into their trap. Demons!"

"Lurking like demons!" Someone yells.

"Savage demons!" Someone else echoes.

Then Mercy Lewis begins to scream.

❧

WE WERE NOT ALL HERE, in 1676. Many of us, like my father and mother and I, and Judah, and Joseph Ingersoll and his wife, came after, at the second birth of this town, when the fort was built and Edward Tyng installed as magistrate. But that is no matter. Because the earth holds what has been as surely as it holds what will be. So all of us remember. All of us know what happened, twelve years ago almost to the day, as sure as if we had lived it. On that day, too, it came first to Brackett's farm.

King Philip's war had been running hot for a year on that summer morning, which people would later say was as beautiful as any they had ever seen. But the fighting was in the south, and no real affair of the Eastward. The sky was pale blue, the wind still and the sun not too hot as the Brackett family gathered. Younger then, Anthony Brackett was fresh from serving in the local militia, which ventured nowhere south of Portsmouth, and mostly did nothing at all. Thinner and full of himself, farm proud, he had seen the second hay cut and turned the day before, sooner than any of his neighbors, puffed though they were. Especially those Lewises who, bloated on righteousness, never let a soul forget how many of them there were, and how long they had been on Casco Bay. That morning though, Anthony Brackett had won the race he ran in his head with them, and as a reward was taking a little ease with his family. His children, wife and sister, and her children and husband were all at the kitchen table.

They were talking about what needed to be done and not done now the hay was in. No one said it aloud, but they were all congratulating themselves on a farm well run and lives well lived —some might say it was God, but Anthony Brackett knew it was his own hard labor that brought such good fortune—when the door burst open, and the Indian they called Simon stood on the threshold with the morning light behind him.

Simon was no stranger. He was a pest, it was true, but a known one. For the last few weeks he had appeared and reappeared, sometimes at the house, sometimes at the barn or at the edges of the fields, a dark figure in cast off clothes, a savage pretending he was something else. The Bracketts kept a good table, and they were kind. If there were scraps, Brackett's wife left them out for Simon, and once or twice Brackett and his brother-in-law and nephews traded some bit of molded tobacco or a mug of soured beer for heavy work, dragging a log or moving the muck heap. When one of the Brackett cows disappeared and later the carcass was discovered beyond a broken fence line, Simon promised he would find the culprit.

Truth be, none of the Bracketts put much stock in it. Indians always grumbled that cattle broke down fences and got loose and trampled their plantings. Which was true enough. But fencing was expensive, and if the cattle wandered, they didn't go far and could be rounded up, and what were a few squash and some half ripe corn husks? Now, Brackett supposed as he pushed himself to his feet, wiping his mouth with the back of his hand, Simon had returned with a name, probably expecting a reward, some bit of rubbish, a button or one of his wife's old ribbons. Indians were easy to please. Captain Anthony Brackett had barely taken a step when the men behind Simon pushed him aside and streamed into the house.

Brackett heard his sister scream. A pitcher was knocked over. His wife grabbed for the children. These men suddenly surrounding him, pouring out of nowhere as if the morning itself had birthed them from pure air, were like none he had seen before. His time in the militia had not, in truth, been much time at all. He had enjoyed the camaraderie, the smell of other men and the talk of forts and guns and battles. But his term had been over almost before it began. Captain Anthony Brackett, as he was by then, had marched about and seen a bit of New England. But he hadn't seen much of Indians. At least, none like these. Yet he knew at once who they were, almost as if he had dreamed, or nightmared, them. Or somehow always known they were close, echoes of the forest that had once covered the land he now called his own.

In their half nakedness, they were lean and hard. Their faces were streaked with black, and there was an alien smell to them. Grease, and sweat, and something else, unnamed but familiar that churned deep in the gut. The north. These men were from the Pentagoet, which everyone had heard of and no-one quite believed in.

Anthony Brackett saw his wife grabbed by her hair, and felt an arm around his neck and a blade at his throat. And in that split second, he knew himself for what he was. A farmer who loved his farm. A man who loved his wife and children. A man who wanted to live.

"You serve us or you be slain by us." Simon suddenly no longer sounded like a cur, a sidling thing you kicked or threw a scrap to depending on your mood, and either way, laughed about later.

Brackett's wife was holding the baby. His eyes met hers, and he nodded.

When his brother-in-law screamed, "Coward!" his throat was cut. He died slowly, gasping like a fish on the kitchen floor.

No one could say later, exactly how many of them there were, or how, exactly everyone knew they had been sent by the sachem, Madockawando, who might even have been amongst them, although since no one could recognize him, no one could say. They moved so quickly, and in such a strange way, running as if their feet barely touched the ground, that no one could be sure, or have time to count, or if they had counted, remember. It was if they were an apparition, a night terror made real. Except for the blood. The cut throat of a grown man is more than enough to soak a kitchen floor.

They took all the arms, the guns and shot and even the axes and the knives from the Brackett farm. Then, leaving the dead man with his wife keening over him, and Anthony Brackett shamed, and his wife and children and even the baby too terrified to cry or move, they went on, along Back Cove and up Cleeve's Neck.

Robert Corbin and his brother-in-law Benjamin Atwell were determined to finish the haying that day. Anthony Brackett was already finished, and it wouldn't do to be shown up by that windbag. They had brought bread and a flask of small ale. Passing it back and forth as they walked to the fartherest field, they started just after first light. The morning had wound on for an hour, probably two, when Benjamin looked up, pausing his scythe in mid-swing. He had just realized what stopped him—the sudden uncanny silence because the forest birds had stopped singing—when a hatchet caught him in the back of the head.

Robert Corbin was dead before he could turn to see what had happened. At the house, his wife and their youngest child were cut down before either one of them could finish a scream. The older girl, who was milking, heard the noise and, without knowing quite why, dropped her bucket, climbed out the back shed window, and ran. She did not reach the Atwell house to give warning before her aunt Alice and all her Atwell cousins were taken. Even as the captives were being turned to begin the long march north, the main war party moved on, running swift, silent, and bloody across the summer morning.

Farther along Back Cove, James Ross and his wife, Anne, a pretty thing named for her mother who was not supposed to have favorites but did, were set on and killed as they broke the day's bread. Anne's father, old George Lewis, who had come from England and been thirty-six years in Casco, was cut down beside his wife, the old lady twining her hand in his shirt before she died. Their Ross grandchildren, like the others who didn't run or get killed, were taken.

Out on the water setting nets, two men from the village finally heard screams, and paddled to raise the alarm. Guessing most of his family was already dead and beyond help, Philip Lewis got his wife, Mary, and their three year old daughter, Mercy, into a boat George Burroughs commandeered. Together with the rest who had a vessel and the wits to get to it, they took refuge on an island in the bay. Trying not to show themselves, they huddled in the tree line, watching the town burn and listening to screams echo across the water.

Finally, as the sun sank on August 11, 1676, a silence fell over Cleeve's Neck. Smoke blurred the reddening air, making it look as if the forges of Hell had burst their doors. Eleven Casco men lay dead, most of them cut down where they stood. Twenty-three women and children had been slaughtered or captured. Of all the families in Casco, the Lewis family, who had been there longer than most, was hit hardest.

Both grandparents were dead with their daughter, Ann. Another daughter, beloved Alice Atwell, has captured, stolen into the forest. Five grandchildren had been killed. The others, save two who ran and hid, were taken. Two sons-in-law had been slaughtered in the fields. A third, Thomas Skilling, would die of his wounds before the year was out. His wife, old George Lewis's youngest daughter, Mary Skilling, survived. Cruel rumor said she was so disagreeable that even the savages didn't want her. But they killed two of her sons. Mary Skilling had only one child left, and her niece, Mercy, her brother Philip's daughter whom she would hold and whisper to. Fasten on, and sometimes even call her own.

Out on the island, Philip and Mary and little Mercy Lewis and the others who had followed short, wild haired George Burroughs, waited through four nights and five days, huddling in the scraggy trees without even a fire for fear of being seen, before they were rescued. Even then, when they were finally rowed back to shore, even though Philip Lewis and George Burroughs and one or two other men were able-bodied and unharmed, there were still not enough people left in Casco Bay to bury the dead.

No, most of us were not there. But all of us knew what happened.

❧

WITH MY SIDE pinched from running and my ears ringing from the bell, I had not noticed Mercy Lewis when I arrived at The Ordinary. Now, I cannot stop looking at her. Judah reaches for my hand. Her nails dig into my flesh because there is something terrible about it. Watching Mercy Lewis is like watching a creature being tortured.

She bends double, holding her stomach. The sound she makes is more of a shriek than a scream. It is endless, as though she does not have to breathe. Mercy's wailing is so loud and so piercing that those around her step back as if the noise is pushing them. Mercy staggers. Then, as she folds in on herself and curls to the ground, it is not her beloved aunt Mary Skilling, or even her own mother, who seems terrified, but my mother who goes to her.

"A cup of water! Water!"

Men are stepping backwards while women flap like hens. Some people are pushing up the steps of The Ordinary, while others mill in a circle. In the space that has opened around Mercy Lewis, I see that my mother is again as she was at Avis Hobbs'. Nothing in her wavers as she bends and grasps Mercy by both shoulders. Mercy tries to twist away, but my mother is too strong. The screaming wail comes again, and again. Mercy's cap is half off. Her hair flies about her face. My mother draws the girl up until she is on her knees. Then she rocks her hand back and slaps Mercy Lewis, hard.

All at once, there is silence. Everyone stops moving. Mercy's eyes are wild. She stares at my mother, and for a moment I am horribly afraid of what she may do. I catch George Burroughs' eye, and see the thought fly between us. He is already moving, shaking off his wife who is clinging to his shoulder, her eyes lit with excitement, when my mother lets go of Mercy's shoulders and puts her arms around her.

Standing, she draws Mercy Lewis up with her. The silence is broken now by the sound of long, horrible, keening sobs. Patting Mercy on the back, my mother turns and walks her away from the crowd.

CHAPTER SIX

"The girl is not witched!" My mother's voice is cross. "She is terrified."

Judah and I sit before the hearth. Despite the heat, we have lit a fire. The pop and jump of the flames, even their warmth on this too warm night, is comforting. My mother stands at the table holding a knife, her hand on a new loaf.

"Those women will drive that child mad."

She cuts a slice, then looks at us as though we have some part in this because Judah repeated what she has heard whispered in The Ordinary all afternoon, that Mercy Lewis is witched.

"Those women," my mother says again, reaching for the block of cheese I brought from the stillroom. There is an uncharacteristic bitterness in her voice, and I know she is thinking of Elizabeth Bourne. My mother spoke for her. My father paid ten coins, one for each stroke that would have landed on her naked back, and arranged her passage south. They saved her from the whip, but they could not save her from the lash of wagging tongues. My mother feels it still, I know. Then it was Goody Buroughs, and the others she commands. Now, she is talking about Mercy's mother, Mary Lewis, and mostly about her aunt, Mary Skilling.

"They are all terrified." My mother shakes her head. "Of Indians. Or as they call them, savages. Or demons. But you do not pass terror on to a child. You do not feed it like mother's milk, drip, drip, drip, until it wears her mind away. Especially after what that child went through. It is wicked."

As she says it, I think of our time in The Greening. I was not much older then than Mercy Lewis was on the morning the village was attacked. But I never witnessed any killing, or even fighting. A few times in the years we spent with Ashawonks, we moved quickly, once at night, because the fighting came too close. But when we moved, our whole world moved with us. Nothing was lost or destroyed. We were not cast into strangeness. And always, I had my mother.

I never, not once, sensed fear in her. Nor was I afraid of the people who surrounded us. They were very strange to me, at first. At first, I could not understand a thing they said. Nor, I know now, could my mother. But we both learned, quickly. And then gradually, because it was how we lived, we came to look and smell and sound more and more like them until, except for our paleness and our hair, we were not different from them at all. So there was no space for strangeness.

When at last the war was over and Ashawonks brought us to where we could see their boat anchored and watch the wherry as it rowed ashore, my father and Captain Alden laughed, and said we were so well disguised that they could scarce tell us apart. I know that was not true. But I also know that, had my father and Captain Alden been strangers, it might have been. We could have been Ashawonks people, not only because we dressed and spoke and smelled the same, but also because we were not afraid.

I think of the sour smell of fear, of the quick fumbling movements it begets, of its broken voice. Of how fear parses out those it seizes, weakening their minds, setting them apart like a fever or a pox. And how, like a fever or a pox, it is contagious. This is what my mother means about Mercy Lewis. Her aunt and mother never allowed her terror to heal. Instead they fed her, and doubtless still feed her, more terror. And it has scarred her. The wheals and sores are in her mind, not on her skin, but they are there. You can smell them in her sweat. See them in her eyes. You can look straight into Mercy Lewis's soul and watch the putrid cankers blossom there.

And, I think, if you get too close to her, if you stay too long, you could catch them. They could jump from her to you the way the pox jumps. Then they would possess you as surely as any demon, so at the whisper of *'savages'*, you too, would twist and shriek. You too, would gibber and grab your waist like a mad thing. Those who gossip in The Ordinary are not altogether wrong. Nor is my mother. Mercy Lewis has been witched by terror.

I cannot rid myself of this idea. Nor of the thought that fear flies abroad. That it arrived here this afternoon, perched on Anthony Brackett's shoulder. Carried in his sleeve. That it hid in his pocket like a familiar, and as he began to speak he loosed it just as imps and familiars are loosed. That he set it free, and bid it run amongst us. I whisper this to Judah as we lay in the dark.

Joseph Ingersoll has closed The Ordinary until tomorrow. Just before sunset, a militia troop arrived from Saco, and like most of the men, Ingersoll went to the fort to meet with them. Which is why Judah is here. She comes when she can, and now we nest in the upstairs room.

My mother made up the bed with fresh linen, and threw the window open. The smell of lavender from the garden mixes with the smell of low tide that drifts up through the birches. As I speak of the fear I can feel gathering as surely as any group of witches, Judah takes my hand. I wince. There is a moon tonight. I can see her face. She frowns and looks down. Raising my hand, she sees the criss-cross scratches I got in the brambles.

"What have you done?" She asks. And I realize that with all that happened today, I had almost forgotten about the song, and Abigail Hobbs.

This time, I tell her everything. When I finish, Judah lays

back on the pillow. Her hair fans like crows' wings. In the center of its black halo, her face is moonlit.

"Why was she there?"

How like Judah to ask this question. I did not even wonder it. In what seems to me now a madness, a daze like those that come from being too long in the sun, I had not wondered anything.

"Why was she there?" Judah asks again. This time she raises herself on her elbow to look at me.

We all know Avis Hobbs allowed Abigail to do more or less as she pleased. The child was always wandering, appearing in doors, and sometimes in other people's houses. Once, when she was serving in The Ordinary, Judah heard Peter Cloyce tell how he and his wife had awoken one morning last summer to find Abigail, standing still as a statue at the end of their bed.

Then, we had laughed at the idea of Peter Cloyce in his night shirt. Now, I would like to ask the Cloyces if, in the pearled morning light, they had felt a touch of ice on their sleep-warmed skin? I would like to ask if Abigail Hobbs was holding a bouquet? Or if, in their dreams or as they went about their chores, they caught the echo of a song, a ditty they could somehow not quite hear? I would like to ask Peter Cloyce and his wife if, when they woke and saw her standing watching them in the half light, Abigail Hobbs was smiling.

CHAPTER SEVEN

"No one has seen us! Come on!"

Judah runs ahead of me, leaving behind the sound of men, and shouting, and the crunch of feet—the chaos the village has become in the two days since Anthony Brackett loosed his imps. Captain Blackman, who commands of the militia at Saco, arrived at the fort yesterday, and every man for ten miles around has suddenly become a soldier. At least the common has been scythed. Terror of savages achieved what we could not agree among ourselves. Now, half the town is marching up and down it, drilling.

I have not seen Mercy Lewis since my mother led her away. I don't know if she still rocks in terror, or if the teas my mother sent have calmed her so she may sleep and not dream of demons creeping from the forest. The rest of the village seems half seduced by fear and half convinced that, now that we have our fort and men marching around it, we are safe. That we have learned the lessons of twelve years ago, and will never again be taken by surprise again. Or if we are, we shall be so well defended that no savage demon will stand a chance.

My mother says what happened in Saco is no cause for fear in any case—that the cows broke through a rotten fence the Saco men could not be bothered to mend, and being loose, trampled three stands of corn, ruining them for the harvest. She says the shots that caused all this fuss were fired, not at anyone, but as a warning. And who could blame the Indians for that? The tithes the sachem, Hope Hood, was promised for the land his people sold to Saco town have not been paid these last three years. So, all harvest is precious. The days are long and hot now, but winter will come. Without every kernel, and without the tithes, the Indians risk starvation.

How she is so sure of all this, I do not know. But I can guess. The last two mornings when I woke at dawn, the house was empty, and the canoe we keep pulled up on the cove was gone. I know, because in my bare feet with only a shawl pulled around me for modesty, I picked my way past the paddock and the milking shed and through the silvered grove to our beach.

There in the wet sand, I sensed the ghosts of footsteps. A plank has been set from where the canoe is beached to the water. At full tide, which had been an hour before, it is easy to pull it down and float it free. Our canoe is not a dug-out, but framed and skinned, built in the manner of the Indians. My father had it fashioned for my mother so she might paddle into the marshes to collect plants, or use it to reach the few farms that back up to the shore when she is needed.

What he never said—and what my mother does not say, but we both know, as my father also surely knew—is that she also uses the canoe to visit the local sachem's summer camps. In winter the cove, and even the water along the shore, freezes. Then, Hope Hood and his people move far back into the forest to trap and hunt. But in summer and autumn, they stay on the coast, harvesting the sea.

In our family, the people are not 'savages', and have never been strangers. John Alden and my father made good trade among them when we lived in Duxbury and now make good trade up and down this coast. This is what took my father to London, and has kept him there these two years. Someone must see that we are not cheated—that the furs John Alden collects and their partner Philip English sends in his ships are properly graded and warehoused.

To keep eyebrows down and mouths shut in the village and at the farms she visits, my mother talks about my father's business with sawmills and shares of ships, and says that is why he must be in London. But we know it is the business they do with the tribes that has made my father's and John Alden's fortunes. It is fur that keeps our roof tight.

Now more than ever though, given what has happened in Saco—and given the marching and wheeling on the common, and the torches lit at the fort—it would not do to have our sympathies, or the true nature of my father's trade, known here. We left Duxbury and came north to Maine in part because no one hereabouts knew that my mother and I had been hidden away in The Greening, sheltered by 'savages' during the war. It's true that people whisper about John Alden. But the sloop he captains is owned by Boston. He sails in the city's name, and his parents were famous—saints among the living. So whispering is all it is. Alden is a name that lends protection. Hammond means nothing. And would mean less if people knew it comes from the French, Hamon. All of this would still be true if my father was here. It is even more true with him gone.

Yet, for all that, I know that my mother has been among those very 'savages' who are so feared and loathed. She has been visiting the sachem, Hope Hood. I feel it in my bones. I have seen it. Although she had been gone for hours, this morning, standing barefoot on the beach, relishing the cool damp of the sand, I could see her, as if she was moving just under the skin of the water, or as if I was a bird, coasting invisible above her.

Her skirts rucked up into her old leather belt, my mother pushed the canoe out. She wore no cap. Her tawny hair was dark in the half-light and shadows from the shore. Wading knee-deep, she climbed into the boat, then sat for a moment, rocking on the day's new water. She reached down to trail a hand across the smoky sea, then straightened, and set out. My mother made each stroke of the paddle the way she was taught by the people, the same way she taught me— deliberate and silent, first one side then the next, until the vee of her going opened behind her like a wing.

Or perhaps I dreamed it. Perhaps my mother just left before dawn as she often does, to clip and harvest the world's secrets in the hour when they are most powerful, and Judah and I will meet her returning any moment now and have to explain why we are starting up the track that leads to the point.

If we did, what would we say? That we are chasing Abigail Hobbs?

It is Judah's idea. And suddenly, I feel a fool for following her. I saw Abigail and William Hobbs yesterday, at the harbor where a shipment of beer was being unloaded. The barrels formed a pyramid, and they stopped to watch as some of the village boys tried to climb them, and were shouted at, and ran away, laughing. Bright in the sun, Abigail's curls, escaped her cap. She swung on her father's hand, hopping and skipping like the child she is.

Watching them, I felt shamed. And worse, suspected I might be mad—that my mind has become as deranged as Mercy Lewis's. I was sun dazed. I had stayed out too long, and dug too hard, and standing up must have sniffed the air and caught the witching fear that was already loosed and running abroad, escaped from Anthony Brackett's pockets as he made his busy way towards the village to set the bell tolling and spread his news.

"Come on!" Judah calls again, dancing ahead of me, flickering beyond the trees where the track that runs up the point begins.

For a second, I almost shout to her that this is a mistake. That I was sun-witched and saw nothing, and that we will do nothing but get caught in brambles. Then it is too late. She is gone, and I have no choice but to follow.

CHAPTER EIGHT

The track seems to have overgrown itself. Any evidence of my headlong bolting, any snapped twigs or kicked-up leaves are gone. Following Judah, I wonder if I was here at all? Or if I dreamed Abigail and her song, and before that, her smile and the cold on my cheek the same way I probably dreamed my mother this morning.

What little of the track there is dwindles as it climbs. Judah waits until I catch her up and walks behind me. We are above the far side of the cove now. If you slipped, the fall would not be far, but the pink glittered rock is sharp. You would tear your clothes, and bark your shins, and skin your hands as you reached to stop yourself sliding straight down into the sea which is dark green here, and deep. I can swim. My mother and I both learned in The Greening. But that is rare, and considered immodest, if not downright wanton. No one here swims. I know Judah cannot. I feel her putting her feet where I put mine, following close and careful.

Unlike Judah, I do not think we will find any evidence of Abigail. There is nothing at the very tip of the point but a clump of wind-bent trees. If I am not mad and Abigail Hobbs actually came here, it was because she is a spoiled, willful child, and had been warned that the point is dangerous, and was told not to play there. I do not think she had any more reason than that.

I am wrong.

The bushes and brambles thin. At the top of the point it is so windy and salt-blown that not much can grow here. Judah walks beside me now. Water is all around us, below the prow of the rocks, and on either side. I imagine that this is like standing in the bow of a great ship. Judah would know, since she sailed all the way from Jersey. The only ship I have been on is Captain Alden's when he brought us here ten years ago, and we were never out of sight of land. So, I am about to ask if this is what it is like, to sail upon the ocean, when Judah stops and cocks her head. Strands of hair have come loose from her cap and whip across her face. She raises a hand to brush them away and wrinkles her nose.

"What is that smell?"

Back at our cove, it was still. But here the wind has taken up residence, as if this is its true home. I can smell salt, and sun on the rocks. Then, lifting my nose like a hound, I realize she is right. There is something. Something rotten.

At the very top of the point, a little ways back from its nose, the rocks are dipped and worn. Enough soil has collected to let a small stand of sea oaks to sink their roots. Their leaves dance and clatter, clinging to their twisted arms, which look for all the world as though they are raised above their heads in alarm. As well they might be. Because, as we turn towards them, following the smell, we see what lies at the heart of their tiny grove.

At first, I think it is just bunches of wilted flowers weighed down with stones. I recognize them. Sea roses, still crimson, their petals curling like babies' fists. The bruised purple-blue smudges of monkshood. All laid in a circle inside the small wind-twisted trees. At first, I do not understand what is at their center. I step closer, and see that it is long and bedraggled, and even in this wind, covered in flies. It is a fish, I think. Or a dead sea bird. Then I realize I am wrong.

I reach out to stop Judah, but I am too late. She steps forward, then gasps as she jumps back and we stand, side by side, looking down at the ravaged body of a small orange cat.

"Percy," Judah whispers, and I nod.

We all knew that Avis Hobbs' cat was no better disciplined, no less given to wandering, than her child. But he was a sweet thing. Perching on the window sill, he would watch you, then jump down into your lap if you were spinning or sitting to card wool or mend. He followed me more than once, when I went to do our milking. I sometimes poured a bowl for him and left it under the lavender bank in the garden where it would stay cool even in the mid-day sun. Avis doted on him. She would walk up Broad Street and around the common and down to the harbor calling for him, then when she found him, lift him and carry him home like a baby, telling him to mend his wicked ways.

Some creature has been at him. Or perhaps a gull, or gulls, or crows. What is left of his pretty orange fur is matted horribly, although his little white gloves are still bright and clean. For some reason, this brings tears to my eyes. It is clear that Percy has been dead for some time. Some of the flowers are fresher than others. I am certain the most recent are the ones I saw Abigail carrying. I may have been sun-dazed, but I didn't dream it. She must have been on her way here. Arranged around Percy in a circle, each bouquet is weighed down with a stone. *A Trisket. A trasket. Four kittens in a basket.* The song spins in my head like a wheel.

Judah and I leave the point quickly, trotting when we can as the track descends and finally widens. We barely speak until we reach the birch grove. I think both of us know we are going to fetch my mother—that what we have found is somehow too large to be kept to ourselves. We never consider telling anyone else. I know that too, because our minds scurry, as we do, side by side. The only choice would be George Burroughs. Again without speaking of it, I know we both touch upon the idea—flit across it the way a butterfly flits across warmed stone—then reject it, and hurry on, heads bowed.

Our hands brush as we come down off the point into the birches. Our fingertips feel for each other, as if we are reassuring ourselves that warm live flesh will meet warm live flesh because, no matter what we have just seen, we are still in the world of men.

My mother is in the stillroom. Her morning's work—the plants she has cut or been given in trade—are laid along the work bench. Some of the branches and long stalks are already tied, ready to be hung from the rafter hooks. Sunlight from the single window falls on her hands as she works. Her head turns at the sound of us, but her fingers keep stripping leaves and straightening stems. At the sight of our faces, they stop.

We try to tell her, describe what we have found. But we cannot. Judah and I speak at once. Neither of us make any sense. Finally, my mother wipes her hands on her apron and tells us to show her.

THAT WAS AN HOUR AGO. We brought Percy back from the point, laid in a basket my mother thought to bring. She bedded it with mint to mute the stink. Now, Judah wields the spade. When the hole is deep enough, it is my mother who bends and places the little cat, shrouded in one of her old aprons, in the earth. When the soil has been shoveled back and smoothed, she looks from me to Judah.

"We will say nothing of this. Not to anyone. Not a word."

Both of us nod. We do not need to be warned. We understand that there is something larger here, the thing that made us fetch her in the first place. I have found a big, flat stone. I lay it on the fresh earth so no fox, or ring-tailed coon, or village dog can dig poor Percy up. It does not hurt that it also disguises the newly-dug grave.

Judah must return to work. Our expedition took far longer than it should have, and the Ingersolls will be looking for her. I walk with her as far as the common, which is empty now, and stand watching her weave down Broad Street through clumps of militia men who have finished their marching for the morning and will soon be looking for beer. I tell myself that I am keeping an eye on her, waiting until she is safely back at The Ordinary. But in truth, I think I am watching for Abigail Hobbs, hoping to see that she is still nothing but a child.

❧

THAT EVENING, my mother lifts the kettle, which has boiled. The wilted bouquets were not the only things we found up on the point with Percy. When my mother lifted him, she found several scraps of cloth, old bits of quilt that looked suspiciously like the one Avis Hobbs was wrapped in when she died, beneath him. In the grass beside the little cat's body, she spotted a stub of burned tallow, and a small, cracked, wooden bowl. Which she now fills with boiling water.

My mother replaces the kettle on its hook and sets the little bowl on the hearth. We watch as the wood swells and seals. She bends and, without touching it, sniffs. Then she dabs her finger in what is now cloudy liquid, and raises it to meet the tip of her tongue.

My mother makes a face and turns to me.

"Hellebore. Soaked in milk." She looks back at the bowl. "I might have thought," she says slowly, "still, even after what we found in the garden, that Avis' death could have been an accident. I would have thought so, if not for this."

Silence hangs between us. We look to the bowl as if it might speak. Which, in its way, it has.

"The cat did not die there," my mother says finally, "where you found him. He would have been nothing but bones, if scavengers left anything at all. She brought him, after she used him as a test for the hellebore. She must have done it at the house and hidden him, then brought him there, with the bowl, so neither would be found at the death cleaning."

"But they were. I mean, we found them, on the point."

"But not in the house. And by accident" my mother says.

The small flames of the fire flicker and dance. Their shadows finger her face, heightening the gold in her eyes.

"Or fate," she adds a moment later. "The turn of the world. God's will." She looks at me. "We are all instruments, intended to do what we must do. A day more, and something would have taken him. Nothing would have been left but the bowl, which would have cracked and rotted and returned to the earth. Then no one would have thought a thing, about the death of Avis Hobbs."

No one but you, I think. Again, I see my mother stopping on the threshold of the fetid room, and feel the moth wings of her question. *Why did they not use charcoal?* She had asked.

Because, I think answering her now, *Goody Skilling is twisted around her own importance. And the world listens because twelve years ago she lost a family, and that makes her appear more than she should be.* But, still, she has no gift. God did not reach down and touch Goody Skilling. She could not see what was before her, and if she'd had her way, if George Burroughs had not come for us, Avis Hobbs would have slipped from life unremarked. And Abigail would be known as nothing but her golden haired poppet, skipping through the world.

Reading my mind, my mother nods. Then she picks up the little wooden bowl and throws it on to the fire.

CHAPTER NINE

That night, I dream it is dawn and I am standing on the tip of the point. Suddenly, the blackness is split by a burst of flame as a mighty angel's wing plummets into the sea. The sky flares as the doors of heaven cast their traitor out. Then they snap shut, leaving behind nothing but a single spark that grows into the sun.

The bright rises fast, and its heat is mighty. I can feel it through the rock with its thin skin of soil. The ocean churns, and sets itself to boiling. All at once, a wind whips across the water. Throwing waves this way and that, it rushes ashore, bending the already bent sea oaks, setting their spindly arms waving.

I would like to leave. To run as fast and as far as I can from here. But a sinew laced into my heart is pulled so tight that I cannot move as one by one the stunted trees turn towards me. Their leaves rise and fall. They should clatter, but I cannot hear them any more than I can hear the wind. I cannot taste salt on my lips, or feel its sting, or even look away.

The trees come closer and closer until I see that their twigs are fingers, and that they are holding something. A lock of my mother's hair. I snatch at it even as I realize its smell is foul. And then it is no longer her hair. Instead, the putrid stink rises from smudges of ragged red, and dark night blue. The trees wave their gifts in front of my face until I know them for what they are—a hundred bouquets of poison flowers.

I wake panting. A sound is echoing in my head, a long, low, howl that might have been a wolf, but was probably me. I am sweating and the bed linen is soaked. Throwing it off, I see at once that my mother's side of the mattress is empty. Light fingers the sill of the open window. No breeze blows. The room is so airless, and so hot that for an awful moment I think that somehow, in our distress at what we discovered last night, we forgot to bank and dowse the fire and that the kitchen is burning. Yet, when I get downstairs, the hearth is cold. I stand for a moment, then take the poker and jab through the pile of ashes, searching for the remains of the little wooden bowl.

There is nothing there. And it crosses my mind that this, too, was all a fever dream. That it was Judah who slept beside me last night, the hollow of her body that I felt in the mattress, and that my mother stayed here in the kitchen or went out to sit under the arbor as she sometimes does. That Judah slipped away at first light without waking me because she has work to do at The Ordinary, and my mother is out searching for mallow and burdock. That we never went to the point yesterday, or buried what was left of Percy, or dipped our fingers in a wooden bowl and tasted the milky poison that killed Avis Hobbs. I have all but convinced myself that this is the case, when I step outside and see the big flat stone. Around it, fringes of earth are still black and damp against the summer grass.

Back inside, I dress quickly and start towards the birch grove. Beyond the columns of silvered trunks, the tide is high. I stop on the top of the bank. Below me, the strip of fine sand is almost swallowed. Even the end of the launching plank is floating. It does not surprise me that the canoe is gone, and I am sure that if I look hard enough, I will see echoes of my mother's paddle, the dips like liquid foot prints. I stand quite still for a moment. Then I turn up the track.

I think I must know already what I am going to find. Part of me wants to hurry, part of me wants to drag my feet, as if not getting there will somehow make all of this, whatever this is, less real. I consider turning back. But I am pulled along, remembering the tug of the sinew, and how, as I lay in the brambles, it stretched between me and Abigail Hobbs, the beat of our hearts traveling along it as if from the same drum.

The thought makes me momentarily dizzy again. *The turn of the world*, my mother said. *Fate. We are all instruments.* But I do not want this turn of the world. Nor this fate. Whatever it is. Still, I walk on. Passing the bramble scree, I shinny into the underbrush that will give way to my hidden clearing. The by now almost familiar silence has come down again, stilling everything, swaddling the world. The lap and stroke of the sea has stopped. The air does not move. I am hardly surprised when, as I step through the last screen of trees, the morning is ripped by the furious scream of a blue jay.

My hidden clearing is hidden no more. The thin covering of sea grass is trampled, as if someone has run to and fro and around and around in a fury. Branches are snapped, twigs are broken. And all of my memory holes are filled with stones.

CHAPTER TEN

I do not know if I would have told my mother what I had found when I returned to the house. I felt dizzy and sick walking back, and mostly, anxious to get away. I did stand for a moment, trying to take in what I was seeing. But even as I did, I knew this for what it was—revenge for taking Percy. And a warning. A powerful rage had turned this place that had been my own into something else. Somewhere infected. Dangerous. Still, I could not help but linger, trying to gather all my broken memories. But they were so strewn and trampled that finally, I backed away.

PICKING my way back down the track, I find myself hoping the house will be empty. That my mother will still be out on the water so I will have the silence of the rooms and the undisturbed light falling across the flagstones in which to collect myself. As I stood on the edge of the clearing, staring, taking in what had been done, I felt as if I had stepped into a snare. Now, away from the place, I think that, perhaps, if I have time to gather myself, I might yet find a way to step out of the deadly circle.

But, coming through the garden, I realize it is not to be. I shall have no solitude to consider how best to wriggle free of Abigail Hobbs. Because we have a visitor. Even before I reach the kitchen door, I hear John Alden's voice.

There has never been a time when I have not known Captain Alden. When they first came from Jersey, my parents settled near his people. My parents' name then was Hamon, Rachel and James. Understanding that in this new world it was best to rid themselves of any whisper of French, they became Hammond, which was what I was born. Susannah Hammond, in the Year of Our Lord, 1671. The first shell inside a shell.

Later, when my parents decided we would come north to the Eastward, my mother scented the wind again. In order that we might fit in when we arrived, that we would cause no comment and that our path might be smoothed, she took the Puritan name Deliverance, and gave me Resolve. With no ordained minister so no baptism, who was to know we had not always been so? Even Judah Lablanc, as she was when she set sail across the sea, turned herself into Judah White when she came here. Ridges of change rise and close around us. In this new place, we became new again.

Yet, for all their name changing, my parents carried Jersey with them. My father and Philip English, who was Philippe Lenglois then, were boys together on that little island, along with Edmund Andros, who is now the King's man, and Governor of this Dominion. My father began his trade with them even before he set foot in this New World, and as soon as he did, he became a partner of Captain John Alden.

Suddenly, I am gripped by the idea that this is why John Alden has come. That there are letters. Or even news that my father is on his way back to us. But one moment standing in the doorway, the sun warm on my back, my hand resting on the jamb, much as George Burroughs' hands rested there a week ago, tells me this is not so. My mother's face is grave and, unusually,

Captain Alden's is even graver. Neither of them look at me. I am not even sure they notice me.

"Madockawando," my mother says.

It's only half a question. Captain Alden shakes his head, then nods, as if he cannot make up his mind, or both things are true at once. Sighing, he slumps into a chair. His long legs in their scuffed boots stretch almost to the ashes of last night's fire.

"No," he says. "But, yes. And Andros bears his part in this as well. It's all woven of the same web." He smiles, but his smile is tired. "He's as stubborn as all you Jersey folk, our good Governor Andros. Try as I might to convince him that he is not the biggest spider, and is in fact facing a master-spider, and a web he may not see but will soon feel, I cannot. So, yes. This is an answer. A slap for a slap."

I know now what he is talking about, or at least part of it. This past spring, before he left for New York where he has been all summer, Governor Andros raised men and sailed north. The French hold Acadia, and one of them, Saint Castin, lives with the sachem Madockawando's people and, John Alden says, is married to Madockawando's daughter. Which makes Saint Castin both things, French and 'savage' at once. Seeing an opportunity to teach France a lesson and to deal a blow to Madockawando at the same time, last spring Andros attacked The Pentagoet.

Madockawando's stronghold is legendary. It is said to be built on a bluff above a steep passage guarded by winds and currents that make it difficult, if not impossible, to sail into. Some say it is guarded by a sea monster the Indians can summon, or by vapors they command, a shield of mist that drops down and swallows the Pentagoet, or bears it away on a cloud. And suddenly, I think, *that is where they were taken.* Mercy Lewis's aunt, and all her little cousins. Twelve years ago this week.

And I want to ask, are they still there? I want to know if, at the Pentagoet, Governor Andros found Alice Atwell and her babes. Or if, like us when we lived with Ashawonks, they have become something else—if they have vanished, changed so completely that no one but a husband or a father could know them? And since their husband and father is dead, cut down by those Alice Atwell and her children have become, there is no one left who can pick them out.

"I told him it was foolish," John Alden says. "I told Andros at the time. No man likes to have his house attacked, and Saint Castin is both a man and France."

"What? What has happened?"

My voice is sharper than I mean it to be. John Alden turns as if he has just noticed me, which, for all I know, is true.

"Ah," he says.

And then he tells me the news. How, barely a day ago, raiding parties moved down the Connecticut river valley from New France, and now, in Northfield, five settlers are dead. It is, he guesses, Saint Castin and Madockawando's answer to Andros. Reprisal for his spring raid. Yet, by chance or not, it comes just days after the incident in Saco.

"So, you are saying that this is their answer? You are saying France has done this?"

"Well," John Alden runs a hand through his hair. His hat sits on the floor, its rim bent and grubby. "The attackers at Northfield were Mohawk. At least some of them, if reports can be believed. Which they can. So the answer comes from France, or those who love the French. Which is one and the same. I think it's clear enough. If you shove a hornets nest, sooner or later the hornets, or the hornets' friends, will come out and sting. Certainly, it will cause a panic." He fishes his hat off the floor and pushes himself to his feet. "I wanted to let you know." He looks at my mother. "Warn you. The mills are safe enough," he adds, pulling a leather purse from his pocket and placing it on the table.

This will be our share of the profits from the sawmills. My mother does not look at it. Her hand taps the oiled wood that I have scrubbed and scrubbed, but that is still stained with the sap of plums. Her cap is untied, as if she pulled it on in a hurry, or never straightened it after crossing the cove and being caught by the wind. Escaped tendrils curl on her shoulder. In this morning light that falls through the wide open casements, she looks like a girl. Like she must have when Captain Alden, and perhaps even my father, first knew her. Again, I am seized by the idea that she is moving backwards through time, that each bout of illness has stripped days and months and even years from her the way winter strips bark from a tree.

"And Madockawando?" She asks, "what will he do next?"

I know that what she is really asking is if we should be prepared to be attacked. If we should leave. Or seek sanctuary.

John Alden shakes his head. "Nothing," he says. "If I can help it. Castin has his ear, and Castin's no fool. No one wants another war." He smiles and jams his hat on his head. "It's bad for business."

John Alden's hair is blonde. There's a shade of gray in it now. But when he was a babe it must have been almost as gold as Abigail's. His eyes are still as blue as hers, but there is no ice, and nothing of the jay's shriek in them. His smile comes easily, and his laughter runs before him. He has a dimple on one cheek. I see it, and remember the rumors I have heard, and all the things I know without knowing. That the trade in furs is richer the farther north you go. That my father, and for that matter my mother, and certainly Philip English, and probably Governor Andros, like everyone from Jersey and for all I know John Alden too, speaks more than a word of French. As does Judah, who has more than once leaned close to me as we have watched Captain Alden's sloop come in and asked me if I do not think him handsome? And told me the whispers she has heard in The Ordinary. That John Alden only married his wife for her father's sawmills, and that there are children in the north, even at The Pentagoet, who have dark skin and his blue eyes.

My mother and I do not walk with him to the harbor. John Alden says he would call on Edward Tyng, our magistrate, to try to head off the panic that will come as night follows day with the news of Northfield, if it would do any good. But it would not as, like Captain Blackman, the man is both stubborn and stupid. Instead, John Alden says, he will spend his words where they will be heard. And for that, he must hurry to catch the tide.

❧

WE WATCH from the garden gate as he strides away up the meadow, passes through the side yards, and is lost in the marching and wheeling of the militia. Then, a bare half hour later, we watch again, this time from the edge of the birch grove above our beach. The tide is spilling, rushing to get wherever it goes when it goes out. A fair wind is building from the southwest. Out beyond the mouth of the cove, we see cats paws dabbing the open water as John Alden's sloop comes into view, her red sail raised as she rounds the point and catches the wind.

"Come."

When I turn, I expect to see my mother already moving back into the birch grove. Instead, she is stepping down the bank. By the time I join her, she has removed her shoes and is hitching her skirts into her belt.

"Quickly," she says. "We must also catch the tide."

I do not have to ask. Even as I ruck my own skirts and we slide the canoe down the plank and into the cove, I know where we are going. While John Alden sails north to try to stop a war, my mother and I will rush to deliver a warning in case he fails.

CHAPTER ELEVEN

I am in the front of the canoe, paddling. I cannot see them, but I know a trail of silver bubbles streams behind us. In the stern, my mother uses a piece of broken plank as a tiller. Normally, this would not be necessary. But the same tide that rushed John Alden out of the harbor is pushing us toward the mouth of the cove. My mother lets it, not guiding us in until we have almost reached the headland opposite the point. Then, just as the current would pull us into open water, she calls for me to paddle hard. I do. I feel us bump a ridge of sand, and seconds later I am out and dragging us to shore.

A shell of hide and silvered bark, the canoe weighs little more than one of my mother's loaded baskets. It barely takes a moment to pull it up and lift it into the brush, where we turn it turtle, tucking the paddle under it. Then my mother shoulders past me. Leading the way into the trees, she starts down a track I cannot even see.

When we lived in The Greening I learned its stories, as all the children in Ashawonks' village did. How the beaver built its dam. How the crow became a messenger between worlds. How the spring frogs learned to hide. The ones I remember best, though, the ones told most often in the winter when the sea froze and the fires burned all night, were about the wolves.

As the shadows flickered, making strange shapes on the lodge walls and the wind howled, whipping snow through the tree tops, the elders told us how the wolves watch over the villages from their star high in the east, which is why it is always the first star to appear in the evening, and the last to vanish come morning. Because the wolves will not leave the people until they have escorted them, safe to a new day. They explained that what white men call 'the milky way' is actually The Wolf Trail—the thousands and thousands of silver paw prints all the packs that have ever been leave as they patrol the night sky. And how, in times of war, the wolves leave their star and race down The Wolf Trail to circle the villages, keeping the people safe inside, daring any enemy to cross their tracks. They told us that if a warrior is wounded, a wolf will come for him and guide him safely home. Which is why white people fear, and try to kill them.

I HAVE NEVER SEEN memory holes here. But, like that forest I grew up in, this one has been the home to so many stories and so many people for so long that it is webbed with paths. They thread through it, crossing and criss-crossing, becoming visible then vanishing as they are used and abandoned over the years. I do not know this place well. But I am certain each path has its own marks, if you know how to see and read them. Which my mother does. She moves swiftly and surely, weaving through trees and across the edge of a marsh.

When we first came to live here, I used to accompany her, especially in the summer, paddling along the shore as she sought out the local people to find the best growing places for plants, and to understand their powers, and how they might best be used. But it was not long, no more than a year, before she stopped me coming with her. She did so, she explained, not because the people she visited were dangerous, but because those who lived in the village believed they were.

It did matter that the attack that took the lives of so many was years ago, and made by Madockawondo's men. Savages were savages. All the same. And the Lewises and the Cloyces and the Mary Skillings of the village would never let the memory of that August morning die. They tended it like a sacred flame. My mother said I was just beginning. That I would live my life here—find a husband, marry, raise my children. So, if there was to be a taint, even a faint hint of sympathy for 'savages', it could rest on her, not me.

What was true then is just as true now. More so. Now, all the Anthony Bracketts and Edward Tyngs and Captain Blackmans also need the memory of that morning—the fall of those hatchets, the blood, the captives, the terror of Madockawando—for themselves. John Alden says that for some, fear is profit. My mother says that for many, fear is purpose. The union of the two is deadly. An unholy marriage indeed. As we hurry through the forest, I think of the militia wheeling and stomping on the common, and know that this, as much as any other, is the warning we bring.

FOLLOWING MY MOTHER, I notice again that she is—I start to think—*her old self.* But it is not that. And again, I am struck by the sense that she is somehow changing, is familiar and strange at once. This morning, she moves quickly, almost loping. Sometimes, she is so far ahead of me that I have to trot to keep her in sight. Once, I stumble on a root, and when I catch myself and look up, she is gone. I blink, gripped by a sudden panic that she brought me here only to lose me. Then, far ahead, I spot a sleek shape weaving through dappled sunlight, disappearing and appearing again behind a stand of trees.

The sun is straight overhead when, at last, the village comes into sight. This is a summer camp. The winter villages are farther inland, better placed, not only for trapping and hunting, but for shelter. There, earth-bound lodges will be humped against the snowfall. Here, on a plateau above the shore, there are summer teepees.

As we break through the tree line, I can see a half moon of them, perhaps twenty, their woven flaps pegged open, facing the east and the sea. The camp is set above a small pebbled cove. Canoes are pulled up below a line of drying racks covered in the splayed carcasses of fish. The tide is still slipping out. On the exposed sheet of sea mud, women flip long shanks of seaweed and dig and collect clams, layering them in baskets. When the tide turns, they will haul them up to the smoking shed and cure them on the racks above the smudge fires that stay lit all summer long.

I smell them even before I even see them, and suddenly I am back in The Greening. My legs are short. My mother looms in front of me. A tiny coracle, I bob in her wake as she crosses the village, her long hair a single plait swinging down her back. If I run and reach out, I will feel, not the linen stuff of the skirts she wears now, but the soft rub of deerskin, the knub of beads, and the pattern of the quilled leggings she wore then.

The moment is so real that I nearly stumble, caught by surprise at the sudden length of my stride and the clomp of my shoes, hard and ugly compared to the beaten skin of moccasins.

❧

I KNOW I met Hope Hood, the sachem of this village, when we first came here. But it was a long time ago, and I doubt I can pick him out. The strange name he is called by the likes of us is no more the name he was born with than Deliverance and Resolve are my mother's name or mine. It seems we all, or at least women and Indians, must negotiate this New England under new names either given to us by English men or designed to appease them. Sometimes I think that before they are finished, those same men will fashion and re-fashion this place, re-making and re-naming it in their own image, molding the land and all of us in it to their own desires until there is nothing they did not create left to disturb their dreams. Before they killed him, they called Hope Hood's father Robin Hood. My mother stops and speaks with an old woman, who smiles, and places a weathered hand upon her arm, then points to the cove.

The sachem is a tall man with a soft face that breaks into a smile as we approach. I hang back and watch as Hope Hood opens his hands in greeting. He is wearing a summer mantle, woven and painted with red markings. A fine row of turkey feathers hang from its shoulder, matching those in his dark hair. His leggings are quilled. The smell of grease—bear, or perhaps eagle, applied liberally in the summer against the sun and sting of insects—rises from the group around him, and again I smell my childhood.

I learned the language of Ashawonks' people. Though I have not heard it for years, somehow the smells—the grease potion, the wafted smoke of the curing huts—freshens it in my mind. The language these people speak is different, but also much the same. So I am able to understand both my mother's greeting and the sachem's reply. And hearing them, I know I am right. She has been visiting often.

Others come to gather around, drawn by the news we clearly bring. An older woman leans close, catching the gesture of my mother's hand. A man older than Hope Hood, stooped and with his mantle gathered over his thin shoulders despite the heat of the day, joins them, and I wonder if this is his wife's father, or perhaps an uncle, since he, too has turkey feathers and his leggings are both embroidered and quilled. A younger woman passes as they bend their heads together. Carrying a clam basket, she picks her way across the pale egg-shaped pebbles down onto the apron of exposed sea mud, tracking the receding rim of the water as it slides back to reveal the cove's glistening underskin. Beside a hank of seaweed, I see a bright spurt and a pin-point hole, the sign of a clam, or a nest of them. Dropping the basket, she sees it, too, and raises her hoe. Because you must be quick. Clams travel through mud faster than seems possible.

I guess that she is not much older than I am, and watching, I long to join her. To pull off my shoes and feel the cool slick of mud across my feet and between my toes. To stand on the edge of the water as the underbelly of the sea is revealed—tiny scuttling things, the shine of seaweed. The bright spurts that tell you to dash and dig, shove your hands down until your fingers fasten around shells and you pull the clams out, and rinse them in a tide pool. She does this now, intent on her work until a little boy not more than three or four years old gallops along the beach and circles her. Throwing himself into the wet sand, he digs his tiny hands into the hole she has opened, and squeals as he pulls out a fat, round clam. She takes it from him, then reaches out and daubs his chin with mud.

The woman must sense me because, dropping the clam in the basket, she looks around, and meets my eye, and smiles. Her face is unpainted, although I can see the red shine of tinted grease in her hair. A long thin scar, pale and looking as if it might have been made by a claw, runs down her left cheek. She laughs as the little boy jumps at her, trying to streak her with mud, then goes back to her digging. I watch as she scoops out three, four, five more clams. Then I hear my mother's voice and, catching the tone of it, look up.

"Now!" She is saying. "Go now, I beg you!"

Her distress is plain, at least to me. Hope Hood listens to her and smiles as he shakes his head.

"HE SAYS the fishing is very good, and the birds are coming into the marsh. It has been so dry that the crop is failing, so they need the fish, and fowl too. The smoking fires are set, and the sea is abundant, so they will finish. Then they will leave. Perhaps."

My mother is walking ahead of me again. She stops and looks back. We have just left the village. The pale points of the teepees rise through the screen of trees. The smell of the fires, the waft of smoked fish, hangs, fading in the air.

"He says he has no desire for war, or to kill anyone, and his people are not bothering anyone and he knows nothing of Saco or Northfield or anywhere else. I tried to tell him it does not matter."

My mother shakes her head and walks on, but her step is slower now.

"I tried to explain that to them—to Edward Tyng and Blackman and the Cloyce brothers—one Indian looks much like the next. He laughed, and said he thought the same of white men. I wish," she says more to herself than to me, "that Yellow Bird was here. If Yellow Bird was here, he would make them understand."

I have no idea who Yellow Bird is, and she does not tell me, so I follow her in silence.

The canoe is exactly as we left it. Dead low, the tide dibbles and dabbles, barely moving as if, exhausted by the effort of going out, it wants nothing more than to sleep in the afternoon sun. Glancing at the pewter plate of the cove, I imagine we do not need a boat at all but could simply step out and walk across it. On the far side, our birches shine white under the green halo of their leaves.

I am watching them, catching their slight waver in the heat, when my eye is drawn up the point. Just for a second, I am sure I see a figure standing where the track runs above the pink, glittering rocks. The back of my neck goes cold. Without meaning to, I raise my hand, and feel the matching coldness blossom on my cheek. Jerking my fingers away, I turn to the canoe, almost tripping, as if turning my back on Abigail Hobbs could make her vanish.

"What is it?"

My mother is watching me intently.

"Nothing," I say, as a blue jay shrieks and flashes across the water.

I bend to feel for the paddle, and grab the side to flip the canoe. But my mother does not move to help me. Hands resting on the wide band of her old leather belt, she stands with her eyes narrowed, staring at the opposite shore.

CHAPTER TWELVE

It is three days later, in the afternoon and we are making bread in the kitchen, lifting the dough, folding and banging it on the scrubbed surface of the table when my mother and I hear a voice ask, "Do you know me, Mistress?"

As one, we spin around.

Neither of us has said so, but we have been waiting for John Alden. Watching for his familiar form to stride down the meadow path, or appear like something conjured in the doorway telling us his errand is achieved, that Madockawando and Saint Castin have no interest in wars or raids. That we are safe.

But this is not John Alden. The man standing in our kitchen door is not much more than a boy. He has doffed his old hat and twists it as if he could wring words from it, make it speak for him instead of having to speak himself. His boots are worn and his breeches, like his face, are filthy with dust. But it's the hands that mark him as one of the militia. It's the grease streaks and the powder burns, black and sore looking from the loading and re-loading.

More of them arrived yesterday. Like the rest of the town, Judah and I watched them pass. All shapes and sizes, some ragged, some short, others tall. Fat men and thin boys and men who look so ordinary it is hard to tell one from the other marched down Broad Street to the Fort with Captain Blackman riding at their head, his new boots and sun burned cheeks shining with importance.

In the three days since John Alden left, his prediction has come true as surely as if he had seen it in a crystal ball. The news from Northfield did indeed spread like summer fire, and its hot wind has fanned a mighty panic.

Now this tall boy stands in our door-yard looking in at us, and suddenly, even though I have not seen him for years and have never so much as traded a word with him, I do know him. This is Thaddeus Hobbs. Avis's oldest son. Abigail's older brother.

My mother must see it at the same time, because she nods. Her hands hover over the dough on the table before she lowers them and wipes them on her apron.

"Master Hobbs," my mother says. But she might as well have said, *I've been waiting for you.*

SITTING AT OUR TABLE, Thaddeus Hobbs watches me pour the pitcher of cider as if he has never seen the stuff before. As he takes the proffered cup, I see that his hands are shaking. He is exhausted. Or terrified. Or both. Perhaps his hair was once as gold as Abigail's. Now, it is dirty brown and in need of a barber. His eyes are blue, but softer than his sister's, almost gray. There is nothing of the jay here. This is a wood thrush, or a cow bird. His linen shirt is old, and sticks to him, and smells. When he lowers the cup, I pour him another. He drinks that greedily, too.

My mother mounds the dough and places it in the waiting bowl to let it rise. Then, her keys jingling at her belt, she steps out into the kitchen yard. A moment later, I hear the rasp as she unlocks the stillroom. When she comes back, she is carrying a bowl of water and strips of the fresh linen we keep for bandages.

The pot of salve I can see in her apron pocket smells strongly of mint and comfrey.

"Let me see."

She takes the cup from Thaddeus Hobbs the way you take something from a child. My mother examines the burns. When she lowers his hand into the water, which is salt, I see him wince. Best for wounds, we keep a bucket from the cove inside the still-room door for just such occasions as this. When Thaddeus' hand is soaked clean, my mother pats it dry. She repeats the exercise with his other hand before finally dabbing the burns with the ointment. All the while, Thaddeus Hobbs watches her and no one says a word.

Finally, my mother puts the pot of salve aside. She nods for me to take the bowl and empty it. I am throwing it onto the gravel of the garden path, using the salt to discourage weeds, when I hear her say, "Your mother left the world in peace." Which is a lie. "But they called me too late," she adds. "There was little I could do for her."

"Or the babe."

It is not a question. I am stepping back into the kitchen and can see my mother's face. She looks at Thaddeus Hobbs, considering, before she nods.

"No." She agrees. "I could do nothing for the babe. How did you know? From your father?"

He shakes his head. "From my mother."

The words hang in the room. And it is then, looking at Thaddeus Hobbs, that my mother and I understand. He knows. I do not know how, but Avis' son knows that her death was not a natural one. Any doubt is dispelled by his next question.

"How?"

"Poison," my mother says, after a moment. "Hellebore. In food. A stew or soup."

"You are sure?" There is pain on his face, and also, strangely, something like relief. I do not understand why until he speaks again. "So, she was not witched?" He asks. "You are sure? You are certain of that, Mistress?"

"Witched?" My mother frowns. "Why would you think that?"

"Goody Skilling says it."

My mother makes a face. "You have seen her?"

Thaddeus shakes his head. "Not here. I have not even seen my father since I arrived. We have been kept in the fort, when we are not drilling on the green. I came to you the first moment I could get away. But it was Goody Skilling, who told me you were at my mother's death. She passed through Saco on an errand, barely a week ago, and she told me. Everything."

My mother and I exchange a look. I cannot imagine what Goody Skilling's 'everything' is, but I am quite certain it bears little resemblance to ours. I do not have time to ponder this, because suddenly Thaddeus Hobbs is babbling. Now that he has started, he cannot seem to stop. Words break from him like a dam giving way, tumbling and falling over one another, so roiled by the storm of his distress that their sense is hard to grasp.

"I heard the rumor before, even before Goody Skilling sought me out to break the news that it was my mother. Gossip said a woman had died here, witched. And I was afraid it was her. I wanted to come at once. But with all the trouble, I was not allowed. But I heard, and after the stories from Boston, I thought—people say, it travels. The witching travels, on the night air. And, I thought—" His words run dry, stopping almost as abruptly as they began.

My mother shakes her head. She reaches for the stool that sits beside the hearth that is dry and strewn with petals of sea roses I have been collecting for their hips. They rustle in my mother's skirts as she pulls the stool in front of Thaddeus Hobbs' chair and sinks down on it. Taking both of his hands, holding them gently so as not to worry the burns or smear the healing ointment, she looks straight into his face.

"Your mother was not witched, Thaddeus. We, too have heard the gossip."

Of course we have. The whole world has heard how the children of a Boston family have been struck. All of them witched. Writhing in pain, and shouting, and rushing about as if their wits have been snatched and put in the Devil's hands.

"This is not what happened here," my mothers says, her eyes never leaving his. "Your mother's soul was never in danger."

Now I understand the look of relief that came over him when she told him about the hellebore. Thaddeus Hobbs has been carrying the burden of his mother's soul, the fear that it was taken from her and she is wandering in torment, searching and searching for it in the wilderness of The Damned.

"Your mother was not witched," my mother repeats. "She was taken from this world before her time, it is true. But by poison. Not witching. By the time I was sent for, it was too late. There was nothing I could do."

After a moment, Thaddeus nods. His next words sound as if he is pulling them from his very depths. As if they are heavy and tied to a rope he is hauling hand over hand.

"It need not have been evil. It could have been in error."

The hope in the words is palpable. My mother says nothing. I know what she is doing—giving him the place in his mind to believe what he will, to believe what will give him peace. But peace is not what Thaddeus Hobbs wants. His next words freeze me to the floor.

"My mother's death could have been an error," he says. "But it was not."

CHAPTER THIRTEEN

My mother does not move. Nor does she let go of Thaddeus' hands.

"I know it was not," Thaddeus Hobbs' voice sinks so low that we can barely hear him. "I tried to warn her," he says. "I tried, and tried. But my mother would not hear me. She called me wicked even to think it, much less speak it. It angered her greatly. So, I said nothing, and stayed away. And now, it is too late. I knew, when I heard about the babe. It was then that I became truly afraid for her. I knew, and I could not save her."

The last is a mewl of pain. Gently, my mother places his hands in his lap.

"Resolve," she says as she stands, "there is still the fowl, from last night. And potage and bread. And cheese."

George Burroughs brought us a fat turkey hen. We plucked and roasted it, and there is more than enough left. I fetch it from the coolness of the stillroom, and the bowl of turnips and carrots, and the end of the old loaf, and the cheese I make from the goats. Thaddeus protests at first, but my mother silences him.

"Eat," she says. "We will talk more when your mind is rested. Now, you need strength."

He starts to object again, but the food is too much for him. I do not know what the militia eats, but I can imagine. Dried biscuit. Dried fish. Thin ale. I pour him another cup of cider. My mother brings him a dish of the sun-dried plums soaked in the Marsala wine Captain Alden brings from Salem. She has topped the plums with a shaving from the sugar loaf that also comes on Philip English's ships.

Thaddeus Hobbs does not say a word. He eats and eats, and when he can eat no more, when I remove the bowl and plate and cup, he lays his head in his arms folded upon our table.

❧

WE KEEP a pallet in the front parlor. Sometimes it is used by Judah, but mostly it is kept, re-stuffed with new straw, in case of a voyager, or someone too ill to be sent back to where ever they have come from seeking my mother's care. Now, we unroll it by the hearth. Between us, we lower Thaddeus Hobbs on to it. Grief has exhausted him. The militia has worn him thin.

"Fear and guilt have done the rest," my mother says in her low voice as we remove his boots and strip the filthy shirt from his bony shoulders, exposing the rails of his ribs.

Through all this, he does not move, and it is then that I realize my mother has given him something, a draft mixed into the plums. A tea or syrup, of valerian and St John's wort, for pain and dreams. It would not have taken much, and the sugar would have masked the taste.

"Into the rag bin," she says, balling the filthy shirt and handing it to me. "We'll give him one of your father's when he wakes. Which won't be for hours yet." She sits back on her heels, watching him. "There'll be time when he's rested."

Time for what? I start to ask. Before I can, she looks at me.

"For him to tell us what he came to say," my mother says.

As she rises I think, not for the first time, that we are bonded so tight that she might as well be another limb, a part of me that moves and speaks and thinks as I do. Yet at the same time, this is not true. Because I know my mother sees and speaks a silent language I do not fully understand. I would have said, for instance, that Thaddeus Hobbs came here to learn of his mother's last hours—to salve his grief in the lie my mother told him that Avis Hobbs died at peace. And that is true. But she is telling me it is not *all* that is true.

I see only half the picture. My mother sees it whole. She reads words written on air. Hears whispers so thin, and catches shadows moving so fast that I do not even feel their passing. Stepping into our shuttered front room, she becomes little more than a dark shape in the open doorway. Watching her, I suddenly realize that I have understood this for a very long time. And that it began in The Greening. That reading the power of blossoms and leaves and bark was not the only thing Ashawonks taught her.

The understanding lands like a bird on my outstretched hand.

I glance at Thaddeus Hobbs, his mouth slack and lost to sleep, and I understand too, that he has been carrying a weight that has all but exhausted him, and that he came here to put it down. To see if he could trust us. Which is why my mother both lied to him, and told him the truth. First about peace then about poison.

She emerges carrying our little writing chest. Setting it on the table, my mother lifts the lid, opens a fresh ink pot, and dips a quill. The nib on parchment sounds like a cat's scratch. My mother does not look up until she is finished.

Then, folding the paper and stamping it with her red wax, she hands it to me and says, "Take this to Edward Tyng. He will instruct Blackman, and will not argue. I have written that I suspect Master Hobbs of having a fever, and that unless I am left undisturbed to cure him he will pass it to everyone in the fort and by the time it finishes there will be no militia left."

She smiles, and I smile back. Because everyone knows that Edward Tyng is terrified of almost everything. Our magistrate fears the sun because he may be sun dazed. He fears the sea because he may drown. He fears the Natives because they may kill him. And horses because they kick. And dogs because they bite. But most of all, he fears sickness. And it is also well known that, while he is wholly terrified of both Captain Alden and my father, Edward Tyng is half in love with my mother because she once cured him of a sore throat. And half terrified of her too, because she knew the cure.

His besottedness is a joke between us, and this will not be the first time my mother has used it to her advantage, especially since my father went to London. John Alden is right. Edward Tyng is both stupid and stubborn. But it can be useful to have a magistrate in your thrall. One that is a fussy old maid and a terrible gossip is doubly useful. Murmur piles upon murmur like rotting leaves. My mother has just added a new layer.

❧

It is twilight when Thaddeus Hobbs turns and mutters in his sleep. The soft whir of my mother's spinning wheel fills the room. I sort berries, dropping them from one bowl to another as his eyes flutter, and open.

At first Thaddeus is shamed, to find himself in nothing but his britches. But my mother settles that quickly. She has already selected one of my father's shirts from the linen press in the front room. Handing it to Thaddeus, she directs him out to our well where linen and soap are left on the summer trough. I wonder, briefly, if he will return. If coming to his senses under the cold water, he might think better of coming here and, being well rested and fed, pick up his burden again and scurry away.

Although he will have to go barefoot, as his boots are at the foot of the pallet.

But he does not. By the time he returns to the kitchen, my mother has lit candles, and there is a bowl of grapes, and my berries, and a plate of fresh biscuits on the table. At the sight, Thaddeus smiles and I notice for the first time that he is handsome. More than that, Thaddeus Hobbs is beautiful. Like his sister. And yet, not like her at all. Sleep has erased the lines around his eyes and mouth. His hair, clean and combed, is longer than it should be. The paleness of his skin and those gray eyes in the warming candle light make him look almost as if he is disappearing. Almost as if he is nothing but the reflection of an angel that has lost its way and drifted to our table.

My mother fetches out the pewter goblets that were part of her wedding portion and a bottle of wine from Philip English's ships. She pours the wine with water, thinking, I suspect, that Thaddeus Hobbs will not be used to such stuff, and might keep his senses better with a weaker drink. And so we sit, the three of us, sipping, sucking on grapes, picking at the crumbled edges of new biscuits while the evening light creeps through the open kitchen door as if the house is sucking it in, making the candles brighter.

"I was not sure," Thaddeus says finally, "I was not certain at all until you told me about the poison. Then—" He looks up from a grape he has been rolling back and forth across the table. "Then," he says again, "I knew. Or perhaps—" He smiles, but it's a smile of sadness, nothing else. "Perhaps I knew the moment I heard, the moment Goody Skilling told me my mother was dead. Only, I did not want to believe it. I would almost rather have believed her death a witching."

Without anyone saying her name, we all understand that he is talking about his sister. About Abigail. And for just a moment then, I am sure I feel her small shape. Am sure that, if I look up and through the open kitchen door, I will see her standing in the garden with the sunset burning her curls into a crown of flames.

CHAPTER FOURTEEN

Thaddeus's Story

The fact that I was born in the spring of 1668, just a scant few months after my parents married, was a source of shame. So they left Wells, where their families farmed and they were known, and moved to Topsfield, where they were not known.

My mother told me that my father began with high hopes. But he did not prosper. Their holding in Topsfield was small, and the ground not good, and the work hard. My father is not a bad man, only a very weak one, and he never quite managed to succeed as he had dreamed. Nor could he rid himself of the conviction that his first son, who had come into the world before he was quite welcome, was, if not a curse, then bad luck. Looking at me, he saw the root of the family's troubles. In short, I became my father's scapegoat. The living talisman of his shame and failure. So when, two years later, the twins were born, they were seen as the true new beginning.

Everyone knows twins bring luck, and being that they were a

boy and girl, and both healthy and flourishing, they were double luck. So my parents gave them their own names. In tiny Avis and tiny William they saw perfect reflections of themselves—everything they wished they might have been, and everything they now hoped their family might be.

Perhaps I should have been jealous. But I was not. The twins brought us happiness, and happiness brings kindness. My father's anger towards me eased. From the start, I loved my brother and sister. I had been lonely, so I loved William and Avis because they were company, and lovable. And because they loved me. Especially William.

He was two years younger, but my brother was a better man than I, even when we were boys. As we grew, we became closest friends. Then, in 1678, in the last days of King Philip's war, my mother fell pregnant again, and gave birth to one more daughter, whom my parents called Abigail. She was a pretty baby, a miniature version of her older sister. Golden haired from the very beginning, Abigail had eyes so blue you could see the entire sky in them.

This was our family in 1683, when, after my father had failed to reach even the status of the most lowly elected town official, my parents decided that Topsfield held nothing for them. The war was ended. King Philip's head had long been stuck on a pike and paraded through Massachusetts. News spread, of how the settlement at Falmouth, with its fine harbor and new village, was rising like a phoenix after being destroyed and abandoned. The Eastward was full of promise. My parents decided to begin again.

They leased their property in Topsfield, and with the money rented a house here that was far finer than anything they could afford to build themselves. I was fifteen when we arrived, and more than eager to be my father's right hand. The twins were thirteen. Abigail was five. Her name means 'my father's joy'. Yet, for that, and for all her prettiness, she was an afterthought, an addition no one seemed to have much use for.

My father was eager to prove himself in this new town, and I was eager to prove myself to him. My brother was a boy, and excited to be by the sea. William loved anything to do with ships. My mother had a new and much finer house, and little time for a child who was no longer a babe but not yet useful. She handed the care of Abigail to my sister.

At thirteen, my sister Avis was still a girl, taken up with girlish things. In a new place with new people, she had no desire to be weighed down. So it is true that, as Abigail grew and was more inclined to follow Avis about and mimic everything she did, Avis was often unkind to her. And because Avis was not only my mother's namesake and mirror image, but increasingly her ally and friend in a new strange place, more often than not my mother turned a blind eye to my sister's unkindness.

For my part, I admit I paid little attention. The squabbling of women, even my mother and sisters, did not interest me. I saw a new beginning here as well, both for myself and for my father. I was anxious for his success, and determined to do everything I could to help him. As for my brother, when he was not about the harbor, or neglecting his lessons, he was with me, or with Avis. She was his twin. They were one and the same. Now, when I think on it, I think that perhaps because of that, or perhaps because of something else, even beyond the fact that she was so much younger and a girl, William never warmed to Abigail.

You must understand. It was not only that Abigail was pretty. Even from the time she was very small, we knew she was clever. Far cleverer than most children of her age. Sometimes it seemed uncanny, as if someone, or something, far older lurked inside her tiny body. She would look at you, and you would see something far larger than she was in her eyes. Other times, she was merely an annoying brat. She remembered everything, and mimicked, and repeated. Abigail was always under foot, always following and peeping and listening at the door. When she was not running wild. Which, in truth, no one much noticed. Or if we did, cared about, especially if it got her out of the way.

That was how our first years here passed. My brother became more and more fascinated by boats. It was as if he was in love. More than that, besotted. He wanted to be a fisherman, but my father preferred he apprentice to a trade. William was big, and strong, so when he turned fourteen, my father placed him with the blacksmith. At the same time, my sister Avis grew prettier and prettier. She was not a bright, hard thing like Abigail. Avis was light and swift, like a brook running fast. She cleaved in all things to our mother, who in turn, I think, saw a second chance at youth in her.

In time, it became clear that my father had failed again to flourish. He planted out land he let from George Burroughs along the Back Cove. But in truth he had no gift for it, and a great gift for The Ordinary. Finally, when I felt his eye falling on me and sensed what I had lived with before the twins were born returning, I took my chance in the militia. I had no desire to be my father's goat again, and I thought I might learn something useful, and even perhaps gain father's respect, if not his love. So, I'd been marching and drilling under Captain Blackman for a year when it began.

As you know, the militia headquarters at Saco is not a day's ride south. I was home now and again. In the winter of 1685, I had a few days leave. I heard of an ox carter delivering hemp, coming north. He was a good fellow, and eager for company, and offered me a ride in return for help loading and unloading. I agreed, and when we arrived, after helping him unload, I made my way home and found the house in an uproar.

William had tripped in the forge and burned his foot. It was almost dark by the time I reached the house, and inside, bitter cold. With all the fuss over the accident, no one had split the wood, or brought it in, nor had they hauled water. My father, seeing his beloved son maimed, had fallen into a panic and repaired to The Ordinary to gather his courage, something I understood he had taken to doing more and more. So it was left to me, with the help of George Burroughs, to split the wood in the pile and see that we did not all freeze.

Burroughs' was generous with his time and effort. That is true. But now, looking back, I wonder if also he did not seek out the chance to speak with me. It was darkening quickly that first evening of my return, so we were working hard. It was then, amid the crack of axes, that I first heard about 'the mishaps.' George Burroughs' spoke by way of conversation, as if he wished to keep our minds off the cold. But there was something in the way he did, in the way he looked at me as he kicked a split log aside and reached for another, and in the way he measured his words, that made me certain I needed to talk alone with my brother.

The chance did not come until the morning of the day I was to return to Saco. My brother's foot was healing, and William was desperate to get out of the house, away from what he called 'the infernal gabbling of women.' Even more than that, he wanted to show me something, a shallop that was being built in the boat shed on the beach. It had snowed overnight, but the day was fine and bright, and I saw my chance. Using a crutch, and with his arm around my shoulder, my brother and I hobbled down the front path.

Getting through the gate and away from my mother's fussing, we turned towards the harbor. As soon as we had gone far enough that I was certain we could not be overheard, I asked about 'the mishaps.' William was not yet sixteen, but he had grown since I saw him last, and was taller than me, in some ways already more like a man. When I told him what George Burroughs had said, he stopped and threw back his head and laughed. 'Oh, that! That,' he said, 'was Abigail! Honestly, Thaddy! Since you've been gone!' He stepped away, wobbling on his bad foot and his crutch so he could look at me. 'She's not a child,' he said. 'She's an animal.' And then, and I can remember his words exactly, my brother said, 'I love mother, Thaddy! You know I do. But I think Abigail is a changeling!'

Those were his exact words. But when I asked him what he meant, William only shrugged and laughed again. He was in great good humor that morning, glad to be outside, and that we were together. 'Nothing,' he said. 'Nothing. Just that no one can control the child, or cares to try. If you do, she scratches and hisses like a bad cat. She's got a bit big now, and she delights in tormenting poor Avis.' Then he told me how, in the autumn, our father had been to Topsfield to check on the property, and on his way back, stopped in Salem and bought Avis some new ribbons. No sooner had they been unwrapped and put on the table, than Abigail snatched them up and threw them into the fire. When Avis jumped after them, the hem of her skirt caught. Our mother was close by, and snatched up a pitcher and dowsed the hem. But the material was ruined, and the ribbons burned, and it had been sheer spite. Avis chased Abigail, tried to catch her and pinch her. But Abigail escaped, laughing. Then, a few weeks later, she tried to push Avis down the stairs.

We had started walking, or hobbling, again. But at this, I stopped and stared. William laughed, and said that as Abigail was only eight years old, there was not that much mischief she could do. Not that it stopped her trying. Avis was sweeping the stairs, one foot on one, and one foot on the next. She had been looking down when Abigail had come along the top landing and shoved her, with both hands, as hard as she could. Avis is swift. She dropped the broom and grabbed the banister.

Abigail had not known it, but William had come back from the forge and was in the kitchen and heard Avis scream. This time, Abigail had not been able to escape. William had raced upstairs and snatched her and slapped her. Like a cat, she clawed and hissed and spat in his face.

'That's what she is.' William said. 'She's a bad cat, and gone wild with it.' He thought it a great joke, and slung his arm again across my shoulder, and told me he was going to fix it so Abigail's tricks, and what our father did or did not do, would not matter any more. That was why he wanted to show me the boat.

She was indeed fine. I could see that at once, although I did not know half as much as William about boats. He explained how some of the Portuguese from Portsmouth had been here in the summer, and he had admired their craft. They had become friends, and had shown him the workings and pointed out the design of their small, fast, ships. So, when William heard that Sylvanus Davis was building a new boat, William had gone to see him and told him all about what he had learned. Having no son of his own, Sylvanus Davis had a soft spot for William, as William well understood, so old Sylvanus let William work on the boat in his spare time.

My brother was in love with that boat, I swear he was. William ran his hand along her sides the way other men run their hands along the flanks of a horse they admire and told me he 'planned to have her.' He pointed out how she had less beam and less draft, and explained why it would make her fast. The mast was to be stepped in the spring, once she was afloat, but the rudder was already set. It was long and deep, and William showed it off as he had made it himself, or, at least the fitting, which he fashioned at the forge.

The tiller was very long, so whomever was steering could hang on to it and still move about the boat. It was fixed with a special swivel pin to the rudder. 'You see, it drops in here,' William said. I remember every word, exactly. William pulled out an iron pin and dropped it back into the fitting. He was especially proud of the way it could be removed, so you could take the tiller off the boat if you were in a strange harbor, and of the way it fixed the tiller to the top of the rudder for easy steering. He pulled the pin out to show me again, and held it up and pointed to a rounded hole, like an eye, in its end. 'The cord ties through here, then onto this.' He tapped a small ring set into the stern that I had not noticed before. 'It's a fail safe, so if the pin works loose it won't go to the bottom. Otherwise, you need to carry at least a spare, if not two. This saves you your pocket, as long as you know your knots. You simply fish it back, re-fix the tiller, and save yourself from the rocks!'

'You've thought of everything,' I said. And he said I did not know the half of it. Then he told me his plan. How he was working all hours at the forge, which was probably why he made the stupid mistake and burned himself. But he'd be right as rain, back again in a few days, and he was saving everything. He told me Avis had begun mending and doing scullery jobs. She was saving, too. William said Sylvanus Davis had hurt his shoulder, so he had agreed to take William on come spring, give him a share in the new shallop, and in the catch. It would not be long, William said, before he would do so well that he could buy off what remained of his apprenticeship at the forge, and buy Sylvanus Davis' share of the shallop as well. As soon as he owned her outright, he'd join the coasting trade, carry cargo when he wasn't fishing.

I could see the joy even the thought brought him. I can still hear his voice, see the huff of his breath in the freezing air. 'I designed her so I could sail her alone, and I'll be able to run clear down to Portsmouth,' he crowed as he patted the boat. 'Before you know it, I'll have made enough that I'll take Avis and mother, and we'll get out of here. Go to Salem, or Boston.'

It was a boy's dream, of course. A fancy born of winter and high hopes. I would have been cruel to tell him otherwise. So I laughed because he was laughing, and I asked him what he planned to do about father and Abigail.

'You can visit.' William punched my shoulder, wobbling on his crutch. 'We'll keep a room for you in our fine new house. But not father. He's happiest in The Ordinary, anyway. He can stay here and his changeling can take care of him. She's plenty old and strong enough, and it's about time she did some work. Or he can take her back to Topsfield, and perhaps she'll fly away. No, Thaddy, we're off! The drunkard and the bad cat can fend for themselves!'

Those were his very words. I laughed with him over them.

Then I heard a noise, and we turned to the open door of the shed, and saw Abigail.

By the time we reached the door, she was gone. We returned to the house, both of us looking at the trail of little footprints in the snow, trying to judge how long she had been standing there, how much she had heard. The carter was returning to Saco, and I had to go with him. My leave was up. My mother had made dinner, but Abigail was not there. William and I both thought we knew why, but neither of us said anything, and no one else remarked on her absence. As I said, she had more or less run wild by then. Still, I searched for her, before I left the house. I wanted to explain, to tell her that William's plans were not plans at all, but merely boyish dreams. That they meant nothing. But she would not be found, and finally, I had to go.

The twins came with me to The Ordinary. I remember it as clearly as if it was yesterday, how I climbed up onto the bench, and they walked beside us until we reached the Cleeve's Neck road. They stood then, and waved, and as the oxen lumbered away, I could not stop looking back. I watched the blue of Avis's cloak and the patch of my brother's hair against the snow until finally they grew so small that I could see them no more. Even when I knew they were out of sight, I kept twisting around and looking. Four months later, they were dead.

CHAPTER FIFTEEN

"George Burroughs sent for me." Thaddeus runs a hand through his hair. It is full dark now. Beyond the pools of candlelight, the kitchen is a cave of shapes.

"It was a great kindness. Burroughs said he would have come for me, except he was needed in the search. There was still hope then, that they might be on one of the islands."

I think of Mercy Lewis and the others after the attack, and shiver. Getting up and opening the cupboard, I pull out more candles than we need. My mother does not object as I light them all.

"I came straight away," Thaddeus goes on. "It was on their birthday, that they vanished. I should say drowned, but I cannot bear the thought of them sinking." He shudders, and looks at my mother. "Did you know?"

"That they were missing, of course. That it was their birthday? No."

Unlike us, the Hobbs are churched and, like the Lewis family, inclined to the Puritans, who do not celebrate birthdays any more than they celebrate anything else. I cannot remember if I ever heard, if anyone ever mentioned that Avis and William fell out of the world on the same day they came into it.

My mother leans forward and pours more wine into Thaddeus's goblet. This time, she does not add water.

"Tell us," she says.

Thaddeus nods. He drinks and wipes the back of his hand across his mouth.

"I wasn't here. So what happened, I can only tell from what others told me. The shallop had been finished for a month, or more, perhaps. The mast was stepped, and she was rigged. The day the twins would have been sixteen was the last day of April. That spring, two years ago, was warm, if you remember? Sylvanus Davis told William that as a gift, he could take the shallop out. He'd had such a hand in her design and building that it was only fitting he be the first to try her on the water.

William promised to stay in the harbor, or in the Back Cove. Of course, Avis wanted to go with him. It had been a long winter. They were both excited. William prepared the boat the day before, as the tide was to be high early in the morning. Avis packed a picnic, in a basket with a pretty cloth. They crept out of the house not long after dawn.

As is common in spring, there was a fair wind that day. But William was an excellent sailor. He still had a limp from the burn, but it wouldn't hinder him in a boat. No one was worried. At least, they weren't until afternoon, then evening, when they didn't return. My mother went down to the harbor to watch for the sail. But there was nothing. My father went out to the Back Cove, but there was no sighting there either. Nor was there all the next day.

By the time I arrived, they were searching the islands, everyone telling each other how you can survive on them for weeks, if you have to. I had been here for two days when one of the Indians, one of Hope Hood's people, I think, came to say they had seen the boat. That they knew where it was." Thaddeus looks at my mother. "But, surely, Mistress, you remember that?"

Indeed we do. We did not keep company with the Hobbs family. Mary Skilling's hatred for my mother was enough to make it unlikely. Judah and I had not really known the twins. Avis was a friend of Mercy Lewis, not ours. Still, of course, we knew what had happened. Everyone in our small world knew when the twins did not return. We joined the search along the coast until it was clear that they had not gone aground in the Back Cove or been blown onto the rocks on the point. From that time, after the marsh and river estuary had been combed, the search for Avis and William Hobbs became a thing of men in ships.

My father went to sea to search the islands with the others. But it was my mother who thought to go to Hope Hood. It was she who asked the sachem to ask his people if they had seen the little boat, or if they knew where the boy and the girl had gone. I don't know if she was worried about Madockawando, if she thought it was possible they had been taken. Snatched and carried away to the Pentagoet. My mother never said, and in the end it did not matter. Because Hope Hood sent word the next day, and the fine little shallop was found exactly where a fishing party of his people said they had seen it, dashed and stuck on a ledge.

The ledge was close enough to an islet, that, if the current was right, Avis and William might have reached it. But, like so many fishermen who love the sea, William Hobbs could not swim. Neither could his sister.

"I went with the salvage party." Thaddeus Hobbs stares into the ring of candles I have placed around the table as if they will protect us. "My parents did not wish me to, but I insisted. I thought—" His voice stops, then starts again. "I don't know what I thought. That I would find them. Or some trace of them. Something." He takes another drink and goes on.

"The boat was hard to reach. She had been swept down on to the ledge. We had to wait for the tide, and then for the current to ebb before we could lower a dory and row out to her. Her mast was still up. But the rigging was fouled, as if someone had struggled with it mightily. She was stuck, hard. The damage was amidships, where she must have been landed by a wave on the rocks. Several of us got onto the ledge, and I was able to climb along her. I got to the stern. It was not damaged, and I could see the rudder. Its tip was in the water, slapping back and forth. But there was no tiller."

Beyond the silence in the room, I hear crickets in the meadow.

"There was no tiller," Thaddeus says again. "That great long handle William had showed me, that he was so proud of, that he said would make the boat so much easier to sail, was gone. Which meant the pin must have worked itself loose. And there was no cord. There was no knot on the ring. Nothing. Not even any fraying. I climbed down. I clung to the stern and looked, and looked. I ran my hand across the plate, to see if there was even a thread, any trace of a frayed knot. But there was nothing."

"So, you believe it came untied?"

Thaddeus Hobbs looks at my mother.

"I believe," he says, "that someone untied it."

We sit in silence, all of us seeing the sun on the sparkling sea that in April is still as cold as ice. We can all but feel the wind, sharp as a slap. We see the picnic basket with its pretty cloth, blown on the water. And we see small, deft, hands.

A fine mimic. A clever listener, who can remember exactly what has been said. Little footsteps in the snow.

CHAPTER SIXTEEN

"I have never told anyone else. No one," Thaddeus says, finally. "Because, although I was afraid, I was not certain. It was why I had to see you. In order to ask."

My mother and I exchange a look. I know we are both seeing the ravaged body, the mangled, matted fur of Percy. And the bits of quilt. The tallow stub. The burning shape of a wooden bowl.

"Yet, when you spoke, Mistress. When I heard the words, I knew." Thaddeus looks from one to the other of us. "No," he says. "That is not true. I knew before. I knew in my heart from the first moment my mother told me I was to have another brother or sister. It was then, that fear truly gripped me."

"But, why?" The question bursts out of me. "After Avis and William were lost, after that, it was widely known, how your mother spoiled Abigail and doted on her!" *Just as*, I think, *she doted on poor Percy*.

But even as I put the pieces together, my mother says, "Yes. And there is your reason. She heard your brother's plan. A dream, to him. A jest to you. But she was only a child. She thought she was to be abandoned, and she could not let it happen. When she learned another babe was coming, she must have feared, mightily, that it would all begin again. That once more, she would be set aside. She would lose all she had gained."

My mother gets up and goes to the window. She stands with her back to us, looking out onto the summer night.

"Hellebore is well known" she says, "for its properties. All children are warned against it, because the flowers are so pretty. Abigail may also have heard how the root, ground, can be mixed with corn and used for killing rats. She may have intended only to hurt the babe. To be certain it was not born. That may have been why—"

She stops, but I know what she was about to say. *That may have been why she tried first with the cat, another small creature, not unlike a babe.* I can see the calculation in a child's mind. What it takes to kill one small thing is what it takes to kill another. Then I remember kneeling on the dim stair landing, looking into the icy clearness of Abigail Hobbs' blue eyes, seeing her smile as behind the closed door, her mother died in agony. And I am not so sure.

"So you believe—" Thaddeus cannot bring himself to finish the question, so my mother finishes it for him.

"That it was Abigail, who caused your mother's death? And that it was not in error, at least the adding of the hellebore, whatever she intended by it?"

My mother does not turn as she speaks. Instead, she lifts her hand to the casement, resting her fingers against the diamonds of glass as if she can feel the night beyond.

"Yes," she says. "Do not ask me how. I will not tell you. But, yes. I am certain."

Thaddeus Hobbs makes a dreadful sound. He puts his head in his hands.

"If I had found Abigail, that day before I left. If I had found her, told her, explained. Perhaps the twins would still be alive." He looks up. "And my mother. I thought I was mad, or wicked, or both to be so afraid for her. But now I see I was merely weak. My father came to Saco, a month ago, and my mother came with him, to tell me her joyous news. That was what she called it, 'my joyous news.' She was so very happy. She hoped, she prayed, even dreamed, of twins. As if Avis and William were angels who might return. I did not tell her, about the cord, or the pin, or what I suspected had happened to the boat. Perhaps, if I had—instead, I only said I was afraid. Of Abigail, for her sake. I reminded her, of what had happened with my sister Avis, on the stairs. I told her I believed Abigail was jealous. I begged her to take care." He looks up. "And do you know what she did?"

His tears glisten in the candle light.

"She told me that Abigail was her blessed, good child, and that I had always been unlucky. She called me jealous, and said I was ungodly. And then, she slapped me. My own mother slapped me, there in the street. Then she turned and walked away. I never saw her again."

❧

THADDEUS HOBBS SPENDS the night on the pallet before our hearth. I climb the stairs, and sleep beside my mother in the big bed in the top room. Or at least, I think I do. It is very late, or very early when I dream. Or wake. The line between the two seems thinner and thinner.

Moonlight pools on the floor below the open window. There is a wind. I can see the shadows of tree branches, dancing. The bed beside me is empty, which does not seem unusual, and I know, somehow, that if I get up and go to the casement, I will see my mother.

The boards are cool under my bare feet, and slightly damp, as if a sea mist has seeped into our room. When I lean out, my fingers leave prints on the sill. The meadow stretches away, up towards the roofs of the village that look like jagged hills. I stare at them until within their darkness, I see another darkness. As I watch, it detaches itself and steps forward into the pale washed light and starts down the path that leads to our house.

The figure seems to grow as it comes closer, as if it is a shadow of itself. Again, I tell myself that Abigail Hobbs is only ten years old. That what, or who, ever this is, it is far too large to be her. And again, I know I am wrong. I hear Thaddeus' voice, whispering as if he is standing beside me. *Sometimes it seemed someone, something, far older lurked inside her tiny body.* And I know that this is what I am seeing. Just as I saw it that morning on the point.

I feel the same coldness now too, as I did then, on that hot, still day. The same urgent need to become very small, and very still. Once more, the world deadens. The shadows cease their dance. The moon seems to have frozen.

The figure is halfway down the path. I cannot make out its features. I cannot see how it is dressed, or even tell its proper shape. I could not describe it. But I can feel it, fixing its gaze on me. And I know it is coming for us. As I shrink back from the sill, it stops.

A shape has appeared from the side of our paddock. As large as a giant dog, it moves along our fence line. Passing across the dark bars of our gate, it appears somehow both inside the garden and outside it at once, and I know, without knowing how, that it has been circling the house. Drawing a ring around the kitchen garden and the milking shed and the wood store. As I watch, it turns abruptly and paces to the edge of the meadow.

Like a hand removed from a cheek, I feel the figure's gaze leave my face, and know that now it is fixed on the creature that bars its way.

I do not know how long they stand, staring at each other. My fingers grip the sill. Finally, I look down at them. When I look up again, the wind blows, and the meadow is empty. Above, the midnight sky is dark, filled with nothing but the wolf trail that glistens like a river of stars.

CHAPTER SEVENTEEN

My mother sends word that Thaddeus Hobbs does not have a fever. His stomach was merely upset. While we wait for the gossip to spread, she cuts his hair. Then she gives him two more of my father's old shirts, and sends him back to the fort. After he is gone, she tells me that Thaddeus came to us in confidence and that what he told us, he told us in confidence. I should, she says, on no account, tell Judah.

I tell Judah. She arrives barely an hour later, skirts lifted and cap askew, dark hair flying as she runs through the summer grass, bringing us news from The Ordinary.

Captain Blackman and all the men were there last night. They called for pitchers of ale, and ate the better part of a side of beef, lunging at it with their knives while it still turned on the spit, snarling like dogs. Judah tells how they shed their coats, and wiped their greasy hair out of their eyes, and talked about how the Indians are gathering at Pennacook, not three days ride away.

Sylvanus Davis shouted that he knows, that he has it on authority that there are two hundred, or seven hundred, or two thousand of them, and they are all warriors. He pounded the table, and upset his tankard, spilling beer across the sanded planks while another man Judah did know, someone who came with Blackman's militia, stood on his chair and declared that with French help the savages have built a fort that covers five acres. Someone else shouted that they are led and drilled by French officers. That they carry French weapons, and that at night all of them gather around their fires, their faces painted red with blood, and speak of war with the English.

Then Captain Blackman climbed onto his chair. The room hushed when he said that was right. Captain Blackman said he had it in confidence that for all their caution, all their instinct not to make war, the older sachems have been swayed by the young bucks thirsty for white blood. And by the French, who everyone knows want to drive the English from the New World so they can seize it and make it a Devil's dominion for themselves and the pope in Rome. And, he said, it is not just them, but also by Some of Our Own. Captain Blackman said the Indians may be persuaded to attack by those who wish to seize the day, to see a war in the name of Catholic King James who will use it as an excuse to keep us under London's heel so Protestant New Englanders may never control the colony. "A wheel," Captain Blackman declared, "turns within a wheel."

My mother and I and Judah know, as everyone knows, as Blackman intended they should, that when he spoke of 'Some of Our Own', he meant Governor Andros. The Massachusetts Bay Company's charter has been suspended these last four years, and Edward Andros was sent by the King, who now has his Catholic son, not only to govern this slice of the New World, but also to keep a brake on the Puritan god. Or, so scuttlebutt says. Being from the Channel Islands as Andros is, we know this is both true and not true. All coins, as my father would say if he was here, have two sides.

"It is a bad time," my mother said when Judah finished, "for him to be away."

And although I knew she was speaking of Governor Andros, I thought again of my father. Then I thought of the tiller that came unfixed from the rudder and killed Avis and William Hobbs. And suddenly, it seemed an omen—as if theirs was but the first small boat cast to the mercy of dangerous seas.

"What do you think will happen?" Judah's cheeks were bright with excitement.

"It is nonsense." My mother shook her head. "No one here wants war."

I knew she meant Hope Hood. But I also knew she was thinking of John Alden. Of the red sail, rushing north. And of Madockawando and Saint Castin.

Judah and I said then that we would go and fetch the goats in and do the milking. My mother nodded absently. When I looked back as we left the house, I saw that she was opening the writing box.

Now, Judah and I stand at the cove. The tide is out. Gulls wheel above the far bank where they have found something dead washed up below the shore. We have been walking up and down the beach, heads bent, collecting pebbles. Small bright ones. Dull ones. Round ones. Pebbles in the shapes of bird's eggs. As we bend and pluck, I tell her about Thaddeus Hobbs.

I tell about the twins, and the 'mishaps.' About Avis' ribbons, burning in the fire, and the scorch of her hem that must have come so close to her legs. I tell about the stairs, and the shallop in the boat shed, and the gust of spring winds, and the cord and the pin, and how Thaddeus Hobbs climbed down on to the ledge to scour the wreck and found not so much as a thread. Only a nothingness he kept to himself until he opened his palm and showed it to his mother, and she repaid him with a slap.

When we have selected the pebbles we need, we make a pattern, an intricate lacing of all that has happened. How we found the cat, poor Percy. How Judah dug the grave and I placed the flat stone. I told her, too, about the hellebore. How my mother dipped her finger into the deadly milk, and how we threw the cracked wooden bowl on the fire. And I told her about my dreams.

Judah knows it all now. Even the memory holes, and the stunted trees with their claw fingers and gifts of poison flowers. She knows about the black figure on the path, and the creature that circled our house before it turned to face him. We work all of it into our pattern, making sure each pebble is placed just so. Then we stand back and watch as the tide rocks and changes. As wavelets creep from England and France and Jersey, rippling up to lick the edges of our design, and suck it all away before the day is done.

❧

"Do you believe him?" Judah sits on a rock, pulling her skirts up, pushing her feet into the cool, wet sand.

"Thaddeus?"

I told her how he looked like an angel. How his shoulders were wings, stretching as he slept, then folded under the fresh linen of my father's shirt.

"Yes," I say. "I don't know what happened to the shallop. How can anyone? But I believe what he told us. I believe he believes it."

"They say a witch cannot drown."

I look at her.

"It's true," Judah says. "A witch cannot sink. The sea cannot take her. Nor a pond, nor lake, nor river. It is a test, and never fails. The devil walks on water."

"Then Avis and William Hobbs were not witches."

"No." She shades her eyes and looks up toward the point. "Do you think she is there?" She asks. "Watching us?"

"Abigail?"

She looks back at me and nods. I know we are both thinking of the day John Alden came, when I found my memory holes blocked with stones. The same day I accompanied my mother to warn Hope Hood, and looked across from the opposite bank and felt Abigail, or whatever the thing that takes Abigail's shape is, here, above the birches on the track to the point.

"No," I say. "She is not here. Not now."

"Then let's go."

Judah stands and stretches out her hand. The tide licks our pebbles, creeping a little farther each time.

"Let's go," she says, "And clear the holes, and mend your memories. We'll collect the stones, and throw them in the sea!"

I start to say, *No*. Start to remind her of the fury I felt the last time I dared to go to the clearing. I start to tell her how Thaddeus looked when he spoke of Abigail, and how my mother, just this morning, stood with her hand over mine on the fence rail, staring at the spot where the figure had appeared last night in my dream as if she had seen it, too. But Judah cuts me off.

"She is a child." Judah reaches out. Her hands, gritty with sand from creating the pattern of our world, rest on my cheeks. "Abigail Hobbs may be a bad cat," she says. "But she is just a child. An ordinary, naughty child. I promise you. Surely you cannot think otherwise? Not truly?"

I open my mouth. I begin to say what I have just allowed myself to think, *Not Abigail. The thing inside her*. But before I can, Judah laughs, and turns, and starts to climb the bank.

❧

For some reason, I expect the track leading up to the point to be changed. Some part of me thinks that in the few days that have passed, it will have overgrown itself, returned to wilderness, as if it prefers to pretend it has never been. As I follow Judah, I find myself looking for small footprints, like those Thaddeus Hobbs saw in the snow. But there are no prints. There are no marks at all. The track is exactly as it was before and has been all summer.

By the time we reach the bramble patch and I shoulder past Judah, leading the way to my secret clearing, I have begun to think she is right. That Thaddeus Hobbs, for all that he looks like an angel, is deranged by the loss of his brother and sister and now his mother. That William was only a boy. He could have forgotten to tie the cord into the pin altogether. Or made a bad knot. Or the cord could have been frayed after all, and all trace of it washed away. In Thaddeus's mind, warped by loss and guilt as it is, it is his mother's death that has made the twins' deaths seem something more than a dreadful accident. A horrible gusting of spring wind that upset a small boat and sent Avis and William Hobbs who came together into the world, out of it the same way. Cast them down, down, down into the arms of the sea.

Judah knows me well. She knows I am prone to dreams and nonsense. The hellebore was wicked, yes. But she is right. Abigail is a child who could not understand how dangerous these things are. Comfort falls like sunlight through the leafed branches and wraps itself around me. When we finally reach the clearing, it is as I saw it last. True, some branches are bent, twigs snapped and broken. But now the grass just looks flattened by a summer shower, although we have had no rain. That, Judah points out, is most likely to have been deer, nesting here with their fawns.

"What was the song?" Judah tugs my sleeve. "Tell me again, what was the song Abigail sang?"

I shake my head. "I can't remember," I say. Although, of course, I will never forget. And for an instant, I cannot hear the sea. Lapping is replaced by the tuneless echo of words. *A Trisket. A Trasket. Four Kittens in a Basket.* A cloud crosses the sun, its shadow dimming the grass. Suddenly, I think coming here was not a good idea.

"Yes, you can." Judah steps into the center of the clearing. "You can remember. You just won't." She swings around and looks at me. "Never mind," she says, pulling off her cap and letting her hair tumble over her shoulders. "We shall sing our own song and drive the other one away! Or use it as a lure to tempt your dream beast!"

She laughs and spins around, throwing out her arms as she begins to sing.

"There was an old man, who lived near Hells' Gate, What happened to him, I will soon relate!"

Judah's voice has a rich, rhythmic, lilt. She raises her hands over her head and waggles her fingers in time to the words, making them dance in the air.

"The Devil he called upon him one day, saying one of your family I must take away!"

She learns these songs in The Ordinary. I know that sometimes she even sings them for a coin or two. The Ingersolls are happy enough, if it keeps men drinking and paying for another pie and pint.

"The Devil did say, it's not your eldest I want for your life, but your scolding old bitch of a wife!"

She lifts her skirts, and jigs.

"So the Devil he slung her over his back, and carried her as a soldier carries his pack."

By now, I am laughing. Grinning, Judah drops her skirts and grabs my hands. Before I know it, I am singing with her.

"He brought her straight up to Hell's door, and said, get along you scolding old whore! When she saw some devils hanging in chains, she ripped off her mittens and dashed out their brains!"

In the center of the clearing we spin around and around, our hair flying out behind us, sky and trees wheeling above.

"So the Devil he threw her over Hell's wall, where she lit on her arse in a hell of a fall!"

We let go of each other and tumble into the grass where we lay, shouting the last verse.

"Which only proves women are far worse than men, for they go to hell and are kicked out again!"

Panting and giggling with the sudden joy of being alive, we spread our arms and fan them like wings.

"That's what happened to Mary Skilling," Judah says when we

can breathe again. "And to Mercy Lewis. They took one look at them and not savages, not the Devil, not even Madockawando wanted them!"

"Nor Sarah Burroughs!"

"I have it on good authority," Judah proclaims. "That George Burroughs tried to sell her. But he couldn't give her away! Now," recovering before I do, she sits up. "What of these memory holes?" Judah demands. "Where are all these stones? Lets collect them and throw them at Abigail Hobbs. Or tie her in a sack with them and see if she sinks."

My cap is hanging around my neck. Untying it, I point towards the far side of the clearing. I am still worrying the knot as Judah gets to her feet.

"Where?" She asks.

"Just there, at the base of the trees."

I pull the knot out and look up. Judah is standing with her back to me. Above her, leaves rattle and chatter in a sudden breeze.

"There," I say. "In front of you."

When she says nothing, I get to my feet. The clearing is a small space. I am beside her in two steps. But everything is wrong. For a moment, I wonder if we can be in the wrong clearing, if there is another one? Or if we are even, somehow, on the wrong point? But the sea glitters through the trees just where it should be. The tops of the pink rocks catch the sun. At our feet, though, there is nothing.

Nothing at all except a few wilting petals scattered on patches of earth. The holes I made and filled with memories of my mother are no longer merely clogged with stones. They are gone.

CHAPTER EIGHTEEN

"Resolve, wait! Wait!" Judah calls.

But I cannot wait. I am running as fast as I can, down the track, and through the birch grove, and up across the meadow, driven by something greater and more powerful than fear. Fury gives me wings.

Because now, I understand. This is not just Abigail's revenge for the fact that we discovered, and took poor Percy. It was not enough for her, to stop up the memory holes. No. Abigail Hobbs may not be able to feed my mother hellebore ground into a stew, but she would take her from me nonetheless. She would erase every word and look and touch. She would rob me of the most valuable thing I have—my memories. Abigail would make me motherless, as she is herself.

I find her at the common, standing on the corner of Broad Street, watching the militia as they tromp and wheel like ragged birds. Any other day, I might think how stupid this is, how these men know nothing of fighting so it is no wonder so many are attacked and left for dead. But today, I do not care. I fasten on Abigail Hobbs the way a hawk fastens on a mouse.

I feel as if I have seen her from far above, and the sinew that stretches between us is pulling me to her the way a line pulls a fish. If I had paused to think on that, if I had not been in such a rage, I might not have done what I do next.

Abigail must have sensed, or seen, or heard me coming because as I bear down on her, she turns to face me. She is smiling when I slap her.

"You!" I scream. "You are a bad, bad cat!"

The blow sends her reeling. But she does not fall. Abigail, as I noticed when I tried to remove her from her mother's room, is as solid as fence post.

"I know you!" I shriek. "I know what you have done! And what you would do!"

I slap her again, feeling the satisfying sting of my palm on her perfect cheek. Then, I close on her, like a thing on its prey. The world disappears as I bend down, creeping forward, putting my face so close to Abigail's that my spittle catches her.

"I know," I hiss, so low that only the two of us can hear. "I know what you have done, and what you are doing. I know. But you will not win! Not from me! Because I know what you are!"

All at once, my temper snaps. My voice rises to a shriek as Judah catches my shoulders, dragging me backwards before I can hit Abigail again.

"I know you!" I scream. "I know you!"

Then, I am lifted off my feet. Arms strong as steel bands close around me, swinging me away. I do not have to look to know they belong to George Burroughs. I remember the smell of his sweat.

By now, there is more shrieking and screaming. Mercy Lewis is running towards us flapping her arms like a chicken. Her mother follows, Mary Skilling hard on her heels. The men on the common have stopped their wheeling and stomping and stand staring like beached fish, mouths open, eyes goggling. Beyond them, I see Captain Blackman.

"Come," George Burroughs says, and I realize he is talking to Judah. "Come, let's away from here, and quickly."

He puts me down, and they turn me as if I am a doll, hustling me towards the side yards of the Broad Street houses. But as my feet move away, my head twists. Mercy Lewis is clinging to Abigail, keening and howling. Goody Lewis is kneeling in front of her, fingering her cheek where, even from here, I can see a red mark rising. Mary Skilling circles them, snapping and bobbing. In the middle of it all, Abigail Hobbs stands perfectly still. As George Burroughs and Judah hustle me into the passage between the houses, she fastens me with her bright blue eyes, and raises her hand in a wave.

❧

"WHAT WERE YOU THINKING?"

My mother is kneeling in front of me, holding one of my feet, which she has plunged into a bowl of the salt water Judah fetched from the stillroom. Driven by furies, I was barefoot, my shoes abandoned when I bolted from the clearing, and did not notice that I stepped on a stone, or a shell, or a branch, or some discarded piece of pottery or blade. Judah tells me later that she would have had no trouble following, even if she had not seen me. Bloody splats marked my path to Abigail.

Now, she stands holding a bowl of clay mashed with valerian and willow root that my mother smears on the wound to seal it. George Burroughs looks on from our kitchen doorway, which seems to be his accustomed spot. This time, he leans his shoulder on the frame, arms crossed. Being a minister, he should surely be upbraiding me for attacking children. But if I expected him to scold or lecture me, I was wrong. He has barely said a word. Judah has said almost nothing, either. Although in her case, I know it is because she can barely keep a straight face. She will not meet my eye for fear of the laughter that I know is about to erupt from her. Normally, it would be as infectious as pox. But I do not feel like laughing. Sitting in the chair before the hearth while my mother bandages my foot, I am both drained and gripped by a growing sense of dread. A terrible unease—like an animal that thinks it has been clever, and instead finds it has walked into a trap.

My mother finishes. She props my foot on the fire stool and sends Judah to wash the bowl and fetch cool cider from the still-room. Then she looks at me because I have not answered her question. What would I say? *She has threaded a sinew through my heart? She watches us? She creeps down our path under the moonlight when she is something else? She has scattered my memories, and would erase them forever, leave nothing but poison petals in their place because she knows when you are gone they are all I will have, and she does not want me to have even that. Because what Abigail Hobbs wants is for me to be all alone. She wants me to be just like her.*

Would I tell my mother and Judah and George Burroughs that I believe her brother, William, was right? That he may have spoken it in jest, but it is true. Would I tell them that Abigail Hobbs is a changeling? Or worse than that, a demon? A witch? That she can turn herself into a shape three times the size of a man? I might have, before today. Before an hour ago. But now, I cannot. Because she laid the bait, and I snatched her lure. Abigail has played, and won. I walked straight into the snare she set. Everyone has heard me shriek like a mad woman. Everyone has seen me attack a child.

❧

THE THOUGHT MAKES me ill with shame. But it is nothing to the fear that knots my stomach. I understand now that Abigail has shown me what she is. She wants me to know. And it does not matter. Because after the way I behaved today, not only will no one believe a word I say about her—they will take one look and decide that it is me—the barefoot screaming madwoman leaving a trail of blood—who is a witch. Not the golden haired motherless child.

I shudder, and am brought to my senses by the scrape of George Burroughs' chair as he pulls it out and sits at the table.

As he lifts his cider cup, I notice that his fingers are short and blunt, giving his hands the appearance of paws. He does not look at us, but studies the scrubbed, oiled boards of the table. Then he says, "You should not be ashamed. I have seen Abigail do this before. Indeed, it is not much different from what she did to her sister."

I close my eyes and see the twins, William and Avis with their hair streaming and their hands joined, wrapped in green water.

George Burroughs looks at me, and again I am struck by his kindness. He would be well within his rights to be angry with me. To suggest a punishment, or at least deliver a lecture. But all I see in his face is worry.

"She is no ordinary child. I have suspected it for some time."

The words lay in the room. Through the open kitchen door, I can smell the garden. Our hive is working. The low drone of the bees sounds like the breath of the world.

"I do not know what to do." George Burroughs looks around the table. "I tried once, during the winter before Avis and William were lost, to speak to her father. I asked him to pray with me. I suggested we pray with Abigail."

Judah makes a noise. George Burroughs looks at her, and smiles.

"Yes," he says. "I was a fool. But, William Hobbs is an even greater fool, and weak with it. There is no help there, not for this. And since Avis and William were lost, he has been a fool and a weakling and broken. And that is when he is not drunk." George Burroughs looks at my mother. "Is it your belief that Abigail witched her own mother?"

"No." My mother reaches for the cider pitcher and pours again into their cups.

Judah takes mine, holds it while my mother refills it and passes it back. My mother seems to know somehow, and no longer care, that I have told her everything.

"It was not witching," my mother says. "It was poison. I am

not sure what she intended—if it was meant just for the babe, out of jealousy, or if it was truly meant for Avis as well. If she meant to kill one or both of them. Abigail is a child. Perhaps she did not know herself."

George Burroughs bows his head. The dark curl of his hair falls forward, like the forelock of a bull. "I was afraid of that," his voice is barely a whisper. "God help me. But I was not sure, when I came for you. Could it have been an error?" He asks, as Thaddeus did. Although, like Thaddeus, there is not much hope in his voice. "Or an accident?"

My mother shakes her head. She gestures towards the far side of the house, towards the milking shed and the fence where the little grave is covered with a stone. This time, she minces no words. She will tell our minister what she would not tell Avis Hobbs' son.

"Abigail killed the cat first, as a test."

"And because Avis loved it." This is the first time Judah has spoken. "We found it. Resolve and I came across it, dead, up on the point."

For a horrible moment, I am afraid she is going to say more. That she is going to tell about the memory holes, and the clearing, and how I hid in the brambles and heard singing. About my dreams of beasts and dark figures. Then, no matter how kind he is, George Burroughs will have no choice but to think me mad, or witched, or both. But, "The poor little puss was laid out," is all she says.

Judah's voice takes on a tinge of French when she is upset, as if her past rises with her blood. "In a bed of flowers," she adds. "And she had lit a candle."

"Jesu." George Burroughs picks up his cup, and sets it down again. For the first time, I see something on his face that looks like fear. "If I go with this," he says, "with what I have suspected and now know, to the Elders in the church in Salem, or Boston, we shall have a panic. There are those children already."

He is right. When the gossip has not been of the Indians and

Northfield, it has been of the Goodwin children of Boston, the same Thaddeus spoke of, who have been possessed and tormented and have writhed and screamed and fought for their souls all summer long.

"They say now it is the washer woman, who witched them, and that there shall be a trial." George Burroughs looks from one to the next of us. "If I speak what I know of Abigail, or venture even to probe at it to try to learn more, the same will happen here. We will have those preachers, the Mathers, father and son, who took over the Goodwin children, and every charlatan and attention seeker who travels with them. It will do nothing but give power to Boston. They will say we cannot conduct ourselves, and that to save our souls they must take a stronger hand in our affairs. And with Andros away. And, all this." He gestures towards the common, as if all these things—the militia marching and stomping, the shots fired in Saco, the raiding and murders in Northfield, Abigail Hobbs, and dead cats, and poison flowers—all this calamity, is spun by the same spider into the same web.

"The child is dangerous," George Burroughs says, a second later. He regards his cup, as if he is looking for comfort in it. "She may even be wicked. But that is a long way, surely, from witching."

Is it? I start to open my mouth. But words do not come, because what, in truth, will I say? What have I seen, or witnessed? I have not seen Abigail Hobbs turn into a black cat or suckle a familiar. I have not seen her fly through the air. Or felt her stick me with pins. All of which they say witches do. Instead, I have run through the town barefoot, shrieked and hissed and slapped a child in front of the whole world. I am the one who has heard strange voices, and dreamed of dark figures and circling beasts.

My mother glances at me. "We have panic enough," she says quickly.

"We cannot have more. Especially with the gossip that is flying. It is too dangerous. Innocent people will be hurt."

No one says her name, but all of us remember Eliza Bourne.

My mother looks at George Burroughs. "We are also from Jersey. Myself, Resolve, Judah. Oh, I know." She waves a hand. "We have taken baptized names, and Judah calls herself White. But in the minds of many, of most probably, if panic blooms, we still smell French. My husband is far away, and I have these girls to protect. No, there is panic enough," she says again, and this time there is iron in her voice. "Strike that tinder," my mother warns, "and the very air in this town will set itself alight."

George Burroughs does not even try to hide his relief at this way out she has suggested. He drains his cider and places his cup on the table.

"You are more than right, Mistress," he says. "What we need is not panic, but peace and sober thought. In truth," he adds, attempting, I suspect, not to appear a coward, "if Abigail was a man, or even a boy, or a crone, she could be questioned. Perhaps even made to answer for what she has done, be it in error, or no. But she is a child." He looks at us. "A golden-haired girl child with a drunkard father who has lost her brother and sister and now her mother and whom all the Goodwives, including my own," he smiles ruefully, "want to prize and coddle."

He rests his paw-hands on the table in front of him. "It is true," George Burroughs says, "that we know what we know. But I think you are right. It must stay here, amongst ourselves."

My mother nods as he gets to his feet. She is watching our minister, but I see the look in her eye and know she is also warning Judah and me. *No gossip. No tattling. No whispering. Not. One. Word.*

"I will watch her carefully." George Burroughs looks at us as if he is making a promise, taking it upon himself as God's agent here to patrol and corral this thing, whatever it may be.

"I have done so before," he says with rather more bravado than I think he feels. "I thought, God Forgive me, that the tragedy of her brother and sister's deaths had brought it to an end, that with her sister gone, Abigail would regret her taunts and tricks, and rest."

Looking up at George Burroughs from where I sit with my bandaged foot on the stool, I realize that he does not even consider questioning what happened to the twins. His suspicions have never darkened to include their deaths. He runs his hands through his hair, pulling it as if he can pull the world back into a shape he likes better than the one he sees.

"In any case," he says, resolute, as if he can leave Abigail behind him, "we have, I think, an even greater danger in Blackman, and the panic that he brews for his own importance. I will do what I can there, too. This Sunday, I shall preach peace and calm."

George Burroughs smiles, though there is more hope than conviction in it. "Peace and calm and order," He says as he steps out the door. "Peace and calm and order."

But it is not to be.

PART II

Love me like a sister

CHAPTER NINETEEN

Lavender fans the sun warmed gravel. The bees protest as I clip the stalks, clinging to the flowers until I shake them off and they whir away into the marigolds, which they like, but not half so much as the lavender. My mother told me how she brought these roots and cuttings with her from Jersey. How, with the pewter plate and goblets and the silver buckles she never wears upon her shoes, they were her marriage portion. As they had been my great-grandmother's. She brought lavender roots with her from France when she crossed to join her husband in the Channel Islands. Marriage portion to marriage portion, flower to flower, the knowledge in them traveled across the glittering sea.

I have never seen The Channel Islands—Jersey and Guernsey and Sark. But sometimes, in moments like these, I think I smell them. Think I can feel the green roll of the hills my mother has told me about, and hear the mighty crash of the sea against the cliffs. I pick up a flower, flick a bee from it, and wonder, if the blossom too, remembers. If in turning to the sun, in leaning to the warmth of the gravel, some part of the plant recalls an island far away, or even France.

This late in the summer, when the lavender hedge is at its

most potent, the smell is intoxicating. I think of all the good things that come from France—lavender, and the ribbons and lace and fancies that find their way to us on Philip English's ships or emerge from the mysteries that are John Alden's pockets, and wonder if they can really be as fearsome as the Puritans say. If it is true, as they insist, that all that is beautiful is but a glove for the Devil's hand.

I am mulling on this, and wondering if I have cut enough lavender, or if my mother will be annoyed if I do not finish the whole row? If she wishes some of the flowers to stay for the bees and thus for the honey, or if she wants the whole for pressing? When Thaddeus Hobbs says, "Don't they sting?"

I nearly drop the shears as I whirl around, almost toppling over on my bandaged foot. Above me, Thaddeus leans on our garden fence, his elbows resting on the rail, and tries not to laugh.

"I am sorry," he says. "I didn't mean to startle you."

Although I know he did. I can see in his face that the temptation was too much to resist. For a split second I remember that he is his sister's brother.

"Do you use it for linen, or for tea?" He is nodding at the lavender.

"Neither," I say. "Oil."

Thaddeus nods again, as if this means something to him, which I am sure it does not. Any fool knows lavender is not used for tea.

"Is it painful?" He looks at my foot.

I look at it, too, as if I am considering the question. Which is a lie, because my foot hurts a great deal. The cut is almost in the center, and more like a stab, as if I stepped on a knife or an arrow tip, although my mother says it was more likely a broken branch. I was in such a fury as I ran that I did not feel it at all until George Burroughs and Judah were hustling me away from the common and back to the house. Whatever it was went deep, which has made it difficult to clean. My mother has re-bandaged and soaked it twice daily for the last two days. But it is still inflamed, and she is not happy. Nor am I. I feel as if I have been stabbed by the Devil himself. I shrug.

"I'm sorry," Thaddeus says, and I realize that when I saw him I had wondered if he was coming to berate me for attacking his sister. But his mission, it seems, is the opposite. "I heard what happened."

I make a face. I have had two days to consider my stupidity, the way I fell straight into the trap Abigail set for me. From what Judah has told me, the whole village, possibly all of the Eastward and most of New England, has heard what happened. How I set upon a child like a mad thing. Goody Burroughs alone has probably broadcast the news across Massachusetts.

"Do they say that I am altogether possessed, or merely that I have lost my wits?"

I turn to face Thaddeus, seating myself on the gravel as if I intended to all along and had not almost fallen over. He smiles.

"It depends on who is telling the story," he says. Then his smile fades. "In truth, though. I am sorry. This is my fault. If I had not come, had not spoken as I did, told you and your mother of my suspicions—"

"It would have made no difference."

We study one another. Thaddeus is too thin. His bones are raised and his features hollowed, whether from grief, or the militia, or both, I cannot tell. As he stands here in the sun looking down on me, I can see something of his mother in him, the shadow of her dying face, as if it was not just a slap but her memory she left upon his cheek that afternoon in Saco. His eyes are as wide and as large as Abigail's. But there, the similarity ends. They are blue today. But not ice. Summer sky. When it is grayed and heavy before the rain.

We stay like this for several seconds. Then I tell him what my mother would not—about the point, and poor Percy, and the little wooden bowl and its milk of hellebore. Nor do I stop there. I tell him about what happened in the brambles. Then I tell him about my dreams. About the storm and the trees. I tell him about the clearing, and the dark figure on the path and the circling beast. And finally, about the memory holes. How they were first piled with stones, then sealed with poison flowers.

When I finish, I close my eyes. There is nothing but the sound of the bees, and the sun on my face, and a weightlessness. As if I have floated free of the world. And I realize, in that moment, that Thaddeus Hobbs is the only person who has felt—who, for all I know still feels—what I feel. Who does not think I am mad if I speak of a sinew through the heart, and my fury at it, and terror of it. Who knows what I mean when I say I am an animal trapped in a snare set by a ten year old child.

Even Judah, even my mother, for all their love of me, would think me fevered or deranged if I were to tell them of my absolute certainty that Abigail tried first to smash my memories, then to erase them. And lace the ground they rested in with poison. Which is the same thing as poisoning my mother, and erasing me.

Thaddeus comes through the gate and lowers himself to sit beside me on the gravel.

"I am so sorry."

I look at him, and think of the angel wings folded tight against his back.

"It is not your doing."

"No," he says. "It is not. But she is my kin." He looks away and almost smiles. "I do not know how. I think I would not believe it, if I had not seen my mother carry her, and did not remember the day she was born. So, I fear William may have been right."

At this we both smile. Changelings are generally thought to be dark things, shadows left in the place of babes, claiming their substance, filling the shell of their skin. But Abigail is a golden thing. Perhaps, I think, the Boston Puritans are correct after all. The Devil does wear beautiful gloves.

"I do not understand," I say. "Why she has fastened on me?"

There is no one I can ask except Thaddeus. I had considered George Burroughs, for, even more than my mother, I believe he suspects what I think I know. *The thing that has taken the shape of Abigail.* But I dare not consult our minister. I think again of contagion, of Goody Burroughs and her whispers. And know I am better off keeping my thoughts, and questions, to myself. Sharing them even with Judah led to my present calamity. I would never have returned to the clearing, but for her.

So, alone these last few days, as I have been working in the stillroom and in the garden—doing what I can for my mother, being lame—I have given all of this some thought.

It is easy to see why Abigail would have been jealous of her sister. Avis and Avis were not just copies, but bonded, as my mother and I are. It is easy to understand Abigail's fear when she heard William's plans. That did not include her. That abandoned her to care for an unlucky, drunken father. Shut her out of the circle of love and protection that was her family. I can understand fear and fury in the face of that. After all, my own fury led me to fly from the point and attack her. But what I do not understand is why she set her snare for me.

"Because," Thaddeus says, "she loves you. And she is afraid of you."

I look at him.

"She is afraid of you," he says again. "And she loves you. The second because of the first, as with all lovers. And, like all lovers, she wishes to possess you."

"But why? Of all people, why me?"

"Because she recognizes you. She knows you are like her. She knows you can see."

I open my mouth, about to admit a squawk of protest—to say that I see nothing everyone does not see. Then I close it again, and think of the moonlight a few nights ago. Of what I felt as I opened the window on the day Avis Hobbs died, how the babe skittered across my shoulder and down my arm. How it lingered in my palm before I wished it free. I think of the flat plate of the cove as my mother and I paused on the opposite bank before launching the canoe, and how I felt the cold, familiar touch on my cheek. My hand rises without meaning to, fingers running across the patch of skin.

"I can feel it, too," Thaddeus says, interrupting my thoughts as if, like my mother, he can read them. "I know you have seen what Abigail is. I knew at once."

I stare at him. Thaddeus Hobbs reaches for my hand. He pulls it away from my cheek, cradling the fingers in his palm as if he can feel the cold they have just brushed against, the mark of his sister's touch.

"She may suspect that I know," he says. "But she is not sure of it. Of you though, she is sure. She has recognized you, and she has toyed with you. She has tried to find out how powerful you are. She did the same with my sister, who did not understand what she was or how to counter her, and paid for it with her life. Abigail dared you, and I think," he adds quietly, "your mother, to challenge and name her, sure you would not because no one ever has. And, though she has won—she has made you an object of gossip—it is a hollow victory and she will not care for it. Abigail thrives on playing the poppet. It is her power. She knows now that you would strip her of it. So you must be careful."

"She cannot hurt me." I wish it did not sound so much like a question. "She cannot hurt me," I say again, and slide my hand away to finger the edge of the basket I have filled with lavender.

"William and Avis and my mother—" Thaddeus says, and I can hear the rest. *William and Avis and my mother thought the same. And they are all dead.*

If he speaks it, if Thaddeus Hobbs lets those words into the world, they will buzz as surely as the bees, and find a place to land, and make themselves come true.

"She cannot hurt me," I say again, too loud. "She is nothing but a child."

Thaddeus nods.

"Indeed," he says, and his voice changes. For, he too, knows the power of words. "In any case," he adds, his voice light now. "It is no matter. Soon enough, my bad cat of a sister will be forgotten. No one will remember that she ever stood beside the common. Or that she is very pretty, and very brattish, and got herself slapped. No one will think twice about it. Not with the news that is coming, which is what I came to share with you, and your mother."

"My mother is not here."

She was called very early this morning, just after first light, to a difficult birth at one of the farms along the Back Cove. She worried about the goodwife there, and told the husband he must send for her at once when the babe announced that it was coming. The man arrived at just past dawn with his own cart, hammering on our door. While I might previously have gone with her, my foot now renders me next to useless. No longer her strong arms, I could barely help with the baskets. The anxious man carried them himself, placing them carefully into the bed of the cart before helping my mother onto the high seat and turning the little bay horse back towards the neck. There was nothing for me to do but stand in the gate, watching them go as the sun rose, promising I would finish the chores she set out.

"Well then," Thaddeus says, standing and reaching to help me to my feet, "I shall tell you."

I allow him to help me up. He bends and lifts the lavender basket and, like a fine gentleman, offers me his arm as we turn towards the open stillroom and the kitchen. Resting my hand, I realize that the linen under it is my father's and the fine stitching is my own.

"It is Captain Blackman." Thaddeus' words match the crunch of the gravel. "I thought you would want to know."

He glances at me, and I understand that he has heard of our history. That somehow our past, the years we spent in The Greening with Ashawonks during the last war, has found us as lost dogs will find their masters even when they must travel great distances to do so.

"Blackman," Thaddeus says as we make our way through the banks of herb beds, "is afraid of not being enough of a commander. He is afraid that in the face of the threats here, and in light of what happened in Saco, he will be perceived a failure, and that old Benjamin Church will be sent to replace him. So, he has put out an order, that all Indians, no matter who they are or what they are doing, should be taken and destroyed."

CHAPTER TWENTY

After Thaddeus left, I made a long, careful circle around the house and the garden and the milking shed and the wood store, looking for paw prints. I saw none. Not even in the freshly turned edges of Percy's grave. Still, I repeated the exercise the next few mornings as soon as my mother left for the Back Cove farm where the goodwife, though safely delivered of a baby girl, is still sickly and requires almost constant care. In the nights, I rose from hour to hour while my mother slept and tiptoed to the open casement where I stood in the shadows, watching the meadow and the jagged outlines of the village rooftops beyond. I saw nothing in the waning moonlight. And remembered that because I could not see it did not mean it was not there.

Busy as she is, my mother barely noticed the sabbath that passed, and I had the excuse of my foot. So we did not hear George Burroughs preach on peace and calm and order. Which apparently Captain Blackman did not hear, either. Or, perhaps he did, and fancies this is how he will achieve it.

Since his order went out, even more militia have been poured into the fort. There are so many that they have overflowed across the village, mostly, it would seem into The Ordinary.

Judah says Joseph Ingersoll now serves them in the door yard and what was the garden, before they trampled it. They have kept her so busy that I have barely seen her since we danced our wild dance in the clearing. Nor have I gone to the village. I tell myself this is because of my foot. But really it is because I do not wish to be stared at. It does not take much to imagine wagging tongues.

The militia patrol constantly. Groups march in and out of the fort and up and down the road along Cleeve's neck. My mother sees them as she comes and goes from the Back Cove. She spots them skulking around the edges of fields. There are so many, and they make so much noise that she has gone out more than once to shush them when her goodwife and the new babe are sleeping. They are, she says, so loud they could not surprise a deaf mule.

My mother smiles and shakes her head as she packs and repacks her baskets. But I know she wishes Hope Hood had listened to her warning. Blackman is an idiot, she says, who cannot see far enough past his own too-big nose to understand that kicking one nest may well bring down upon him—and us—more hornets than he has ever dreamed of. But kick he will, and with John Alden gone, nothing it seems can be done to stop him. So, we wait, dogged by an unease that would be foreboding if we were certain of exactly what is to come.

THE CART WAS EARLY AGAIN this morning. This time the little bay horse was driven by the son, no more than a boy, with a lick of ginger hair and sun dots across his cheeks and a mangy little dog called Tom who sits on the bench beside him. My mother says the babe is strengthening, and the mother, too. She says she is hopeful, and does not add what we both know, that hope is no cure for birth fever. After she had gone, with her baskets in the back and the dog between her and the boy, I did the milking, and brought new curds to the stillroom, and set the new milk, and changed the cloths for the cheese I am making.

As if sensing our mood, the animals are fretful. Our cow does not want to come out of the shed while my goats patrol the paddock, hopping and butting the rails. Yesterday I saw an owl, at noon, sitting on the last of our fence posts, staring up the meadow with its great unblinking eyes. I even thought, this morning, that I saw a paw print, larger than one of the village dogs', in the dusty edge of the cleared space behind our wood shed. But when I bent to look, I lost my balance and staggered, stepping where I thought I had seen it and if it was there at all, brushed it away with my skirts.

Today is hotter than it has ever been. The pain in my foot has become an ache. Poultices of willow bark have eased it, but it dragged at me as I limped to the well, feeling as if my punishment for being foolish enough to attack Abigail Hobbs is not only my self-imposed exile and shame, but a flipping of the coin that is my mother and me. Now, she is well and strong and out in the world and I am lame and cloistered.

Feeling very sorry for myself, I hauled up the well bucket. Regarding Percy's small grave with its stone that I have laid marigolds around because they are precious to the dead, I drank my fill. Then, without thinking what I was doing, I lifted the bucket and poured what remained over my head.

The dress and cap I put on this morning are my oldest, and very worn, and it is so hot that I knew they would dry even before I returned to the house. My hair came loose and stuck in a mat to my back. There was not much in the bucket, no more than when my mother washes my hair. My foot ached, and the ache made me long for wet sand. Without thinking, I dropped the bucket and began to hobble towards the birch grove.

The tide had reached its highest point and was beginning to slither out. On top of the bank, I took off my shoes and unwound the bandage from my foot. I began to hitch my skirts into my old leather belt. Then, I stopped and looked about.

Sometimes there are fishing shallops in the mouth of the cove, but there were none today. Behind me, there was nothing beyond the grove but our paddocks with the cow and the goats. Almost before I knew what I was doing, I undid my belt and reached back to loosen my laces. I pulled my cap off and, shedding my dress like a skin, slithered unsteadily down the slope and onto the beach.

The water felt like a kiss. As I waded deeper, the pain in my foot seemed first to fade, then to vanish altogether. Because it is so hot, the first touch of the summer sea is always icy. But, basking as it has, it is warmer this year than usual. I went in up to my knees, then a little farther. I was relishing the blessed cold of it when I stepped on a rock, teetered, and fell.

I landed with a splash, my shift billowing around me. I started to scramble up, then I felt the coolness, and stopped, and sat there, floating my hands on the water, holding them flat and watching it run between my fingers. The gulls were so high that I couldn't hear them. Above me, the white blades of their wings sliced the pale, hot, sky. There seemed to be no sound at all, as if the world was emptied and I was alone with the coolness and the glitter that danced across the surface of the cove.

I don't know how long it was before I saw the seal. The slick dome of the dog-shaped head and the comical old man whiskers appeared suddenly, so close that I felt if I stretched I would be able to stroke it, to run my fingers down its slick pelt. Even as I thought this, it turned and looked at me, its eyes wide and brown and beckoning. I watched those eyes as they watched me, and before I knew it I had leaned forward. I rested on my elbows. Then on my hands and knees. Then, I was swimming the way I had not swum in years, following the seal as if it had come just for me.

I learned to do this as a child in The Greening. We all did. It was easy, to go from washing, to splashing in the shallows, to chasing one another until we tripped and fell and were caught and cradled by the river. Then, almost without meaning to, we were slicing through it, arms and legs turned to fins that set us flying on the current.

The English do not swim. I know my mother can, because she and all the other women in The Greening did the same thing. There, it was not considered ungodly. It did not mean you were a witch. It meant you would not drown. But once we returned to Duxbury, and once we came here, it was no more mentioned or thought about than our old names—the Rachel and Susannah we slithered out of and left at the water's edge as we stepped ashore to begin new lives in the shelter of Deliverance and Resolve.

Now, I find I have not forgotten. My limbs remember, all too well. My legs kick and my arms reach, and there is no pain in my foot at all. I dive down, and everything around me is soft and green and silent. Rising, I stroke the water with my fingers. I close my eyes and roll, floating on my back, feeling my hair fan around me. Staring into the sun that is directly above, I am almost overcome by an unruly joy, a knowledge that I have not altogether lost the creature I was, the creature that once knew how to do this.

I do not know where the seal is. Having lured me, it has vanished. I know there are stories like this, in Jersey. I suppose my mother must have told me, or perhaps my father, so long ago I do not even remember. They come back now, like the memory of swimming. Tales of Selkies. Seal people who shed their skins and come ashore. Jersey is rife with stories of maids besotted and despoiled by handsome fishy suitors. Of husbands whose wives suddenly find their skins again, and desert them for the sea. Of strange singing. And men and women whose clothes are abandoned on the shore and whose bodies are never found.

I dive again, wondering if I will spot the flash of a fin, or feel a whisker on my cheek. If a smooth sleek hand will reach for mine. But there is only greenness. I open my mouth and let bubbles rise. Then follow them, and lay on my back, as if I am sleeping, arms spread, face to the sun.

The water ripples. The tide is moving. Finally, I open my eyes, thinking to look for my seal, and roll, first toward the opposite bank, where my mother and I hid the canoe, and where now there is nothing, then back toward our beach. Where a figure stands on the sand.

For one awful moment, I am sure it is Abigail Hobbs. Then I see it is Judah.

Relieved, giddy almost, I raise a hand. But she does not wave back. She does not even move. It is not until I am in the shallows, suddenly robbed of the grace I had in the deep water, not until I scrabble, attempting to stand and wade to the beach, that I see the look on her face.

"What?" I hear myself ask. "Did you think me a witch, or a selkie?"

Smiling, laughing, I wring out my hair as I come towards her, my shift clinging about my legs and across my belly. But Judah is not laughing. She is not even smiling. She blinks, and then, quickly, so fast I almost do not see it, touches her hand to her forehead, chest, and shoulders, making the sign of the cross.

I stop and stand staring at her. Judah is not Catholic. But she would have known this gesture, on Jersey, as a child. She would have seen it used even by those who do not follow Rome, as I have seen it used, like a horseshoe nailed above a door, to ward off evil. As loud as if she has spoken again, I hear what she said, bare a week ago in this very place. Fast and sure as a blade, the remembered words slip between us. *A witch cannot sink. The Devil walks on water*.

JUDAH RECOVERS FIRST, stepping forward, her hands on her hips.

"Anyone could have seen you!" She hisses.

I look over my shoulder at the plate of the cove, then up the bank to the birches. Anger fizzes through me—whether at myself because she is right, or at her for saying so, or out of fear, hard and bright as a jay's wing in the noonday sun, I am not sure. My voice, when it comes, is sharp.

"That is fine, coming from one who sings about goodwives' arses and the Devil."

Judah glares at me, then turns and scrambles up the bank. For a terrible moment I think she is leaving. Abandoning me here, dripping and all but naked in my shift, convinced I am a witch. But all she is doing is collecting my clothes. She slithers down the bank again.

"Come!" She says, holding them out to me. "Come, hurry. Do you not know? Haven't you heard?"

Tottering up the squelching sand, trying not to trip on my bad foot, which, deprived of the cold and with my weight on it, has started to hurt again, I begin to ask how I could have heard anything. But Judah is already wiping at me with the skirt of my old dress. She gives up, tutting.

"Take it off!" She says, ducking to grab the hem of my shift and pulling it over my head. Dropping it into the sand at her feet, she bundles me into my dress and turns me around as if I am a naughty child.

"Here." She hands me the wet hank of my hair to lift as she does up my laces, then rolls it and stuffs it into my grubby cap. "Come!" She says, buckling my belt, pulling it tighter than she needs to. "Come! We'll miss everything!"

Judah grabs my hand. She is dragging me up the bank. We are hurrying through the birch grove, stooping for my shoes and the discarded bandage, before I finally ask her where we are going, and what has happened.

"The harbor!" She says, as if I should know this. "Everyone is at the harbor! They have captives."

I stop dead. *My mother.* I see her climbing into the cart at first light, the little bay horse turning and trotting away. I see the owl on the fence post, in broad daylight. An omen. And imagine the Back Cove farm—the sick goodwife, the ailing baby, the distracted husband and the boy who is only a boy. And Madockawando's men.

"No!" Looking over her shoulder, Judah shakes her head. "No!" she says. "We have captives! The militia have captured twenty savages, and Hope Hood is among them!"

CHAPTER TWENTY-ONE

Out in the harbor, Captain Blackman's ship rides uneasy at her anchor, as if suddenly uncertain of her purpose. She is, after all, a sloop, not a prison. Yet that is what she will be used for, since our village has no jail and the fort is filled to bursting with militia. Who are very proud of themselves. Puffing their ragged breasts like so many motley chickens, they march down the beach, their captives in their midst.

Judah and I arrived too late to watch them parade along Broad Street. The best we could do was join the crowd at the water's edge. From the smell, most of the others surrounding us are fishermen, which explains why our cove was empty. News of the captives must have come before the tides changed, after they had come in and before they were ready to go out again. Some of the townspeople are down here, too. Others are lined up along the common. Yet others, mostly boys, follow the militia and the captives, shouting and shaking their fists at the savages. Who do not look particularly savage.

Rumor says there are twenty of them, and from what I can see—the dark heads surrounded by sweat stained shirts and slouched hats—most are women. I cannot see any young men.

No one who looks like a warrior. Only one head rises above the militia and their shouldered guns. Even without the turkey feathers laced into his braid and the red line along his crown, I would recognize Hope Hood. He stares straight ahead, his long face impassive.

The group we are standing in shifts. Judah and I nudge our way towards the front until we are almost at the waterline. Looking up to the fort, I see more militia, presumably those who were not out on patrol, standing against the stockade. They are too far away for me to make out faces, but I find myself hoping Thaddeus Hobbs is among them, that I will not pick him out among those who presumably captured, and now escort, the captives.

No more than a few yards from us, Edward Tyng is standing on the beach next to Captain Blackman. Both of them wear dress coats. Sweat leaks from under the brims of their hats. They are so close to the water that the tide worries their boots, but they do not move. Side by side they stand frozen, as if they have been struck to stone. Or, more likely, having given this order have no idea what to do now that it has been carried out.

"Scrawny!" One of the fishermen behind me says as the militia and their captives come down the beach. "And they stink."

He spits. The splat hits an upturned wherry.

A ripple runs through the crowd, a restless quiver of disgust and interest. They jostle. I feel myself pressed from behind, and hear mutters of "stink" and "savages" and "animals." There is a guffaw of laughter. It is not a sound with any humor in it.

Edward Tyng hears it too, and looks sideways. Seeing his face, I realize he is terrified, and suddenly I wish Captain Alden was here, or my father, or even my mother. Eleven years ago in Marblehead, a ship came in bearing Indian captives, hoping to ransom them. When they were disembarked and marched through the town, a group of women blocked their way, and set upon them, and tore them to pieces. No one stepped forward to help them, or even protest. They say that when the women were finished, there was nothing left of the Indians. Scraps of cloth. A hank of hair. A bead rolling in the street.

I feel my hands begin to shake.

Judah looks at me, her face creased with concern. "Is it your foot?"

I shake my head. She puts her arm around my shoulders.

"They cannot hurt us," she whispers, as if this is a secret only she knows. "They are surrounded, by men and guns."

I look at her, and see that her color is high. Her cheeks are pink, not from the sun. Her eyes, which are deep green today, sparkle with excitement.

"They cannot hurt us. We have them," Judah repeats. And as she squeezes my shoulder, I feel the blade again, like a shard of ice slipping between us.

The procession reaches the water's edge and comes to a halt, face to face with Edward Tyng and Captain Blackman. No one seems entirely certain, now, what to do. Captain Blackman salutes the leader of the militia company. The leader of the militia company salutes Captain Blackman. Behind him, his men shift uneasily on the shingle. They are standing three abreast in front, and three abreast behind, and ten in a line on either side of the captives, boxing them in. I can still only make out Hope Hood. The others are lost behind and between the bodies of men. The fisherman was right. The scent of bear grease, which they will have slathered on against the sun and insects, hangs in the still, hot air mixing with the smell of boats—of ropes and nets and gutted fish.

Captain Blackman steps back, almost putting his boot in the water, its heel sinking. He gestures behind him to the harbor, and says something I cannot hear. The militia commander nods and looks over his shoulder. Following his gaze, I see that a wherry has left the sloop. The men rowing her dip their oars in unison, straining as they pull against the outgoing tide. As if on cue, everyone looks towards the boat. The boys who followed the procession have stopped. Intimidated perhaps by the sight of Blackman and Edward Tyng, they linger at the top of the beach. Then one of them reaches down, and picks up a stone, and hurls it.

It flies wide. But everyone hears the smack when it lands. Two of the militia men whirl around, their guns raised. The boys do not move. They just stand there. Slowly, another reaches down, and picks up another stone. Heat shimmers and rises and time seems to stop. Then Captain Blackman shouts, and the sloop's wherry hits the shingle, and the sailors who had been rowing her leap out to hold her steady.

A second wherry is coming up behind the first. There is a smacking sound as she beaches. Her crew also jump out, splashing up to their knees. Realizing they will be able to take all of the captives to the sloop, I feel a tide of relief, and then agitation. Because the crowd from the common has moved down Broad Street and is standing behind the boys.

I see Anthony Brackett, holding some kind of staff. Beside him are Peter Cloyce and the Lewises. Mercy hovers next to her father, her cap askew, her eyes fixed on the knot of captives and militia. Her shoulders are stiff. Even from where I am, down by the water, I can see that she is so excited she stands on tiptoe. One hand rests on her father's arm. The other holds a stone.

"Back! Back up!" The shout is as abrupt and loud as a gun shot. It comes from George Burroughs.

I don't know where he has been, but all at once he is striding up the beach in his shirt sleeves, arms raised, flapping as if he is herding geese or unruly cows.

"Back!" He shouts.

The boys look at him. They think about disobeying. But George Burroughs does not even break stride.

"Drop those!" He commands.

Startled, the boys drop the stones.

"Do not be unGodly!" Our minister stops before his congregation. "Have you no business to be about?" He demands. "Are you idle? Have you nothing better to do than stand gawping? The Lord's eye is upon you, and His work will not do itself!"

The crowd stares at him.

"Go! Go with God," he says more quietly. "There is nothing to be done, and nothing to see here."

They hesitate. Then, slowly, they begin to turn away. I see Mercy Lewis's father place his own hand over hers on his arm. Anthony Brackett lowers his staff. Peter Cloyce is the first to leave, his hand reaching for his wife's. I close my eyes. When I open them again, the sailors are still steadying the wherries and the militia men are leading the captives to the boats, shepherding them into the shallows.

With the formation broken, I can see more clearly who these people are. I was right. With the exception of Hope Hood and two other men—both of whom are older than he is and neither of whom are dressed to suggest his rank—all the rest of the captives are women. And children. Almost half of them must be children, or barely older than children. These are the savages Captain Blackman ordered, no matter who they were or what they were doing, to be destroyed.

I watch as they are led into the water. A young woman climbs into the closest wherry. Lowering herself, she turns and holds out her hands. And that is when I see the scar. The line, like a long pale scratch running down her left cheek. I stare as a militia man lifts the little boy and hands him to her. The child throws his arms around his mother's neck and buries his face in her chest. She covers his head with her hand, and looks up, and meets my gaze. We are still watching each other as the last captive is loaded and the boats pull away.

CHAPTER TWENTY-TWO

"Come."

I do not know how long I have been standing here, squinting into the sun.

"Come," a voice says, and I expect it to be Judah's. But it is George Burroughs'.

I had not noticed him beside me. He reaches for my elbow. I let him take it, and think that this is becoming a habit, for our minister to take me by the arm and lead me home. As we turn, I look up and see that Judah has wandered away down the beach and is talking with one of the militia men. I hear her laugh before she turns and runs to join us.

"He says they will take them to Boston." Her voice is breathy and high. "Tomorrow. They will sail at first light. Tonight they will keep them here, at anchor, because the shoals are too dangerous to navigate in the dark with a dropping tide."

Judah's face is lit with excitement, whether because of the captives or the militia man, I don't know. She turns to George Burroughs, falling into step beside us as we climb the harbor beach.

"Do you think they will be sold?"

We all know this happens, that captive Indians are sold, and sometimes even captured for the purpose of being sold, either to the Indes, or sometimes to the Spanish islands in the Atlantic. Philip English says they do not survive. He says that, set to work on the great plantations, they pine, and suffer, and die.

"I hope not," George Burroughs says, and I think I feel him tighten his grip on my arm, as if he is willing me to keep quiet. "I hope that this will all be resolved, and we shall have no further panic."

"Well, this will teach them a lesson, at least."

Judah is bouncing from foot to foot. Her hair coming loose curls about her face. I think again how many barrels of beer John Alden says he would trade for her beauty.

"I have heard," she says, "that it was but a fishing party, and the poor things are so stupid that they did not even run. They just came when they were called, like good dogs, and allowed themselves to be taken."

We have reached the edge of the common. Judah spins away, the events of the day lighting her step and her voice. Laughing, she says captives are good for business. The Ordinary will be heaving. The Ingersolls will have her hide if she does not hurry. Running down Broad Street, Judah raises her hand in a wave.

"Come," George Burroughs says, as I stand looking after her. Then he says again, very gently, "Come away."

THAT WAS THIS AFTERNOON. Now, I lift the dipper from the well bucket and fill and stopper each bottle before placing it in the basket at my feet. Lit by just one candle, the stillroom is dim and shadowed. It is late. The last bell has rung. I hear nothing but the owl and the distant bark of the fox who has her den on the far edge of the meadow.

I cannot be certain of the exact moment when I knew what I was going to do. I am not sure if it was when the scarred woman's eyes met mine as she placed her hand over her son's head. Or, if it was when the wherries became lost in the bulk of the prison ship. Or when Judah laughed, and called them stupid good dogs who came when they were called. Thinking of that, I feel the blade that sliced between us this morning, and the fear that comes with knowing that, despite my best efforts, it has lodged itself in my heart.

The thought is so distressing, as if I have pressed on a bruise and found instead that the bone is broken, that I shove it away. Placing the last bottle in the bottom of the basket, I look to the shelves, wondering what else I can take. I choose two loaves, the last we have, and a small linen sack of venison I cured last winter. I pick up a wedge of hard cheese that was sent from Salem, then reject it, and choose instead a bag of dried plums. They last longer, and are lighter. Unless I am careful I will make the basket so heavy I will not be able to lift it.

My mother is asleep. She returned just before dark. I heard the cart—the squeak and whine of the axle and the faint jingling of the little bay horse's harness—from where I stood in the kitchen. Going to meet her in the summer twilight, I could see enough of her face to know she had heard the news.

We did not speak of the captives as we made our way to the house. Instead, my mother told me how the babe is thriving, and the goodwife, too. How the fever has abated. She does not believe she will be needed again. I heard the relief in her voice as she said this and, as we entered the kitchen and the light from the candles I had lit, I saw that she was exhausted, and understood how much this particular caring, going on as it has for days, has taken out of her. She looked ill, pale and unsteady as she lowered herself into her chair. I felt a stab of fear, then, followed by a greater stab, of anger, at my father for being so long away. Reaching for the kettle I had set to boil, I shoved both aside. They will still be here tomorrow, my fear and my anger. But if Judah is right, and I suspect she is, Captain Blackman's ship will not.

My mother ate a little, then drank a tea and said she would

sleep. I watched her climb the stairs and heard her climb on to the bed, the creak and rustle of it. By the time I had cleared her plate and cup, washed them and set them back on the dresser and crept up to look in on her, she was asleep. She had not bothered to remove her clothes, or even her cap. I bent, and took off her shoes, which were dusty from the farm cart. Then, I unfolded the coverlet and pulled it to her shoulders, even though it is warm tonight. Carefully, I plucked the knot of her cap. She did not move, her lips parted only slightly in dreams as I removed it, and set her hair loose upon the pillow before I leaned down to kiss the warm brow of her forehead.

Now, I look about the stillroom, wondering what else might ease a journey into slavery. My hand falls upon a pot of salve. For a moment I think, *they will not know what to do with it, if they have sores or wounds.* And then I hear Judah, *the poor things are so stupid*, and almost laugh aloud at myself, remembering that it was they who taught us how to make these salves in the first place. The pot is added to my basket. I blow the candle out.

Pulling the stillroom door shut behind me, I am careful to press the latch down hard and turn the lock. I take the key back into the kitchen and hang it on the hook beside the tinder box. Then, I blow out the last kitchen candle, and step outside. The latch on the kitchen door is stiff. I ease it down with my thumb. There is a very faint breeze. The crickets are quiet tonight. Scent rises around me from the garden, cut lavender and the pepper of marigolds mixed with the tang of sea mud which tells me the tide is dead low. I close my eyes, and open them, and close and open them again. This is another trick I learned in The Greening, how to come quickly to seeing in the dark. Away towards the village, beyond our meadow and the roofs of the houses on Broad Street, there is a faint orange glow in the sky. It is not fire, just the torches they keep burning now along the ramparts of the fort. I bend for the heavy basket, pad quietly across the gravel, and turn towards the cove. As I reach our paddock fence, I hear the sharp bark of the fox. I am not surprised when the dark shape of the owl appears, gliding ahead, as if escorting me into the birches.

I hear Judah's voice as I pick my way. *They will sail at first light. Tonight they will keep them here, at anchor, because the shoals are too dangerous without a moon.* She did not mean them to be, but those words were my map to opportunity. The village harbor is safe anchorage for fishing boats, shallops and wherries. But anything larger, certainly ships and sloops like John Alden's and Captain Blackman's, must be unloaded at its mouth because at low tide the water becomes shallow and treacherous. Larger boats can drop anchor there, but they cannot ride for long because the bottom is not safe holding ground when the currents shift.

Captain Blackman's sloop has been laying south of the village, in an inlet down the coast. That was safe enough, with a small crew aboard, when the ship was empty. But I do not think he will take her there tonight. Not in the dark. The shoals are too dangerous. Tonight, with such a precious cargo, he will have her moved to the safest deep water anchorage close by. And that is the mouth of our cove.

❧

I WORRY the militia have posted watch. That they might be on the point, looking over their prize, guarding it through the night, until the sun rises and it is safely on its way to Boston and Captain Blackman's greater glory. But had they done so, they would have had to cross our meadow. I pretended to work in the garden, snipping and raking all afternoon. But no one came down the path. After sunset, I heard nothing until the return of my mother.

My next fear is that they will have sent crew from the ship to post guard along the point. If that is so, whatever vessel they used will be beached in our cove because there is no other place to come ashore. I slip through the birch grove, holding the heavy basket high to avoid it catching the grass or a fallen branch. The owl has vanished, or flown up into one of the trees where it sits, watching me with its yellow-moon eyes.

A few feet from the edge of the bank, I set the basket down and sidle forward. The beach below is empty. No militia guards have beached a wherry here, and this is the only place. Turning, I look to the cove's mouth. Even though it is black and almost moonless, I see the solid bulk of the sloop against the liquid bulk of the sea. The spire of her mast rocks between the stars. She is exactly where I thought she would be, riding at anchor just inside the headland.

The canoe slides silently along the launching board. The only moment of panic I have is as I lift the basket in, and find it so heavy that I am not certain I will be able to climb over the side and settle myself without capsizing. But I manage. My father has set hooks on the underside of the plank seats for the baskets my mother uses for the plants she harvests from the marsh and for her curings when she paddles to the Back Cove farms. I hook the handle of this basket, fixing it firmly amidships, then grasp the paddle and settle myself.

I gave some thought to what I should wear—my darkest dress and no cap. My hair is in a braid down my back. As for shoes, I decided finally that my bandage gave good protection, so I would bind my other foot, too. The linen looks white and strange, as if my feet do not belong to me. I push away from the beach, once, twice, three times until I can no longer feel the bottom.

If Blackman has posted a watch on sloop's deck and the watch is vigilant, I will be seen. I have already decided that, if that is the case, I will play the coquette, claim I am bringing sustenance to our brave militia men. But it is very late and the day has been long. I am certain Captain Blackman, who will have spent the evening in The Ordinary boasting of his triumph, will be loath to leave the comfort of Edward Tyng's fine house where he usually stays. Rather than laying down amidst savages, he will sleep there, well washed in ale, and come aboard tomorrow to sail his prizes away. In the meantime, I am counting on inexperience and the puffed confidence of too easy victory over their captives, whom, like Judah, they consider stupid, to make the crew stupid in turn. My paddle slices the water. Once, in the glassy darkness, I think I see the head of the seal. Then it is gone, and I am alone on the cove, closing fast on the sloop.

I was aboard John Alden's ship only once, when it brought us here. But I remember it well. A hold too shallow for a man to stand in ran the sloop's length. Goods had to be lowered into it. Our cabin, the only large place for sleeping and eating, was in the stern. I do not know if Captain Blackman's ship is the same, but I doubt that even his militia would be careless enough to allow their captives to stay on deck when they are at anchor and it is dark and they are so close to home.

As I come near, the ship grows huge. Her anchor is set towards the cove's mouth, out in the deepest water. She has swung her seaward. I know I am at most danger of being seen when I am out on the water and away from her. As she looms over me, I see the stern rail plainly, and have a sudden terror that any moment the white moon of a face will peer over it. That I will hear a shout. Running feet. The flash of a lantern will blind me. But there is nothing. I stop paddling and glide.

The spars creak gently. Above me, the rigging is a fretwork pricked with stars. The sail folds like a sleeping wing. There is no footfall, no sound from the deck at all. If I did not know of this ship's horrid cargo, I would think she had been abandoned. I would think I was alone on the cove with a ghost ship.

The prow of the canoe bumps the top of the sloop's rudder. Dipping the paddle, I push hard over, bringing myself flush to the stern. For an awful moment, I think I have miscalculated, that there is nothing to hold on to and I will have no way to fix myself to the sloop. Then I see the reflection of glass. In the cabin of Captain Alden's sloop there were ports, like little windows, one on either side. This ship has them, too, and given the heat of the night and what must be the press of bodies within, they are open. If I stretch, I can grab a sill. Even as I do, I smell it. Wood smoke and bear grease and tanned hides. The scent of my childhood.

"Are you here?" I whisper as loudly as I dare, reaching for the language that has been locked inside me, the remnants of that same childhood. "Are you here?"

There is a movement, an intake of breath. Then a hand touches mine in the dark.

CHAPTER TWENTY-THREE

The face that appears is Hope Hood's. I can tell, even in the dark, that he recognizes me. Still, I speak my mother's name, knowing instinctively which one it is she uses with them.

"Rachel," I whisper. "I am the child of Rachel."

He nods, looking beyond me, as if searching for her shape.

"I am alone," I say. Then, "Dangerous."

Some part of me, I think, had hoped that the port hole would be large enough. That somehow I could bear at least some of them away. In some fevered part of my mind, I realize now as I kneel in the canoe, I had dreamed that they would be able to climb out. That, as Blackman's militia slept, full of ale and self congratulation, I would steal their captives, ferrying group after group to the headland, and freedom.

I must have known it was unlikely, because I packed the basket. Still, a part of me sinks in disappointment, threatening a distress that, unless I am careful, will undo me.

"I have food," I whisper. "I have water."

I rehearsed the words in the stillroom, dredging them up and murmuring them to myself as I filled the bottles and chose the provisions. But they are rusty, and their shape is strange in my mouth.

"Here."

I nod down to the basket, realizing as I do that it will not fit through the port hole. And that if I let go of the sill to hand the contents up, I will drift away. I should have brought a line, or at least a cord. Again, distress washes over me, threatening the whole enterprise. Then I think of my belt, which will not be long enough. Even so, I begin to unbuckle it with my free hand.

Seeing my problem, Hope Hood shakes his head. His face vanishes. I hear whispers, then more movement. A moment later, his arm appears, a strip of deerskin in his hand. It is soft and braided, and as I take it I realize that it is not one belt but two, tied together. I snag my end quickly on to one of the canoe's hooks. Then, I free the basket and begin, wordlessly, to empty it, feeding items one by one through the port hole.

The opening is small, otherwise, even Blackman's men would not have left it open. An arm can reach through, and perhaps a shoulder, but not much else. Feeding my supplies in is like feeding darkness. I hold an item out, stretching through, and it is taken from my hand. Too soon, I have passed the last water bottle.

"I am sorry," I whisper. "I am sorry. That is all I have."

I can hear murmuring and rustling, the movement of bodies and soft voices, several speaking at once in the close dark of the cabin. Again, I feel a pang of frustration. I should have brought tools, an ax. I should have tried to hack through what seems now a thin skin of wood that is the only thing between them and slavery. The endless sea voyage. The heat and pining and labor and death far from home with no hope of freedom.

But I did not think of it. And I realize that if I had, it would probably only have got us all killed. There are men on this ship who are armed, and I am sure they would be happy for any excuse to slaughter savages. I think of the crowd this afternoon. Of the look on Mercy Lewis's face, the way she rose on her toes like an excited child, the stone in her hand, and feel a pang of pure terror.

I wonder how long I have been here. How much noise I have made. My courage leeches away like sand from a broken hour glass. I am bending to unhook the braided deerskin, to stuff it back through the porthole, when a face appears. Somehow, without even looking up, I know which one it will be.

Her scar is paler in this darkness, looking less like a scratch than a line that divides her. I cannot see her eyes, but I would like to look away from them. I am shaking my head before she even speaks.

"You must take him."

I am still holding my end of the belt. Gripping it, balancing myself in the canoe, the now empty basket beside me, I start to say it is impossible. I cannot. It cannot be done, and even if it could—

Then she vanishes, and the next thing I see is a small pair of feet.

The soles are pale. Legs follow them. Then hips, and a stomach. I realize what they have done. They have run their hands down their bodies, across their hair, making them slick, then rubbed him with as much grease as they could so his little shape can slide out of this dreadful prison and into my arms and freedom.

I rehook the belt and reach for him.

He is as slippery as an eel, and for an awful moment, I think I will drop him. That he will slither away from me down into the dark water, like Avis and William. In the next awful moment, I wonder if that was what she was planning. If I had not come, would she have slid her child out and into the sea rather than letting him be carried away and sold like an object?

She has held his hands above his head so he cannot resist and try to cling to her, or flail and catch his elbows. His shoulders come, followed by his terrified face. The top of the little window scrapes his brow and I almost cry out, although he does not. His arms, stretched above his head, come last. For one brief moment, in the dark of the porthole, I see his mother's hands, holding his. Then she lets go.

❧

I AM KNEELING in the canoe beside the empty basket cradling the boy. Hope Hood's face appears in the small dark space that delivered this child.

"Go," he says.

I nod. Placing the boy in the bed of the canoe, I whisper to him to lie down. Without a word, he does. I lean over and unhook the belt that has bound me to them. The pale trail of deerskin dangles towards the water.

"Go!" Hope Hood whispers again. And I feel as much as see his eyes on me as the canoe begins to drift.

The boy does not move. Laying at my feet, he is rigid with terror. Which may be just as well. At least he does not cry, which would finish us both. The paddle is slick in my hands from the grease. I grasp the top of it, and don't look back. I don't listen for a shout, or for the ringing of a bell, or for the sound of a shot. Instead, I paddle as fast and as hard as I can for the headland, fixing on the bulk of it, on its outline against the stars, looking for the place where my mother guided us ashore. Because all at once, I understand that this is the only thing I can do.

I cannot take this child to my mother, or to our house, or even to our shore. I cannot hide him in the milking shed, or wait for daybreak. If I try, he will be discovered, and he will be finished. And so will we. I have only one choice. I must take him home.

CHAPTER TWENTY-FOUR

Darkness reaches for us, pulling us in as we approach the shore. My eyes have grown used to the reflections on the water, to the pinpricks of light that bounce from the stars, and to the night shine that drips from the paddle and streams from the prow of the canoe. Above me on the headland the forest opens, shadowed and deep as a mighty mouth. As we come close, I smell trees and damp earth. There is the faint sound of life, of small things moving, and the ripple of water on rocks.

I have tried to judge where it was that my mother brought us in, and I hope I am right. I cannot stop paddling and glide because the tide will simply push us down into the center of the cove. This shore is steep in parts. Some of it is sheer rock. Other parts are bitten with shallow inlets of bog. If I am wrong and traveling too swiftly, if I hit something, I could damage or even rip the skin of the canoe.

I take short strokes, nudging forward, and feel my heart sink as I hear the prow scrape stone. Then we swing sideways, and bump the bank. Reaching for a branch, I hang on, pulling us in. In the bed of the canoe, the boy still has not moved. I clamber over him. Hand over hand, branch by branch, I move us along until the slope dips and widens enough that I can climb out. The earth I cannot see is soft and slippery. Holding the boat with one hand, I reach my other to him.

"Come," I say. "You are safe. But we must walk now."

I can see his head turn, but I can't make out his eyes or his expression. All at once he rises up, and without touching me scrambles onto the bank. I start to shout. I start to tell him to wait for me or he will be lost. But sound travels too easily over water, so instead, I hiss, sounding like an angry cat. "Wait! Wait for me!"

Then I turn my attention to the canoe. If I do not get it secured on shore and hidden, I shall have to swim back when the time comes. I scrabble along the bank until the land falls away and is marshy enough that I can drag the boat on shore, pulling it up, out of the water and into the trees so it is out of sight. I flip it over and secure the paddle underneath, then turn and look for the child.

Part of me is certain he will be gone. That like a wild animal, a fox or a hare loosed from a trap, he will have dashed mindless, simply running, into the forest with no thought but to get as far away as possible. He is so small that I wonder if something will snatch and eat him. If he will be lost and wandering. Or fall into the river or the marsh and drown in the darkness.

"Where are you?"

I never intended this. I only thought that I would bring some food and water, perhaps be able to deliver a message. At best, ferry one or two of the women, or the old men to the headland. I never thought that I would be handed a child, or have to try to remember how to find the camp in the dark.

I have the sudden sense that I am on a wheel, spinning. Tears prick the back of my eyes. I realize I am wringing my hands.

"Where are you? Please! I won't hurt you," I hiss. "Please, let me take you home."

The rusty words must sound almost as odd to him as they do to me, strange from lack of use, sticking and stumbling on my tongue. I think of his mother, and wonder what I have done. She has given me her son, and I have lost him.

The trees thicken. As I feel my way inland, away from the glimmer of the water, I have the sense of the forest breathing, as if it is a great beast and I am burrowing into its hide, into its very belly. I bang into a rock, and abruptly sit down.

"Please," I whisper. And then, before I realize it, "Please, don't leave me."

When the tiny hand touches my shoulder, I nearly shriek. He is standing right beside me, a small dark shape in the darker forest. He moves in front of me, staring into my face. Then, slowly, he reaches out. I feel his fingers touch the tears that are running down my cheeks. He pats at them, and at my lips and my chin.

"Home," he says. "Home." And takes my hand.

WHEN I CROSSED the headland with my mother a bare few weeks ago, in what seems another world, it was daylight. Even then, following her, I did not think I could have found the path on my own. Now, in the pitch dark, I have no idea where it is. And I am not confident that this child does either. For a while he leads me on, weaving through the thickening trees. Then he stops and simply stands looking up at me. I kneel down. My eyes have adjusted enough to see his face.

"Do you know where we are?" I ask.

He looks at me blankly.

"Home," I try. "How do we get home?"

Nothing. He must be exhausted. I am asking too much of him. He is, after all, little more than a babe. One who left his home, this morning or the day before, with his mother and Hope Hood and aunts and uncles and older children, probably cousins or even half brothers and sisters, to go to a fishing camp somewhere on one of the streams or rivers. I remember the joy and excitement of these summer outings from my own time in The Greening. His family will have gone to the same camp since he could remember. Everyone looks forward to it, but it is a special treat for children. There would have been berry picking, and the setting and emptying of nets. Fish speared from the pools, cleaned and packed in wet reeds, ready for the journey back. Fires lit on the stream shore, and splashing in the shallows. Until white men appeared, and called for them. And they went. To answer a question, or offer a greeting, or perhaps thinking to give help. And now he is here.

I stand. When I reach down and pick him up, he does not protest.

The little boy sits easily on my hip. He is smaller than I realized, a tiny person, and I think he has probably three years, not four. I smooth the hair back from his forehead, my fingers running across the scrape on his brow, and wonder at the terror he must have felt when hands lifted him towards the sloop's porthole. What did his mother whisper to him as she held his hands above his head while someone else held his feet so he could not struggle and yet other hands ran grease over his skin so he would slide through the space that would separate him from her forever?

"You are very brave," I say. And then, "My name is Susannah. What is your name?"

He looks at me, unblinking.

"Do you know which way it is from here?" I ask. "To go home?"

He stares at me for so long that I think he is not going to answer. Then he nods, and points. He is looking over my shoulder, his face still and grave. Something in his expression makes my skin turn cold. I feel hair rise on the back of my neck. Very slowly, I turn around.

AT FIRST, I don't see anything, just the shapes of trees, and darkness, the great mouth of the forest. But it's there. I can feel it. We are not alone. In my arms, the boy doesn't move. I can't hear anything but my own breathing. Then, I see it. Or rather, them. Two yellow stars. Eyes, not ten feet in front of us.

The wolf is larger than any I have ever seen. Not that I have seen many, and the few I have seen have been at a distance. On the edge of a field. Once, bounding across a snowy, frozen marsh. Usually, they are shy. They do not seek out humans, or come near farms and settlements. But I am not near a farm. I am deep in the forest. I am in their settlement, and the stories I was taught as a child suddenly seem just that—stories.

The creature stands completely still. I can make out the great head, the powerful shoulders. Those eyes, which seem fixed on mine. I remember that they live in packs, families like our own. That they never hunt, or travel alone. And I wonder where the others are, and how soon they too, will melt out of the darkness, and surround us.

I could scream. But my mouth is too dry—and who would hear me? I could run, but not carrying this child. And anyway, even if I dropped him, even if I left him to be devoured, they would easily outrun me. They would catch me, their teeth sinking into my flesh, and drag me to the ground.

I tighten my arms around the boy. The wolf does not move. And I can sense no other movement, no other presence. In fact, the forest seems suddenly completely still, as if, like me it has stopped breathing. I have the sense that, if I looked up, the stars would be frozen—nothing but distant pricks in an ice-still sky. I don't know how long we stay like this before the wolf turns, and walks into the woods.

I feel my knees go weak with relief. I start to step backwards, ready to spin and blunder back the way we have come, find some place to hide until daylight. But the boy's hand rises again to my face. He places it against my cheek, his little fingers covering the same spot Abigail once touched, turning what was cold, warm.

When I look down at him, he shakes his head. Then, he points, and says, "home."

"No," I shake my head. "No," I whisper, "we must—"

"Home." He frowns, still pointing into the trees, at the spot where the wolf has gone.

I look at him. Then, I take a breath, and step forward.

❧

THE SHAPE IS ALWAYS in front of us, and never quite visible. I catch the flick of a tail. See the sinuous bend of a figure, weaving through the dense growth of pines. Sometimes my foot is so painful, I am limping so badly that I think I cannot go on. Once, when I stumble, I swear it stops, and looks back, waiting until I see the flash of eyes in the dark, as golden and bright as stars.

We walk for an hour. More. I don't know. I have no sense of time. Any more than I have any sense of where we are. Sometimes, the trees open above us and I see the far away glitter of the summer sky. But mostly, I keep my eyes on the path that seems to unwind as if by magic, and on the dark shape that moves ahead, always almost out of sight. Each time I think it is gone, that I have lost it, I find it again, like a tune hovering on the edge of memory.

I am not sure where we are when I sense dawn. There is a faint lightening, and the stirring of birds. The breeze changes. The forest is un-frozen, moving again. Then, I smell the smoke, and stop. The pungent odor of the smudge fires, of mussels and clams, mixed with the dry, sweet scent of sun-dried wood fills my nostrils. It twists around me as sure as a skein twists around a spindle, and, as surely, draws me in, and back to The Greening. Once more, I am following my mother, watching her moccasins, their tread soft as paws on the dew-damp earth. She weaves through the trees, shifting in and out of shadows, and all the time the smell grows stronger, as we near the summer camp.

When finally I return to myself, feeling the weight of the

child heavy in my arms and on my hip, I look up and, sure enough, ahead of me the trees have thinned. Beyond them, I can see the slight heave of the sea, as if the water is turning in its sleep. In a few steps more, I make out the curve of the little cove and its beach filled with egg-shaped pebbles. As the light creeps from night to morning, I see the smoking huts, and the lodges. I take a step, expecting the dark shape, the shadow in the deepening shadows of dappled light ahead of us. But the wolf is gone. The path ahead is empty.

The child's head is lolling on my shoulder, his arms dangling when, a moment later, I break through the treeline and step into the circle of teepees.

CHAPTER TWENTY-FIVE

For a long moment, nothing happens. The teepee flaps are folded back and the morning fires are lit. A kettle hangs over one, hissing hot steam into the mist that rises from the damp grass. An old woman bends over another, feeding kindling and fanning the flame. In the crescent of the little beach the water is placid and tinged pink. Sunrise happened when I wasn't looking. Now, for a moment, the sea beyond blazes, and I think of the story The Puritans tell, about how every day begins with the angel Lucifer, cast out of heaven yet again.

It is then, for some reason, that I realize how tired I am. I have been carrying this child for what seems like hours, and although he is small, he suddenly feels as if he may be made of lead. Just when I think I am about to drop him, the old woman looks up. She freezes, then stands and shouts, and all at once people appear and are moving, then running, toward us.

The boy is taken from my arms. I think at first that they may think he is dead. But he wakes, and looks around, confused. Realizing he is safe among his own people, he begins at last to howl. Two women carry him away. The old woman who had been tending the fire and saw us first is in front of me, staring into my face. She reaches up, slowly, to touch my cheek, and although the language Hope Hood's people speak is not exactly the same as that I learned in The Greening, I understand what she says.

"Rachel?" She speaks my mother's name. "Rachel?" She asks.

I shake my head, struggling in my tired mind for the right word. Finally, I mutter, "Daughter."

The old woman smiles and nods. She turns and shouts something. More women appear. They surround me, taking my arms and my shoulders, until there are so many hands on me that I wonder if they mean to pick me up and bear me away.

"Hope Hood," I say. And, "Captive."

But I see from their faces that they already know. Word has traveled, as it always does. When the party did not return, someone will have gone to the fishing camp. Someone will have seen the abandoned nets, the burned out fires, the dropped spears and rotting fish still wrapped in river grass. Someone will have understood, and rushed back, bringing word. Or someone escaped. Someone did not come forward like a good dog, but darted away into the woods then turned and ran, carrying the news.

The lodge the women steer me to has its flaps pinned back like all the others. A bed of furs and blankets, recently vacated and not yet rolled away for the day, covers the floor. The last thing I think as they half ease, half push me down onto it is, *There are no men here. Where have all the men gone?*

❧

I HAVE no idea how long I sleep. When I wake, I think it must be late afternoon, because the shadows are long, and the sun is thick and heavy. I remember being fed, a soup of some kind. I dreamed of someone brushing my hair. I dreamed of my feet being soaked and salved. I dreamed of a great weight, and darkness and trees rising all around me, closing me in, then cracking open to reveal the north star. I dreamed of a ship swinging at anchor, and of the smell of sweat and terror. And I dreamed of yellow eyes, and of the deep softness of fur, rubbed against my cheek.

I raise myself, resting on my elbows. Two women are sitting in the lodge's opening, their backs to me. Hearing me, they turn and smile. Even so, I am not sure if I am a guest or a prisoner. It did not occur to me, when I set out to bring the boy home, that it might be dangerous. That they might try to keep me as a captive of their own, a chip to trade or bargain with. I was simply thinking I had to bring him back. Now, I realize the equation may not be so simple. I look down. My hands are not tied. I am not bound. But I know this does not mean I am free to go. When I try to stand, the pain in my injured foot is so sharp that I sit back down with a gasp.

One of my watchers jumps to her feet and runs off. I can hear her calling something, but the language is still foreign enough that I can't understand what she is saying. The other woman comes into the lodge and sits beside me. She is handsome, with very dark hair bound in sinews threaded with tiny shells. She puts a hand on my forehead, feeling for fever, and with the other reaches for my foot. Even her light touch feels like fire. I look down, and see that the lower half of my leg is very swollen and very red. I twist my calf. A bright red line creeps up my ankle. As I watch, I am convinced I can see it move. I feel a throb of fear.

I am still staring at my foot, and at the line, still fixated on it, as if it is something that has crawled into the lodge and does not belong to me, when the old woman who had been tending the fire appears in the opening. Behind her are the second woman who had been sitting outside and the strangest looking man I have ever seen.

He is short, bandy legged, and bent as if his back is hunched. His face is streaked with bright yellow. He wears a high shell collar that comes almost to his chin and a cloak decorated with what I realize are small bones. The delicate legs and hands of rabbits and squirrels, the spines and tails of mice and tiny woodland things are sewn in lines across his shoulders and chest. Claws, that I see as he comes close must be the skeletal feet of birds, hang above his heart.

The bizarre fringes rustle and click as he moves. He raises his hands, holding them on either side of his face, and I see that they, too, are decorated with elaborate yellow markings. His fingers are short and his nails long and curved. With his pelt of black hair, he is more like a bear, a half human-half creature, than a man.

I shrink back. He says something to the old woman. She replies with several words. Most, I do not understand. One, I do. "Medicine".

She smiles and nods as she repeats it, and reaches out to stroke my arm, trying to reassure me. Then she moves aside, and before I have a chance to protest, the man takes my foot in his hands. The pain is searing. I squeal, but he does not let go. He holds my foot as if it is a struggling, wounded animal. Finally, he says something to the women that I don't understand. The one who had been sitting outside ducks in and gives the old woman a cup. She takes it in both hands and, smiling again, holds it out to me.

"Medicine," she says. "Medicine." And adds, "Do not be afraid. Help."

I have a choice. This old woman, and the woman who sits next to me with shells threaded through her hair like pearls—neither of them are Ashawonks, and this is not The Greening. But it could be, and if these people wanted to kill me, they would have killed me. If they wanted to bind or hurt me, they would have done that, too. "Rachel," the old woman had said, running her hand down my face. I came here with my mother, and these people are her friends. I think of my leg, and take the offered cup gingerly, cradling it in both hands. The liquid smells of the forest, of green things—plants, and leaves and some kind of bark tea. I count to three, and drink it down.

This time, I do not dream. Instead, I feel a warm, deep, cradling, as if the furs have curled around me and wrapped me tight. Just once, there is a lightning bolt of pain. Then, nothing.

CHAPTER TWENTY-SIX

When I finally wake, it is dark—the profound velvety blackness that comes before first light. The lodge flaps are pinned open. Through the gap, I can see the morning star, hanging almost in front of me above the shimmering water of the cove. A shadow bounces. There is a fire outside. The smudge fires in the smoke houses will be kept burning all night. But that's not what this is. This is the dancing of new flame. A cooking fire. I smell bannock and roasted corn, and realize I am hungry.

Before I can sit up, the woman with the shells appears in the lodge entrance carrying a torch. I have the sense that she may have slept here with me, and that even if she did not, she has been close by and has only just pinned back the lodge flaps. It is a sign to get up, a signal that morning is coming.

This time when I try to stand, my foot does not sear with pain. Instead, from the knee down my leg feels numb, as if it is made of wood. I have the odd notion that I could stick a pin in it, and feel nothing. The torch light wavers. There is enough for me to see that my legs, both of them, have been bound and laced tight in deerskin leggings. My feet are enclosed in the soft gloves of moccasins, high-topped winter ones that rise above my ankles, over the leggings, and are also laced tight. Wordlessly, the woman with the torch offers me her arm.

It is warm out, even this early. Still, I am loathe to leave my fur cocoon. Sleep does not want to peel itself from me. But hunger drives me on. A group is gathered by the newly lit fire. Light shimmers over their faces. As we approach, I see that they are all women. Above the sea, the darkness is shrinking, tinged with violet. I let go of my guide's arm, making for the treeline to relieve myself. I totter a little, but I can walk.

As I go, I look at the cove again, remembering what is not there, the line of canoes pulled up above the tide mark. Perhaps they returned while I was sleeping, and have already gone out again, to fish in the lee of the islands. But I do not think so. Once again, I wonder, *Where are all the men?* The only one I have seen was the creature, the half man-half I Am Not Sure What with his cloak of bones and his yellow streaked face and hands. He was so strange that perhaps I dreamed him, for even he is not in evidence now. I remember the gossip Judah heard at The Ordinary, about the great fort at Pennacook, and the war council of two hundred, or five hundred, or a thousand. For the first time, I think it might be true.

By the time I am finished, my eyes have lost their night blindness. Day is coming quickly from the east. The morning star fades as I watch. At the cook fire, the corn has been roasted. A place is made for me in the circle of women. We peel back the charred husks and bite into the cobs, letting the juice from the fat, sweet kernels run down our chins. Bannock, the crisped cake made of corn and nut meal, is lifted from the flat stones where it has been cooking, and broken into pieces. When we have finished, there is a silence. Almost as one, we lean back, resting on our hands and twisting to watch the sun as it rises like a mighty bird, trailing flaming feathers across the sea.

"You must go." It is the old woman who speaks. The words are not unkind. She speaks slowly, so I can understand. "We are leaving this place," she says. "Now. You must go back."

I nod. I know she is right. Obviously, I cannot stay here. Anymore than I can go and fetch my mother and insist that we return, and hide again in this new Greening. Although, I feel the pull of it. For a moment, I think of the wolf—of the waking dream that somehow led me here carrying the boy in my arms, and almost laugh. Because time seems to repeat. Fifteen years ago, it was my mother who carried me to the safety of Ashawonks' camp. Now, it is I who have carried another child here. Wheels turn, but nothing is new. Lives fold and bleed into one another.

"I know," I say, forming the rusty old words carefully, hoping they will be understood. "I know I must go."

The old women nods, but she must see something in my eyes, a faint panic at the thought of navigating my way through the forest. In daylight, oddly, it will be harder. If I was going at night, at least I could keep the north star at my back. Or wait for the wolf to come and fetch me and lead me home again. Even as I think this, I know it is mad. I know it was the fever that must already have been coursing from the wound in my foot, racing through my blood and whispering in my brain.

The old women laughs and shakes her head. "We will take you."

Even as she speaks, my two watchers, the woman with the shells in her hair and the other who sat with her, get up. I see that they have pemmican bags already tied to their belts, food for their return, and that they too are wearing the high, tightly laced moccasins, the same ones I have been given, that are best for walking. One of them produces a walking stick, straight, and hard and made of polished hickory. She hands it to me.

I would like to see the boy, and say good-bye to him. But no one else is moving in the camp. The old woman rises with me as I get to my feet. I am struggling to find the phrases I should speak to thank them for their kindness and their care when she reaches up and as she did when I first appeared, ragged and exhausted with a stolen child in my arms, touches my face.

"Rachel," she says again.

I nod as the message passes between us. *I will tell my mother that you spoke her name.* Then her hand drops to my chest. She lays her palm above my heart, and for a moment, I am sure I feel something hard there. Her eyes look straight into mine, and seem to have no color at all.

"Ciplahq," she says.

I have no idea what this means. I begin to ask, but something in her expression suggests I might not like the answer. *Leave? Go? Death?*

"Ciplahq," she says again and this time she turns me sharply, and pushes me. I grasp my stick and stagger forward. When I look up, it is not a wolf, but the two women who are already moving away, threading between shafts of sunlight into the forest.

THIS TIME, the journey goes quickly. I would have found my way back eventually, not because I can see the trail now, but because I would, in the end, have wandered long enough to reach the far side of the headland. My guides, however, know exactly where they are going. They are swift and sure and we walk without speaking. The stick helps, and the odd, numb feeling of my leg wears off a little. But it still feels weak, even laced tight into the legging. I have hitched my skirts into my belt to walk more easily. For all my clumsiness, I am glorying in the feel of the moccasins, in the forgotten sense that they connect rather than separate me from the earth, as if the fact that they are deerskin changes the way my feet fall upon the world.

I remember feeling this as a child. Thinking I could run faster in moccasins than in stockings and shoes because deer do not wear stockings and shoes. Even so, I am unusually slow. Or at least slower than my guides. More than once, they stop to wait for me. I am tired, I think, with all that has happened. As we get closer to the cove, I have a sense that the air is thickening and I am laboring, climbing through a barrier as I pass from one time, from one world, into another.

And then we are there. I have no sense of homecoming, no hint of it until I feel the glitter of the sea through the trees. At the same time, I realize my escorts have stopped. Standing well back in the forest, they move aside, giving me room to walk past them into my own life.

I pause, awkward, wishing I had a gift or a token, anything to give in thanks. But I do not. The woman with the shells in her hair reaches out. She places her hand flat on my chest as the old woman by the fire had, and again I am sure I feel something hard pressing against my heart. Then they are gone, fading soundlessly back into the web of trees and secret paths.

I stand, staring after them, trying not to feel abandoned. Without thinking, I raise my own hand to my heart, and realize I was not wrong. Something hard presses against me. Dropping my stick, I scrabble at the neckline of my dress. Sure enough, there is a slit. A small opening has been sliced into the layered fabric of my bodice. A single stitch of the thinnest filament, the sinew of some tiny animal holds it closed. I pluck, and pull out what feels like a disc. It is made of some kind of stone, black and shiny. Almost as thin as a shell, it is no bigger than a large coin.

I hold it up to the light, turning it over and over. Etched on each side is the figure of a bird.

Its wings are spread. Its beak is long and sharp. Its eye seems to look straight into mine. The wafer of stone is heavy, and feels comfortable in my palm, warm, almost as if it is part of me. For a moment, I imagine that I can feel it throbbing. As if it carries the memory of my heart beat. Or has one of its own.

CHAPTER TWENTY-SEVEN

The canoe does not want to budge. It feels stuck, as if, in the space of a day its bark skin and wooden frame have taken root. I have slipped my bird disc back into its pocket, pulled and knotted the sinew to secure it. Now, I rock and tug at the canoe. In the dark, I pulled it farther up the marshy bank than I realized. The place was safe. It will not have been seen. But by the time I get it righted and in the water and lower myself into it, I am so tired that I am not entirely sure I will be able to paddle. Whatever drug I was given has not entirely let go of me. My hand goes to my chest again. I feel a flood of relief as my fingers find the stone, although am not entirely sure why. Perhaps because it is proof that I have not dreamed, or imagined, everything.

Luckily, the tide is coming in. If it was running out, I think I would have to wait, or risk being taken out to sea. The current eddies in the pocket formed by the marsh, spinning the canoe like a leaf so I have to drag my paddle to right the prow. Finally, as I come free of the little inlet and clear the bank, I see that the mouth of the cove is empty. Captain Blackman's sloop has sailed, taking her terrible cargo with her.

I dally out into the current, then have to paddle hard to get across. I'm so tired that I tempted to give up, let myself be swept down into the Back Cove. My arms feel as if they are made of lead. I put my head down and pull, one side then the other, keeping the prow aimed at the center of our beach which refuses to come any closer. At last, I cross the mid-point of the cove, gather speed, and come in fast and hard, hitting the sand. For a moment I sit there, panting. Then I pull myself out, splashing in the shallows, and drag the canoe ashore.

When I finally get it up to the place where we keep it, I am almost too tired to flip it over. My back is sore. I left the walking stick on the far bank, and my leg and foot feel numb again. My head hurts. I lift the empty basket out, then grab the side of the canoe and heave as if I am trying to roll a mighty stone. After it flips, I tuck the paddle under it and sit down on the sand. Then, I fling my arms out and let myself fall backwards and close my eyes.

I am still laying there when I feel a shadow fall across my face. Someone is standing, looking down at me.

"I know you," I say, and open my eyes to stare up at Abigail Hobbs.

❧

We stay like this—me laying in the warm sand, my arms outstretched as if I am dead, Abigail standing above me, studying me as if I may be dead—for I don't know how long. Finally, I sit up, resting on my elbows. Abigail is watching me with the same stillness, the same interest I remember from the day Avis died.

"What are you doing here?" I ask.

"Waiting for you," she replies. Then, a moment later, she says, "I know where you have been. You have been in the dark woods. I go there, too."

I regard her. I very much doubt this. She would have no way of getting there, for a start.

"I do," she says, reading my mind. "It is the truth. I always tell the truth. I do not lie. Lying is sinful. I may be wicked, but I am not sinful. I go and talk with the black man. I am not afraid of him," she adds. "He is my friend. He wears a hat and gives me things."

I remember what my mother says, about the nonsense spewed by Mary Skilling and her friends. How it is a witching that grows and spreads of its own accord, winding about the minds it touches like some kind of poisonous weed. I imagine Mercy Lewis listening, wide eyed and hang-mouthed, while her aunt spins stories of black men and devils coming out of the woods to offer sweetmeats and jewels for the souls of children. I imagine her whispering to Abigail, who probably heard in any case, loitering in a doorway or standing on the stairs. I know, just by looking at her, that Abigail wants me to ask 'what things?' So I don't. Oddly, I find I do not care.

"Help me up," I say, stretching out a hand.

Abigail looks at it. "I will," she says, "if you promise you will love me like a sister."

I consider her, and wonder if I am dreaming again. If this is nothing more than another effect of whatever potion the man with the yellow marks and the bone cape gave me. It occurs to me that too might have been a dream, and any moment I will wake dozing in the chair before the hearth and find my mother standing in the doorway, returned from the Back Cove farm, frowning because I have not done half the chores I promised. Then I remember the bird. This time, my hand does not need to rise to my chest to feel its heart, beating against mine like the beat of wings.

"I thought," Abigail says, still looking at my outstretched hand, "that you loved me like a sister. I truly believed it, on the day my mother died, when you held me in your arms, and wept."

And you did not weep, I think. *You did nothing but smile.*

"I thought so, then," Abigail says. "But after, you were cruel. You took Percy. You took what was mine."

"And you took what was mine!" I snap before I can stop myself.

"Because I was angered! Because you had betrayed me! The bible says an eye for an eye."

I make a sound very like a snort. We stare at one another. Abigail Hobbs is a child of ten. And yet she seems older, not by days and weeks, but by years. For a moment I see, coiled inside her small frame, a woman, a crone, a timeless thing grown restless that would emerge into the world. The idea should terrify me. I should recoil. Scrabble away from her. Then I remember what I said to Thaddeus. Only, now, for some reason, it feels true. *She cannot hurt me.* I stretch my hand farther.

"Help me up."

The words come out as a command. Abigail and I stare at one another.

"I know you," I say, although I am no longer entirely sure what I mean by this. "Now, help me up."

We both look at my hand, which is still outstretched, as if my arm is a tree branch, or is stuck. "I will," Abigail says finally, without moving. "I will help you up. But you must not slap or pinch me, or call me a bad cat. Because I love you like a sister. So, if I am to help you, you must love me like a sister. The bible says—"

"Yes! Yes," I snap. "An eye for an eye. Leviticus twenty-four. I know."

I start to add that I also do not care. That the bible says all sorts of things, and I am not sure I believe any of them. Perhaps it is the memory of the yellow man in his bone cape, or the touch of the old woman's fingers, or the bird stone, or the lingering effects of the drug. But sitting here in the sand negotiating with Abigail Hobbs, I am gripped by a strong desire to laugh.

"Alright," I say, finally, when she still does not move. "I will. I will love you like a sister."

Abigail considers for a moment before she steps forward and

takes my hand. Hers is small and cool. It feels more like polished stone than flesh. "Do you promise?"

"I promise."

"Forever and always?"

I roll my eyes. "Forever and always."

"You must mean it."

Abigail tightens her grip, and I feel myself blush because, of course, I mean no such thing. "You must mean it," she says again. Then, with surprising strength, she pulls me to my feet.

❧

WITHOUT MY STICK, I have to lean on Abigail. With her arm around my waist, we scramble up the bank and into the birch grove, and again, I am surprised by her strength. Stopping among the silver trees, I unhitch my skirts from my belt and let them fall, hiding the now soaked leggings and moccasins. Abigail hands me the empty basket she retrieved from the beach.

As we approach milking shed, I know something is wrong. The animals, the goats and our cow, have not been let out to graze. I look up the paddock and see that the gate to the kitchen garden is wide open. The normally raked gravel is smeared with boot prints. The kitchen door is open, too, and there are men standing outside, peering in.

My mother! Something terrible has happened to my mother! The sickness has returned, and this time it has taken her. Or some awful accident has befallen her. Suddenly, I am sure that is what the old woman was trying to tell me. This is why she sent me back, why she spoke my mother's name. This is the word she murmured that I could not understand. Grasping the gate post, I shake off Abigail and try to run but end up hobbling, dragging my numb leg.

The men who had been peering into the kitchen turn to stare. They are Peter and Thomas Cloyce. I have no idea how I must look, limping like a crab, without a cap, my hair in its braid now matted, my face dirty, my eyes wild. Nor do I care. Like cows interrupted chewing cud, their mouths fall open and their eyes pop. They step back as I come close.

"My mother!" My voice is huffed and raspy. "My mother!"

As I shove past them into the kitchen, stumbling through the space they have made for me, she is the first thing I see. My mother is not laid out. She is not wrapped in a winding sheet, dead and white. She is not writhing in pain, or propped in her chair waiting to meet God. She is rising from the kitchen table, where she has been sitting among the men who crowd the room.

I take in Edward Tyng, perching on the hearth chair. Sylvanus Davis and George Burroughs hover by the open casement. John Alden, returned at last, stands at my mother's shoulder. I stop, confused as I realize that all of them are staring at me.

Then everyone is speaking at once.

"Thanks be to God!" Voices chorus. "Thanks be!"

My mother reaches me first. I smell the familiar scents of chamomile and lavender and sun as she takes me by the shoulders, and holding me at arm's length, looks into my face.

"Are you alright?" She asks. "Are you hurt? Are you truly safe?"

I nod. I am not sure what has happened here, but as I look into her face, I know my mother is trying to tell me something. Tired and confused as I am, I cannot understand her message.

"I have been so worried," she says. Her voice is measured, as if she is reading aloud. "We have all been most alarmed. We were mightily afraid, that you were injured, or lost. Or had been taken. Everyone has searched. All these kind gentlemen have come—"

John Alden's voice rises above the others, who are still chattering, cutting them, and my mother, off.

"For God's sake, Girl!" he thunders. "Where have you been? Half the town and the militia have been out these two days and nights, searching for you."

Two days and nights? As I look around the room, it occurs to me that I thought I only slept for one day and one night at the camp. But in truth it could have been more. In truth, I have no idea how long I have been gone. John Alden is looking me up and down. The dress I set out in was my oldest. Now, it is wet and the skirts, undone from my belt, are sagging and torn. My back and arms and hair are clotted with sand from the beach. I am sure my face is dirty. Before I can open my mouth to ask what day it is, or answer his question, John Alden goes on.

"You have caused an almighty panic," he booms. "Your mother has been frightened half to death. What do you have to say for yourself? Did you run away? Were you lost? Were you captive? Did you escape? Where have you been? How did you return? For God's sake do tell us. Half the town and half the militia thought you dead, or taken in retribution by the savages."

Looking at his face, which I know so well, I see the warning in his eye, and understand that he is speaking so none of the others can. Suddenly I wonder what, exactly, the other half of the town and the other half of the militia, those who did not think me dead or captive, thought.

Unease ripples through me. I imagine the bright eyes of Mary Skilling and the wagging tongue of Goody Burroughs. What do they say? That I turned into a black cat or a crow? That they saw me fly away? *Think, girl!* John Alden's eyes are saying. *And think fast!*

When I set out, I did not think about accounting for myself to anyone but my mother. In truth, I did not think about accounting to her, either. I knew that if she woke and found me gone, she would take one look at the stillroom and guess what I had done. My mother would know the truth.

But there can be no truth here. Not in the face of this jury. And there is no mistake. That is what they are. John Alden and George Burroughs will be here to give help and friendship. As for the others—Edward Tyng has his lust. The Cloyces breed jealousy like fleas. Sylvanus Davis's dislike of my father and distrust of the French beat through his heart with every breath. I have a sudden image of the captives, caught between the crowd and the water. Of a stone, thudding on the beach. Of the sailor's spit, and of Mercy Lewis with a rock in her hand, rising on her toes in anticipation.

The chatter has stopped. The room is absolutely silent.

"Forgive me." I do my best to make my voice wobble. It isn't hard.

Standing in my own home, I feel the fear I did not feel at the sight of Abigail. What would they do to me, these men whose families were cut down and whose wives and children were taken by Madockawando, if they knew the truth—that I had stolen one of their captives, even if only a very small one? I know the answer.

If they find out what I have done, they will kill me. Or their wives and daughters will.

"I went, without my mother's knowledge." I drop my eyes, fix on my twisting hands, and allow myself to whine. "I am very sorry. Before dawn, I took the canoe, thinking to get into the marshes, to harvest both new reeds and the first cattails. I meant to save her labor, as she was tired from her work for the babe and mother on the Back Cove."

We save lives, I mean to say. *We are not enemies. We save lives with our skill and labor, and never ask for pay.* My words speed up. They stumble into one another and fall in unruly heaps. I let them.

"I thought to be back by the time my mother woke. But the tide was both high and fast, and, in my weakness, the paddle slipped from my hands and I was swept down into the marshes. It was too deep to wade. By the time I got to firm enough ground, I was exhausted. And lost. I could not see above the reeds. And, having no idea where I was, and knowing savages were abroad—" The word sticks on my tongue. But I spit it out, then let my voice waver and drivel off. "I thought it best to try to hide and, I don't know—I was lost and foolish and afraid. I am sorry, I meant no harm. Nor to cause worry. I am—"

I raise my eyes enough to look around the room. Edward Tyng is disappointed. I suspect he thought he could ride to my mother's rescue, console her for the drowning of her idiot child when my body washed up, and now I have robbed him of the chance. Sylvanus Davis is staring at me as though I have risen from the dead. The Cloyce brothers have stuck their heads through the door, the better to catch every word that their wives and sister and daughters will demand on their return. They glance at each other and then at me as if I am a particularly stupid sheep.

The only one who does not stare at me is George Burroughs. He is studying the floor, as if he has suddenly found his boots and our flagstones fascinating. I feel a nervous bubble of laughter rising, and tamp it down with what I hope sounds like a sob.

"Forgive me," I say again. "Before God, forgive me."

My mother pulls me to her. She runs her hand across my tangled hair, and I feel her still. She can smell the camp on me. The familiar scent of grease. The smudge fires, and the furs I slept in. Looking down, we both see the toes of moccasins peeping from under my sodden skirts.

"Gentlemen," my mother says quickly, turning to the room, holding me behind her. "My daughter is returned, Thanks be to God."

There is a general, if grudging, murmur of agreement.

"She has been both foolish and disobedient. But by God's mercy, she is safe. Her return is a blessing, a reflection on each of you and a reward for the righteousness of this town, and for our endeavor here. My thanks to you, and to God, can know no depths. But as you can see now, she is exhausted from her foolishness and this ordeal. I must care for her."

The excitement is over. The explanation banal. Everyone already knows that I am either witless, or such a dreamer as to be the same thing. Nothing but a silly girl, which is what becomes of female children when they are too long without a father's hand. We may be from Jersey and scented French, but it is fecklessness, not traitorousness that marks us. Already they are moving toward the door. John Alden opens his arms to herd Edward Tyng and Sylvanus Davis. The Cloyce brothers are turning away, shaking their heads.

I have no doubt my mother had to suffer their wives, possibly through the night. They will have bustled away at first light to straighten their houses and pass on everything they saw, and ate, and touched here. Even now, they will be tending their whispers. Feeding all the other village women, and anyone else who will listen, on the rich broth of my mother's sorry state—abandoned by her too fine husband, and now even by her idiot child. They will call it a lesson, because my mother thinks herself too fine and clever. I can only be grateful they were not still here when I returned. The men do not appear to suspect the truth. With the women it would not be so easy.

For all that, I find that the one face I am surprised not to see here is Judah's. I tell myself she has come and gone. That she spent last night with my mother, and has to be at The Ordinary now, but will return at the first opportunity. Or that she is out searching for me.

Yet it was Abigail Hobbs who was standing on the beach. I cannot rid myself of the idea that, as she waited for me, she read all of the patterns Judah and I have made there. Studied all our secrets and lies and dreams. I shiver, and look up. This time, George Burroughs meets my eye. He has not moved.

"Praise be to God in His mercy and wisdom that you are safely returned from your ordeal," he says. Then he follows the others into the garden where John Alden is already shepherding them out the gate.

Captain Alden's familiar voice bounces back, loud and boisterous. He is talking about ale in The Ordinary and stupid girls. Over my mother's shoulder, I watch as they start up the meadow. The rolling walk of the Cloyce brothers, so alike that from a distance they could be one another. The broad green back of

Edward Tyng's too fine coat. Sylvanus Davis's old hat. John Alden's pale hair, now half silver, half gold in the sun. George Burroughs trails behind them like a tired terrier behind a pack of boisterous hounds.

He has reached the gate, when he stops, his hand on the post. George Burroughs looks up. Following his gaze, I see a small singular figure, still as a statue, standing at the edge of our meadow. A sick feeling washes over me, as I understand. Abigail followed me. She sidled up behind the Cloyces, or snuck around to crouch below the open kitchen casement. Hovering in the garden, or under the window. Pressed against the wall behind the stillroom door, Abigail Hobbs heard. She heard and will remember every lie I told.

CHAPTER TWENTY-EIGHT

My mother pulls the kitchen door closed and slides the bolt. She crosses to the open casement, and stands watching until the men have disappeared. Until their voices have faded, and they have passed along the side yards and turned down the common, making for The Ordinary and the generosity of John Alden's deep pockets. Then she waits a moment more before she closes the shutter and turns to me. The room is so dim that I can barely see her face. But I feel her expression.

"I'm sorry," I whisper. "I'm sorry, I'm sorry, I—"

"I know." My mother's voice is cool and still. "I know," she says again. She lights candles, then moves to the hearth and the kettle, laying her hand against it to see if it is still warm. "I know where you were. And what you did. I would have come for you. But the fuss broke out."

I look at her.

"Savages," my mother says. "There has has been endless wonderment and excited amazement at the Godlessness of savages—that one of them would throw her own child overboard rather than see him sold into righteous Christian slavery."

I cannot tell whether it is humor or fury in her voice. Or both.

"Sit." She points to the hearth chair that is still warm from the bulk of Edward Tyng.

"I would have said nothing." My mother takes a bowl from the sill. "I knew you would return unharmed. But Judah came looking for you. So, I was left no choice but to feign surprise that she could not find you. She ran to the fort with the news that you were missing before I could stop her. And so, the fuse was lit."

My mother places the bowl of warmed water at my feet before going to the cider pitcher I had not noticed on the table.

"Blackman and his ship sailed at first light, but not before they sent word that the savages had thrown a child overboard. That, and Judah's news that you were missing, sent the town into a frenzy. They were sure you had been taken in retribution, and were afraid you would not be the last. Their commiseration," she adds, "ate me out of house and home. But, we have a little left." She smiles as she pours a cup of the cider and hands it to me. "I had no idea sympathy was so greedy."

Then her voice, and face, sobers. "My greatest fear," she says, "was that they would blunder into the camp. They are too stupid to find it. But I was afraid they would fall over it, and destroy it, and you in it. I think," she adds, pulling up the fire stool, "that you had best tell me what happened."

I nod, sipping from the cup, feeling the sweet cider run down my throat, washing away the salt and the tiredness.

MY MOTHER WASHES my face and hands as I speak. She unbraids my hair and combs it. When I tell her about the animal-like man, about the cape and the yellow markings, she surprises me by smiling.

"Yellow Bird," she murmurs.

She mentioned him as we returned from our visit to Hope Hood, and I would like to ask her more about him, but she motions me to go on with the story. So I tell her about the strange heavy sleep, and the old woman, and my journey back through the forest. When, finally, I tell her about the disc that was sewn over my heart, she holds out her hand.

"May I see?"

I nod and pluck it from my dress.

"What is it?" I ask, suddenly both afraid and anxious to have the answer. "Do you know?"

My mother turns it over, examining it in the dim light. "It is a manitou."

I shake my head. I don't know what that means.

"A manitou is link," my mother says, answering the question in my face. "As a link in a chain, but between worlds. The world of creatures and their spirits, and the world of humans." She runs her finger across the engraving.

"Between worlds?" My voice sounds strange, as if I am speaking from far away.

My mother nods, still studying the stone.

"Yes. A manitou is—" she pauses, trying to find the language, the words to bridge our world and theirs. To reach from The Greening into this room with its pewter plate and writing chest and bible locked away.

"A manitou is both an opening, a door, and a path," she says, finally. "And, more. A messenger, and a message at once." My mother looks up at me. "A harbinger, if you will. Both of the wearer, and of the path they take." She frowns. "I do not know how else to say it. We do not have anything quite like it, except perhaps, an amulet. But this is different. It is, a being, if you like, in and of itself. It gives the bearer power. Or rather, channels and forms what is already there. Do you understand?"

I shake my head. My mother looks at me. Her features flicker in the shadows of the candles and, once more, as I have in these last few months, I have the sense that she is leaving.

Moving from the center to the very rim of this world, until one day she will slip over the edge, and vanish. For a moment, she does not even look like herself, but like a wavering shape. A creature, threading its way from light to shadow. Her voice, when it comes again, almost startles me.

"Ashawonks taught me that in the world, there is only so much power, and that it is never gone. It only changes. Like sand in an hour glass, it flows between and within us. And between and within the world. And worlds, which overlap, like circles in the sand. The manitous are its conduits. They are creatures, spirits. Each offers its own protection. Each leads its human down its own path. It is a prayer and a being—" She looks at the stone in her hand, "And a destiny at once."

"Does everyone have one?"

My mother shakes her head. "Only—" her voice hesitates, "only some."

I start to ask if that means her, if she also has a disc of stone above her heart, but something stops me.

"A manitou is only given to those who can receive it," my mother says. "And the match must be perfect. They must find one another, like a stone that is chipped then reunited with the piece it lost." She smiles. "Then, as a candle to a spark, or a curing to an illness—two sometimes opposites create a third—a flame, a life, even a death. That is what a manitou is, and does. And the power of each is different."

My throat is oddly thick as I ask the next question. "What is this one? Do you know?"

"Yes." My mother looks at me. "I thought at first that it was what they call Kwimu. He is a bird, and a messenger, and a spy. His call is the report of the doings of men. But I think it is not."

She runs her finger over the image, the engraving with its outstretched wings, its fierce eye and mighty beak.

"I think," she says, "that this is Ciplahq. He is strange. Both good and bad, like all manitous. Only, perhaps more so. One story says the stars fell in love with a girl, and asked Ciplahq, who owed them a favor, if he would fetch her to them. Agreeing, he soared down and snatched her. But when she reached the stars, all she did was cry. So, Ciplahq stole her back, and brought her home."

She hands the stone back to me. "Ciplahq is also called The Night Spirit."

Ciplahq. The word the old woman spoke that I did not understand. When I repeat it, it feels both strange and familiar on my tongue, like something I once tasted a very long time ago.

CHAPTER TWENTY-NINE

Now I find myself wishing that if it is The Night Spirit who travels with me, he would see fit to call up the moon. Because the dark is total, inky and thick. It is past midnight and too warm for a shawl, but I have pulled one over my head anyway. The wool scratches. Sweat pricks the back of my neck. Swaddled like this, I am nothing but a shape moving soundlessly through the birch grove.

Even as the men left the house this afternoon, my mother and I both understood, without speaking of it, what had to be done. In their presence, both those who came to help and those who came to spy, I was forced to make up my story on the spot. While neither my mother nor I believe it raised undo suspicion, it has one major flaw. Thanks in no small part to John Alden, none of the men were given enough time to think about it. If they had, they might have thought to ask how I returned to the cove? How I got the canoe back after I lost the paddle?

I would have said I fashioned a branch, or even used my hands and the outgoing tide. I would have made up some nonsense about weaving reeds into a makeshift paddle. But if anyone thought to check, if anyone was suspicious enough to go and search our beach, they would know at once that my entire story was a lie. They would know I had not lost the paddle, because they would find it, tucked neatly under the hull. And they would know it is ours. I could not claim to have found, or stolen, or come across it. Because my father branded an *H* for Hammond into the handle. So, we knew we had to get rid of it.

Probing my wounded foot and leg, my mother had decided to leave the leggings and moccasins. She says they are a bandage, part of what she believes to be a poultice that must be given time to work. Even so, I am still lame. So my mother said she would come to the cove and dispose of the paddle herself. But I pointed out that if a well-wisher, or more likely a spy—a Goody Burroughs snuffling for scandal—called at the house to ask after me or congratulate her on my return, it would be easier for my mother to claim she had given me a tea and put me to bed than for me to explain why she was absent. So, we waited until it was fully dark. Then, swaddled in my shawl and hobbling on an old crutch kept in the stillroom, I set out like some strange three-legged creature.

Now I stop, blinking, playing my old trick. As my eyes adjust, I see the birch trunks rising in their pale, slender columns. There is a rustle. Something slips past and vanishes towards the point, the fox or one of her cubs. I cross the grove, stepping gingerly. I can barely make out the edge of the bank, and have no wish to fall down it. Stars shimmer in the mirror of the cove. The tide is high, the beach nothing but a pale rim on the plate of the sea. As I start to make my way down, a call breaks the night —the long sorrowful sound of a water bird. Kwimu, spying on the events of men.

Reaching the sand, I pause to smell the night wind. Above, moonless black cradles the heavens. I think about Ciplahq, and wonder if the girl he stole was cold up there with the stars who loved her, and if that was why she cried. Then I pick out the pole star, and think of the boy whose name I do not know, and his mother, and wonder if he is asleep and dreaming of her. And if whatever prison she is in, be it a ship or the Boston jail, has a window she can gaze through as she dreams of him. My free hand feels for the manitou. I close my fingers around it, caress it through the cloth of my dress, and picture her with her scar, and send her a picture of her son.

Despite the trouble it has caused, I don't regret what I did. Yet the specter of Eliza Bourne looms large. She feels so close that I am sure that if I turn and look back through the birches, I will see her. If I am discovered, if anyone suspects what I have really done, my mother and I will be, at best, banished. At worst? I think of the women in Marblehead, of the crowd on the beach, of the stone in Mercy Lewis' hand. And shudder.

DOWN HERE BY THE WATER, the night seems less dark. Upside down and cradled in the sea grass at the end of the beach, the canoe looks like the belly of a giant fish. I pad towards it. Letting the crutch fall, I drop to my knees. Almost laying in the sand and prickly grass, I shove my hand under the hull. My fingers meet pebbles, and the sharp edges of reeds. They find the basket hooks, and the smooth plank of the seat. But not the paddle.

I was so tired when I hauled the canoe from the shallows that it felt heavier than ever before. I had barely been able to flip it because my arms and back ached so. Perhaps I shoved the paddle farther towards the bow? Or left in in the bottom of the hull, so it has fallen and is balanced on the underside of the seat planks?

I wriggle as close as I can and poke my arm upwards. My fingers find first one smooth sanded bench, then the next. But there is nothing resting on either of them. Pulling my arm out, I scuttle like a crab towards the prow, and try again. Again, there is nothing.

My heart is beginning to beat hard. The paddle could have fallen to the far side of the canoe. I could have forgotten, and dropped it in the reeds. I was, I think now, not quite in my right mind, sluggish with whatever drug had made me sleep for two days. Slightly drunk with the sense that I had battled from one time and world to another. I get to my feet and hobble around the upturned hull, my hands trailing across its pale, silvery skin as if I could beg it to give up its secret. But there is nothing in the reed grass on the far side except a small pile of drift wood and broken shells. Finally, in frustration, I drop to my knees and, fueled by the strength of growing fear, grab the canoe and flip it over. This time, it rolls easily. But when it rights itself, it is still empty. The paddle is gone.

I feel tears rising, and a deep, terrible despair. Someone, one of the men—Peter or Thomas Cloyce, goaded by their wives, or Sylvanus Davis who watched me as if I was a phantom, or even Edward Tyng or George Burroughs himself—did not believe me. Someone was suspicious. Someone didn't drink as much ale as John Alden intended, and thought about it, and saw the flaw in my story, and came to check for themselves. Someone found the paddle with its tell-tale H. And now everyone will know I lied.

It is probably already on display in The Ordinary, held up as evidence that I was not drifting. That I was not lost. Everyone knows our sympathies. And those who don't will be reminded. The story of our past in The Greening will rise as the dead always do. It will not take much to guess that it was me who helped the captives. That I was not in the reed beds, but staying and sleeping and eating among our enemies. Which makes me a traitor, because I returned a child to those who have killed our children.

I close my eyes, wondering if they are meeting now to discuss what to do, if they are on their way? Or have they already come and found my mother alone. Did she glance out the window after I left and see the orbs of torches bouncing down the path from the village?

Then I think of something else. The small figure standing at the edge of our meadow. Abigail. Who sees everything. And forgets nothing. Who was waiting. Who saw me arrive at the cove. Who knew I had been in the forest. Abigail, who may be wicked, but always tells the truth, so will tell again, if she is asked. Abigail, who takes an eye for eye, and whom I lied to.

Despite the heat and the shawl, I begin to shiver. I wonder if I should return to the house at all? Or if I should take the canoe now, and try to get back to the camp. Where there will be no one, because they were leaving. Or perhaps I should try to find John Alden, or George Burroughs, or—

"Are you looking for this?"

The question hangs in the dark. I cannot see where it comes from, but I recognize the voice. It is only when she steps out of the shadow of the bank that I see she is holding the paddle.

"I told you," Abigail Hobbs says, "that I would love you like a sister."

CHAPTER THIRTY

For the second time in less than a day, and in almost exactly the same place, Abigail helps me to my feet. She helps me, too, to roll the canoe, turning its fish belly back to the stars. Then, she retrieves the crutch from where I dropped it and hands it to me.

"Come," she says, picking up the paddle again. "We should not stay here. We are too easily seen."

She is right. The paleness of the beach and the shimmer of the water beyond makes it too easy to pick out our shapes. Abigail scrambles up the bank. I follow with my crutch. She leads the way through the birch grove to the start of the track up the point. There is more undergrowth here. The birches give way to scrub oak and hawthorn, so, like the fox, we can disappear if we need to. As we sit, I wonder if she is nearby, surrounded by her cubs, watching us.

"You heard?"

My question is not really a question. Although I cannot see her, I know Abigail is nodding.

"Men do not pay attention to children," she says. "Even less so if they are girls. Girls are nothing. They might as well be air." I feel her glance at me. "My father thinks I am in bed now,"

Abigail says. "The Cloyces think me little better than a hound or a kit. They are so accustomed to me being underfoot that they never see me at all. This afternoon, they did not even know I was there, or think about it if they did. They were too busy peering at you and wondering if you were lying, or looking for signs that you are a sorceress. Goody Cloyce says your mother can fly."

I am not surprised by this. The whole town knows Goodwife Cloyce is as fond of ale as her husband. And that she is friendly with Mary Skilling, who will say anything about my mother. If someone dies, my mother has witched them. If they live, she uses sorcery.

"I crept away," Abigail says, "before they knew I had been there. When I was certain they were gone, I came and made certain this was gone."

She strokes the paddle that lays between us as if it is alive. As if it is a kit. I see her small white hand in the darkness, and think of Percy.

"Why did you?"

The question is a whisper, but Abigail hears it, and knows what I am asking. There is a pause before she answers.

"To be certain," she says. "Of the hellebore. I meant it only for the babe, and a kit is not much bigger than a babe."

I know she is looking at me. That, even as her fingers with their pearly nails caress the fine grained wood, those ice blue eyes are fastened on my face.

"You do not understand," she says. "You are loved."

"But Avis loved you! Everyone knew you were your mother's poppet!" I blurt the words before I can stop myself.

Abigail seems to consider them, to turn them over as if they are shells and pebbles that hide a design.

"Only when there was no one else," she says, finally. "She loved me when everyone else was gone. If the babe had come, no one would have loved me all over again. My mother is not sad," she adds. "Now that she is filled with God."

And what of your sister and brother? What of the twins and the shallop and the untied knot? Were William and Avis filled with God as the green water wrapped around them and pulled them down, down, down?

I cannot ask it. This is not the same as struggling to dredge up the old rusted bits of Ashawonks' language. There is no well in me deep enough to plumb for the words I should say now to Abigail Hobbs, to find the questions I should ask her. Perhaps George Burroughs would do better. Certainly my mother would. But I cannot. So I say nothing at all.

"I am sorry for Percy." Abigail's voice comes out of the dark. "He was a very good kit, and I did love him. That is why I gave him so many flowers. And was so angered when you took him."

"Abigail—" I am reaching towards her. I would like to still her small hand, stop it stroking the smoothed oak of the paddle. Which I would also like to snatch from her.

"I came here," she says, "as soon as the men left. As soon as I knew they had gone to The Ordinary. I came and took the paddle. Then I waited, and watched."

My hand stops moving as something twists in my heart. An even deeper coldness than the one I felt earlier is creeping over me. The night is close. The wind is warm, as it often is in these last days of summer. I pull my shawl around me, as if it can protect me from what Abigail Hobbs will say next.

"I sat here, behind the hawthorn, in the twilight," she says, "just before it turned to dark. There were shadows, but I could still see. Everything was so quiet."

Abigail's voice begins to change, becoming low and deep and dreamy, as it was when she sang Trisket, Trasket. This time, though, the words are not a song, but a story.

"She didn't make a sound coming through the birches. Weaving without touching a twig, as you can only do when you know somewhere so well you can walk it with your eyes closed. I have done that. In our old house, I could walk clear across the kitchen with my eyes shut, and not a touch a thing. So, I was not surprised. But I stayed very still. I spread myself like air, and watched. Which was as well, because it was a good search. She began with the canoe. Underneath, and on each side. Turning it up and dropping it back. Then she searched the whole beach, even the shallows. After that, she looked along the bank, lifting the tall grass. Then, finally, she climbed back up, and worked her way through the grove. Once, she was so close to me that we might have touched. Then, she went to your milking shed. I followed. She was angry by then. Because she could not find it. I had made sure. You were never in danger."

The coldness I feel now is not making me shiver. It is freezing me to the bone.

"Even when she is angry, she is very beautiful." The small, cool, hand reaches for my frozen one. "She is very beautiful indeed," Abigail Hobbs says. "But Judah White no longer loves you like a sister."

CHAPTER THIRTY-ONE

I know how it happened. I can see the men throwing open the door to The Ordinary, their unruly laughter running before them like a pack of dogs. I can hear the calls for pitchers of ale, and the thump of tankards. And the repeating of my story. I can see the fading gold of John Alden's hair, the fall of his coin. Hear the boom of his voice and stretch of his arm as he reaches for Judah as she passes and shouts that she is The Beautiful Jersey Maid!

I can see the Cloyce brothers and Sylvanus Davis, and Edward Tyng unbuttoning his too tight coat as he tells how, disobedient and willful and stupid with it, I took the canoe and, like the fools all women are, fumbled the paddle and was swept away into the marsh where I lay two days, lost and terrified of savages.

What a good tale it must have been, told and retold, embroidered and elaborated until, aided by pint upon pint thanks to John Alden's deep pockets, it became truth. Which no one would think to question. Except a Jersey maid so beautiful she is worth how many barrels of that same ale.

A Jersey maid who knows me as well as she knows her own

fair flesh, and the lines we made in it when we cut our palms and mingled our blood, and swore to love each other like sisters. Which means she knows that I am not afraid of savages. And that even if I was, I would never fumble a canoe's paddle. And that even if I did, I would not let myself be swept into the marsh. Or become lost, or hide for two days, or fail to return to my own beach. Because I do not need a paddle, or even a canoe to bring me across the water. Because I can swim. She has seen me.

I want desperately to believe that on hearing the story and knowing at once that it was a pack of lies, Judah, fearing my mother and I had somehow missed the crack in the story, slipped away to search for the paddle in order to bring it to us. But if that was so, why not come to the house and knock on the door? Why search the beach, and creep through the grove, and pry and poke in the milking shed?

This, in turn, makes me wonder what else Judah did. Tiptoe up the garden path? Try the stillroom latch? Put her ear to the kitchen door, or crouch below the closed casement to hear my mother and I talking about manitous and Yellow Birds and Night Spirits?

Laying awake, the thought terrifies me.

But, surely, if it had happened, Abigail would have seen her, and Abigail would have told me? I comfort myself with this idea, and with the knowledge that there is no proof now, of anything. Abigail and I made sure. After she had finished her story, we sat for a long time. Then, we went back to the cove. Without speaking, we went back down the bank, and stood on the beach, where Abigail handed me the paddle. I held it for a moment, running my thumb across the H my father had burned into the smooth, polished wood. Then I threw it. I threw it as hard as I could, so it turned end over end against the stars, before falling into the current that waited to bear it away.

I DID NOT TELL my mother that Abigail was standing beside me as the paddle cartwheeled towards the stars. Or what I, what we both, now owe her. Nor did I tell her what I had learned about Judah.

If she wondered why pulling a paddle out from under the canoe and hurling it into the cove took me quite so long, she did not ask. When I finally returned, she simply made me a tea, and asked if my leg and foot were hurting. The true answer was, not much. But I said, "Yes." I used that small pain to cover the great pain, the terrible twist of the blade in my heart, which is no less painful this morning as we sit in the cart on our way to the Back Cove Farm.

Before we left, my mother unlaced the moccasins and the leggings. She said we could not risk someone seeing them, and she must check the wound. After she had untied the knots and peeled back the deerskin, she looked up at me.

"Did it hurt a great deal?" She asked.

I shook my head, then remembered the lightning bolt.

"Yes," I said. "No. I don't remember."

My mother smiled.

"I suspect they gave you enough willow and valerian that you were lucky not to sleep for a week. Even so," she gestured to my leg, "this would have been painful."

I looked down, seeing it for the first time since it had been treated in the camp. It was no longer swollen, and no longer red. But there was a white crusted line, like a seam a handspan long, running from my ankle up my calf.

"There's a poultice on it," my mother said, reaching for a linen bandage. "I'll leave it and cover it again. We'll wash it in a day or two. On your journey to the camp, the wound in your foot got something in it and became poisoned. The poison was moving up your leg. In order to stop it, they lanced it. Then cauterized the wound."

I have never seen this done, but I have heard of it. The

wound must be opened, with a blade, and the poison drained out. Then it is cleaned, and sealed with fire.

"You will have a fine scar," my mother continued. "But you will not lose the leg. Or your foot. You have Yellow Bird to thank for that."

The creature with the cape of bones. My mother says I am honored to have been treated by him. Apparently, he does not care for white skinned people, and must have agreed to care for me only because I returned the boy. When I asked if she thought he was the one who gave me the manitou, my mother had looked at me for a long time before she nodded.

"Yes," she said finally. "That can only have been Yellow Bird."

"Why?"

I had the feeling I should not be asking this. That even speaking of it we were crossing a line, like the line of yet another snare. But there seem to be so many now, it felt as if one more hardly mattered. I could feel the stone in its secret pocket, beating against my chest, egging me on. My mother had stopped what she was doing. For a moment, she stood perfectly still.

"Was it a reward?" I insisted. "For returning the child?" Even as I asked, I knew it wasn't.

My mother shook her head. "That was the cure," she said. "That was the medicine that saved your leg."

"Then why?"

My voice was high, and childish. I knew I should stop. I could see it in her eyes. But I couldn't. I was pushing the same way you push on a fragile piece of wood, knowing it will give way, and that when it does, it will be broken forever.

"If it was not a reward, then why me? And why Ciplahq?"

Through the long previous night, I summoned every memory I had of Judah. And with each one, I felt the blade in my heart twisting a little more. At some point, in the dark, I reached for the thin disc that I had taken out of my dress and hidden under my pillow, and held it. Without being quite sure why, I had run my fingers over its image, tracing its line with every memory I dredged up, each more painful than the last, until finally I fell asleep with its shape pulsing in my veins.

"Why Ciplahq?" The name, so recently alien, fell off my tongue as if I had always known it. "Why did Yellow Bird give The Night Spirit to me?"

"Because," my mother said finally, "he recognized you." Then she left the room.

❧

NOW, as the cart leaves the common and the fort and The Ordinary behind, I run my fingers over my other scar, the one Judah and I made three summers ago when we stood in the cove, and think this is what time does. It engraves the past upon you so you cannot forget, even if you try.

The boy is driving again today. Again, my mother sits on the bench with him and the dog called Tom. I sit in the cart bed with the baskets. The boy's name is Henry Smith. He announces this proudly, looking over his shoulder and almost dropping the reins, which makes no difference because, in truth, the little bay horse could come and go on her own. He is Small Henry, he says, because his name is the same as his father's. And his grandfather's. And, though he was in Scotland, his grandfather's father before that. Looking at his ginger hair and sun speckled cheeks, I imagine a great, bright chain of Henrys, a small and a large and a small and a large, laid end to end, grasping ankles and wrists as they stretch down the years and across the sea.

At the Brackett Farm, we turn north, skirting the Back Cove. It is only when we are within sight of the farm house that I realize where we are. This used to be the Lewis family land. This is where, almost exactly a dozen years ago, on a morning that was probably not very different from this one, Mercy's grandfather, old George Lewis, and her grandmother, were cut down.

This is where their daughter, Anne, and her husband James Ross, and their son-in-law Benjamin Atwell were killed. These fields were the last glimpse of her old life that their second daughter, Alice Atwell, had before she was taken. And this is where Mercy's cousins, Mary Skilling's children, were put to death.

CHAPTER THIRTY-TWO

The house is not as gracious as the one my father built for us. But it is large and well kept and, I suspect, more than the Smith family could have hoped to build for themselves. After the attack, what remained of the Lewis family had, like everyone else, left Casco Bay and Cleeve's Neck until the fort was put up and the village rebuilt. Gossip says they never set foot in this house again, and that the land and its memories were sold cheap. Farther out even than the Brackett farm, it must now be one of the last settled properties to the north. These fields mark the line between Godliness and what lays beyond.

Yet, the place is not gloomy. I noticed as we approached that the fences are in good repair, the fields recently harvested. When we enter, the house is clean and swept. Goodwife Smith has been out of bed for several days now. A pale woman with hair the color of the moon, she is still not strong. But there is joy in her face, probably at the mere fact of being alive and having her babe alive with her. The tiny girl lays in a cradle by the hearth. She waves a fist and lets out a howl, then a gurgle as my mother picks her up, cooing her name, "Hannah, Hannah, Hannah," which is also her mother's name.

We have brought sugar shaved from the loaf sent to us by Philip English, and spice cakes baked with the ginger and nutmeg that also come in his ships from the Indes. These are delicacies, and while my mother insists that they are necessary to build up the strength of Goodwife Smith and Tiny Hannah, I know too, that she has brought them as a celebration that the two are thriving.

I love ginger, and also the woody sweetness of nutmeg. I have always loved the parcels that come from Philip English's ships—the ribbons and bits of lace that it is not politic for us to wear and yet are a pleasure to own and finger, to fix at the throat of a dress merely because they are beautiful. And the other things, a bowl from London. A silver spoon. Malaga wine from the Spanish islands. I love them all. Everything that makes life sweet.

And yet, this afternoon, watching the pleasure on Goodwife Smith's too thin face, and the excitement of Small Henry, and even the pleasure and pride of Large Henry as he holds his baby daughter and dabs a sugared finger to her kitten tongue, I find all of it turning to sand in my mouth. Lifting a ginger cake I baked myself, I see, not the room around me, but the narrow porthole and the cabin beyond, crowded with bodies. *They do not thrive in the Indies on the great plantations. They pine and suffer and die*. I drop the cake to my side, letting the little dog, Tom, take it untasted from my hand.

We stay all that morning and into the afternoon on the Smith farm. My mother boils a kettle, and cools the water and unwraps a bar of fine milled soap—another treat from Philip English's ships—and instructs Goodwife Smith in the washing and wrapping of her tiny daughter. I help with the clearing and cleaning of dishes, and when Small Henry comes in, sent by his father from the fields to see if we are ready to return, he shows me the barn where the cows and the bay horse live, and where doves coo and nest in the rafters. As we finally prepare to leave, Big Henry lifts the now empty baskets into the cart bed. Before helping her up onto the bench, he takes my mother's hand in his roughened dirty ones.

"We are strangers here," he says. "Newly come for a new beginning. My Hannah and I, we wish just for a good life on this land. We are not wealthy, and we are not churched, and have few acquaintances in the town. You have been good to us, Mistress. We will not forget it. The boy and I—" He nods at his son who has already taken the reins. "This winter, or come spring, when you need work."

My mother thanks him. He hands her up, then lifts me to the cart bed as easily as if I am a straw poppet. Fastening the back, he raps the board to tell the little bay mare she may go on her way. Henry Smith waves as we start down the track through the fields. With his broad shoulders and carrot hair, he is a red giant of a man, his son but a smaller version of him who will one day stand as tall, and have a son of his own to call Henry Smith, and perhaps a daughter to call Hannah. Two more links in the chain.

Geese are settling in the marshes that rim the Back Cove. In the next moon or the one after, they will be gone, flying like so many arrows shot south. I wonder if the place they land looks like this. If they go to Virginia or Carolina, and what those places are. I have never been to Boston, or even to Salem where Philip English has his docks. I have never been anywhere except here, and Duxbury, and The Greening. Even Judah can remember Jersey.

At the thought of her, the blade twists again. I think of the paddle, and know that I could believe Abigail is jealous, and was lying, that Judah was never there at all. But I do not. For a start, strange though it is, I believe Abigail when she says she does not lie. God knows, she is honest enough about any number of things most of us would never speak of. But even beyond that, I remember how pleased Judah was when the captives were taken, what she said when she walked with George Burroughs and me. I remember her excitement, that was not just for the militia man she had been speaking to on the beach. And I remember the look on her face when she saw me swimming. The fast darting motion of her hand to her head and heart and shoulders—the sign that wards off evil.

So I believe Judah came and searched for the paddle. She did not warn us. That was not why she was there. If she had found it, she would not have returned it, or thrown it into the cove for the tide to take away. I understand that she wanted it for herself. And she wanted it badly. What I do not understand is *Why?*

We are past the Brackett Farm, have turned down Cleeves Neck and are well down the road to town when we see the figure running towards us waving his arms above his head. As he comes close, I realize it is Thaddeus Hobbs. Thaddeus grips the horse's harness, as Small Henry stops the cart. Bent and out of breath, his words are little more than a gasp.

"You must come! Captain Alden says you must come at once, Mistress Hammond!"

Before my mother can ask why, or what he means, Thaddeus has clambered over the side of the cart and is throwing himself down beside me.

"Hurry!" He commands Small Henry. "Captain Alden says you must come as fast as you can to the harbor!"

CHAPTER THIRTY-THREE

The sight that greets us is the strangest I have ever seen.

When we saw Thaddeus, I thought, and I know my mother thought, there had been some kind of accident. That a half-built shallop had collapsed in the boat shed, crushing someone's limb. Or a fisherman had gone over the side and been pulled from the water. Or that something had happened at the fort with gun powder.

My mother asked if we should not return to the house so she could fetch supplies from the stillroom? But Thaddeus, winded and red faced, shook his head.

"To the harbor!" He insisted. "Captain Alden requires you at the harbor, as fast as you can!"

So, we had clung to the sides of the cart as Small Henry, looping an arm around Tom so he did not fly from the bench, gee-ed the little bay horse into a canter and we tore along the Common and down Broad Street and, slowing to a trot, finally stopped above the harbor beach.

As on the day Captain Blackman's captives had been paraded there, a crowd had gathered. Seeing them, I felt queasy, as if I had lived this before, and now must relive it. Before I could ask what was going on, Thaddeus helped me down. Then he helped my mother. Taking her elbow, he shouted for the crowd to make way. They fell back as he led her to the harbor, Small Henry with Tom in his arms and me with my crutch following in their wake.

❧

THIS TIME, the townspeople have not come close. Instead, they throng the top of the beach, as if they dare not set foot on the pebble or wish to stay back in case they have to turn and flee. It takes me a moment, as we pass through them, to understand why.

Ahead of us, John Alden stands at the water's edge. George Burroughs is beside him, and Edward Tyng. As we come close, I see that the magistrate's collar is crooked and his fine green coat has been misbuttoned, as if he has woken from a nap and stuffed himself into it on the run. Glancing towards the fort, I see the motley collection of militia left behind when Blackman set sail with his prize for Boston. Lined up under the ramparts, they shift uneasily. As well they might. Because the harbor is filled with canoes.

These are not small, light canoes like ours. They are huge. I take in their white shapes, their birch skins glistening in the sun. Figures are painted on their prows—a wolf, a serpent, a bird in flight. Each is manned by four, five, perhaps as many as six men. Although I have never seen one before, I know these are war canoes. Remembering the crescent of empty cove below the teepees, I think, *So, this is where the men have gone.* Then, I am completely distracted. Like everyone else, I cannot pull my eyes from the figures who stand facing Captain Alden, and George Burroughs, and the by now openly sweating Edward Tyng.

There are five of them, and they are the most singular sight I, or I suspect any of us, have ever seen. The man who is obviously their leader is very tall. Hope Hood may be the same height, but this man, who must be twenty years his junior, seems twice his size. His head is shaved, save for a magnificent cockscomb, stiffened with deer bristles and reddened with ocher, that runs from his forehead to the nape of his neck. Like the men who stand on either side of him, his face and chest are also reddened. His torso is painted with patterns of animals. I can make out a bear, and what may be a deer or a wolf. A serpent twists around and around, winding down his arm. His moccasins and leggings are finely beaded. His mantle, which is clasped on one shoulder by the claw of what must be a bear, is quilled with zigs and zags of lightning. In his left hand, he holds a fan of turkey feathers.

The men who stand on either side of him are not as finely dressed. Indeed, they are barely dressed at all, wearing only leggings and breech clothes. Like their leader, they are tall, and their bodies are ochered and patterned. Their heads are shaved except for dark top knots that are tightly wound and oiled and laced with feathers. Bows and loaded quivers are slung across their chests. Each carries what must be a war club. In closest canoes, I can see that at least half of the men carry guns. It is safe to bet the others are also armed.

John Alden looks up, and extends a hand to my mother, beckoning her forward.

"Mistress Hammond," he says, "I would like to present you to the Sachem, Egeremet, and his sons. They have come to speak with us, but I can't understand a word they're saying. I only pray to whatever God exists that you can."

My mother stands for a moment without moving. Then she steps in front of John Alden. Between the two men, she seems insubstantial, almost translucent with her pale skin and white cap. When she speaks, her voice is so low that I cannot hear what she says. Holding Tom, Small Henry sidles close to me.

My mother bows her head. She holds her hands together, raised as if in prayer. When she has finished speaking, she looks up at the tall man with his painted face and tattooed arms. His eyes are so black in the afternoon sun that I can make out no expression in them at all.

I don't recognize the words he uses as he replies. His voice is strangely accented. He does not sound at all like Hope Hood's people, and I could barely understand them. I can tell that my mother is having something of the same problem. She cocks her head, frowning. He speaks again, gesturing with his fan. The feathers catch the sun. Finally, my mother nods. She turns to John Alden. This time, her voice is clear and loud.

"He says they have heard that you have taken Hope Hood and many of his people. They are unhappy because the promised tributes have not been paid for the land deeds they signed, nor for the damage done to their crops and stores by wandering beasts. And now, this taking of captives further saddens their hearts. They wish only peace. They have come here today to ask why Hope Hood and his people have been taken."

For a split second, I almost think John Alden is going to smile. He turns slowly to Edward Tyng.

"You heard the question, Magistrate." John Alden opens his hands, as if he is presenting a gift. "I was not here when the captives were taken. I am not the authority, and gave no order, nor know the reasoning. So, the answer must be yours."

I remember the day Thaddeus came to the garden and told me how Blackman had ordered that all and any Indians, no matter who they were or what they did, should be taken. Edward Tyng seems to be remembering the same thing. Unable to look at the five visitors, he swallows hard. He tugs at his coat and, realizing it is mis-buttoned becomes flustered. He lets go of it, and stamps his boots.

"We, we took the captives as hostages to our peace. For our security." Magistrate Tyng coughs and splutters, then puffs himself up. "In light of the dreadful killings in Northfield."

John Alden considers him for a moment. I notice that George Burroughs is shifting his gaze, watching the canoes that seem to have stilled on the water, and the still figures in them that are nothing but silhouettes. There must be fifty or sixty men, each with a hatchet and a war club and quivers and bows, and as many again with guns. George Burroughs glances back at the twenty or so militia men who shift uneasily in front of the fort as if they are tempted to dash inside and slam the gates. I wonder which of them is Judah's, or if he has gone with Captain Blackman.

No, I think. *He has not gone. He must still be here*. Or else she would not have come looking for the paddle. The thought comes unbidden. My mind has been worrying it like a dog with a bone, and now, all at once, I understand. I know *Why?* The paddle, proof of my lie, was to be Judah's gift to him, so he could run with it to his commander and be a hero for uncovering not only a traitor, but also a thief. For surely to steal a slave, even a very small one is as bad as stealing a plow, or an ax, or a horse? Or a roll of table linen. Did Judah really wish so much to see me with a T sewn onto the back of my dress? Did she wish me whipped?

The thought makes me sick, and I am glad to return my attention to John Alden, who is gesturing to my mother, telling her to relay Tyng's message. She nods, then turns to the sachem, Egeremet, and speaks again. Again, there is a pause before he replies. The men on either side of the sachem appear motionless, yet somehow, they have moved closer to him. I feel a tightening of the air, as if an invisible crank is being turned. I wonder how many in the crowd above the beach feel it, too. How many step back, and begin to creep away. Making for their houses so they may bar the doors and windows and reach for their axes and their powder bags. Or send their wives and children out to the fields and down into the root cellars to burrow like tiny animals when hawks circle the sky.

When Egeremet finally speaks again, his voice is low. Again, I cannot understand the words. But my mother does. She turns to John Alden and Edward Tyng.

"He says that Northfield is very far away. And that the attackers were Mohawk and French. He says he is Abenaki, and Hope Hood is Abenaki, so they are not French, and have no love for the Mohawk. They have wished nothing but peace. But now their people have been taken. He would like to know where they are, and what is going to happen to them."

"It was Captain Blackman's plan! Captain Blackman conceived of it entirely!" Edward Tyng blurts this out almost before my mother has finished speaking. "The militia—" He waves at the fort as if it is some alien thing he has never seen before. "You must tell him! You must tell him! It was a plan entirely conceived and carried out by Captain Blackman!"

My mother nods and relays the message. John Alden folds his arms and regards Edward Tyng. George Burroughs looks as if he is silently counting the throng of canoes, judging how close they are and how quickly they could come ashore—and not liking the answer.

"They would like to know," my mother says, when Egeremont has listened and replied to her, "where Captain Blackman is, and when they can speak to him. They would like to know where the captives are, and when they will be returned, since they wish nothing but peace."

John Alden turns to our magistrate and raises his eyebrows. But for the fact that we may all be slaughtered, it is almost possible to believe he is enjoying himself. Edward Tyng is not enjoying himself. He shifts from boot to boot, squelching wet sand and crunching pebbles. He pulls at his crooked collar, and becomes even more red in the face.

"I shall—" He sputters. "Tell them we shall, send immediately to Boston. For instructions. Tell him—You must say, that the captives are safe. That they are being very well cared for. Very well. Assure him that they are being shown every courtesy."

"Oh, yes," John Alden mutters. "Do assure him of that."

George Burroughs glances up. My mother relays the message.

For a moment, Egeremet and his sons do not move. Then, bowing, almost as if he is a courtier, the sachem takes my mother's small folded hands in his large free one. Beside me, I feel Thaddeus tense. John Alden and George Burroughs stiffen. Alden's hand goes to his belt where there is a knife sheath. But

Egeremet is not pulling my mother toward him. Instead, he is bending toward her. Raising his turkey fan to shield them, he speaks so quietly that only she can hear him. When he is finished, he lets go of her, and straightens.

The sachem looks at the white men in front of him. At John Alden with his hand hovering at his knife, at George Burroughs in his shirt sleeves with his wild black hair, and at Edward Tyng who seems to be sputtering without making a sound. Then Egeremet turns so swiftly we barely realize it is happening. In an instant, he and his four sons are in the shallows, boarding a canoe that has nosed up out of nowhere.

With their sachem in the center, the warriors raise their paddles as one and strike the water. Bubbles stream from the wolf's smile with its bared teeth that is painted on the prow. Two of Egeremet's sons twist in the stern to face us on the beach, bows off their backs, arrows notched. Strings pulled taut, they scan for any movement, anything that might herald the firing of a weapon. In seconds, all of the canoes have turned and formed around Egeremet, gathering like a knot of leaves in a storm. As they paddle fast for the harbor mouth, we stand frozen, too terrified to move, bewitched by a fleet of silvered birch.

CHAPTER THIRTY-FOUR

As the last of the mighty war canoes swings behind the island in the harbor mouth, which is little more than an outsized rock, George Burroughs lets out a sigh. He raises a hand to his face, murmuring something that might be a prayer. For a moment, I think he is going to fall to his knees. Edward Tyng staggers slightly, then grabs his coat as if he can right himself with it, and puffs out his chest, fumbling with his buttons. One pops off and lands at his feet. It lays there, winking like fool's gold in the wet sand.

Now that no arrows are aimed at them or hatchets are within throwing distance, the militia men begin to rumble. They bustle to the fort gates as if they are going to do something important. John Alden turns to my mother.

"What did he say?"

She has been staring at the harbor mouth, at the dark blotch of the islet which looks like a black hole in the shimmering sea. Finally, she looks at him.

"He said that it is their fondest wish that Hope Hood and his people, who are dear to their hearts even as family, should be returned. Quickly and unharmed. He said that they wish it because they wish peace."

John Alden stares at her for a moment. Then he turns on Edward Tyng.

"Do you hear that?" He bellows. "Do you hear that, you fat fool! This is where your antics, yours and that idiot Blackman's, have got us! Now, if you wish not to be murdered in your bed and the whole town murdered with you, I suggest you set what brains you have to making the sachem's wish come true!"

❧

AFTER THE SCENE at the harbor, and the hour we have all just spent standing in the baking sun wondering if we were about to die, our house looks like an oasis at the bottom of the meadow. My mother's garden floats around it, making it look slightly unearthly, as if it is perched on a cloud and might drift away and leave the world behind.

Thaddeus was called by John Alden, who went striding off toward the fort. Small Henry insists on driving the cart down to our gate. When we get there, the little boy clambers over the driving bench to hand out our baskets, then jumps down and trails us through the garden and into the kitchen. Trotting ahead, Tom pauses to inspect the mint and the drift of chamomile I have not yet cut, before darting inside to sniff the corners of the kitchen.

"Will we be safe?" Small Henry blurts, as we cross the threshold. "Are we going to be attacked by the savages?"

I imagine this question being asked in every house, every room, at every meeting, with every tankard shakily poured and unsteadily lifted in The Ordinary. I had been so intent on Egeremet and on my mother, on trying to understand even a few words, and if not that, then at least the meaning of what was going on in front of me, that I had not bothered to look at the crowd. They hung well back this time. There was no hissing, or spitting, or name calling. War clubs are quite different from a bound and barefoot fishing party. Despite what I had realized about her, I had not even looked for Judah. Much less, Abigail. Although I am sure both of them were there, along with Mercy Lewis, who is probably at home even now, screaming about demons and rolling on the floor in a fit.

My mother shakes her head at Small Henry's question. She has lowered a dish of water to the floor for Tom, who abandons his survey of the corners to lap noisily.

"No," she says, plucking two of the ripe plums from a plate on the table and handing them to the boy. "We are not going to be attacked. But it is best that you start for home, in order to tell your parents what has happened. And perhaps suggest that your father close the barn before dark, and shutter the windows and bar the door tonight."

Small Henry's eyes grow huge.

"You are saying they will come?"

"No," my mother says again. "But it is best to be careful. Just for a day or two, until their friends are returned to them. And there is no one but you to take the message to your family."

Puffed with sudden importance, he pockets the plums and starts towards the door, calling Tom.

"Do not forget," my mother calls after them as they run up the garden path, "to stop at the stream and let the horse drink!"

When they are gone, she sinks into a chair. I fetch the cider pitcher and pour a cup for each of us.

"What else did he say?" I ask as I watch her drink. "At the end?"

I could not catch the sachem's words, and would not have understood them if I had. The strangeness of the accents and the differences in the language are too much for me. But I know that Egeremet was talking for too long for the message to be solely what my mother relayed to John Alden.

She lowers the cup and looks at me.

"He said Yellow Bird sends his greetings, and is glad my daughter is safe and that her wound is healing well."

❧

TOWARD SUNSET, there is a knock on the kitchen door, which, for once, we have closed. I expect it to be John Alden. But it is Thaddeus. He stands with a bundle slung over his shoulder. As I pull the door wide he looks at first uncertain, then resolute.

"Captain Alden sends his regards," he says. "He is billeted at the fort, but wishes—I wish—" Thaddeus's cheeks flush. He stops and starts again. "We think it better that I should stay here, Captain Alden and I. Since you are two women alone."

We have taken out a haunch of venison, another gift from George Burroughs that, despite the heat, we had roasted the day before, turning it on the summer spit behind the house. There is a jar of walnut pickle. My mother is cutting bread at the table. She looks past me and smiles.

"If you do not mind the pallet again, you can have the front room." She nods toward our parlor, where the chests are now kept because it is never used since my father is gone.

And so Thaddeus Hobbs comes into our home.

John Alden does appear. I am bringing the goats in not an hour later when I see him striding down the meadow, raking a hand through his hair, his shirt sleeves rolled. Thaddeus has been hauling water from the well. We assemble in the kitchen, where my mother has already fetched a bottle of the Malaga wine. As the sun dims and the twilight creeps up from the cove, we listen as John Alden tells of his visit to The Pentagoet, and of his conversations with Saint Castin and Madockawando.

I do not know when I first became aware that the Pentagoet was part of his, and thus of my father's, trade. I think perhaps I had always known. Our place in The Greening during the last war was, after all, secured by the trade they did with Ashawonks. But it is only recently that my understanding of the meaning of it has fully blossomed. John Alden and my father, or at least a facet of them, are in conversation, in trade, and thus in sympathy, with the "savages." Which also means with the French.

Now, I wonder as I watch John Alden roll one of our pewter goblets between his sea-roughed hands, if doing business with the enemy makes them privateers. I suspect it does. The idea is new to me, but not surprising. Listening to him, I also come to understand that John Alden has taken Thaddeus under his wing —that Abigail's brother is now his 'man' in the same way they say Governor Andros is 'the King's man.' While this is certainly better than being under Blackman's heel, I wonder if it will cause Thaddeus the same kind of problems it has caused the Governor —whispers behind his back about allegiance. And I fear it will.

"Saint Castin does not want another war. Nor, he says, do the French. I believe it of him, Saint Castin. Of his masters, I am not so sure." John Alden lifts his goblet and pushes himself back in his chair. An empty dish of what had been venison mopped with bread sits before him.

"Nor is Madockawando itching for a fight. At least if he is not provoked, and the English move no farther north. The two of them, Castin and his father-in-law, don't mind a skirmish now and then. But they made their peace with Andros, and they thought they had an agreement. It would not take much to convince them otherwise. I fear that if our good Governor does not tear himself away from New York soon and see fit to put his hand on this unruly Dominion, they shall indeed be provoked. That was the warning Egeremet delivered today." John Alden nods, half to himself and half to us. "Make no mistake about it, Egeremet speaks for the Pentagoet as well as for himself. His word is Madockawando's. And Castin's, at least the Indian half of him. What they are saying is, strike one, you strike them all. And, if that comes to pass, we shall have real trouble."

He takes a long drink.

"Blackman is a fool. A small man, and glory hungry with it. And he's being used by Boston, and the Mathers and all the Godmongers who would rather be dead than ruled by a Catholic. An option," John Alden adds, smiling, "I fear they may soon be allowed to exercise, if things go on as they are."

"I have written to Philip English." My mother's voice is quiet. "I told him what was happening here. And what we fear. Although I am sure he already knows. I begged him to implore Andros to return."

"Well, Philip English may succeed where others have failed. They grew up together. And coin speaks." John Alden drains his wine and reaches for the bottle. "Let's just hope it speaks without delay. And that those idiots have done nothing with those captives. I have sent word to Boston, today. And just finished standing over your admirer, Tyng—" he smiles at my mother, "guiding his fat hand across the page as he wrote the order to bring them back. Not that he took much convincing. He was simply too terrified to form the words. They were impressive," he adds, "were they not?"

He is speaking of Egeremet and his sons, not of Edward Tyng's words.

I think of the canoes with their prows painted with bears and wolves and birds, and of the dip of paddles, flashing them through the water. They say that when there is a war party, the warriors sing in time to the strokes. They say that is how they speed themselves to battle, and that if the wind is blowing in the right direction, you can hear their song under the tide, beating like the heart of the sea.

"What will they do? Egeremet and his men?"

It is Thaddeus who asks. John Alden shrugs.

"I don't know," he says. "It depends a great deal upon what we do. And on how fast we do it. If we return the captives, and none of them are dead, probably nothing. If not," he shrugs. "Our fate is in our own hands." He raises the pewter goblet. "We shall see," he says, "how we conduct ourselves, and what the gods decree."

❧

IN THE DAYS that are to come, I will think back upon those words. Perhaps they struck me then as portentous. But to be honest, I think they did not. John Alden left soon after. He said he had a billet at the fort, and that it was a good thing as he could keep an eye on the militia—which, with a smile at Thaddeus, he called "a rag-tag bag of scoundrels,"—and more importantly on the supply of shot and powder. He bid us bar the door when he left. We did not, but my mother did shoot the bolt. Then, we lit the candles and latched the shutters, and then, all at once, as if the day had landed suddenly upon us, we were tired.

Thaddeus made his bed on the pallet in the front parlor. My mother and I climbed the stairs. I would like to say that I lay awake. That I had some great premonition of what was to happen, what was happening even then, beyond our four walls. Beyond the summer cloud that was our house and the garden and the milking shed and meadow and poor little Percy's grave. But that would not be true. Instead, I slept, curled against my mother's back, breathing in the scent of her, and of the summer night. I may or may not have clasped the manitou in my fist. If I felt the brush of Yellow Bird's wing against my cheek, if I rode The Night Spirit into dreams, if I hovered, lost and cold among the stars, I do not remember it. Nor do I remember hearing any sound, any lick or whisper or jangle of tiny bones from the cove, or on the beach, or in the birch grove.

So, it was not until the next morning that I suspected anything at all unusual had happened, and not happened, at least to us.

For once, I woke before my mother. Light crept through the shutter cracks, fingering the smooth paleness of her cheek, brushing the faint rise and fall of her chest. I watched her, thinking of the spring and the sickness and willing myself to believe that it was gone, not just hiding—crouching in the corner, waiting to amble out again with its tail switching.

Then, remembering Thaddeus was in the house, I slipped

out of bed and pulled on my dress and stuffed my hair under a cap. I would go to the shed, and we would have fresh milk. And if I had enough corn meal left, and could find some berries above the cove, we would have hot bannock with it. This was what I had in mind as I went barefoot down to the kitchen and padded across the flagstones to draw back the bolt.

It was a beautiful morning. The sky was already translucent blue. The bees were at work. Their buzzing followed me as I retrieved the pail from the stillroom and crossed the garden. Once more, we had not had rain, and there almost no dew in the meadow. I wondered if, and when, we might need to worry about our well running dry. Spiders had woven their webs into the corners of the fence where the posts met the rails. Ahead, I could see the flat stone of Percy's grave, and I thought that later I would cut some of the Queen Anne's lace that edged the meadow, and leave a bouquet upon it.

The earth was warm beneath my feet as I wandered down the paddock. I had not brought my crutch. As if Yellow Bird's message made it so, I was certain I was healing, and hoped that soon the scar on my leg would seal itself once and for all, and I could take the linen wrap off and walk as I used to. These were the things that preoccupied me as I reached the milking shed, and saw the door. As my fingers opened and the pail fell, thudding, onto the summer grass.

Without warning, the world stilled around me. As it had that day on the point, and again the night I saw the figure, and while I was swimming, and in the forest as I faced the wolf. This time, the fence line and the milking shed, the drying grass of the paddock, Percy's grave, the spires of the birches rising from the grove—all of it looked suddenly flat and too bright, like a reflection on water. One that rippled as I watched, as if a faint wind, or a giant wing, had brushed across it.

Without realizing, I raised a hand, covering the stone that nested, still sleep warmed, against my chest. My other hand went to my cheek, fingers splaying in unconscious imitation of the marks that ran down the door and covered the shed wall facing the cove.

Bright yellow, glistening in the morning sun, they seemed to move. To writhe. As if, at any moment, they might slither down. Leave the rough wood and take to the grass. Come and wrap themselves around my bare feet, and twine up my legs. Embrace my body in coils of yellow snakes as they licked their message onto my naked skin.

I stepped back. Once. Twice. Then I turned and ran for the house.

As I came around the corner, I saw my mother, dressed and standing in the open kitchen door with Thaddeus behind her. At first I thought that somehow they knew—that they too had seen the yellow snake marks. Then I realized that they were not watching me. They were looking to the meadow. Grasping the paddock post, I stopped.

The Smiths' little bay mare was cantering down the path. Even from a distance, I could see that she was wild-eyed, her harness flapping, the cart bouncing behind her. The driver was hunched over, and at first I thought it must be Small Henry, and that something had happened to Hannah or Tiny Hannah and he had raced to fetch us, his shirt billowing around him. Then I realized that was not right. It was Hannah herself who was driving, clutching the baby and fumbling the reins, trying not to fall off the bench.

We ran, reaching the gate together, Thaddeus, my mother, and me.

The mare jerked to stop. Thaddeus grabbed her harness. My mother jumped, grabbing the baby from Hannah Smith who was tumbling out of the cart, her colorless hair wild, tears streaming down her face.

"I did not know where to go! I did not know where to go!"

Thaddeus's eyes met mine as, words spewing from her, Hannah fell into my mother's arms.

"Just at first light," she babbled. "We had barred the doors.

But night was past, and they had to do the milking. We thought it was safe. Henry and Small Henry went out to the barn. And that's when they took them. From the barn!" She wailed. "The savages just took them!"

PART III

THE DEVIL'S GLOVE

CHAPTER THIRTY-FIVE

All day, reports come in. It is the same from almost every outlying farm and house. In the hour before dawn, the Indians had come and plucked husbands and boys. Picked them like ripe fruit as 'hostages for their peace,' as Edward Tyng had put it. An eye for an eye, a heart for a heart, to keep until their own were returned.

A militia patrol went out, gingerly, and came back with its sometime commander, one Captain Walter Gendle, missing. Snatched, they said, from before their eyes. One moment he had been there. The next, he was gone. By sunset, the tally is sixteen.

We gather at The Ordinary. My mother stays at the house to care for Hannah and Tiny Hannah, so I go with Thaddeus. The bell has rung through the afternoon. Edward Tyng's ordered the summons, but we all know we have come to hear John Alden.

People are milling in The Ordinary dooryard and in the dusty street where Joseph Ingersoll has set out a board and barrel. Stacks of tankards are at his side. Calamity is good business. Ingersoll taps the cask and does the pouring while his wife collects the coin and Judah hands out the ale. I see a burly man slap her on the arse and another grab for her waist, and I wonder which, if either of them, is her militia sweetheart. She is laughing, her face lit with excitement, her cheeks so pink that I think at any moment she will lift her skirts, dance a jig and burst into song as she did in the clearing.

Perhaps her man is, after all, safe with Captain Blackman, and Abigail was lying. Judah never came searching for the canoe's paddle. If her happiness is anything to go by, her sweetheart cannot be among the captives. If he exists at all. For a moment, I entertain the idea that he does not. Imagine that I have woven this hurt, this betrayal, out of thin air. But it is not true. Because in the next second I see again the quick dart of Judah's hand, the same one that bears our scar of sisterhood, as she crossed herself at the sight of me. And I hear her words. *The Devil walks on water*.

If Judah has noticed me, she is ignoring me. Thaddeus takes my arm. We sidle through the crowd, edging past Peter Cloyce and his wife, who is already holding a tankard. Sylvanus Davis stands with them, his old hat pulled so low that he looks as if he has no eyes, just a bulbous nose. Thaddeus finds us a place at the side of the steps. Above us, John Alden leans in The Ordinary doorway, his arms crossed. In front of him on the top step, Edward Tyng, who has polished his boots for the occasion, waves a piece of paper toward George Burroughs, who finally snatches it and begins to read, his brow furrowed. Across from us, his wife is talking so fast that it is hard to imagine words keeping up with her lips. Goody Burroughs bends towards Mercy Lewis's mother. Mercy and her father are nowhere to be seen. But I do catch sight of William Hobbs, and Abigail. She is hanging from his hand. She looks over her shoulder, and it may be my imagination, but I am sure that when she sees me, she winks.

Then George Burroughs raises his arms. I can see Tyng's paper, stuffed hastily into the pocket of the black coat our minister wears for preaching—which seems to be what he is going to do now.

"We are gathered under the eyes of God!"

Harvard College may not have ordained him, but George

Burroughs has an impressive voice, the more so because it comes from such a small man. The crowd hushes.

"We are gathered here under the eyes of God, in this place, seeking peace!"

"Bah!" Someone shouts from back by the road.

Another joins in. "The savages don't seek peace! Who seeks peace in the face of demons?"

"Our Lord!" Bellows Burroughs. "Our Lords seeks peace and the love of all mankind. Especially those who, ignorant of his grace are savage in their actions, but not their hearts! It is our job, our duty in this new land, to open their eyes and write His grace and peace upon their hearts that we may live together. Or else, surely, we all shall perish together."

A murmur runs through the crowd, though whether of approval or not, I cannot tell. Nor do I have time to wonder because John Alden has straightened. Unfolding his arms, he steps forward.

"Well said, Minister."

He places a hand on Burroughs' shoulder, then looks out over the faces that have turned toward him. The lowering sun catches his hair, burning it bronze, then golden. For a moment in the last light of this day, John Alden looks like the boy, and the young man, he once was. He looks probably much as he did when my mother and father first met him on their arrival from Jersey.

"Good people of Falmouth, you'd do well," he says, "to heed your Minister, for he is wise. If you seek this war, if you move to fight, you will all be dead."

"What of God's love?" Someone shouts from the shadows.

The sun is setting. There is a while yet before dark, but Ingersoll directs one of his stable boys to fix the first torches to the brackets on the dooryard gate. Flames jump above the crowd, making it look like holy fire is dancing on air.

"God's Love," John Alden shouts back, "will be a mighty comfort, I am sure, in the face of Madockawando."

At the mere mention of the name, the crowd falls silent.

Finally, someone murmurs, "Then, what shall we do?"

I sense that this is the moment John Alden has been waiting for. He comes to the front of the top step, all but pushing Edward Tyng aside.

"How many?" He raises his hands as if he too is preaching. "How many," he asks, "taken today?"

"Sixteen," someone calls from back in the road.

"Sixteen." John Alden nods. "And how many did Blackman take?"

No one answers.

"How many?" He asks again, then answers himself. "Twenty. Your militia, in its Christian wisdom, took twenty. Half of them women and children and the other half of them old, except Hope Hood. Their leader. You took him, too. For no reason. What had those people done to you, except sell you land you have no wish to pay for? And then, what did you do? Did you keep them here to bargain with? To trade? No! Though you've a perfectly good fort. Instead, you sent them to Boston! And who among you can say that you know what will happen to them in Boston? Though you'd better," he mutters dropping his voice, "damn well hope it's nothing."

"It was Blackman's doing! Blackman's, not ours!"

I cannot see who shouts, but I fancy the voice may belong to one of the Cloyces. The light is sinking now, quickly, as it does at the end of summer. More torches are lit, but half the faces are lost in shadow.

"It was Blackman's doing," John Alden agrees. "You're right there. That's what happens when you let the militia rule. But—" He raises both hands, holding his palms up in a calming motion. "That is what Egeremet knows, too. That is what he was told, and what he believes, and that is why he has done this. He has taken like for like, not to hurt them, or kill them, but to be certain that our good magistrate here—" John Alden waves towards Tyng, all but hitting him in the face. "To be certain that our good magistrate keeps his word. And recalls Captain

Blackman with his ship of captives. When the sachems see they are returned and in good health, they will return those they have taken. Like for like. Because, as with you, the last thing they want is another war."

There is quiet, then murmuring as the crowd chews this over.

"But the French do!" Someone shouts. "The French want war because they are Catholic! And wish to rule us all and make us bend our knees to Rome! And the savages belong to the French!"

"This has nothing to do with the French!" Alden snaps. "No one caused this but Blackman. When Blackman provides the remedy, it will cease."

"And what do we do in the meantime?" It is Sylvanus Davis who blurts the question, the words smeared with ale, and fear.

"Not panic." John Alden barks. He looks at the crowd. "We must wait," he says more gently. "And not panic. Panic will get us nowhere. We must wait until Egeremet contacts us, or Blackman returns the captives. The sachem will know when Blackman's ship comes in sight. Then, we will negotiate. If they had wanted to attack us," he adds, "they would have attacked us. Yesterday. This morning. As we slept. There are more of them than us. It would not have been difficult. But they did not. And they will not. Nor shall they harm your brothers and husbands and sons. So long as we keep our word, and do not panic. Panic, gentlemen. Panic," he adds, "is oil to flames. And once this fire is lit, believe me, it will burn so hot it will consume us all, Christian and savage alike."

There is silence. Flames flicker across upturned faces, catching some, drowning others. John Alden turns on his heel and walks back into The Ordinary. Edward Tyng bustles after him. From where we are standing, I can see them, nothing more than shapes against the candles that light the hall and front room.

George Burroughs mounts the steps again. Again, taking advantage of the hush, he raises his hands and asks that we pray with him, for the pain of families in their distress, and for the captives' safe return. I notice that he is careful not to say which ones.

Thaddeus bows his head as the words begin. Which is when I look up and see Judah starting down the side of The Ordinary towards the back where the washing is done, a basket of empty tankards in her arms. Touching Thaddeus's shoulder to let him know I will return, I slip from his side and follow her.

CHAPTER THIRTY-SIX

The back yard of The Ordinary is lit by yet more torches flickering from brackets set in the stable wall. I can see the dark rumps of the horses Joseph Ingersoll rents shifting in their stalls. One looks out and puts his ears back, then turns away as I approach. Judah is beside the well, bent over a tub she is filling with tankards. She does not hear me until I am almost close enough to touch her.

When she looks up, something like fear flashes across her face, and the blade in my heart twists again. For a moment, I am tempted to reach my hand out, palm up, showing the thin line of the scar that binds us. Instead, I ask just one word.

"Why?" I think I know the answer, but something in me needs to hear her say it. "Why?" I ask again.

Judah White straightens, the ale-stinking tankards at her feet. Her cap is pushed back. Dark curls stick to her brow and flushed cheeks. She raises both hands to brush them away as she faces me.

"Why did you come searching for the paddle? Who were you going to give it to?"

"You lied." In the shadows thrown by the torches I cannot tell if, this evening, Judah's eyes are gray or green. "I know you lied," she says. "I knew it the moment I heard the story. About losing the paddle and being lost in the marshes. And if I could have proved it, then they could have made you tell where the savages are. I know you were with them." Judah laughs, but there is no warmth or humor in it. "Where else could you have been? If I had proved you were lying, they could have made you tell where their camp is, and we would have attacked it, and none of this would have happened."

I feel a surge of rage, sudden and unexpected.

"What do you mean, none of this would have happened?"

"This is your fault." Judah stares at me. There is bitterness in her voice, something close to contempt. "We choose sides," Judah says. "All of us. And you chose yours. You sided with the savages instead of us. I am not surprised. But if you had told the truth, if, for once, you had been on our side, and told the militia where you had been, where the savages camp, then they could have killed them all, and none of this would have happened. All those men and boys would be safe."

I stare at her.

"You are mad."

"No. Not me."

I am preparing to tell her what happened. To explain that there were no men in the camp, so attacking and killing a group of women and children and old people and Yellow Bird, whether he is old or not, which I do not know, would have not only done no good, it would have made things worse. Would truly have been oil upon the fire. I want to tell her that, in any case, it would not have happened, no matter what I said, or who had the stupid paddle... Because the camp would have vanished. They were preparing to move even as I left.

The words are on my tongue when Judah speaks again.

"You are only lucky," she says, "that I did not tell them all I know of you, and your family. Or else they would have come for you, and forced you to tell the truth."

In the dying light, with the jumping flames of the torches,

her face is both very pale and dark at once. She is more of a shape, a furious thing standing in front of me, than the person I know. Or thought I knew. Suddenly, I hear my mother's voice, as clearly as if she is standing beside me, and remember how she warned me not to tell Judah too much, or possibly anything at all. For the first time, I understand what my mother must have seen, or guessed, or simply felt. And I know what the blade in my heart is. It is not just the knowledge that Abigail Hobbs is right, it is that I have known it for some time, too. I cannot trust her. Because not only does Judah White no longer love me like a sister, now she may even be an enemy.

When did it happen? When did the change take place? Was it when I told her what I had dreamed? Or when I slapped Abigail? Did she secretly think me cruel, or deranged, or both? Or was it when she saw me swimming? Did she think me witched? Or, worse, bewitching? Or has it been there ever since I told her about our time in The Greening, a poison seed waiting to sprout and twine itself around her heart.

Cold runs through me. *No,* I tell myself. It must be the militia man, whomever he is, whispering in her ear. Is he jealous? Or merely looking to curry favor with Blackman, and sees her as the route, since she is close to us and half the world knows we are close to the sachems. Are these his seeds, the poison flowers he has planted and now plans to harvest? In which case it is he who is the true enemy. Not her.

"Who would you have given it to," I ask. "The paddle. If you had found it?"

Knowing seems suddenly important, as if it will explain everything. Judah frowns, confused.

"The paddle," I say. "Who would you have given it to? What is his name?"

A slow smile spreads across her face, as if a point has been proved.

"Why does it matter?" She asks. "Are you jealous?" Judah leans towards me. Her eyes shine in the torch light. I think she is going to laugh. "You do not know him," she says. "But he loves me."

"How can he love you? He barely knows you!"

The words are cruel, and out of my mouth before I can snatch them back.

"You wouldn't understand!" Judah spits. The smile is gone now. "You are a traitor, just like your mother, and still everyone has always loved you both. Your father, Captain Alden, oh yes—" She is so close that I can feel the heat of her breath. "Just look at how he looks at her!" Judah exclaims. "Even George Burroughs is the same! Are you blind as well as stupid? It does not matter what you do, either of you! And now you have that milk sop you call your angel who follows you around like a moon cow!"

It takes me a moment to realize she is talking about Thaddeus. Before I can say anything, she goes on.

"Well, I had nothing," Judah spits. "Nothing and no one. Except scraps from your family table. Charity and kind words, when your parents saw fit to give them to me, so long as I was grateful. And kind to you. And only because I replaced Elizabeth Bourne, who was a thief. But now, I am loved! I am no longer your creature!"

I feel as if I have been slapped. The tide of her anger, this rage released as if from a broken dam, hits me so hard it takes my breath away. I want to raise my palms. To stop the water, and remind her of the scar. Of the mingling of our blood. Of all the patterns of all the shells we have laid down to be swallowed by the tides.

"I know—" I say.

But, in truth, I do not know. And even if I did, Judah cuts me off.

"You know nothing!" She spits, and I am sure I see tears on her face. "You," Judah White says, "do not even know who you are."

"Do you love him?" My question is barely a whisper, as if I

cannot gain enough breath to speak. "Do you love him?" I ask. "Is that why?"

That, at least, I could understand. I could comprehend betrayal for love. Judah looks at me as if I am a fool.

"I do not need to love him." Her voice drops to something like a hiss. "That is how stupid you are, that you cannot comprehend. I do not need to love him. I need him to love me. I need him to believe me. I need him in debt to me. Then, he will marry me."

Judah straightens. She steps back and looks at me with something almost like sadness in her face. "He will marry me," she says again, her voice suddenly flat. "And buy my indenture. And then, like you, I will be free."

CHAPTER THIRTY-SEVEN

"We all wish to be free."

I have told Thaddeus what Judah said. This is his reply.

"We all wish to be free," he says again. "But it cannot be. We fall into the world ensnared in God's love, and live entangled in our love for one another." Thaddeus flicks the reins, geeing the little brown mare into a trot. "Only angels are free," he says as we pass the Brackett farm and turn north along the Back Cove.

Despite the furor of the day, and night, before. Despite the taking of captives, and the yellow snake marks that no one else could see. Despite John Alden's fine words at The Ordinary, and my confrontation with Judah, the world goes on. And the Lord's creatures go on with it. Henry and Small Henry may have been taken, and Hannah and Tiny Hannah may have fled, but the Smith cattle still need watering and feeding and milking. Which is what Thaddeus and I have set off to do.

After she was finished last night, Judah had turned away from me. She had reached for a block of lye soap and bent to her filthy tankards while I stood, as dumb and stupid as she had accused me of being, until finally I recovered myself enough to speak, to try somehow to reply to her. But before I could form a word, she had raised a weary hand.

"Leave me alone," she had said, not even looking at me. "Go away."

And so, I had.

I trailed up the passage beside The Ordinary, and found Thaddeus waiting for me, talking with a militia member I did not know. George Burroughs was gone, and his wife, and the Lewises. There was no sign of William Hobbs or Abigail. The board that had held the cask was bare and the coin pot was empty. The night smelled of spilled ale, and burning pitch, and fear.

Thaddeus and I walked up Broad Street and crossed the common that is now trampled flat. I do not know how much he guessed, of what passed between Judah and me. He did not ask, and I felt numb, so we walked in silence while behind us torches and more torches flared despite the fire risk.

Our house floated ahead of us as we came down the meadow, and again I thought it was like a ship, barely anchored on the cusp of another world. Candles flickered in the windows. The stars swam in their lazy river, and all around fireflies sparked the tall grass. My mother had not put out flares, and I knew that when Thaddeus and I arrived, the gate would not be chained. Nor would we have to knock at the kitchen door, which would be unlatched. Because we were not, and are not, and will not be, in danger. At least not in danger from 'savages.'

I told Thaddeus then, as we walked down the meadow, about the marks on the shed door and on the wall. And I told him how, yesterday morning as my mother settled the Hannahs and he ran to the village with the news that the Henrys had been taken, I had taken a pail with rags and a lump of lye soap and a jar of vinegar and gone back to the milking shed. But when I got there, the door and the wall facing the cove looked as they always have. The snakes were gone. But I understood the message, the same one delivered by Egeremet. Yellow Bird is watching over us.

So, in her way, Judah is right. Perhaps we did not choose, but we have been chosen.

❧

THE SMITH FARM does not look any different. Nothing is burned or plundered. The fences are not broken. No sacks and jars of foodstuffs are trailed across the yard. A father and son were plucked from this place just yesterday. A dozen years ago, lives were taken. But the fields are still green. Wild flowers still bend in the wind. Looking down from the cart's driving bench I do not know, if I walked across this land, if I would feel any memory at all.

The little horse pricks her ears as we reach the house and climb down. She meanders towards the trough even before Thaddeus can free her from her harness. Inside the barn, cows are lowing. They have not been milked, and their udders will be swollen and sore. There are two of them. Small Henry told me their names were Bess and Belle, but I find when we open the barn doors that I cannot remember which is which.

It takes me almost an hour to do the milking. After I have finished, we cap the pails and lift them into the cart. Then I find corn and spread it for the doves before I follow Thaddeus into the house to look for the things—swaddling cloths, and a spare dress, and two aprons, and a hung turkey that will spoil if it is not cooked—that Hannah asked us to fetch. She and the babe both slept as if half dead last night with, I suspect, some help from my mother. They are in our front room now. Thaddeus helped us take out and set up our second bed. He fitted the head board and tightened the mattress ropes of what had once been my parents' marriage bed while I aired and swatted the bolsters, puffing their goose down, and my mother found a basket big enough for Tiny Hannah. The pallet was rolled and unrolled again in its old place by the hearth before my mother and I climbed the stairs.

Now I feel like a thief going through Hannah's things, opening her chest and fingering her marriage goods. Some of the linen is yellowed with age. I suspect it was her mother's, and even her grandmother's, before it was hers. An H is embroidered in every corner, and I wonder if they are all Hannahs to match the Henrys, and if so, how far the chain of them, woman to woman, hand to ankle, will one day stretch.

When I have collected what we were sent for, I latch and bar the shutters and the main door. I find the key where Hannah said it would be, under the tinder box that sits on the hearth shelf, and let myself out, locking the kitchen door behind me. Thaddeus has been busy, too. As well as the milk and the belongings I have packed, a sack of grain has been loaded into the cart. Bess and Belle nose it with interest. Thaddeus has collared them and tied them to the tail gate. The doves can care for themselves, the cows cannot.

We risked coming this morning in no small part because of Yellow Bird's signs and the disc I wear above my heart. But no one knows what will happen in the days ahead. So Bess and Belle must come and live with us in the paddock that adjoins the milking shed. My goats will not like it, but our cow will not mind. She was happy enough to share her stall with the little bay horse last night, and will be glad to have the company of others of her kind. Not two hours after we arrived, we set off again with the cart loaded and the cows plodding behind us. Thaddeus holds the reins as I sit beside him, thinking we must look for all the world like a little family setting out to find its future.

We have almost reached the end of the Smith farm track when I hear the noise. At first, I think something must have startled the geese who are still feeding in the shallows before they fly south. But it is not honking. It is more half whimper, half yap. Thaddeus is whistling. I reach for his arm.

"Stop!"

He looks at me, then pulls the horse to a halt. The yap comes again, louder now. Before Thaddeus can speak or ask me what I am doing, I clamber down. My leg and foot are better, but I still cannot jump. Making my way to the back of the cart where Bess and Belle stand shifting their big hooves in the dust, I raise my hand to my eyes. The sun is directly behind us. The farm is a silhouette, fences criss-crossing back towards it. At first, I don't see anything. Then, trotting along the track in our wake, his tail dragging as if he is too tired to lift it, I see Tom.

The little dog must have recognized the cart and the horse. I wonder that he did not come out when we first arrived. And then I think that perhaps he has only just arrived himself. When I pick him up, he is covered in burrs and I can tell that he is so exhausted he can barely stand. I have heard stories of dogs, and even cats, that have traveled miles to be reunited with their families, and I wonder if Tom tried to follow Small Henry when he was taken. If he was chased from a camp, or finally could not keep up, or was left when the captives were put into canoes. Perhaps he even tried to swim, and finally turned back and made his way home, arriving just in time to see us leave.

I cradle him in my arms and stroke the top of his little head, and hand him up to Thaddeus while I climb back onto the driving bench. Then I take Tom in my lap, and spend the drive home picking burrs out of his coat and dropping them by the wayside. Before I am near finished, he is asleep.

We have turned down Cleeve's Neck and across Ware Creek and are half way to the village, turnip fields stretched on either side of us, when I see Judah. At first, I do not recognize her. I merely think it is a canoodling couple and that they are taking a chance, close as they are to the minister's fields. If Goody Burroughs is out with her hoe, she will spot them, and who knows what stories will be all over the village before sunset. Then I see the curls of black hair and the familiar sway of the hips, and know at once who I am looking at.

Thaddeus sees them too. His face stiffens. They pull apart, Judah slapping the man in mock anger as she jumps away over a plowed furrow. I know she has seen us. We are the only cart on the road. But she looks away, laughing, and bends down to adjust her shoe as we pass. The man is tall and brown haired. He is older, though I cannot guess how old, and has his musket slung across his back, so perhaps this passes for a patrol. He turns toward us and raises a hand in what looks like mock salute.

"Do you know who he is?" I ask after we have left them behind, but Thaddeus does not reply.

FOR THREE DAYS AFTER THAT, nothing happens. The militia marches around the fort, but does not venture out of its sight. The fishing boats do not go out. The hay has mostly been brought in. No one works the fields. At night, the torches are lit. Every morning the harbor and the sea beyond are empty. John Alden grumbles as he and Thaddeus stand in their shirt sleeves mending our fence where the goats, angry as I predicted, climbed on it and broke a rotting rail. He doubts Edward Tyng sent his letter to Boston, and calls him a liar. When by the third night there is still no sign of Captain Blackman or his ship, we fear he might be right. Then, on the fourth morning, Captain Walter Gendle comes back from the dead.

I am not the least bit surprised that the person who finds him is Abigail.

CHAPTER THIRTY-EIGHT

I have finished the milking, which takes much longer now that there are three cows, and am bringing the goats back from the meadow when the small figure bursts from the birch grove. I know Abigail has been on the point. I have not seen her coming or going, but I have felt her there. More than once in the last few days—as I have been hanging laundry or lifting a pail of water, finishing the garden cutting or raking the gravel—I have felt the sinew's tug, and found myself looking towards the grove and the start of the track almost as if I can hear her calling my name.

Now, she is running.

Abigail's cap has come loose and hangs about her neck. Set free, her gold mop sparkles in the sun. She does not hold up her skirts. They are a child's still, and short. Instead, Abigail runs with her hands lifted at her sides, her small legs churning and her arms flapping as if she expects to take flight.

"A black man!" She cries, her voice high with delight and excitement. "They have given us a black man!"

At the sight, and sound, of her, the goats startle and buck. They scatter as Abigail hurtles into me, nearly knocking me off my feet.

"A black man!" She is jumping up and down, clapping her small white hands and snatching at me. "Come see! Come see!" She cries. "The savages have brought us a black man!"

And that is indeed what Walter Gendle looks like when we find him, staggering down the track from the point. His face is filthy. It is only later that I realize it is covered in soot, or mud and ashes—a trick John Alden says the Indians use when they wish to move white captives at night. Gendle has black hair, and a black mustache. He is wearing a black coat that might once have been fine but is now ripped and flaps about him like crows' wings. He wears dark breeches and still has his black boots. His hands, which stretch before him pathetically, as if he is blind, have also been blackened. The overall effect is exactly as Abigail says.

She dances around my mother and me as we stand staring at the apparition that weaves toward us through the birches, uncertain because, not being acquainted with the man himself or the Saco militia, we do not yet know who, or what, he is.

"A black man!" Abigail shrieks. "A black man!"

It is Thaddeus, when he comes running from behind the shed where he has been mending harness, who both recognizes Captain Gendle and tells her to shush. Abigail shows him her tongue, poking it out and waggling her fingers at him before skittering away. She slides down the bank to the cove, disappearing as the poor creature we now know has been a captive finally collapses at our feet.

"A black man! A black man! He came from Hell as fast as he can!" We hear her singing from the beach as we half carry, half drag the militia commander back to the house.

❧

IT IS NOT until after Thaddeus has fetched Captain Alden, and we have washed Walter Gendle's face and his hands, and watched him drink near a pitcher of cider that, in dribs and drabs, the story begins to come out.

"I know the ministers preach that we are all God's children. But I would be a liar if I said I believed it! I never did. And I never will!" Walter Gendle babbles.

I look at my mother. We have seated Gendle before the hearth. Hannah hovers at the kitchen table where Tiny Hannah sleeps in her basket, undisturbed by our voices. Thaddeus pulls out a chair for her, then sits himself. John Alden leans against the far wall by the open window, his arms crossed.

My hand is upon Walter Gendle's brow, wiping away the last remains of ash and mud with a cool cloth. He is obviously exhausted, and when we got him back to the house was either too terrified, or too distracted to say anything. Now, I wonder if, although I cannot feel it, he has a fever? Or has been hit in the head and had his brains knocked loose? I wonder if I should make up a willow tea, or fetch a compress?

John Alden intercepts the look I throw my mother, and shakes his head. He raises a finger, telling me to be silent.

"I came as soon as I heard! That the sachem had come, with his army. The devil! And by water, too, so they could not be pursued. Cowards! I heard what he'd said, the threats he'd made, and I knew Blackman was gone to Boston. I knew the militia would be needing an experienced hand, in his absence, and came to offer my services. I came to do my duty!"

Walter Gendle looks from one to the other of us, as if waiting for us to agree. When no one says anything, he fastens on my mother, who nods and smiles her encouragement.

"I know the ways," he says. "Of the savages. I've had some experience. And I've a wife to home. So, as soon as we had news of captives taken, I thought it best if I took a patrol south. I thought it best to take my men that way, seeing I knew the road. I'd ridden, of course, and we were marching. I had them make haste, double time. And when we arrived, I knew! I knew at once," he says, "that something dreadful had happened!"

"Your wife?" My mother asks.

Walter Gendle shakes his head.

"My mill! All my workmen, every one was gone. And my negro! The place was still as a grave."

By the window, John Alden twitches. I wonder if he is thinking, as I am, of the farms and houses Gendle must have passed, marching double time without stopping to check if captives had been taken from them, if they needed help, or if the inhabitants were even still there.

"I sent my men." Walter Gendle says. "I told them to go around back, to check the wood lots, make sure no savages were hiding there like the coward rats they are. Skulking dogs who will not come out to fight. And I, I went to be sure the coin chest was where it should be. It was as I was coming out. They were everywhere. They held a knife to my throat—"

His voice quivers. I grasp the cider cup just as Walter Gendle lets go of it to raise both hands to his neck.

"I thought they were going to cut it. I thought myself scalped and gutted, right there in the door of my own mill! There had to be twenty of them. And before I knew what they were about, before I could draw a firearm or sword, they had me. I was borne away, and the next thing I knew I was gagged and bound and run through the forest like an infernal dog!"

I cannot help but look at Tom, curled under the table.

"Infernal!" Walter Gendle says again. "They marched us all that night, into the foulest of swamps. Then, at morning, they boarded us into canoes. There were six, seven, of us in the group I was in by then. All men and boys, including my negro. It was on the island, that I saw how many there were, a dozen or more captives, and no hope for escape. It is a war camp! Swarming. There are hundreds of them. Demons upon demons! The place is Hell itself!"

"My husband!" Hannah can contain herself no longer. "My husband, good Henry Smith. And my son, a Henry too. A boy.

Did you see them? They have flame colored hair, and are alike, one a smaller copy of the other. Did you see them?"

Walter Gendle looks at Hannah as if he has only just realized she is in the room. He stares at her for a moment before he nods.

"Aye," he says, confused at having his story interrupted. "They were there."

"And are they well? Are they safe? Are they—"

Hannah cannot finish the questions. Walter Gendle is staring at her, goggle-eyed, which makes me wonder again if he has been hit in the head.

"For God's sake man!" John Alden snaps, "Tell the woman! It's her husband and her son!"

Walter Gendle jumps at the sound of his voice, then nods.

"Yes," he says finally. "Yes." Now he is nodding as if there is something wrong with his neck and he cannot stop. "Yes. Yes. They are unharmed."

He glances at John Alden, alarmed, as if he is afraid Alden will wring the words from him if he does not speak them fast enough.

"No one was injured that I saw," he says. "No one. And we were fed. Venison. Fish. We slept before the fires. Even my negro." Gendle gestures at the cider cup. "Have you anything?" He asks, as if this is The Ordinary and talk of food has reminded him that he is hungry.

My mother goes out. When she returns from the stillroom, she has a wedge of bread and a turkey leg. Walter Gendle reaches for the trencher with both hands, like a child, and sets about tearing the meat as if he has not eaten in a week. When I look at Hannah, she is staring at him. Tears roll down her cheeks.

"I didn't speak to them, as such," Gendle says, swallowing and wiping his mouth with the back of his hand. "But I assure you Mistress, they are well. You've no need for tears."

"Thank you. And Thank God!" Hannah's voice is barely a murmur as she buries her face in her hands.

"And then?" John Alden glances out of the window, then looks from my mother to Gendle. Thaddeus gets up and goes to the open kitchen door.

"Tell us, please," John Alden asks. "How do you come to be here?"

Gendle nods. "By canoe," he says.

John Alden snorts. "Well, I didn't think you swam, man!"

"They blindfolded me!" Gendle drops the turkey bone. "In the middle of the night! The savages raised me up from my sleep, and they blindfolded me and placed me in a canoe!"

"How long?"

John Alden is glancing out the window again. Now, I can hear voices. Men are coming down the meadow. News of our visitor has traveled. Abigail.

"How long," John Alden asks again, "were you in the canoe?"

Gendle shakes his head. "Hours!"

"No," Alden says. "It is not yet noon. And you've been here an hour or more, and were on the point before that. When you were in the canoe, where was the sun? To which side, when it rose?"

"I told you! I was blindfolded!"

"You felt it on your cheek. Left or right?"

"Left," Gendle answers, before he can think.

Alden nods. "So, you came from the north. And how did they drop you? At the cove? The beach?"

"No!" Gendle shakes his head. "No, it was fearsome. I felt the scrape, as the canoe came alongside. And I knew it was rock. I thought they were going to leave me on a Godforsaken rock to be consumed or drowned!"

John Alden snorts again. "What the Hell would they do that for?"

"But it was a cliff!" Gendle exclaims. "A great cliff! They tore the blindfold off, then they pushed me out. And I was clinging to the rock, and begging them. But they turned away, and I cannot swim! I cannot! The savages did not care. There was nothing for me but to climb."

I know where this is, exactly. It is the pink rocks below the clearing where I dug my memory holes. The place where, years ago, mussels would be collected and cracked before being taken up to the smoking fires. The rocks are not a cliff. But Walter Gendle is right. They are steep. Still, there would be little chance he would fall off, if he could climb at all. And there would be little point in returning him if they wished him dead. They had another purpose, I have only just realized. John Alden, as usual, is ahead of me.

"Why?" He asks quickly. "Why did they bring you back? What is the message they sent with you?"

Walter Gendle stares at him. He starts to open his mouth, but before he can answer, Thaddeus is stepping back as Edward Tyng's heavy bulk fills our kitchen door.

CHAPTER THIRTY-NINE

Walter Gendle's second version of his story is quite different from the first.

Edward Tyng has brought so many people with him, what looks to be half the militia as well as half the village men, that we must all move outside. My mother installs Walter Gendle on the bench under the arbor while Thaddeus fetches a chair for magistrate Tyng, who, stuffed into his green coat, is sweating so heavily and is so red in the face that he looks as if he might faint.

Fortified by the turkey leg and the audience, with his face and hands bathed and stripped of the coat that we now know he ripped in his climb up the rocks, Walter Gendle warms to his theme. The resulting tale is far more elaborate. He did not volunteer, the militia called for him. In fact, it was an order left by Blackman himself. The patrol Gendle took out did not march in double time straight down the road to his own mill, but moved stealthily across country, checking every farm, knocking at every door to comfort and reassure distraught families. In fact, they reached his own mill merely by chance, almost by accident. On their arrival, leader of men that he is, Gendle ventured alone into the back wood lot where ten, or more likely twenty, savages ambushed him. He fought valiantly, and shot and possibly killed at least two of them. If not three. Then he volunteered to be taken captive, nobly requesting his men be spared. The war canoes were a fleet, and though the island was again a war camp, it was an even bigger one. It was only Captain Gendle's knowledge of savage ways and his persuasive negotiation that convinced them to release him. There is no mention of 'his negro'. Or of venison, or fish. Or, of course, of his abandoned wife, who doesn't even get a mention in the second version.

When Walter Gendle is finished, there is a silence. Edward Tyng leans back in his chair as if he has just finished a particularly rich meal. The militia men glance between themselves, and it crosses my mind to wonder how many of them were with Gendle and know the truth, and untruths, of this story. The details of the camp were especially lurid the second time around. Scalps hung from branches. War drums beat through the night. There was wild dancing. And all of the captives were bound and gagged and tied to trees. It is a good thing Hannah remained inside with Tiny Hannah, who had woken and begun to fuss.

"And did you come bearing any message?" Tyng asks. "What is it they wish? What are your impressions of their intent?"

Walter Gendle straightens on the bench. "They speak peace," he says. "But no savages can be believed. It is their way, to say one thing and mean the other."

"You believe it is a ruse," Edward Tyng straightens, obviously pleased by the idea of this duplicity, which might absolve him of any responsibility for the mess we find ourselves in. "The taking of the captives? You think it a trick?" He asks, hopefully. "In order to lure us to this island that they may attack us?"

"Why would they do that?" John Alden asks, "When they could have attacked us already? And when they know that if they do, there will be no chance of Hope Hood and his people being returned?"

The question is met with silence. Walter Gendle looks unhappy. He fidgets, and mutters about savages. Edward Tyng nods, as if someone has said something important. Then he heaves himself to his feet.

"We must send to Boston," he says, "at once."

"I thought you had already sent to Boston. What of the letter I saw you write?"

Edward Tyng ignores John Alden again, taking Gendle's arm as if he is an invalid or a child. "Come," our magistrate says, looking around as if he is not altogether certain my mother's garden will not immediately be over-run by savages. "Come, come, we must get you to the fort!"

❧

"HE IS A BALD-FACED LIAR," John Alden says, leaning on our garden gate, watching the group make their way up the meadow, bearing Walter Gendle away as if he is a prize they have claimed.

My goats stop grazing and watch as they pass.

"He was convicted of treason in the last war. And cowardice. Sentenced to run the gauntlet and banished from Boston. We can't believe a word he says. And," John Alden adds turning back to us, "he's an ambitious git. Eager for heroism to redeem his name."

"You think he lied. You think they are not alive?" My mother is barely whispering.

We all glance towards the house where Hannah feeds Tiny Hannah and sheds tears of joy at the news that her husband and her son are alive.

"Not about that," John Alden says. "But we know that. Egeremet isn't stupid. Neither is Yellow Bird. They didn't take captives to kill them. They took them to bargain with. Twenty white men and one poor negro won't be much use if they're dead. It's everything else he's lying about. Why, of all people, would they use Gendle as a messenger? I suppose they don't know any better and he told them he was important." John

Alden lets out a bark of laughter. "Or perhaps they just couldn't stand him any longer, so they sent him back."

"Is it true," Thaddeus asks, "that he keeps a slave?"

"My negro?" John Alden makes a sour face. "Yes. Fancies himself a planter, our Walter. Fond of indentures, too. One was a chit. Aged five. A neighbor's girl. Parents died of the pox. He indentured her until thirteen, out of the kindness of his heart, as a household servant. The child died before she was ten, and Gendle came into her estate. Not that there was much of it. But every little helps. Gendle's a cat with nine lives. Every time a neighbor dies, he profits. Land, sawmills, trading grants. He's made no friends among the sachems. They know all about his sharp ways. My bet is, they shadowed him all the way to his wretched mill and were waiting for him. Militia patrol, my arse. He meant to have a guard for his property. I wonder how much that poor negro promised Egeremet if they would take him and promise never to return him."

There is silence as we watch the group reach the first houses and thread their way through the sideyards. Any minute now, I think, the bell will begin to toll, summoning the village to come hear whatever version of the story Walter Gendle decides to recite next from the steps of The Ordinary. Joseph Ingersoll is probably already setting out his board and sending Judah for fresh tankards. Readying his coin pot. And still there is no sign of Blackman's ship, or its cargo.

"I'll wager," John Alden says, "that Egeremet sent a message. One Gendle does not want to deliver. Otherwise, why release him."

"Why?" My mother asks.

"Why doesn't he want to deliver it? I don't know," John Alden shrugs. "Profit, somehow, probably." He straightens and slaps the gate post. "Or because it reflects too well on the sachems, is altogether too reasonable for 'savages'. I don't know," he shakes his head. "But if it's true, and I'll wager it is, I think it's best we find out what the message was."

"Gendle will not tell you."

"No, Rachel." John Alden looks at my mother, his face softening, her old name rolling off his tongue without thought. "No indeed," he says. "So, we shall have to seek it for ourselves."

❧

THEY LEAVE two hours after sunset. Virtually the entire village is occupied at The Ordinary. While no one was paying attention to anything but Walter Gendle's latest performance, Thaddeus found two paddles in the harbor boat shed and "liberated them," as John Alden calls it. They are not as fine as the one my father made, but they will do. And though it has no wolf's smile, our canoe is strong, and will be fast with two men paddling.

We have packed food, and my mother has sent medicine—salves, bandages, soap—should they, or anyone else need it. With their faces blackened with charcoal, wearing the oldest of my father's clothes that I have rubbed with dirt and ashes, John Alden and Thaddeus Hobbs look like a pair of Abigail's Black Men.

The thin moon hangs like an empty smile as they push the canoe down the launching plank. My mother and I stand on the beach, watching as they wade into the shallows and board quickly and quietly. The water sparks and glistens, night shine trailing from their paddles as they take the first strokes. Within minutes, all we can see is two dark shapes and a silver skin. Then they are gone, and the cove is empty save for mirrored stars.

CHAPTER FORTY

I dream of wolves. Of the high-pitched note of their song, and the soft pad of their journey through the forest. My sleep is filled with the rustle of leaves and glint of yellow eyes. When I wake, I hear them breathing, faintly, in the darkened corners of the room.

The wolves come near the village only rarely, and only in the deepest winter, because they are hungry. When they do, the men go out at twilight with their guns. They patrol the edges of the fields, walk the boundaries of the farmed land as if they are walking the line between holiness and damnation. But they always come back at dark, and they always come empty handed. On those nights the village closes its shutters and listens beside its fires, telling themselves they are safe inside while outside in the snow, the wolves sing.

The memory drives sleep away. It is dark, I don't know how long before dawn. The nights are cooler now, but not much. When I feel my way downstairs, the kitchen is hot and stuffy. I fancy that, with the Hannahs asleep in the front room, the house is warmed by too many bodies.

Unlatching the kitchen door, I step out onto the gravel and make my way to the bench below the arbor where, this spring when she felt unwell, my mother sometimes sat the whole night through. Like the paddle that is now floating who knows where, my father made this bench. Lowering myself onto the smoothed slats, smelling the sweet scent of the grapes that hang in their heavy bunches above me and the woody thatch of the hops that twine between them, I wonder where he is and if he ever thinks of me. Then I wonder where Thaddeus is, and replay in my mind the conversation we had two days ago, in the strange, still time before Abigail's Black Man stumbled down off the point.

❧

I HAD BEEN SETTLING the goats. Our cow, who is a sweet creature, has welcomed both the little bay horse and Bess and Belle. But the goats feel no such generosity. Annoyed, fractious and argumentative, they refuse to be milked. I had loosed them into the paddock, hoping to improve their temper, and was scrubbing the trough before refilling their water when I sensed Thaddeus behind me.

Some men are incapable of moving without rocking the earth. Thaddeus Hobbs is not one of them. He goes silently through the world, barely parting the air. When I looked up, he was leaning on the fence, his shirt sleeves rolled to reveal the summer brown of his arms. His long, almost girlish hands with their perfectly formed blunt-clipped nails that are almost exactly the same as his sister's, picked at a patch of moss. Looking at them, I wondered if the twins, William and Avis, also had those hands, and those nails. If those were the fingers that intertwined as the shallop tipped and breached and they hit the waves, catching their last glimpse of the sun.

Thaddeus looks up. For a second, I think he has seen my thoughts and feel a flush of shame, that I should hang those deaths about him like a garland. But that is not what he is thinking, or if it is, not what he wishes to speak of, because he says, "James Parr."

I frown, not understanding.

"Jamie Parr." Thaddeus stops picking at the moss, letting it drop. "That's his name. The one who is courting your friend."

I think of the young man we saw as we returned from the Smith farm, the slick of sun on his brown curls, the musket over his shoulder, the mock salute and smile he had thrown as we passed.

"How old is he?" I do not know why this is important, but I ask it.

Thaddeus shrugs. "Older than me. His family is from Cape Elizabeth. His father, he says, is a locksmith. I do not know if it is true."

I stop scrubbing the trough. What Thaddeus is not saying hangs in the air between us. Even the goats sense it. They are watching him as carefully as I am.

"He is a bright fellow," Thaddeus says. "A friend to most. He is a good story teller, and not a coward. There are worse men you could have at your side. He dreams of being a farmer, and shall be. Or so he boasts. Because he is betrothed. His soon to be father-in-law owns a great deal of land, south, near Ipswich. Jamie says it is very fine land, and as his promised is an only child she, and he, shall have it all. Her name is Anne. He wears an A, embroidered inside his jacket, over his heart. He shows it off when he is drunk. They are to be wed when he finishes his militia term, in the spring."

Thaddeus is watching me as he speaks.

"I am sorry," he says. "I did not know if I should tell you. It is common knowledge in the fort. Gossip says there is another girl, a fishmonger's daughter on Great Island. Or, there was, when the militia was in Portsmouth. The same gossip says she was ruined, cast out, and has gone south. I am sorry," he says again after a moment. "But I thought it better to tell you. I don't know if you are in a position to warn your friend, or if she will listen to you, if you do. But I do not believe Jamie Parr will give up his betrothal. It is not merely that he boasts of it, and of the wealth and land he will gain, it is also that he cannot afford to. His family has debts. This marriage will be their fortune, and their future. Jamie himself says as much."

I sit back on my heels, the scrub brush idle in my hand.

"And you believe him?"

Thaddeus nods. "Yes. I do. More than one man has lent him money, and been assured that, come spring, it will be repaid."

So, although Judah's sweetheart will be in a position to buy off her indenture, it will only be because he is married to someone else. To say James Parr is unlikely to keep his promises to her is to sell the story short. Thaddeus knows that. So do I. What neither of us know is if Judah will listen to me if I try to warn her.

I had thought of going to George Burroughs. He is our minister, after all. Responsible for our immortal souls, even if he is not ordained. I had thought of speaking with John Alden, even of going to Edward Tyng. But any of that would risk a public commotion. And I know Judah. If she suspects that I have gone behind her back, or that I wish to harm Jamie Parr, her rage will know no bounds. Any attack on him will only make her defend him. But, I must do something. *I need him to love me. I need him in debt to me.* I fear what that may mean. And that I may be too late. *She was ruined, cast out, and has gone south.* My thumb rubs the scar on my palm. Skin to skin. Blood to blood. Heart sister to heart sister.

SHE IS COMING up from the harbor. I thought I would find her here. Although the fishing boats are not going out—or if they are, they are only the small ones that do not venture out of sight of the harbor mouth and the fort towers—we still need salt. The pans are still being set. This heat and endless sun has been good for that, at least. The Ingersolls send Judah each morning for

The Ordinary's portion. That is what I was counting on. And I am correct.

Back along the shore, I can see Mercy Lewis. She, too is coming from the salt shed, carrying a pan in both hands, frowning at it as if the contents might jump out and run away. Behind her, Abigail stands on the beach throwing pebbles at sea gulls. She nearly hits one. The bird, angered, turns and swoops towards her. For a moment, I think Abigail will stand her ground. I imagine her fixing her blue gaze upon the gull, causing it to drop stone dead into the water. Instead, as it swoops close she lets out a mock shriek and leaps and spins and dashes along the beach, running straight into Mercy Lewis. Who screams and drops her salt pan.

"You are a wicked beast!" Mercy shrieks. "You did it on purpose! You are a demon!"

Abigail laughs, and hops, and sticks her tongue out. When Mercy lunges for her, she darts away, disappearing behind a line of upturned wherries.

Judah has stopped to watch. I see she has a new cap. The linen is fine, soft and creamy. A set of crimson ribbons, also clearly new, and fine, lace through the bottom of her bodice, showing above the top of her apron. A matching set threads through the tops of her sleeves. Any brighter, and they would be indelicate. Wearing them in Boston, she would be fined. As it is, they will catch Goody Burroughs' eye, if they have not already. Mercy picks up her salt pan. She holds it for a moment, then drops it again and puts both hands over her face. Judah turns away. She is almost upon me when I speak her name. She stops at the sound of my voice. I am not sure if she truly has not seen me, or if she was merely pretending.

"I must speak with you. Please," I add when I see the look on her face. "Just for a moment."

We are standing below the corner of the common. Judah looks away up Broad Street toward The Ordinary.

"The baking has begun." She glances at me, her voice cool. "They will need the salt."

"Just for a moment," I repeat. "It will not take long. I promise."

And that is true, because my courage will not last long. I will only be able to say what I have to say once. Judah shrugs. I sense that she is about to step past me.

"It is about Jamie Parr."

She stops. A faint smile plays across her beautiful face, as if even the mention of his name is a triumph. I nod toward the common, trampled now to dust and empty since the militia, Jamie Parr among them, gave up drilling after Captain Blackman left.

"Please."

Over Judah's shoulder, I can see that Mercy Lewis has retrieved her pan and is coming toward us, her face red and blotched with either tears or fury, or both.

"That child!" Mercy exclaims as she reaches us. "You can stop smirking! That child is a torment. She is a demon!"

She stomps past us, past the old Hobbs house, the empty salt pan swinging at her side. Judah sticks her tongue out at Mercy's back. Then she turns to me, laughing.

"What about him?" She asks. " What about Jamie? Did the moon cow tell you his name?"

"Yes."

I step backwards, leading Judah away from where people might easily overhear us.

"Yes," I say, deciding not to take up Thaddeus' defense just now. "And that is not all he told me."

Judah nods, her eyes sparkling.

"So, the secret is out," she glances down at the ribbons. "I suppose I should not be surprised. It is after all a joyous thing."

"A joyous thing?" I stare at her.

"To be betrothed. I suppose James boasted of it. Men will do that. Although, we had thought to keep it secret. Until he buys out my indenture. But now the moon cow has told you."

"Betrothed?"

"Yes." She looks at me. "What did you think? You came to wish me happiness, did you not? I told you he would marry me. And now he shall."

"He cannot!"

I blurt it out. I had no idea, exactly, how I would say what needed to be said. How I would warn her. Now I feel as if I am in a runaway cart and the reins have been jerked out of my hands.

"He cannot marry you! You cannot marry him!"

Judah looks at me, amused.

"But I shall. I told you I would."

"No! No, you cannot. Judah, he is promised. To someone else. The date is set."

She stares at me. Then she begins to laugh.

"It's true," I say. "Thaddeus told me. He did not want to, but he had to. It is known. Everyone knows. Her family is from Ipswich. They are wealthy, in land at least. She is an only child. Her name is Anne."

"This is fanciful." Judah smiles, but there is no kindness in it. "Even for you. I know you are jealous. But I did not think you spiteful. But no matter what lies you concoct, or stories you tell, it will not change a thing. James Parr has asked me to be his wife, and I have said yes."

She raises an arm, fluttering the ribbons in my face. "These are my betrothal gift," Judah says. "We had planned to wait, to make our announcement. But now, I suppose you will try to spoil that, too! But it does not matter." She leans her face so close to mine that I can count the summer sun spots scattered across her nose. "You will not ruin this," she says. "Or take it from me. No matter how hard you try."

"He wears an A, embroidered inside his coat. Above his heart."

She leans back as if I have slapped her.

"He does, doesn't he?" I say. "What did he tell you it was for? Who? His sister? His mother?"

"You are wicked."

"No." I feel anger rising in me, an oily swell, mixed with grief. Because I know she will never forgive me for this. "Not me," I say. "It is not me who is wicked. Ask him. Ask James Parr what the A stands for. And ask him about the girl from Great Island. The one who had to go south because she was ruined, and cast out."

Judah steps back.

"He loves me." Her free hand touches the fine new cap, then falls to finger the ribbons at her waist. As she speaks again, I can see tears swelling. The drops cling to her lashes. "He loves me," she says.

I reach toward her. "I am sorry," I whisper. "I am sorry. But it will be alright. Truly, it will. We love you. I love you."

Judah looks at my outstretched hand as if it is a dead thing.

"I do not need your love."

Judah White steps away from me. She turns and walks, very carefully, with her back stiff, as if each step is painful, to the edge of the common. Then she sets foot on Broad Street, and begins to run.

Standing in the middle of the trampled common, feeling the loss of her like something that has been ripped out of me, I close my eyes. When I open them, the village is burning.

In front of me, the roof of the old Hobbs house is in flames. The house behind it has half collapsed. Fire licks the walls of the boat shed. It sputters and flickers from the top of the fort. Yet the sky is clear. There is no smoke. No one is running, or shouting. There is no bucket line on the beach. The bell is not ringing. Nothing moves but the flames.

I gasp, and blink, and they are gone. The Hobbs house with its rickety gate and over-grown garden is in front of me. Judah is still running down Broad Street, carrying the salt pan, the crimson ribbons trailing behind her like falling petals. I feel a small hand slot itself into mine. When I look down, Abigail is standing beside me. She stares after Judah, then looks up.

"You have seen it, too?" She asks.

I nod, my mouth dry. Abigail squeezes my hand.

"Do not be afraid," she says. "It will not hurt us. It is only The Black Man's fire."

CHAPTER FORTY-ONE

A butterfly lands in the honeysuckle. Its wings open and close as it draws the nectar. As if in imitation, the baby's hand does the same thing. Tiny Hannah spreads her fingers then closes them around my thumb, then spreads them again, as if holding on and letting go is a marvelous game. She looks at me and gurgles.

I know all girls are supposed to think about babies, but in truth I do not, much. When I consider them at all, they seem a prize to be gained only if they and their mother live. And a price to be paid if one or both do not. There is a midwife on one of the outer farms who manages most of the births hereabouts. My mother is only called if things go wrong—the child must be turned, or fever sets in. So, for women snared in childbirth the sight of her is half hope, half warning. She is both angels. Janus faced, my mother opens the door to life and death.

Looking at Tiny Hannah, who is now flapping her hands as if she would like to fly, I wonder if that was what Avis Hobbs felt when we arrived, if she even knew we were there. I wonder if the sight of us was a flicker of light, or the closing of a shutter. I remember the presence at my shoulder as I opened the casement, the skitter that ran down my arm, the barest breath that hovered in my hand before that babe—sister or brother to Thaddeus and Abigail both—took flight. The butterfly rises from the vine, circles, and is gone.

I am sitting under the arbor with Tiny Hannah in her basket on the bench beside me, watching my mother and Hannah Smith as they kneel before the chamomile bank, snipping the last blossoms. I was on my way to do the job when, almost shyly, Hannah Smith told me she would like to "be of use." It would be a favor to her, she said, if for an hour we changed places, if I would sit under the arbor with Tiny Hannah and give her my basket and sharpened shears. A moment later, my mother came out to join her, Tom trotting in her wake.

Now, having inspected the garden, the little dog has made himself at home under the bench. Scraping a place in the gravel, he turned in circles before flopping down and, in moments, began to snore. The sound melds with the hum of the bees, and with the voices of my mother and Hannah Smith. With the snip of shears and the crunch of gravel as they move the basket along the unruly bank of flowers.

My mother laughs, and I realize with a shock that it is a rare sound. I cannot hear what caused it, but watching their backs, the faded blue of my mother's old work dress and the warm mustard of Hannah's smock, seeing their heads bent together, I think that my mother does not have many friends. Me, of course. But that is not the same. Since my father went, she has not had the companionship of anyone of her own age, except for John Alden, when he appears and, from time to time, George Burroughs. Which is not the same, either. Male spiders spin different webs.

All the village women know my mother, of course. They speak to her, and are civil. But none of them seek her out to share their secrets. And some, perhaps more than some, fear her. I think of Abigail telling me how Goody Cloyce whispered that my mother can fly. And I know that, in truth, it is not just

Goody Skilling who mutters 'sorcery' if a bone my mother sets knits straight or if she pulls someone from death's shadow.

Again, laughter threads the summer air. This time, it is Hannah Smith. Since hearing that her husband and son are alive and well, since knowing John Alden has gone to discover what it will take to see them safely returned, Hannah Smith has opened like a flower to the sun. My mother moves the basket between them. I see her smile at whatever joke they share, and think again of The Greening. Watching the two women kneeling together, their hands busy in the flower bank, their voices twining like the chamomile stems, I understand that it was not just safety we found and left behind in that place. I close my eyes, feeling Tiny Hannah grasp my thumb again, and see my mother and Ashawonks, walking together, their heads bent as they discussed some plant or recipe. Breathing in the woody scent of the hops and the sweetness of the honeysuckle and the grapes that hangs heavy on the drowsy air, I remember the hours they spent cutting and distilling or completing some other chore while I orbited around them, lost in my child world.

I remember the women in Hope Hood's camp who cared for me, the feel of the old woman's finger on my cheek and how she spoke my mother's name, and I understand why my mother goes. Why she pushes the canoe out and paddles alone to the headland. She is not just in search of remedies and knowledge—salve for a burn, or the correct way to soak the first catkins so their healing may be released. She is also in search of friendship. I think of the great wolf, alone in the forest. And of the song I dreamed—the high lonely wail full of longing.

WE ARE RETURNING to the house. I have stood and lifted Tiny Hannah's basket. Tom has woken and stretched and is poking his nose out from under the bench. My mother has taken the chamomile basket, which is almost full—some of the blossoms will be steeped, and the rest dried and jarred—and is on her way to the stillroom. Hannah is behind her with the shears, asking something about sedge, if it can be cut and milled like wheat grass, when we hear it.

At first, I think the deep, hollow boom is cannon. That something has been seen in the harbor, or beyond. That more war canoes have appeared from behind the islet and the militia have finally used the fort guns that are kept pointed out to sea, although all our danger seems to come from the forest. Then it comes again, and this time the boom ripples, making a sound like someone slapping the surface of a giant drum.

We all stop, frozen. It is Hannah Smith who says it first, her voice hushed, filled with something like awe.

"Thunder," she whispers. "Thunder!"

The rain begins an hour later. At first, it is a shy pat-pat, delicate as a kitten tapping a ball of wool. By the time John Alden and Thaddeus return in the late afternoon, it is a spigot opened from the heavens.

They come running through the birch grove, heads bent, one hand holding their hats. I only see them because I am locking up the goats. The horse and the cows came in quickly, before the rain began. But the goats refused. Leaping and hopping, they seemed to be dancing to the thunder claps. I chased them for a few minutes, then gave up. But now it is raining hard, and I want them in. They come grudgingly, one by one. I am just fitting the last shutter on the shed, snugging the windows against the downpour, when I see the figures. For one split second, my heart stops. Then I recognize them. By the time I follow them to the house, they are standing, dripping on the hearth.

"It is a blessing, is it not!" Thaddeus turns to me, grinning as I come through the door. His shirt is plastered to him. Hat removed, his hair stands up. Rain beads his face. He wipes it with the wet arm of his sleeve, making it wetter.

"And blessed, too," John Alden says. "For no one is out on the water in this. No one saw us. Not that it matters," he adds.

"They'll know soon enough. But I'd as soon have a moment. Or for that matter, an hour."

"Here." My mother comes from the front parlor where she has been opening chests. She carries two sets of clothes—breeches, stockings and shirts. My father's. She hands one each to Thaddeus and John Alden.

"Use the stillroom," she says. "Have those things off, and we'll clean and dry them."

The clothes they are wearing, the same they left in, are soaked and filthy, still streaked with the mud I rubbed into them and smeared with ashes. While they are gone to strip them off, I fetch the tinder box and make up the fire. The room will steam, but we had soup last night from the remains of the turkey and the first wild rice and the chill of even summer rain is best banished by hot food.

Hannah bustles about preparing the table, the baby on her hip. They have become so much part of us in only a few days that it seems hard now to imagine this house without them. Any more than I find I can imagine it without Thaddeus. When I look up, he is picking his way, barefoot, into the room. Through the open door, I see the old clothes, piled in a sodden mass beside the stoop, rain already starting the washing I will finish later.

❧

"THAT WAS GRAND!"

John Alden puts his spoon down and dabs a bread crumb from the table. I push the pitcher towards him. He pours himself more cider and passes it along to Thaddeus before reaching for the pipe and the tobacco pouch my mother placed beside him. One more vestige of my father put to use. John Alden tamps the pipe, then stands to light it at the hearth before turning to face us.

"Gendle is a liar plus ten," he says. "But before that

Mistress," he bows to Hannah, "your husband and your son send you all their greetings, and reassure you they are well."

"You saw them?"

Hannah has not spoken since we sat down. When I look at her, I realize John Alden frightens her. To us, of course, he is familiar. But he is an imposing figure, with a story that runs before him. His father and mother both, The Good John Alden and Fair Priscilla, are legends of a kind, almost mythical creatures. Hannah glances at him sideways from where she sits with Tiny Hannah, as if she is not quite sure what will happen if she actually looks at him.

"Saw them," John Alden assures her, "and spoke with your good man at length. Indeed, it was he who told me first what the message was, that Gendle was actually sent to deliver."

"Perhaps," my mother says, settling herself at the table, "it would be best if you began at the beginning?"

So, John Alden does.

CHAPTER FORTY-TWO

John Alden's Story

I was not certain, when we set out, where the island was, or even if it was an island. Gendle is such a fool, and unobservant with it, that it could have been a peninsula, or a neck, or a cove on the mainland and I daresay he would not know the difference. But I was certain that it was north, and not more than a few hours, so we turned up the coast. Which is all you can do in the dark in a canoe in any case, follow the coastline, unless you are also a fool. In truth, I hoped they would find us, and that is how it went. We had been paddling a bare two hours when Thaddeus here, who has sharp wits and sharper eyes, whispered that he thought we were not alone. And indeed, moments later we had an escort.

I have never known, exactly, how they do it. I know they have scouts, as you do for any army. But I have never spotted them. Some say they can speak with the birds, and that is how they gain their intelligence. Others insist that, like Yellow Bird, they are flighted creatures themselves, at least some of them.

That they can take to the air like hawks, or move through the forest in the guise of brother wolf when they are not being men. I do not know if it is true. There are more things in this world are than we understand.

Oh, yes, the Puritans! I know. The Mathers and their ilk are convinced that their good book holds all the secrets. Or at least all those worth knowing, and that anything else is devilish. But, I'll tell you, they would be sore surprised if they ever stuck their noses out of their God houses. Philip English swears one of his ships netted a mermaid somewhere off the Indes. But all she would do was sing, and her singing made the crew so forlorn that the captain ordered her thrown back overboard. Stranger things have been seen under heaven.

All I know is that our forest friends move across water just as they do through woods. I'd not care to try to outrace or hide from them amid waves any more than among trees. That's when you understand whose land, and sea, this truly is. The first time I made my way to The Pentagoet, I was solitary when I set sail. Then, their escort picked me up almost half a day out. It was the same last night. All at once, war canoes surrounded us like sea ghosts or silent silver whales.

By dawn, we were in sight of the island. It is an island. Gendle was right about that much. Of course, we were surrounded and merely went where we were guided, so I could not tell exactly which island it is, or precisely how we came to be there, which was the point.

It is a big camp. I know the rumors about Penacook. They're not right. The location is wrong for a start. But as with most gossip, it's not all fancy, either. I would say—and Thaddeus agrees, I think—that there were several hundred men. And that was merely those we saw. I don't know what's inland, or on the other side of the island, for that matter. We were welcomed at a west-facing beach, and kept there.

As I said, Gendle is an idiot and a liar—how great a one, you'll see. But he's not wrong about one more thing. This is a war camp. No mistake about it. There wasn't a woman in sight. Not one I saw, and not Thaddeus, either. And we kept our eyes open. Nor, except for Yellow Bird, were there old men. Although who knows what Yellow Bird is. The men we saw, all of them, were either young or in their prime. And, no, they are not just Egeremet's people, either. He couldn't raise those numbers alone. This is a gathering, a confederation. I would say all the sachems were represented, from as far south as Cocheco, at least. As far north as, well—Madockawando. He was not there himself. But his men, or at least a handful of them were. I'd guess they were sniffing the air. Judging how things go so they can report back to him and Castin.

The Pentagoet group is led by one of his sons—Madockawando's, not Castin's. I know him, which was a good thing, as we wished only to visit, not volunteer ourselves as permanent residents. It was fortunate that he was present not just to vouch for us, but also to translate. You know I can't make head nor tail of Egeremet. Can't understand a word of his lingo. And Yellow Bird, although he's of Hope Hood's people and I can understand them as a rule, is short on words. Oh, I know he's not mute. He can speak, Yellow Bird, or so I'm told. Although I've yet to meet anyone who's heard him. They say he won't converse with Whites. In my experience, he prefers to hover on the other side of the fire. But perhaps that's just so no one will see him spread his wings.

Truly. That is what they say. They swear that at night he opens that dreadful cape of his and takes to the wind, buoyed by the spirits of all the forest creatures that adorn his body. They say that's what the marks on his face and hands are—tribute to those who have given him their bones. They say he's a night spirit, that's why his curings are so powerful. But Rachel would know more of that than I. I don't dabble in gods. I'm just a plain sailor, and a businessman. Which was what they wanted, to conduct business. That's the message the liar Gendle didn't bring.

They've met among themselves and decided that they are sorry, for the loss of labor the taking of sixteen men and boys this close to harvest has caused. They say they have no wish to see our fields ruined and us all starving. So, they told Gendle that they wish us to set a price, a cost for the loss, and they will pay it, in full, before any exchange of captives takes place as a gesture of good faith. All we must do is decide the amount, in beaver preferably, as they are short on coin.

That's the message the liar Gendle was sent to bring. That's the goodwill, that's the offer of peace he so conveniently forgot.

In truth, I think they fear we will sell Hope Hood and his people, and hope this will deter us. Some are afraid it is too late, that we have already sent them as slaves to the Indies. If that is the case, they have not decided what they will do. At least, that is what Madockawando's son told me.

No. Don't fear for your son and husband, Mistress Hannah. I did not mean that. They will not kill their captives if their people are not returned. But they may ransom them—sell them to us, as we have sold their people. If that's the case, it will be expensive, and will take time. And we'll need Andros for that.

But it does not have to happen. As I said, they want us to name a price, now, for the time and labor that has been lost by their taking of our men, and they wish to meet to discuss it. Then, when we are agreed, they will pay, in advance of an exchange of captives, to grease the wheels so to speak, in beaver and any other pelts we ask. They hope this will forestall any ideas of slaving. And show their desire to avoid a war. That's the message Gendle was sent to bring.

They also told him that, as a further gesture of good intent, they will free any two hostages we name. Turn them over at negotiations. In fact, they thought, when Thaddeus and I arrived, that was what we had come for, to name the two. That was why they found us so fast. They had been watching for us, and wondering why we were taking so long.

When they finally understood that we had heard nothing of

any of it, that Gendle had failed to say anything at all or give any part of the message that was the price of his freedom, they were, as you can imagine, sore distressed.

❧

JOHN ALDEN TAMPS THE PIPE. He fiddles with the tobacco and leans back in his chair. The rain is not a spigot any more, but a soft scrabble running across the roof and dripping from the eaves. For a moment, no one says anything. Then, somewhat to my surprise, it is Hannah Smith who speaks.

"Why?" She asks. If I was right and she was afraid of John Alden, you cannot hear it in her voice now. Now, all there is, is anger. "Why would Gendle lie like this? Why fail to speak? This could be the freedom of my husband and son!"

Hannah leans forward, cradling Tiny Hannah who looks from one to the other of us with wide dark eyes, as if she is surprised to find us in her world.

"I do not understand," Hannah Smith says. "Please explain to me. Why anyone would lie about such a thing? Surely, to do so will endanger, or at least prolong the captivity of every man and boy who has been taken? If you speak true, and I believe you do, this is a gesture of good faith and an attempt to avoid conflict. To obstruct it is nothing but wickedness. Pure wickedness!"

Hannah's voice is filled with a force I have not heard in it before, but recognize. It is the fury of wife, mother, lover. The surge of blood that pushes away all fear.

"I do not understand," she says again. "Why?"

A look flashes around the table. I think of our journey to the summer camp, of the warning my mother tried, and failed, to deliver, and realize we are witnessing the marriage we feared—the dreadful union of purpose and profit. It is John Alden who finally answers.

"Because, Mistress," he says. "I fear it is a truth that there are those who see calamity as opportunity. In their eyes, when things break there's profit to be made, not in mending the whole, but in selling each piece separate. They're like rats—the greater the panic, the more things are broken, the more bits and pieces there are to scrounge, the fatter they become."

"And the more death they spread." This is my mother, her voice as angry as Hannah's.

John Alden nods. "And men who have been disgraced," he adds, "men who have been accused of cowardliness, men like Gendle. What they see in war is not death, but redemption. He was an unfortunate choice indeed, as a messenger. They told me he put himself forward for the task. I think," John Alden looks around at us, "that now we know why. Anyone else might have delivered the message. And we'd be talking pelts and sums. Instead Gendle is in The Ordinary babbling God knows what while Tyng sits on his arse in his parlor wringing his fat hands."

"What will you do?" My mother asks. For, of course, we all assume John Alden will do something.

"Go see him." John Alden slaps both hands on the table, as if he hopes to startle some sense into the town. "I shall go see Edward Tyng," he says. "Yet again. I shall apprise our magistrate of the situation as we now know it to be. And suggest he come up with a number. Because Egeremet and his people intend to arrive, and hear our answer, tomorrow."

CHAPTER FORTY-THREE

It is almost sunset when John Alden departs. What he has to say will not be gentle and is for Edward Tyng's ears alone, so Thaddeus stays here. He comes with me to the milking shed. As we walk down the paddock, I realize that the days have grown shorter. It is almost harvest. Summer is slipping away.

As I do every time now, I look closely as we open the shed doors. But there is no trace of yellow on the gray, weathered wood. What I saw, I saw in the strange, stilled world that seems to hover, as bubbles hover in the water, next to this one. A world I now seem to enter, or be pushed into, the way others step, or are pushed, over the threshold of an open door. I wonder if I will ever be able to push that door open, step over that threshold at will. Or if I am destined always be caught off guard, to be shoved and stumble through unprepared.

I remember the small hand in mine as we stood on the common watching Judah run down Broad Street, and have the uncomfortable thought that this is yet another thing Thaddeus' sister and I have in common. Another way in which we are bound. Abigail Hobbs also saw the flames, which means she also crosses the threshold. I realize, as I lift the rail that keeps the animals in, that in fact I suspect Abigail comes and goes from any number of worlds at will. *As does my mother.*

The idea hits me so suddenly that I almost drop the rail. Judah is right. I am a fool. And more than that, a coward. Too afraid to ask my own mother if she too, was given a manitou. Because I know the answer.

I decide I will find it. The next time I have a chance, I will rifle her clothes. Search out the hidden pocket so I can run my fingers over the small disc I know is there, and feel the shape of the creature etched into its polished stone.

❧

WITH THE DOORS FLUNG OPEN, Bess and Belle and our old cow to amble out of the shed and stand under the shower that falls so gently it is barely there. Blinking their great brown eyes and swinging their heads, relishing the unaccustomed cool, they do not even bother to graze. The goats flock to the far corner of the paddock. Disappointed to find the fence mended, they snip and shove at one another. But there is no anger in it. They are only pretending. Of all the creatures, it is the little bay horse who finds the rain most glorious. As I watch, she paws the earth, then lowers herself to her knees, and finally her belly, and rolls in the newly wet grass.

I lean on my pitch fork, watching her. Then turn to Thaddeus, who has just finished throwing hay from the loft and climbs down to stand beside me.

"Why do you think he did it?" I ask.

"Gendle?"

He reaches for the second fork and begins turning the old straw, shaking out the dung and banking the clean bedding so the earthen floor may be scattered with sand and raked.

"Because he is a small man," Thaddeus says.

He has rolled his shirt sleeves. The damp linen sticks to his upper arms. I raise my wrist and push the loose hair off my forehead before turning back to the shed.

"He has a small heart. You can see it in his eyes. And he is afraid." Thaddeus is shaping a drift of straw, fluffing the golden strands as he banks them.

"Many are afraid," he says a moment later. "Sometimes I think this whole new world we say we are building here is afraid. Many claim their god gives them strength. But I think the Puritan god is a god of fear. That is the currency he and those who follow him deal in. And dealing in it, as all good traders do, they create and multiply their coin. So dread begets dread. It is a circle. Or rather a whirlpool. Like those that spin in the sea, waiting to suck under any ship that sails too close."

He stops and looks at me. "That is what I believe," he says, shrugging. "I believe they must create fear to justify their own fear. And from that, their own vengeance. Because if they do not, then their god is wrong. He is a false god. And they are wrong, and false with him. And they could not bear that."

I stare at him. Not because I disagree. I do not. But because I am surprised. Not that Thaddeus thinks this—though I would never have guessed him for a firebrand—but that he dares say it. Because we both know who, and what, he is speaking of. Boston. The Mathers. The preachers. The men in black who rule that world. And would rule ours, here in the Eastward, if only they could rid themselves of Governor Andros and reinstate their charter. Free New England of its Catholic loving King and claim it for their angry god.

As John Alden says, as my father always said—most of us have come here, to the Eastward, because we are more interested in fishing and trade than tending our souls in the meeting house. We do not even bother to have ordained ministers, which surely proves it. Many here, I am sure, agree. But few dare say so. Thaddeus shrugs as if he can read my mind, and smiles.

"I may be wrong," he says. "What would I know? I am nothing. Yet, I cannot think well of a man like Gendle who claims to own another man. I cannot say his heart is large. Or true. I spoke to him, you know."

He tosses straw into the air, catches it with the fork, and tosses it again.

"Not Gendle, the negro," Thaddeus says. "Gendle's slave. He has a name. Taylor. He says Gendle won him, in a law suit, some dispute over property that was settled and Taylor was the settlement, or part of it. As if he was a chair, or a table, or a horse. And Captain Alden was right, Taylor did ask Egeremet to take him. He told me so. And told me he has made the sachem promise that he will never be returned. Taylor says he has found freedom with them. Or, as much freedom as a man can have."

"Since he falls into this world tangled in God's love and lives it tangled in his own?"

Thaddeus laughs as I return his words to him.

"Just so," he says. "Just so."

For a while we work in silence, listening to the rain patting the shed roof and to the drips from the shingles. The little bay horse has stood up, and shaken. The cows have begun to graze. Soft snipping mingles with the sound of the rain and the rustle of straw. Beyond the paddock, the apples in our orchard have begun to redden. I can smell them. Mud, manure, and the scent of wet leaves and grass and salt from the cove flood the twilight air. We did not see the sunset today. But it must have come and gone, because the light is sinking. Shadows lengthen in the shed. At most, we have a few minutes before it will be too dark in here to continue our work.

"Was it strange?" Thaddeus asks.

"Strange?" I have scattered sand from the bin and picked up the rake. I don't have to see to make a pattern on the floor.

"In the Greening. When you lived there. With the she-sachem, during the last war. Was it strange?" Thaddeus asks, "To be among them?"

I pause, wondering how he can know about this. Or at least know about it so completely. We, my mother and I, are aware, of course, that it goes about the village—some idea, or rumor, that we have been close to the people and the sachems. But to call it The Greening. To know of Ashawonks.

Before I can think more on it, Thaddeus says, "Captain Alden told me. As we paddled. I had asked him why he was so certain, of how the captives would be treated. And he told me what he knows of the tribes and of the sachems. Then he told me how your father sent you and your mother to Ashawonks, during the last war, for safe keeping."

I nod and begin to rake again.

"No," I say. "No, it was not strange. At first, perhaps. But quickly, not. Because we were not strange. We became so like them there was no space for strangeness."

Thaddeus seems to think about this. Finishing my pattern, I set the rake aside. Thaddeus unbanks the clean straw. Together, we make a bed for the beasts.

"So, you think it is true. That a man, or a woman—a being," he laughs, "can become something else? Can move from one world to another?"

"Yes."

I look over my shoulder at him, wondering if he is more like his sister than I realized. In the shadows, inside the rain, we are nothing more than shapes.

"Yes," I say again. "In Duxbury, I was Susannah. In the Greening, I had another name. Here, I am Resolve. My mother is the same. That is why John Alden calls her Rachel. We carry worlds inside us. And we are, all of us at once, more than one being. Or we can be."

I stop, uncertain where my words have come from. They taste as if they have arrived in my mouth of their own volition. And I think, *John Alden is right, and I have always known it. It is not just Yellow Bird. Any one of us can choose to step to the other side of the fire. Anyone of us can spread his cape, and fly through the night sky on the music of its bones.*

"We can be more than one thing at once. We can move through worlds," I say again. "If we will it." Then, I add, "Like Yellow Bird."

And Thaddeus looks at me and says, "Like Abigail."

We do not talk much after that. The animals are brought in, and the shed shut up for the night. When it is done, we walk back, side by side in the misty rain. Ahead, the house sparks with light. A lantern and candles burn in the windows.

"You will take care of her?"

I do not need to ask who Thaddeus is speaking of. He stops, reaching for my arm.

"She has no one," he says. "And she is only a child." I feel him smile. "Whatever else she is," he adds. "Abigail is that, surely. A child." His voice sobers. "My father is a drunkard and a sloth. He will re-marry, and soon. I don't know to whom. But he will find some woman to care for him because he will not care for himself. And then she will be cut out again. And alone again."

I look at him in the gathering dark.

"And murderous again?" I ask.

"Not if she has you."

I had meant it half in jest, I think. But clearly, he does not.

"Not if she has you," he says again. "If she has you, she will have no reason to be murderous. Because she will not be alone in the world."

I start to say, *What of you? You are her brother. You are her blood. Surely she has you?* And then I stop. Because I see, as clearly as if it is before me. The small boat hits the wind. The sail will not untangle. The wave rises. The picnic basket floats free. And their two perfect hands with their pearly white nails entwine as they sink, down, down, down. Unwilling vessels too soon filled with God.

Anything can be lost. Any cord can fray. That is the lesson

the twins taught Thaddeus. Anything, no matter how beloved, can vanish without a trace.

"You will care for her? Do you promise me?" Thaddeus Hobbs asks.

And I reach out, and run the tips of my fingers down his wet cheek, and say, "Yes."

CHAPTER FORTY-FOUR

The next morning is perfection. A world washed clean. The garden smells of cut chamomile and damp gravel. A haze of green skims the meadow, as if new shoots have just been waiting to push through the summer-burnt thatch. Even the sea smells new, the salt tang mellowed and almost sweet.

We have agreed that, from dawn, we will take turns watching from the point. When the first canoe is sighted, Thaddeus will run for John Alden, who will come hauling Edward Tyng. Egeremet said they will come to our cove and our beach. On their first visit, they had the advantage of surprise. This time, having taken their own captives, they have no wish to be within range of the fort's guns.

Before leaving yesterday, John Alden told us that he would invite himself to sleep in Edward Tyng's parlor. He would, he said, lay across the door if necessary, in order to be sure Tyng did not send word of the sachems' arrival to the militia.

"We want this negotiation done quietly and quickly," John Alden said. "I'd forsake Tyng altogether, but I do not dare. We must have some force of law. So I shall hang on to him, and when Thaddeus comes for us, I shall march him to the spot. All the sachems want is a price, and an agreement. Then they will pay it, and Blackman will be lured back to claim his share, and the captives will be peaceably exchanged, and all this will be over, and our lives resumed."

We had all nodded as he spoke. But I do not know if any of us believed him.

❧

HANNAH INSISTS on taking the first watch. She has changed, since she came to stay with us, and particularly since she heard the Henrys are safe. Hannah Smith has grown stronger, and not just in body. Left with Tiny Hannah after her men were taken, she could have chosen to wither and sink. To become another Mary Skilling, lost in the angry madness of grief. Or a Mercy Lewis, wandering in the terror of her own shadows. Or she could turn like a ship before the winds and unfurl into the world. As she has done.

I walk with her as far as the paddock fence. A faint mist hangs like smoke in the birches. Before Hannah sets off for the point, she hands me the baby.

"Care for her," she says, her voice sharp with determination and anger, that I know is not aimed at me. Hannah has focused her fury on Walter Gendle, fueled it with thoughts of what his lies could have done, and indeed may still do, to her husband and son. She has grasped on to her disdain for him and used it to haul herself up, hand over hand.

I watch as she disappears, weaving through the ghostly columns of the birch grove. Then I look at the babe in my arms, and think that, twice in the space of less than a day, I have been given this order—to care for some small, potentially abandoned, female. Tiny Hannah looks back at me, her eyes as black as Abigail's are blue. She gurgles as if we share a secret joke.

❧

THADDEUS WILL TAKE the watch after Hannah. Then me. Then my mother. We shall repeat this all through the day, and all through tomorrow, if we must. Although I doubt any of us think it will be that long. Certainly, John Alden hopes it will be not be, for he does not know if he can keep Edward Tyng sequestered. Keep him, as he says, from "squealing like a pig" at being imprisoned in his own house. Or keep others from wishing to speak with, or consult, him. And wondering what is amiss when they cannot.

In the event, we do not have to find the answer to any of these questions. Because it is not an hour after Hannah vanished into the birch grove that I hear her call, and look up to see her, running. I have just left the baby in her basket in the kitchen with Thaddeus and my mother, and am on my way to release the animals for grazing.

"They are here!" Hannah calls. "They are here! I have just seen them, coming fast from the north!"

I turn and run for the house. Moments later, Thaddeus is racing across the meadow.

❧

WAR CANOES ARE FAST, but there is still time for John Alden and Edward Tyng to arrive. They come, the magistrate in his green coat almost trotting to keep up with Alden's long stride. Thaddeus strides behind them, as much a guard, I think, as an escort, in case Tyng thinks better of this enterprise or is overcome with terror at the idea of facing savages again, and tries to turn tail and bolt.

The morning bell has not rung yet. People are about, but they will be lolling in the coolness, taking their time over chores to savor the almost forgotten smell of the rain, and the dampness on the beach stones, and the stilling of dust on the road and in the side yards. This morning, sweeping will be slower, the walk to the salt shed more leisurely. There is a good chance that no one at all will have seen Captain Alden and the magistrate hurrying across our meadow. Or so we hope. Because, as John Alden said, it is best that this is done quickly, and without extra consultation.

To be fair, Edward Tyng seems amenable when they arrive. With a few notable exceptions, no one wants another war. And this negotiation will bring not only peace, but also profit for the village from whatever payment is agreed, as well as a way to save face over the debacle of captives. All of which Edward Tyng will happily take credit for. He is almost jolly as they set off for our beach—the Captain, the Magistrate, Master Hobbs with his angels wings folded under his shirt, and my mother, without whom they will not be able to understand a word.

I watch from the kitchen door, Hannah standing at my shoulder. She has taken Tiny Hannah from the basket and rocks her, swaying from foot to foot.

"Go," she says.

We had agreed that I should stay at the house with the Hannahs. It is best not have too many people crowding the beach. Beyond that, we must keep watch, in case someone did notice John Alden and Tyng, and comes down the meadow looking for them, or for my mother, or just to snoop. Should that happen, we have agreed that Hannah will delay them while I slip out and run to the beach with a warning. Now, she gives me a little push.

"Go," she says again. "I see you wish to. You can watch from the grove. I will be fine here." She smiles at Tiny Hannah. "I can see and give a warning as well as you. I can even run, if I have to."

And so I pick up my skirts and hurry through the garden. It is only as I pass the milking shed and begin to trot that I look down and realize that early this morning, even before first light, I pulled the moccasins Yellow Bird had given me from where my mother had hidden them and put them on.

As I approach, I see that the little group standing on our

beach does not look much different from the group I found so extraordinary at the harbor. It is true that George Burroughs is not here, and no silver drift of war canoes floats in the cove. This time, there are only three, each paddled by three or four warriors instead of five or six.

As I come through the birches, I see Egeremet. Two of his sons stand with him at the water's edge. John Alden and Edward Tyng face them, with my mother and Thaddeus. Another person is there, too. Yellow Bird. The same marks run down his cheeks and along his hands. He is still wrapped in his cape. Its fringe of tiny bleached bones, the fingers and legs and tails of creatures glisten in the morning sun. No one looks up as I edge closer to the top of the bank. Then, I stop.

I cannot see them. But I can feel them as surely as I can feel Abigail when she tugs the sinew that binds our hearts. My eyes slide towards the thick undergrowth, towards the mouth of the track that leads up to the point. Nothing moves, not even a leaf. Yet, the air throbs. I do not know if there are fifteen, or twenty, or fifty of them. But I know they are here. I can feel their heart beats, and their arrow tips, and hatchet blades. I can feel the points of knives and muzzles of weapons aimed towards the house. And towards the beach. And towards me.

I am not surprised. This is why they chose our cove as their meeting place. It was not just because of the fort guns. And there are not just three canoes. There are five, or more likely ten, or fifteen, all lingering at the base of the pink rocks where they deposited Walter Gendle and bid him climb. You will not see them from our beach. But they are there. Egeremet and his sons and Yellow Bird will have continued down into the mouth of the cove while their companions climbed the pink rocks, and crossed the clearing where their ancestors camped and spread themselves down the point to guard their leaders backs.

I wonder if John Alden knows we are surrounded. I am sure he does. That is another reason he wants this completed as quickly and as quietly as possible. A fool might assume that, with our fort and guns and militia, we have the upper hand. But it is not the case.

By the time I reach the top of the bank, the negotiation has begun. My mother is speaking, her hand moving in time to her words. Egeremet is listening, slightly bent towards her since she is so much smaller. Thaddeus and Edward Tyng are listening and nodding, while out in the second of the canoes that drift off the beach, Henry Smith and his son sit between a pair of warriors.

I wonder if John Alden arranged this, too. If he made a bargain, or suggested the Smiths should be the two captives returned as a gesture of good faith, and did not say so for fear the arrangement would not hold and Hannah's hopes would be dashed. Or did they somehow know? Did Yellow Bird dream their connection to us? Did he spread his cape and bid his tiny bones fly him across the water. Ride the stars to look down on us, and see the Hannahs here. Even as I think it, he looks up.

The others do not notice me. The conversation is going on in earnest now. A redemption price seems to have been arranged. Egeremet speaks, and my mother speaks. Edward Tyng speaks, and even stretches out his hand. Egeremet takes it. Then, one of his sons turns towards the water, and gestures. The canoe carrying the Smiths comes to the shallows. Something is said. Henry Smith hesitates. Finally, he throws a leg over the side, then another. He drops into the water as his son sits, a warrior's hand on his shoulder, holding him in place as his father wades ashore.

I am not certain how I know what is going to happen next, but I do.

I am already edging forward, already at the lip of the bank when Thaddeus steps past my mother and says, "Tell them they do not need to keep the boy as a bond. Tell them to release him. In return, they may take me."

"No!" I do not mean to shout. It simply happens. "No!" I shout again. And I am slithering down the bank and running along the beach.

Egeremet, and my mother, and John Alden and Edward Tyng, and Henry Smith with his great rough hands and carrot hair, Egeremet's sons and Yellow Bird, all of them turn toward me. But I can only see Thaddeus Hobbs.

The morning light catches his hair, picking up the whisper of gold that runs through it. The linen of his shirt is white and crisp. His beautiful hands reach out to me.

"Please," he says as I come close.

We are face to face when I stop.

"Please," Thaddeus says again, the blue in his eyes almost gray, and pleading. "I could do nothing, for Avis and William. For my brother and sister. Or for my mother." His voice is little more than a whisper, the words a plea for me alone. "I could not save them. But I can return this boy to his mother and to his sister. I can make this family whole again."

I understand now that I was wrong. Last night, in the rain, when he passed the pictures of the twins from his mind to mine, when he sent the images of their drowning to make me promise to take care of Abigail, it was not because he feared fate, or an accident. It was because he knew what he was going to do. Thaddeus Hobbs has seen a chance to mend a rip in the world. And he means to take it.

I beg of you," Thaddeus' fingers brush the back of my hand. "If you love me at all," he says, "let me do this thing."

For a moment, we stand so close that I can feel his breath. Then, he turns and walks back up the beach.

Thaddeus does not join the group. He does not go to stand beside John Alden, or my mother, or even Egeremet. Instead, he goes to Yellow Bird, who has not taken his eyes off my face. I stare back at the strange bent creature that is half man and half something else, focusing on the yellow marks, and on the bones —the tiny interconnected lines that once formed a web of life in the forest.

Out of the corner of my eye, I see the canoe carrying Small Henry nudge into the shallows. One of the warriors steps out and stands, thigh high in the water. Small Henry is lifted into his raised hands and carried as lightly as a twig to the beach. As the child is placed beside his father, Yellow Bird reaches out, his cape spreading like a wing, and places a claw hand on Thaddeus' shoulder. We stare at one another, this shaman, this shape-shifter and I until Yellow Bird lets go and Thaddeus Hobbs is escorted through the shallows to the waiting canoe.

The world stills, and narrows. Reaching into the front of my dress, I lift the Night Spirit from its place against my skin and hold it up.

"Care for him." I dredge the words from some long memory of The Greening. "Care for him," I say. "He is in your charge."

The marks on Yellow Bird's cheeks and hands come alive as I speak. They shimmer and writhe.

"You care for him!" I shout. And I raise the Night Spirit, thrusting it at Yellow Bird. "You care for him, or you answer, to me!"

For a moment, Yellow Bird appears as frozen as the rest of the world around us. Then, he nods. Slowly, he raises both arms. The tiny bones jangle. Yellow Bird's nails flash in the new sun as he opens his wings and splays his fingers. His hands turn to talons as he runs them down his cheeks, across the symbols of his power, and holds them, palms out, to me.

Then, Yellow Bird turns and splashes into the water.

What happens next happens very fast. No one else has moved. Thaddeus is in the canoe. Small Henry is clutching Large Henry's leg. Edward Tyng is staring, open mouthed. My mother and Egeremet and John Alden are all watching Yellow Bird when we hear Hannah scream.

CHAPTER FORTY-FIVE

"Militia! Militia! Militia!"

Skirts clutched, hair flying, Hannah is hurtling down the slope from the milking shed. "Militia!" She shrieks just before they race past her, and into the birch grove, and the shooting starts.

John Alden bellows and shoves my mother. Edward Tyng wails and falls to the sand. Large Henry yells, "No! No! No!" And throws himself up the bank.

I have time to see Walter Gendle, running through the birches with a sword raised and a swarm of men behind him before my mother grabs me and Small Henry and drags all three of us down behind our upturned canoe. There is firing, the sharp bang of shots, and a terrible scream. Egeremet's warriors are pouring out of the thick underbrush above the grove where they have been waiting in case exactly this happened.

Small Henry screams, "Pa!" as Henry Smith is hit and falls, rolling down the bank to the beach.

My mother and I all but sit on him to keep him down. I can't see Hannah Smith, or John Alden. The hump of Edward Tyng's green coat is like a giant turtle huddled in the sand. Egeremet and his sons and Yellow Bird and Thaddeus Hobbs with them, are gone. I have just a glimpse of silver streaking up the cove towards the open sea before I hear another shriek, and look back in time to see Walter Gendle hit with a hatchet in the back of the head. He falls, face first, at the top of the bank and sprawls there, arms outstretched, still holding the sword. Behind him, I can make out figures among the birches—men running, and men falling. There are more shots, and more screams. And then it is over, as fast as it began.

Suddenly, there is utter stillness. In front of us, Large Henry is curled on the sand. Hannah appears out of nowhere and slides down the bank, calling his name. Small Henry wriggles free and runs to join them. This time, we do not try to stop him.

I am not sure how long it is before I stand up, gingerly. Looking toward the place where the track leads up the point, I see that not even a leaf is moving in the undergrowth. The Indians are gone. Vanished, as if they have been sucked into the earth. Nothing is left but blood, and the acrid stink of powder, and dead men.

My mother pushes past me, going to join Hannah, pulling her back, so she can examine Large Henry. Stumbling from behind our canoe, I feel deafened, wrapped in a sort of juddering stillness. Thaddeus' footprints, and Egeremet's, and Yellow Bird's are still on the sand in front of me. But already the cove is still as glass. There is not even the ripple of a prow or the reflection of a wolf's smile on the sunlit water. I hear John Alden's voice, unexpectedly gentle, behind me.

"Come," he is saying. "Come, Old Friend, stand up. Stand up. You are safe, and not injured."

I turn to see him helping Edward Tyng to his feet, reaching to brush the sand off his green coat, handing him his hat, which is squashed after being fallen on. Behind them, a faint pall of smoke hangs in the birch grove, making the figures of men who wander there look ghostly. Slowly, I begin to hear groaning, and the sound of someone crying. Then my mother calls my name.

"Resolve!" She shouts. "Quickly, as fast as you can! The stillroom!"

Her words, the very sound of her voice, shatters the cocoon that has woven itself around me. Suddenly, I see blood. A lot of it, on the sand around Large Henry. And then I am running, scrambling up the bank and dashing through the grove.

Someone is leaning against a tree. Two other men are sitting. I see a fallen man out of the corner of my eye, and dodge past a hand that reaches out to me. But I do not stop. I lift my skirts and run, as fast as I can until I am pulling open the stillroom door and grabbing the baskets, the one full of curings, and the other filled with linen. All of my father's old shirts, and our old sheets and aprons, bleached and stripped and rolled, ready for just such a calamity as this.

I am out the door and into the garden, a basket in each hand, before I remember the baby.

I see Hannah in my mind's eye, flying down the slope below the milking shed. Her skirts were lifted, bunched in each hand. She did not have Tiny Hannah with her. I drop the baskets to the gravel and spin towards the house. Seeing the kitchen door open, I feel a terrible rip of dread. *Mary Skilling's children. Alice Atwell's babes, all cut down before they even walked.*

I am at the door, setting foot on the threshold, when I hear a deep growl.

Tiny Hannah's basket is on the kitchen table. Between it and me, Tom stands stiff-legged with his hackles raised. His teeth are bared and the noise he makes is far bigger than he is. I pause until he recognizes me, and lets me come forward. The baby is fast asleep, her little fist curled on her blanket. I kiss my finger and dab it to her forehead before I step back and bend to pat the little dog. Outside, I latch the door. Leaving Tiny Hannah with her protector, I grab the baskets, and run.

❧

ON THE BEACH, my mother holds out her hand for a bandage. "It is his shoulder," she says. "Not his heart, nor stomach. Thank God."

Hannah has taken off her apron, wadded it up, and pressed it over the wound as my mother instructed. Little Henry sits in the sand, one hand on his father's leg, his eyes as wide. They have got Henry Smith sitting up, somehow. He is pale and dazed, looking more surprised than anything else. My mother begins to bandage, her hands deft.

"We'll get him back to the house. Then take this off, and get the shot out and clean the wound." She nods at me. "We're alright here. Go up and see who else needs help."

I do not want to do this, and my mother sees it.

"Go," she says. "Now, Resolve. Quickly!"

And so, I do.

Clambering up the bank, I stay well away from the fallen figure of Walter Gendle. The sword looks like a child's toy clutched in his dead hand. I make an effort not to look at the hatchet that is lodged in the back of his head, and fail. One of the militia men sits not far behind him, just at the lip of the grove, cradling his arm, rocking back and forth and moaning. A mere glance is enough to see, from the peculiar angle it hangs at, that the arm is broken.

Beyond him another man lays face down. A dreadful dark stain covers his shoulders, and seeps and pools at his waist. Yet another militia man, the one I glimpsed as I ran for the baskets, lays beside him, his musket flung in front of him, his fingers reaching for it as if he tried to crawl through the grass before dying. Because they are both dead, I know it. Even so, I crouch and, as my mother taught me, feel for the flutter of the soul at each neck. Nothing. Standing, I hear John Alden's voice again and look up to see him helping a young man, barely more than a boy, who has a cut on his cheek and stares like a frightened horse.

"This one's alright," John Alden calls, and Edward Tyng

comes and puts his arm around the boy's waist as they get him to his feet.

Tyng's hat is back on, a little flattened, and strangely tilted. He murmurs something to the boy, pats him with his free hand, and does not seem to worry that he may get blood on his fine green coat. Together, they turn and begin their slow way back to the village. Ahead of them, I can see three others, two supporting one in between. I watch as they make their way up our fence line and around the garden, beginning their ragged retreat to the fort.

John Alden appears beside me.

"There are no Indian dead," he whispers. "Just ours. That fool, Gendle, led them straight into an ambush. Why could they not have waited? Why? And how did Gendle know? How?"

He shakes his head. There is a streak of blood on his cheek and chin.

"It did not have to happen." He wipes at the blood and looks at his hand. "And look what it's got us. We had a price, an agreement. The deal was done. A moment more, Egeremet would have been gone. And now, this."

John Alden sighs, and pats my shoulder, and moves towards the man who is sitting cradling his arm.

"You're alright," he calls. "It hurts like a whoreson, boy, I know. But Mistress Hammond will make it right as rain. You just hang on," he shouts, and vanishes down to the beach.

A second later, I hear a yelp of pain and see Henry Smith, helped up by his wife on one side and Captain Alden on the other, half clambering, half being dragged up the bank. My mother appears, carrying one of the baskets. Small Henry follows her, lugging the other. She stops and crouches by the man with the broken arm, speaking to him, trying to pry his hands away and calling to Small Henry who is staring in fascination at Walter Gendle, Abigail's Black Man with a hatchet in the back of his head. As I turn away, I hear the village bell begin to toll.

❧

THE SWARM of men I thought I saw running behind Walter Gendle was not really a swarm at all. There were probably not more than nine or ten. But enough to fill our birch grove with death. It seems a life time ago that Judah and I lay here on our backs, staring up through the leaves, exchanging stories about the death of Avis Hobbs. I look down, and wonder how many pebbled patterns of memory lay beneath these bodies and this blood. The villagers will come to collect them, Walter Gendle and the other poor men shot in the back. They will bring a cart and load them like sacks of flour. By this afternoon, the graves will be dug. Tomorrow we will all stand and listen as George Burroughs tells us they are filled with God.

Suddenly, I wish that I could run down to the cove, tear off my cap and apron and dress and throw myself into the cold water. That I could swim out, and wash this day off me. Lay my hand upon the current and feel the echo of paddles and silver prows, read the long vee of their speed across the water, and know where Thaddeus has gone.

He planned it, I think again, watching the water shimmer beyond the birches. He probably decided at the war camp. He had probably been thinking of it all the way back, paddling through the dawn as John Alden told him how we had lived in The Greening. I think of my mother, and of my father's leaving, and of how we are all circles within circles, journeys within journeys. I think of the touch of my fingers on Thaddeus Hobbs' cheek, just last night, and of what he made me promise. And feel a wave of anger.

My birch glade is covered in death. The beach is marked with blood. The tide will wash away the foot prints, but it cannot wash away the sour aftertaste of violence done by men. Trembling with something that is rage, or grief, or exhaustion, or all three, I pick up my skirts and start toward the milking shed. I must let the cows out to graze. I must help my mother and

Hannah. I must care for Tiny Hannah, and my goats, and even Abigail. I must tend to all the things women tend to so men can leave.

I am almost out of the birch grove when I notice the figure.

At first, I think it is a log or a branch brought down by the rain. Then I step closer and see that it is a man, another member of the militia. This one has fallen backwards, into the bushes, and lays on a bed of crushed elder and hawthorn. I did not spot him because of his dark britches, and the darkness of his shirt. Which is covered in blood.

A great cascade of it runs down his chest, and down his arms, and into his empty hands. Standing here, breathing in the copper scent that mixes with the sweetness of damp leaves, I can see exactly how it happened. He would have been following Walter Gendle. He must have had his eyes fixed on the stupid raised sword, and run too far to the side of the grove, too close to the bushes. So all it took was for a hand to reach out. And grab those lustrous curls. And pull him backward off his feet. And cut his throat.

Drained of blood, his face is white, his lips parted, his teeth bared in protest. His coat flaps open, the lapel thrown back, revealing the stained embroidery of a single letter stitched above his heart.

CHAPTER FORTY-SIX

I *must tell Judah.*

She must hear it from me, not from gossip. Or worse, from the militia, who know what James Parr has done, or at least what he will have boasted about. The tales he will have told beside the fire or over a pipe, to impress or raise a laugh about Judah White. She must not be shamed that way. And she must not see him. She must remember him as he was, not as he is now.

Turning away, I hurry out of the grove.

I don't know what I expect, but the village seems unusually still. The bell has stopped tolling. I can see a throng of people down by the fort, but Broad Street is empty. Perhaps everyone who has not rushed to the fort has gone to The Meeting House, or gone home to bar their doors and fasten their shutters against the threat that never was. *But now may be. For violence follows violence as thunder follows lightning.* I shove the thought aside, and make for The Ordinary.

When I get there, I half expect to find the yard gates closed and chained. But they are open. So is the front door to the tap room, although no sound comes from inside. In an hour or two, certainly by sunset, once the bodies are retrieved and surprise is replaced by fury, the rumors that are even now being planted will be brought here to be fed and watered. Nurtured, so they can grow into God Knows What. For now, though, it is still.

I hear the clatter of kitchen things, and smell baking, and the smokey tang of meat roasting—a goose or turkey for tonight's pies—as I make my way down the side yard. Mistress Ingersoll usually oversees the cooking, shouting and bossing the kitchen boy. I hope I will not have to go inside to ask for Judah. I don't. She is in the back, hanging linen.

A wash tub, half filled with soap-scummed water sits beside the well. A cord is stretched from the end of the stable to a post outside the kitchen door. Judah's sleeves are rolled up. She stands on tiptoe, stretching to peg a cloth. I am half surprised, and half not surprised, to see a flutter of crimson. Jamie Parr's betrothal ribbons, still caught in her apron knot.

She finishes and, as she bends to the basket, senses me and spins around. For a moment, neither of us says anything. Then Judah shakes her head and frowns.

"For God's sake! You are enough to scare anyone witless, creeping about like that on your savage paws."

I look down and see my moccasins below my skirts. I had forgotten all about them.

"I'm sorry," I say.

Judah shakes her head, lifting a cloth from the basket. There is another flash of crimson, ribbon laced through her sleeves.

"I should think so," she says. "You're as bad as Abigail, which is probably no surprise. What do you want?"

Judah turns her back on me, putting two pins in her mouth, reaching for the line again. And that is when I realize. She does not know. I look down at my dirty apron, then at my hands, as if somehow they will tell the story. Save me from having to open my mouth and form the words.

It seems impossible that everyone should not know what has happened. And yet, why should they? It has been less than an hour since Yellow Bird raised his wings and drew his talons down his cheeks. Since Thaddeus was swallowed by a wolf's smile, and Hannah Smith came screaming through the birch grove.

Those at the fort will have seen for themselves as the wounded limped back. And those who ran to the bell will have heard the news. But it will not have had time to filter through the village.

"What is it?" Judah turns. "You look as dense as your moon cow. And," she frowns and wrinkles her nose, "you are very dirty, even for you. I have work to do." She picks another piece of linen out of the basket. "What do you want?" She asks again. "Why have you come?"

I want to say that I want nothing. And just in that moment, more than anything, I wish I had not come. I had forgotten we are no longer friends. I need no more reminder than the tone of her voice. I blink.

"I'm sorry, Judah," I say. "I thought you knew, that you had heard. There was a fight. An attack, this morning, by the militia. At the cove."

Her hand, which had been reaching into her apron for another pin, stops moving. She looks at me as if I am a strange animal that has suddenly appeared in the yard, something to be afraid of.

"An attack?"

I would like to back up. I would like to leave. To turn and run up Broad Street and home across the meadow. But I cannot, any more than I can turn back time. A squawk erupts from the kitchen. Mistress Ingersoll shouts, and there is a bang. I nod.

"Yes," I say. "I am sorry. An attack. The militia came, and they were attacked, and James Parr is dead."

Judah drops the square of linen. For a moment, I think she is going to scream. That she is going to shout at me to leave, to get away from her. I see it in her face. Then she sits down, hard, on the cobbles, her hand catching the basket and tipping it over.

"I am sorry." I step toward her. "I am so sorry."

Judah raises a hand before I can touch her. She looks

stunned, as if she has been slapped. Taking a deep breath, drawing it in as though the air is thick and heavy as soured cream, she looks up at me. Today, her eyes are dark gray, and now, expressionless.

"What happened? Please," she says as she sees me begin to protest. "Please. You must tell me exactly what happened. Exactly."

I open my mouth, thinking how to form the first words, where to begin this story.

Before any sound can come out, Judah snaps, "Tell me! For God's sake, if you care for me at all, tell me. I must know," she says, her voice low and pleading. "I must know, exactly. Because I caused this. This is my fault."

I stare at her.

"No," I begin to protest, "It cannot—"

"Yes," she says. "It is. I did not intend it to be, I promise you. But it is."

I feel as if the world is fracturing. Cracking like a broken looking glass, the pieces flying, helter-skelter. I know Judah does not want me to touch her, but I come close. I crouch so my face is even with hers, so we may look into each other's eyes, and whisper so no one else will hear us.

"Judah, what do you mean?" I ask. "How did you cause this? Why?"

"Because," she whispers back, "I wished to be free."

CHAPTER FORTY-SEVEN

Judah White's Story

You cannot understand what it is, to be indentured. Oh, you may try. You may listen and nod. But you cannot know, any more than you can know Jersey, or what we came from. Not your parents and people like Philip Lenglois, who now calls himself English as I now call myself White. I do not mean them. They are not 'we'. They are not people like me.

My parents left me before I ever knew them. "Taken by God", is the phrase, I think. Well, I can tell you, God took plenty, and for the likes of us, left precious little. I went to an aunt and uncle, who were not bad people. But they could not feed me. They could barely feed themselves. So I learned to beg almost before I could walk. That's where Philip English found me, on the streets of St Helier, in a doorway.

He took pity, the way you take pity on a starving dog. So he bought me. No, I was not his slave, nor his plaything in bed. It is not as you think. It was an act of kindness. He is a kind man, although there are those who fear his tongue, which can be sharp, it's true. Philip Lenglois as he was then, had me taken into his house out of charity. He had me cleaned and clothed and trained. I could not have got an indenture otherwise. Who would pay to be saddled with an untutored, unclean, useless beggar child? There are plenty, believe me, with ample skills, who come first in line. In the Lenglois house I learned to be a kitchen child, and to say "Yes Sir, No Sir," and to curtsy. I learned to be useful, or useful enough that someone might want me.

It was in that house that I first heard of New England. When the Lenglois decided they would begin anew here, I was bare eight years old. They brought me with the rest of their baggage —with their chairs and tables and beds. It was Philip English, as he became, changing half way across the ocean as if the very air transformed him, and later his wife, Mary, who is also a good woman, who brokered my indenture. Mary's mother owned a tavern in Salem and knew the Ingersolls. So they knew when poor Elizabeth Bourne was sent away, and arranged for me to be sent, as a replacement, the way you send a friend who has broken a dish a new dish.

They told me my indenture was a start in life. A launching, as if I was a small but hopeful ship. I was sold for fifteen years.

I do not know if your mother's family knew Eliza Bourne's family in Jersey, but they knew mine. My grand-parents worked for yours. You are surprised? Your mother never told you. That is like her. But, it explains why, when I came here, she was duty-bound to care for me. Everyone knows your mother is kind to strays, and good at mending broken things. I lied, when I shouted at you. Your home has been a refuge. I could not ask for more. You shared everything. But there is one thing you cannot share with me. You cannot share your freedom.

Joseph Ingersoll and his wife paid good money for me, to save them labor. Oh, I'm not complaining. They are not cruel. I am not worked like a beast. I was allowed to visit you, and sleep in your bed and eat your food, when they did not need me. And no, it is not for a lifetime. But it is slavery, nonetheless, of a kind. Even if it has an end in sight. I belong with them, but am not of them. I am not equal, any more than I am equal to you.

No, listen! It's true. I've always known it, even if I allowed myself to think otherwise because I wanted to. To believe that you and I were exactly the same. I kept the mirage, the fancy of it as we stood on the beach and raised our palms to mingle our blood. As we laid out shells and pebbles and said they were our lives. Then I heard you speak of Thaddeus Hobbs, and it was like the cracking of a glass. Or a shell. The pattern broke. It flew apart, because I realized that if it was not him, it would be another.

I saw everything laid out. You would be married, living in your father's house. And where would I be? Who would I be? I could not know, or even guess. Because the decision is not mine. If the Ingersolls leave, I have to go with them. Be taken, as you take a dog or a cow or any other possession. And when my indenture is up? In eight more years, when I am hard and weathered with work so no man will want me, what will I have? A spare set of clothes. Perhaps some cooking pots and tools, if Mistress Ingersoll is feeling flush. A sack of corn.

Oh, yes, I know. Philip and Mary English will help me. They will give me a bit of this, or a bit of that. Set me to be married to someone who needs a working wife. William Hobbs, perhaps? I could be Abigail's mother and your mother-in-law, have you thought of that? It won't happen because Hobbs won't wait that long. But who I'll find will be no better. Not here. Because this place is nowhere, especially when you are no one.

So, yes. When I heard you speak of Thaddeus Hobbs and his angel wings, I was jealous. Not so much of him, but of your freedom to choose him. And I was afraid. I wanted wings of my own. So I set my sights on Jamie Parr.

I knew he gambled. He's good at it. He wins coin, and other things, and he is generous when he does. He told me he would be wealthy, and I believed him. No, I didn't know about her, or about the ruined girl you spoke of. I didn't understand that a betrothal was his route to riches. Not until you told me. I just believed him because I wanted to. And because I thought that if

I could snare him, if I could bewitch him, he would use his winnings to buy what is left of my indenture. It's not much, if you have anything. But it's a great deal if you have nothing.

And then, when he had bought me, he would marry me. And we would leave this place that is no place on the edge of nowhere and I would be someone. Even if it was only Goody Parr. And I liked him, well enough. That was my plan. Until you shattered it with an embroidered letter.

I was very angry. But you know that. What you do not know is that I did not tell him what I had discovered, because I decided I did not care. I decided I would snare him anyway. It was simple. I am here, and she is not. My snare was well laid already, and when I had him in it, I would pull it tight. And he would do what I wanted, or I would ruin him. I would run to George Burroughs, and Edward Tyng. I would write to my patron, the now mighty Philip English. I would stand up in The Meeting House and shout and scream from the roof tops what had been done to me. If I did not become his wife, I would make sure that no father in New England would allow his beloved, landed daughter, or any other daughter, to marry James Parr.

But it was not quite time yet, to pull the wire tight. I needed just a little more time, to be sweet one day and salt the next, until he was mad enough to do anything I bid.

This morning, it was salt.

I had gone down to the harbor early. Abigail was there, skipping along the beach, throwing stones again, at the gulls. I didn't pay her any mind. Then, I saw Jamie come out of the fort. I knew he had seen me. Abigail had given up the gulls by then and was dancing about me. She was very excited, and singing one of her songs. Something about a secret. Out of the corner of my eye, I could see Jamie coming along the beach toward us. Everything was cool from the rain. We went walking in it, last night, Jamie and I. Just for a few moments. I slipped away, and we walked in the rain and I let him kiss me. So, this morning, I turned my back on him.

I waited until I knew he was close enough to hear, close enough to know I was ignoring him, before I said to Abigail, "You have no secrets! What secrets could a chit like you have?"

That made Abigail puff up like a little quail.

"I do have secrets," she said. "And I will tell them. But only if you give me something. Only if you pay a price."

At that, I remembered the story about Abigail and her sister's ribbons, and I had Jamie's ribbons, so I thought at once I could let him know how little they mean to me. I saw a chance to rub more salt in the wound of my disinterest, which would make him long all the more for sweetness to take the sting away.

So I said, "I will give you one of these ribbons. Are they not fine? I will give you one. But first you must tell me your secret."

As I did, I unlaced my sleeve, and fluttered a ribbon before her. Abigail jumped for it. She snatched like a kit at a ball of yarn, and I laughed and finally let it go. And when she had it, Abigail said, "Well, you have earned it then, for I never lie and always keep my word. There are Indians. That is my secret."

She was weaving the scarlet ribbon between her fingers as she spoke, making a cat's cradle.

"There are Indians," she said again. "Many of them. More than I can count. They have come to the cove to talk with Mistress Hammond. And there is a yellow bird with them who flies through the air in a cape of bones. And they have captives, also."

By this time she had broken the cradle and was hopping about, waving the ribbon like a flag, and seeing Jamie had stopped and was staring at us, I thought it was enough. So I said loud enough so he could hear, "Abigail, you are a wicked and terrible liar."

And she shouted, "I am not! I am not! Wicked I may be, but I do not lie. There are Indians and captives on the cove beach this moment. I have just come from there. You go and see for yourself!"

At that, Jamie made a sort of gasp. I thought he said my

name. But when I turned around, intending to smile, to give him a dollop of sweetness, he was walking away. Then he was running toward the fort.

❧

JUDAH'S VOICE STOPS. I lean back on my heels, my hands over my mouth.

"Oh, Judah."

She looks at me, her eyes clouded with tears.

"I meant to go after him," she whispers. "I meant to tell him I was only toying, that I was sorry, about the ribbon. I thought that was why he ran. I thought I had stung him, and I meant to put some sweetness on the wound. But that was not it, was it?"

No. I shake my head, *No,* I think. *That was not it at all.*

CHAPTER FORTY-EIGHT

W*hy?*

The memory of John Alden's voice flickers like a candle in a draft. *Why could they not have waited? And how did Gendle know? How?*

Well, I have the answer to that now. Walter Gendle knew because he heard from Jamie Parr, who heard Abigail Hobbs tell Judah White that there were Indians and captives at the cove. A secret and a taunt, ending in blood.

Jamie Parr may have thought to curry favor. Or perhaps he thought it his duty to tell Gendle, who for good or ill, was a captain. And Walter Gendle must have thought to seize the day —prove himself the hero he was not. So, Abigail's Black Man picked up his sword, and his men followed him. All for a scarlet ribbon.

Yes. I have the answers now. But I will not share them. Not with John Alden, nor anyone, even my mother. This, at least, I will do for Judah. If what she did becomes known, she will be shunned, or worse. So, I will keep her safe. Even if safety is not possible for us. Which, standing at the edge of the village burial ground, I fear it may not be.

Barely a day has passed since Yellow Bird spread his wings

and shots were fired and hatchets thrown. Four great holes have been opened to receive the memories of the lives that will soon be lowered into them. I have heard that in Boston they stand silent at a burial. That they are so afraid of Catholicism and time wasting that no words can be spared for those abruptly filled with God. In the Eastward, we pause to offer up a word or two. We speak the names of the dead. Bare a day ago, they would have answered. George Burroughs opens his book.

Head bowed, Edward Tyng stands behind our minister. As the bell begins to toll, all our heads are lowered. We are supposed to be in prayer, to be rejoicing on behalf of James Parr, and Walter Gendle, and the poor man whose dead fingers could not reach his musket, and the one who lay face down beside him, that they are lucky enough to have met their maker. Yet, I hear nothing but Judah's warning.

She had just finished speaking yesterday morning, we were still hunkered nose-to-nose in The Ordinary courtyard, when Mistress Ingersoll began to call for her and Judah struggled to her feet. I picked up the basket, and was trying to wipe off the last piece of linen which was soiled from having been dropped, when Judah snatched it from me, and hissed, "You must go! Quickly! You must not be seen here!"

She waved at me as if I was a reluctant cur. Which I suppose, by that time, in a way I was. Back by her side, trading secrets again, I wanted nothing more than to stay there, turn back time so we might be as we had been. But she made it plain I could do neither.

"Go!" She said. "You must go, and not come back here, or if you can help it, even into the village. This story will grow, and grow. And anger with it."

Judah leaned close then, lowering her voice to little more than a breath.

"They already say your mother is a witch. They say she loves the savages more than us. And that her ability to speak their language is a sure sign that their demons speak through her.

They already whisper that there is no way to know what the sachem really said that day at the harbor."

I frowned, and Judah nodded.

"Yes," she said. "There is much talk. Much murmuring. They say that when your mother said Egeremet was promising peace, he was really promising war. That she helped him by saying the opposite, and none can know the trick she played, not even Captain Alden, as only she can speak the devil's language. Now, soon, they will say she planned this, if they are not saying it already. They will say that she set the trap to destroy the militia. As she would destroy all of us."

When, stunned, I had said nothing, Judah shook her head and pushed me towards the side alley.

"Go!" She hissed again. "And stay away!"

"But, why?" I finally managed, even as her hand was at my back. "Why would they—"

"Because they are afraid of her. Because she deals in death as well as life, and your father trades with the savages, and he loves the French, and the French want war."

I had turned then, pushing her hand from me.

"But, it is not true," I protested. "You know! My mother did not—"

Judah shook her head, her voice low and urgent.

"It does not matter what is true—what your mother did or did not say, or do. Truth has no place in this. Don't you understand? What matters is that now they will all be certain it is true. They will take this attack as proof she played a trick. They already say she is a witch. Now, they will blame her for these deaths. She is dangerous for all of us. All of us from Jersey will be painted with the same brush. So, go. And stay away!"

I HAD BARELY TAKEN it in then. All I had thought was *It is not true! It is not true!* The words beating time as I hurried up Broad

Street and across the common and down the meadow. Now, standing by these graves, I feel the village crowd that both surrounds and shuns us, and I fear Judah is right. What is, or is not, true does not matter. The restless ghosts of those killed and captured twelve years ago, the fear and loss and sorrow at Egeremet's taking of husbands and sons, be it justified or no, the deaths of Walter Gendle and these men and the wounding of the others—in sum, all the terror and anguish of this place, has taken to the air. Like a mighty bird of prey it flaps and circles, and fixes upon a place to land. And that place is us.

They watch us from across the open graves. Eyes swivel under the brims of hats and around the edges of freshly stiffened caps. Standing directly across from me, nothing but a hole opened for a dead man between us, Mercy Lewis trails a hand up and down her neck. Beside her, Mary Skilling shifts from foot to foot, pleating the edge of her apron. Goody Burroughs holds her prayer book high and pretends to recite a psalm while she whispers with the Cloyces, never taking her eyes off my mother. A man whose name I do not know holds up two fingers in the hex sign that wards off evil. At the back of the crowd, Abigail leans against her father's leg. He slaps her hand as she tries to reach inside his pocket. I see several people make the sign of the cross.

As the first body is lowered, George Burroughs' voice intones, "Peace and Glory and Holiness are the Lord's."

Glancing at the faces around me, I think, *Peace and Glory and Holiness. And also, Vengeance is His.*

Judah is not here. As soon as Walter Gendle is lowered to his final rest, Mistress Ingersoll whispers to her husband, and slips away. The Ordinary will do good business this afternoon. Someone must make sure the board and tankards are laid out and the beer barrels tapped. I imagine Judah sweating in the kitchen and shouting at the cook boy as she kneads the pastry and minces wood pigeon for pies.

The last to be buried is Jamie Parr. As Anthony Brackett, and Ingersoll himself, and two militia men I do not know lower him into the earth, I am surprised to find myself hoping that beneath his winding sheet he is still wearing his coat. That, for all Judah may wish against it, the embroidered *A* will rest above his heart when he faces God. At the thought, I glance around, half expecting to see a face I do not know, a girl pale with grief come to see him on his way. But all I see are the eyes of the village.

I hear it as the first clod of earth hits Jamie's grave. Another sound mingles with the dull *thwamp* as Joseph Ingersoll swings his shovel. A low hum. At first, I think it must be a swarm of bees—that they have come from our hive or another, have been drawn by the fresh turned soil of the burial place. But there are no bees.

The noise comes from the villagers. From our neighbors. It comes from the Cloyces and the Skillings and the Lewises. From Sylvanus Davis and his wife, and a dozen others, all of whom have now shifted their focus from the graves to us.

As the tuneless drone passes from one set of lips to the next, as it gathers and rises, growing louder and louder, my mother looks up. John Alden reaches an arm around her shoulders. His eye meets mine. He jerks his head toward the common behind us and our meadow beyond that. We step back. The village steps forward.

They move as one, humming in menace, joined in threat like some great beast. Mercy Lewis has stopped scraping her neck. Her hands hang straight at her sides. Goody Burroughs has lowered her prayer book. With her eyes hard and bright as a crow's, Mary Skilling is smiling faintly. As the sound gathers, George Burroughs, who has been staring at the graves, his mouth moving in prayer, looks up. His congregation, this motley group of souls consigned to his care, shifts and ripples while Edward Tyng, his face reddening, sidles away.

"What is—" our minister says as the crowd steps forward again and out of the corner of my eye I see John Alden reach under his coat where his knife hangs at his belt.

The drone increases. They are spreading out now. They are

beginning to flow like water around the graves so they can surround us. So they will be in behind and in front and beside us, and we cannot escape. Over my mother's head, John Alden's eyes meet mine. Then, Abigail Hobbs explodes.

Shooting as if from a cannon from her father's grasp, she careens through the village crowd, her arms windmilling in a parody of flight.

"I am a jay! I am a goose! I am the chick you all let loose!" She screams as she slams into Mercy Lewis, who staggers and wails.

Shrieking, Abigail turns on Mary Skilling. Raising her hands in claws, she shouts, "Bad cat! Bad cat!"

She jumps at Goody Burroughs, snatching for her prayer book. Pulling it out of the minister's wife's hands, Abigail raises it above her head, spinning away as she sings, "I have a poppet! I have a book! I'll steal it like a naughty rook!"

Attempting to chase her, her father slips in the damp grass and falls down. Bending double, Mercy Lewis begins to scream. Goody Burroughs is shouting, "Wicked! Wicked!"

"Quick!" John Alden spins us around, one hand on my mother's elbow, the other grasping mine.

As we reach the edge of the common, I look back. George Burroughs is helping William Hobbs to his feet. Edward Tyng is hurrying towards his house. Anthony Brackett stands with his spade raised, as if he no longer knows what to do with it. Several of the women seem to be trying to calm Mercy Lewis. In the pandemonium she created to allow us to escape, I see no sign of Abigail.

CHAPTER FORTY-NINE

"By the Holy God!" John Alden's hand is not shaking, exactly. But it is not steady either as he reaches for the cider pitcher. "That child is mad."

We hurried back across the meadow and are in the kitchen where Captain Alden, son of Honest John and the sainted Priscilla, commander of Boston's sloop *Mary,* is pretending to be rattled by the behavior of a ten year old. I say 'pretending' because I do not think that is the truth of it. I think it is the villagers, with their humming and their bright fixed stares, I think it is our good neighbors who were only distracted by the antics of that same child, who have rattled him.

I look from John Alden to my mother.

"We should not have gone."

My mother shakes her head.

"We owe that much to the dead," she says, pulling off the cap I starched and stiffened with chalk this morning. Unpinned, her hair falls about her shoulders. Another time, I might be surprised that she does this in front of John Alden. Now, I barely notice.

"And," she sighs, "it would have done no good. If we had not gone, they would have thought that proof as well."

As she speaks, I realize she knows what is being said of her.

"This nonsense is my fault." John Alden downs the cider and pours himself another cup. "If I had not asked you, if I had not insisted that you come when Egeremet was here and made you translate, they would not think this."

My mother looks at him, and smiles.

"Yes, John," she says. "They would. And if I had not come, you would have stood there like a deaf mute with no idea of what was being said or any thought as to how to reply to it." She shakes her head, and I notice that her hair has no gray in it. That, if anything it seems tawnier and fuller than I remember.

"There is no matter to it," my mother says. "Whether we had gone to the burials or not. This vine has deep roots. They have always thought this, in this village, of me. Or wanted to think it. They fear what I am able to do, and they cannot forgive me for speaking out for poor Elizabeth. The difference now is that they have found their reasons. Now they can count themselves doubly righteous, as I am both a witch and a traitor."

"What will they do?" It is Hannah Smith who asks.

She is standing in the doorway to our front parlor. Henry Smith's wounds are not as bad as they might have been. He was hit in the shoulder, most likely by one of the militia guns as he attempted to run up the bank. He was lucky that, unlike Walter Gendle, he was not in the way of a hatchet blade flying through the air like an unleashed star. And lucky also, my mother said when she had finished picking the shot out of his wound—an operation that took almost an hour and required both powder of poppy and John Alden to hold him down—that the aim had not been a few inches lower and hit his heart. Or a few inches closer to his neck where veins would have opened and let all his blood pour out instead of merely the substantial amount he lost.

Over Hannah's shoulder, I see that he is sitting up, drinking beef broth. Tiny Hannah lays in his lap. Small Henry is sprawled across the end of my parents' marriage bed watching his parents as if he may never let them out of his sight again.

"What will they do?" Hannah repeats the question, this time glancing towards the open kitchen window as if she expects to see an army marching down the meadow.

"They won't do a thing! They won't dare! Not while I'm here and have breath!" Large Henry shouts from his pile of cushions.

"And me, and Tom!" Small Henry echoes.

John Alden smiles and puts his cup down.

"Nothing," he says. But I notice that he too, glances towards the window. "Nothing," John Alden says again, and his voice sounds too hale and hearty. "They are full of hot air and humming and nothing more. They are afraid and riled, not least because they have been so stupid, and do not wish to know it. The harvest will be better with this rain. They all have fields. Give them a day or two, and they will go back to work and forget about it."

A few minutes later he takes his leave, saying he must call on Edward Tyng and has business at the fort. I walk with him up the garden. When we reach the gate, he passes through, then turns to me. John Alden nods as he sees that I already have the chain and lock in my hands. Then he goes without speaking.

Later, when my mother has gone upstairs to rest and the Smiths are in the front parlor with the door closed, I collect all the kitchen knives. Then I go find the ax at the woodpile, and spend the afternoon at the whetstone, sharpening blades.

❧

NOT THAT KNIVES, however sharp they may be, will do any good. When they come for a witch, they come armed with God. And for a traitor? The punishment for witching is hanging. For a traitor, it is flames.

I reach for the Night Spirit, finger the outline of its shape, and just for a moment think I hear the jangle of bones as I make my way to the milking shed. Relieved of his duty guarding Tiny Hannah, Tom follows me. Like his master, he is only small. But he is comfort and company. It is almost sunset. I am later than I should be. Along with the sharpening of blades, I had my mother's chores to do.

Whether it is caring for Large Henry, or the poisoned fruit of the rumor vine, or simply all that has happened, all the stones that have been piled upon us in the last month, she is exhausted. And, though I try to resist the thought, I find myself hoping it is only that. As she made her way upstairs, her hair falling about her shoulders as if she no longer had the energy to hide it, I watched my mother's hand on the rail. And felt a dark twist in my gut as I tried to tell myself that I had not caught another motion. That the thing that comes for her was not crouching on the top step, kneading its claws and twitching its tail.

My leg is all but healed, and my work goes quickly. Belle and Bess and our old cow and the little bay horse that has no name crop the refreshed grass without looking up. They amble good naturedly when I shoo them in, and shoulder each other gently at the hay rick. The goats, however, sense my mood. They walk stiff-legged, butting each other when I call. I have raked the floor and laid the straw. As I go to fetch the water pail, I realize with a pang that the last time I did this was with Thaddeus. Bare two days ago, in another life.

Closing the shed door, I look towards the cove as if I expect to see him, returning from wherever he has gone, walking with his wings folded, silent as an angel. For a moment, I am sure he is there. Then, the light wavers, revealing nothing but the end of the day. No figure hovers above the blood stained grass. No man is coming through the birch grove.

But there is a man coming down the meadow.

Trailing along the fence, less than eager to go back to the house, I have bent to lay a hand on Percy's grave, to feel the flat, warm surface of the stone and ask him if he too enjoys the rain, when I straighten and see him. With the sun low behind him, he is nothing but a dark shape. As I watch, he stretches and grows.

This time, the world does not go still. Nor does it ripple.

Instead, it seems to flicker around me, as if all the air is suddenly alive and dancing. I hear a scream, then another. Sparks fly from the jagged line of the village roofs, spangle like stars, and gather into a column of flame. From where I am, I should not be able to see the fire that licks first one house, then the next. But I can. Something cleaves the shuddering air. Doors buckle. Windows crumple inward. My cheeks and forehead burn. The great fire shakes the world the way leaves shake a windy forest. I feel it burning my throat and my eyes, which are fastened on the figure of the black man, who comes closer and closer.

Then it is all gone. My skin is cool. The only flames are the flames of the sunset. And the man is John Alden.

I take a breath and close my eyes. Opening them, stepping gingerly back into this world, I notice a motion. Or rather, the lack of one. Animals come out now. As the light tips towards dark, the fox and the ring-tailed coons in their black masks and the deer break cover. Once, I saw a small bear foraging for berries above the cove. All of them scurry, or trot, or turn and run with the coming night. Even now, Tom is scampering to meet John Alden. But this small shape, which was so frantic just a few hours ago does not move at all.

Abigail stands at the far side of the meadow, in the same spot where I have seen her before. Even from this distance, I feel our eyes lock, feel the promises we have made thrumming between us. This time, it is me who raises my hand. When Abigail raises hers I see a flash of scarlet at her sleeve.

❧

My mother is upstairs. The Smiths are in the parlor. The rustle of bedding and soft voices filter under the closed door. Then the line of candle light goes out, and there is silence. I feed John Alden.

He came, he says, because he could abide neither the fort nor Edward Tyng's hospitality for one more moment, so thought he would rest with us. I give him a stew Hannah made, a rich broth of rabbit and turnips—Hannah is a good cook—and a portion of the day's bread, and a wedge of cheese from my goats. I open a bottle of the Malaga wine. Though he claims to be nothing like his father, John Alden is a man of courage and honor, at least to those who know him well. He is also a sly fox. And a terrible liar.

As I started to shutter the window that looks onto the meadow, he said he preferred the night air, and told me to leave it open. Some time after that, as we listened to the peepers singing in the tall grass, I offered to unroll Thaddeus' pallet, since the Hannahs and the Henrys have the marriage bed and we have only the one bed upstairs. But John Alden claimed the hearth chair was comfort enough. Indeed, he insisted it is almost as good as a bed, if he pulls out the old fire stool and uses it as a foot rest. So when he has eaten and I have cleared away, I leave him there with a candle and the bottle. It is only as I am climbing the stairs that I look down and see he has taken out his pistol. Primed, it lays on the table with his hand resting upon it as he stares through our open window into the darkness.

CHAPTER FIFTY

It was then that I knew we were leaving. I felt it in John Alden's blunt fingers as they rested on the pistol butt. And in his gaze, fixed on the opened window. In the years to come, I would think perhaps I had always known. That even as we arrived in the Eastward and built our house between the meadow and the sea, we were already leaving. Much as we were leaving The Greening even as my father first delivered us into Ashawonks' care. Folding shells within shells, we slid from each world to the next even as we entered them and they overlapped. So I should not have been surprised when I reached the top of the stairs, and found my mother waiting for me.

She too, had left the window open and unshuttered. A pale wash of moonlight fell on the floor and across the bed, where she seemed at first to be asleep. In the strange light, her face looked even younger than mine, and again I had the now familiar sense that she was moving backwards through time. From the doorway, I glanced around the room, not wanting to wake her but looking, I think, to see if the thing I knew would take her from me had come again and was sitting twitching in the shadows. But there was nothing, only her dress folded across the linen press where she must have dropped it, too tired even to lift the lid and put it away. I felt my hand go to the neckline of my own dress. I had taken my shoes off downstairs. As quietly as I could, avoiding the board that creaked, I padded across the room.

My fingers probed and dug. They felt along each seam, and in the hems. But they found nothing. No smooth stone. No shape or etched design to tell me I was right, or wrong. It was only when I let myself sigh in frustration that I looked up and saw her watching me. She had pulled herself up to sit against the pillows. Her hair flowed over her shoulders, and I realized it must have grown since I last saw it loose. In the half dark room, her eyes were not brown, but amber, almost golden.

"Did you find what you were looking for?"

There was no anger in her voice. I shook my head. For a moment, we watched one another. Then my mother patted the bed. "Come," she said.

I climbed onto the high frame. As I settled beside her, my mother reached up and stroked my head.

"What did you mean?"

My voice sounded strange to me, as if it was not quite my own. It sounded fluttery, like all the moth words I had been collecting and carrying were escaping, flying away and leaving me hollow, emptied of their wings which I had grown used to beating around my heart.

"What did you mean," I asked again, "when you said Yellow Bird recognized me?"

My mother looked at me. Then she nodded, as if she had decided something. When she spoke, her voice was very soft.

"I am not the first of my family to have the gifts I have," she said. "And you are my only child. Power comes down. It distills, like wine." She regarded me for a moment. Then she stroked my head again and said, "That is what Yellow Bird recognized."

"Did Ashawonks recognize you?" I am not sure how I know

this, but I understand now that it was the bond I had always felt between them.

"Yes. Yes," my mother said again. "That was her gift to me. Ashawonks knew me before I knew myself. It was she who introduced me to Yellow Bird. People say he is her father, although I do not know if that is true."

I twisted around to look at her.

"How old is he?"

"No one knows." My mother shook her head, and I knew her answer was also the answer to the question I had not asked, *What is he?*

"He taught me everything," my mother said. "It was there, inside me, waiting. But I could not reach it. Could not grasp what was at my fingertips. He will teach you, too, if you let him. Although, I wonder if you will need it."

"What do you mean?" The question felt dangerous, like stepping on to spring ice.

"You know more than you think, Susannah."

At the sound of my old name on her lips, I felt tears welling, bubbling inside me like an overflowing spring. Because I knew part of what she was telling me was that I did not need her any more. I shook my head.

"Don't go," I whisper. "Don't leave me."

"I will never leave you." My mother stroked my face. "I will never leave you," she said again. Then she smiled and plumped the pillow. She pushed me gently onto it and lay down beside me the way she did when I was very small. My head felt heavy on her shoulder, as if I was already dreaming. I felt her fingers smooth my hair. Felt her voice wrap around me.

"I will never leave you, and I will always keep you safe," I thought I heard her say. And then something else, but it was barely a whisper. "I promise," my mother said. "Always. Remember."

When I wake what must be hours later, the room is completely dark. But I know I am alone. I sit up, my bare feet finding the floor. The window is still open. Beyond it, I can see stars.

On the stairs, I pause. The candle has guttered out. John Alden sits, his head in his arms on the table, fast asleep, the pistol still primed beside his hand. No sound comes from behind the parlor door. Not even Tom is moving. They are bewitched, I think. The kitchen door is open.

Outside, the garden is nothing but dark shapes against darkness. I can smell lavender and chamomile and mint where they have overgrown and been crushed on the gravel. My mother sometimes comes to sit under the grape arbor at night, but I know she is not here. Instead, I turn toward the cove.

The paddock fence is a jagged line in the darkness. At the end of it, by the last post, something glows faintly. A bunch of Queen Anne's lace has been laid on Percy's grave. I pass the milking shed where the animals are silent. Ahead, the birch grove seems more silver than it should be. The night has changed. The moon seems to have vanished, but the stars are brighter, and lower, as if they have swung down to light the earth. The great river of them the people call The Wolf Trail is so low and close that it is almost part of the grove. It almost looks as if I could pull myself up and walk its shimmering road.

I start to raise my hand, as if I think I can finger the stars, feel the cold pinpricks of their light, when I see my mother, just the white shape of her, standing on the bank above the cove. By the time I get there, she is gone, down to the beach.

Below me the water glitters. The tide has stopped, as if the sea is waiting. My mother stands on the sand, and for a moment I am sure I can see all the shells and pebbles, all the patterns I have made spread around her bare feet. I want to run to her. But I can't. I can't move at all. As I watch from the top of the bank, she grabs the hem of her shift, pulls it over her head, and drops it at the water's edge.

My mother's hair streams down her back. Her shoulders and waist are still narrow, her legs long and fine. She looks like a girl. As she steps into the cove, I want to shout to her. I want to tell her to wait, that I am coming with her. But nothing happens. I am as frozen and helpless as if I have been turned to stone.

She wades until the water is at her waist, then her shoulders. My mother stops and spreads her arms, resting her hands on the starlit sea. Then she begins to swim. Her strokes are strong and sure. There is no weakness, nothing of the sickness that has plagued her. Her body is a pale shape, moving away from me. And again, it seems the sky has lowered, the stars and their reflection merging into one great shimmering orb.

Suddenly unfrozen, I clamber down the bank and step on to the beach, trying to see better. The starlight seems to be revolving now, spinning until the cove glows with it. I raise a hand to my eyes as one does to the sun, and stare as my mother reaches the far shore, which is no longer dark and shadowed, but lit with a strange, cold light. I squint, both hands raised, trying to shield my eyes from the brightness. But I cannot see her anymore. I cannot see anything except the shapes of the trees, swaying gently, rocking in an invisible wind.

My feet are in the water, but I do not feel the cold. I raise my arms. Standing in the shallows, I reach out as if I could stretch across the cove. Once, I am sure I see something move, catch a glint of gold, blinking in the shadows. The air is filled with a deep, sweet, familiar scent, chamomile and lavender and something else, the smell that comes to me just before I drift into dreams, the loam of the forest, the faint tang of winter fires, the perfume of The Greening.

I don't know how long it is before I wade back to the beach and bend to pick up my mother's shift. The linen is still warm. I raise it to my face, and feel a hard, familiar shape. The manitou throbs like a beating heart as I slip it out of the tiny pocket sewn into the neckline. Defender. Guardian. Maker of circles. The guide who comes for lost and wounded warriors, and leads them home. The stars are still low, and still sparkling. But I do not need their light to recognize the creature etched into the polished stone.

CHAPTER FIFTY-ONE

It is dawn when John Alden finds me on the beach where I have fallen asleep clutching my mother's shift. I hear him and sit up, disheveled. He looks as ragged as I feel. His shirt is untucked, his hair tousled. He holds the pistol. Without a word, he clambers down the bank.

I get to my feet, holding out my mother's shift. As John Alden takes it from me, my fingers uncurl. The stone I have been clutching is smooth and plain. It is nothing more special than the dozens of others Judah and I found here over the years and arranged into the pattern of our lives.

❧

THAT WAS THREE DAYS AGO. Although, it might have been three years. Or three minutes. Time is no longer orderly in my mind.

In the village, Goody Burroughs and Goody Skilling and everyone in The Ordinary says my mother drowned herself. That she was a sister to the savages, a speaker of demonic words. A traitor. A liar. A lover of the French. A witch whose wickedness was only proved by her knowledge and, of course, by her beauty. She was a wearer of The Devil's Glove.

They say her death is proof of it all, and that she killed herself rather than face the accusations, the trial, that was surely coming. I am sure it is also whispered in The Ordinary after a pint or two that, in the end, she did them a favor. Saved them all a great deal of unpleasant trouble, and the meddling of Boston. Never mind the fuss of a hanging, or the building of a pyre. I am sure they say all that.

We say nothing at all.

I don't know what John Alden knows, or Hannah Smith senses. Sometimes I am not even sure what I know, beyond the fact that she is gone. That she went, as she promised, to keep me safe. To stop the village vendetta. Twice now, deep in the night, I have half fallen asleep then sat straight up in the dark, sure I can hear the long lonely call of a wolf. But in the morning, no matter how hard I look, there are never any tracks.

I am thinking on this, sitting in the arbor playing cats cradle with it in my mind, trying to sort through what I saw and did not see, what I dreamed and what I know and if the two are different, when Mary English arrives.

I don't know how I know it is her, but I do. Like me, she is tall. But there the resemblance ends. Mary English is the finest creature I have ever seen, and she stands like a mirage at our garden gate.

I blink, then blink again. But she does not go away. The chain is only looped over the gatepost. There is no point now, in locking it. I watch as she lifts it with a gloved hand. Her skirts ruffle with an unfamiliar sound as she crosses the gravel. I catch a glimpse of silver buckles on her shoes.

I know I should be straining curds, or winding bandages in the stillroom ready for the next disaster. Or I could spin, or collect berries from the brambles at the edge of the meadow, or use the still newly sharpened ax to split kindling. But a strange lethargy has come over me. I cannot seem to move far from this bench.

I have not seen Judah, or even Abigail, though I fancy sometimes that I feel her close by. Watching me. Loving me like a sister. No one except George Burroughs has come to offer their condolences. The Smiths are here, of course. And John Alden comes every night to eat Hannah's stew and drink Malaga wine and sit in the hearth chair and stare through the window, although he no longer bothers to prime his gun.

Large Henry is up and about these last two days. He is not strong yet. But he has taken to doing most of the work in the milking shed, and says that one day soon he will harness the little bay horse and drive the cart down Cleeve's neck and out around the Back Cove to tend to the fields on his own farm. In the meantime, Hannah has gone up the path and into town, when it has been necessary. She returns with what we need, salt or a flagon of vinegar. But for an hour after, her lips are pursed and her movements quick. Whatever it is she hears, she does not repeat it. I know it anyway. I hear it on the wind.

"Do you mind, if I sit here?"

Mary English's voice is as pretty as she is. Her words are light and well formed, as if each one is a drop of clear water. She does not wear a cap, but instead a cape made of some light silky stuff, and a hood, a lined one, the kind you can be fined for wearing in Boston. As she pushes it back, I see that her dark hair is not like Judah's. It is not wild and curly, but dressed high, and sleek as seal's fur. Her eyes are the same color, brown and bright. It is only as she sits that I think to wonder where she came from, and look up to see two men standing talking on the meadow path. One is John Alden, and one, I know right away, is Philip English. He wears a fine black coat, and the tall hat that can only be worn by men who pay taxes of more than two hundred pounds a year. No one here has a tall hat.

At first, I think the hand Mary English extends to me is pale and jeweled. Until I see the fine kid of her glove, and the colored embroidery that runs around the wrist.

"You must be Susannah," she says.

"Resolve."

"Of course."

She smiles as she settles herself with the same strange rustling her skirts made when she walked. I smell a scent, as strong as cherries, that I think must be perfume. Mary English studies me for a moment before she pulls off her gloves, one by one, tugging each finger. Then, she reaches out and lays her hands over mine where they are folded in my lap.

"I am a friend of your father's," she says. "And was a friend of your mother's. She was very dear to me."

When I do not answer, Mary English pauses, studying my face. Then, she goes on.

"My husband and your father are partners. You know that. They have known one another many years. Since they were children in Jersey. They are as brothers. And your mother's father, your grandfather, was my husband's godfather. Which makes your mother a sister to me. And you, a daughter."

I start to pull my hands away as she says this. But she stops me, shaking her head.

"I know you are not my daughter," she says. "I have two fine daughters of my own, and I am not your mother. Nor could I be. But I will be your friend, if you will let me."

When I do not answer, Mary English continues.

"Your father wrote to us, some time ago, when he went away. He asked that, if you and your mother should feel unsafe, if things should become—" she hesitates before choosing the right term, and finally settles on, "dangerous. That, since he is not here, you and your mother might come and live with us. Until he can return. What," Mary English asks me now, "would you think of that?"

What I would think of that, I think, *is that it is a lie. My father did not write to you, or anyone. Nor has he given a thought to us. He probably never even planned to return. He abandoned us, and worse. He left my mother to bear the weight of his allegiances. That,* I think, *is what I think of that.*

But looking at her sweet, pretty face, I cannot say it. And, looking at the men, at the way they stand talking on the meadow path, I think I understand what actually happened.

I do not know if John Alden had business at the fort or with Edward Tyng after we were hummed at the burials, or if he rushed to compose a letter to be sent south by fast rider. But I do know that he is behind this. It is not my father who wrote to Philip English and his wife. Not my father who told them we needed protection—that Captain Alden sat through the night with shot and pistol at the ready in case our dear neighbors found their courage at the bottom of a tankard and decided to seek some retribution for the dead, and for their own mistakes.

No, it was John Alden who thought to plan for our safety, our escape. And it is John Alden who probably hired another fast rider three days ago and arranged this. John Alden with his wife who owns sawmills, and who, as Judah pointed out, has always loved my mother. Who thought to try to save her from the witches' rope, or worse. And who now, for her sake, has tried to arrange a refuge for me. He is the one who has done this. Who else can it be? Who else do I have now?

It is only when Mary English reaches her hand to my cheek that I realize I am crying. That tears are streaming down my face and my shoulders are heaving.

"Oh, my Dear," she says, as she pulls me to her. "Oh, my Dear. This has been too horrible. It has all been too much. This is no place for you. You must come to us. You must let us love you, and take you to a place of safety."

And so, that is how it happens. That is how I leave. The Englishes do not spend even one night in the dingy rooms of The Ordinary. It has all been arranged. The small, fast, ship that brought them—one of a fleet of twenty Philip English owns, is at anchor beyond the harbor. A fine stern cabin stands prepared. We will board at the turn of the late afternoon tide. And by midnight, when the sickle moon smiles her thin smile down on the point and the cove and the road that runs along Cleeves Neck, we will be gone.

It is not for good, John Alden says. Just until tempers cool. Just until I am old enough to marry, and return, and take up the inheritance that is mine. And will always be mine, standing at the bottom of the meadow above the birch grove, waiting for me.

He explains that the Smiths have agreed to stay at our house and tend our land. It is safer, just now, for them to be closer to the village. Large Henry will go out to tend his own fields by day, and return each evening. Hannah will take over my goats, and the milking, and the garden. The stillroom will be locked up. Nothing will be touched until my father is returned, and all bad feeling is forgotten. Until life here can be resumed. On that happy day, time will fold itself upon itself and all shall be as it was.

None of us believe this, but we all agree to it. Because, in truth, there is no other choice. After that, it goes quickly.

Hannah helps me pack our chests, and reaches out, just once to touch my cheek.

"I will care for everything," she whispers, "until you send for it. Or return yourself."

I would like to walk through the grove. I would like to run my hand down the birch trunks, and lay once more on my back to look up through their leaves. I would like to say something to Judah, who has not come in the three days since since my mother walked into the starlit water. I would like to stand on the beach one last time, staring hard into the forest on the opposite shore, willing golden eyes to stare back at me. I would even like to go up to the point, follow the track to the clearing above the pink rocks and kneel down to see if I can find the scars of my memory holes.

But the tide does not wait for memories, or echoes, or grief. In the end, all I can do is ask Hannah if, sometimes, she will remember to place some Queen Anne's lace or a handful of field daisies on Percy's grave.

Philip English, whose hair and eyes are as black as his fine coat and boots, goes back to the harbor to send word to his ship and ready the wherry. Large Henry and Small Henry catch the little bay horse, who has grown fat and lazy, and harness her to the cart. John Alden helps them load our chests. Only when that is done does he turn and look back at the house, and the open kitchen door where I know we both half expect my mother to appear.

"Rachel," he whispers. Just once. Then he swings the gate open, and takes my elbow and ushers me through.

The Smiths do not come with us to the harbor. They stand in our garden which, I think as I look back, is now their garden. As I start to turn away, I remember Alice Atwell, taken these twelve years ago, and wonder if she had time, even a moment, to look back, to promise her old life that somehow she would return to it. Did Hope Hood? Or the boy's mother with her scar-split face? Did Thaddeus? Did he even glance over his shoulder as the shooting began and the silver war canoe bore him away? *I will find you*, I think. *I will find you.* And in that moment I know I am promising not just Thaddeus, but all of them.

Mary English sits on the bench while John Alden leads the little bay horse. Our chests fill the cart bed, so I walk behind. We are halfway up the meadow when I see George Burroughs, hurrying down the path. For a terrible moment, my step falters. I see John Alden falter too, see his free hand go to the pistol tucked into his belt, and imagine him pulling it out, imagine him telling the minister that, come what may, I am leaving this place.

But it does not happen. George Burroughs raises his old hat in greeting. He speaks briefly to John Alden, then comes to walk beside me behind the cart.

"This is best," he says in a murmur so low I can barely hear it. "It is best," George Burroughs says again, and nods as certainty grows in his voice. "Where you are going, to live with the Englishes, you need have no fear. They are your protection. In their great house you will be comfortable and cared for. It is what your mother would have wished, beyond all else. To know that you are safe."

And with that, he turns to me and smiles, and reaches for my elbow.

So we pass through the sideyards, and across the common, and make our way to the harbor. I can feel eyes on us. I can feel faces at windows, and figures inside the boat shed. But I see no one. Not even Edward Tyng appears in his green coat. Only Philip English waits for us on the packed pebbled sand.

A fine wherry is drawn up. Two crewmen sit in it, their oars raised, as if we are people of importance. Four more crew stand beside their master. Out beyond the mouth of the harbor, I can see the ship, swinging gently at her anchor. And suddenly, I want to turn and run.

I want to race up the beach, and across the common, and down the meadow. I want to fling myself into the birch grove and down the bank and grab our canoe and paddle away. North. Or to the islands. Out to sea. Or up to the stars. Along The Wolf Trail. Anywhere the Night Spirit leads me. Anywhere but where we are going.

The pull is so strong that I start to tremble. I feel suddenly sick, as if I have been struck by a fever and may fall down. My brow and palms are clammy.

It is Philip English who notices. He has helped his wife down from the cart and turns toward me as John Alden and George Burroughs begin to unload the chests. When he comes to my side, his hand is firm and cool on my arm. His face is not unkind, and neither is his voice as he leans to me and whispers, "It is difficult, I know. But have no fear. I promise you, we take you to a place of safety."

❧

THE WHERRY IS DEEP KEELED, unlike a canoe, and far enough out that I think we will have to wade. I watch as the crewmen lift my chests and splash through the shallows with them. I am preparing to bend and remove my shoes and stockings, waiting for a sign from Mary English, ready to do as she does when I notice the chair. It is an extraordinary contraption—a fine carved armed chair with poles on either side that stick out in front and in back of it, and a sort of gate across the front. I do not understand until the crewmen splash back with it, and Mary English steps forward. The chair is lowered, and she sits. Lifting her skirts, she places her feet on a little step and with one gloved hand closes the gate across her lap. Then she nods, and the four men bend, grasping the poles, and splash through the shallows, carrying her to the wherry.

Beside me, Philip English is taking John Alden's hand. George Burroughs steps forward too. The men bend their heads in conversation as the crew splash back with the chair. I am next. I am about to step forward when I hear a shout, and spin around, a wave of hope rising in me. That it is Judah. Or somehow all a mistake, or one of my dreams, and I will see my mother, or even Thaddeus running down the beach, shouting that they have come to take me home. Instead, I see Abigail.

She runs as before, legs churning under her short skirts, arms flapping as if she might take flight. As usual, her cap has come off. It hangs around her neck, setting her golden curls free to bounce and stream in the sunlight. As soon as she is close enough, Abigail throws herself at me, hitting me like a cannonball.

For a moment, she stands clutching my legs, burying her face in my skirts. Then she lets go so I can kneel on the damp sand, my face level with hers. I expect her to be angry. To hiss at me, or spit, or threaten. Perhaps even to slap me, as I once slapped her. But instead, as she did on the day her mother died, she studies me with her icy eyes, and smiles.

"Love me like a sister?" She whispers.

I nod, not quite trusting my voice. "Love you like a sister," I finally manage.

"Do you promise?"

"I promise," I say, and am surprised to find that, despite everything, or perhaps because of it, the words are true. *But,* I think, *even as I speak them, I am breaking that other promise. I am abandoning her, leaving her alone in the world so I can be spirited away to a place of safety.*

Before I can apologize, or try to begin to explain, Abigail leans back. Shaking her head, she places her cold, pearly little hand on my lips.

"Do not think it." She says, reading my mind, thrumming the sinew that runs between us. "Do not think it, for it is not so. We shall not be apart for long, I promise. I am coming where you are going," Abigail Hobbs says, smiling at me. "We shall be together again, soon. In Salem."

THE END

ABOUT THE AUTHOR

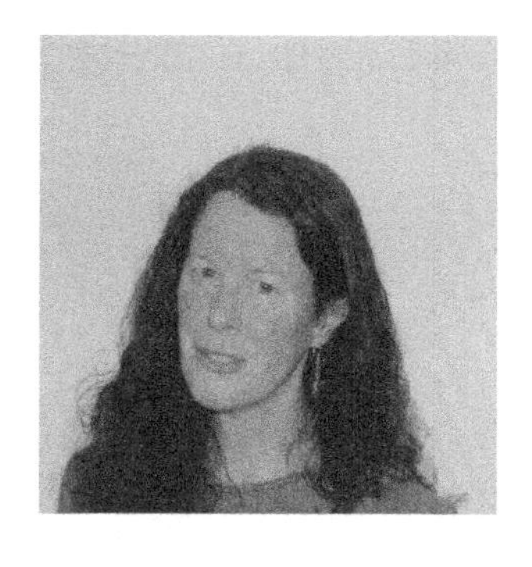

Lucretia Grindle is an award winning author whose captivating novels have won the hearts of readers worldwide. Her intricately plotted stories, richly described settings, and multi-dimensional characters have made her a beloved author in the genres of mystery, thrillers, and literary fiction.

Her six novels, including the best-selling *Villa Triste*, have been translated into numerous languages and won her critical acclaim. Her ability to keep readers on the edge of their seats while weaving complex narratives has earned her numerous accolades, including the first Inspector Pallioti novel, *The Faces of Angels* being named as one of The BBC's Six Best Thrillers of the Year in 2007. Her books have been short-listed for the Agatha Awards, The CWA Steel Dagger, The CWA Gold Dagger and the Edgar Awards. In 2014, she won the Lorna Sage Award for literary non-fiction for her memoir, *Fireflies.*

In addition to her work as a novelist, Lucretia is committed to written history, and to teaching. She holds an MA with Distinction in Biography and Non-Fiction from The University of East Anglia. She has been the Writer in Residence at the Wallace Stegner Foundation, and has led workshops in both Fiction and Non-Fiction. She has held additional fellowships at

Hedgebrook, The Hambidge Foundation, The Hawthornden Foundation, and The Canadian American Foundation at the University of Maine, Orono, where she was an Instructor in the History Department.

A masterful storyteller who creates immersive worlds and unforgettable characters, Lucretia Grindle is the perfect choice if you are looking for a thrilling read that will keep you up late into the night.

For more info, go to Lucretia's website www.lucretiagrindle.com.

ALSO BY LUCRETIA GRINDLE

Villa Triste

The Lost Daughter

The Faces of Angels

Nightspinners

Made in United States
North Haven, CT
31 October 2023